Surviving On A Whisper

Emilee King

To Arie—thanks for sharing your story with me
I owe you everything

1

I've always wanted to see Chicago. Sears Tower, Buckingham Fountain, Cloud Gate—the whole nine yards. I'd always imagined if I ever got the chance to go, I would've gone with my older brother. Out of the two of us, he was more adventurous, and his enthusiastic spirit would've given me the confidence to push myself out of my comfort zone and make something memorable. We would've had so much fun.

I've always imagined that if I ever saw Chicago, it would be on a trip with my best friend in the world, not while I was running for my life.

My heart pounded painfully in my chest as I weaved my way through the crowd, trying to be fast but still casual. Blending in was key: my pursuers couldn't catch me if they couldn't find me. The consequences of failure were too high and I had to treat every chase as life or death, as if they even saw me they could unravel the mystery that followed me everywhere.

The pier was crowded with people enjoying the carnival that had come into town. Brightly colored candy wrappers littered the ground and the air was tainted with saltwater and popcorn. Teenagers wearing dark red shirts called from the game booths, half-heartedly asking for players. Children were screaming in delight as parents shouted after them, not wanting to lose them in their excitement. For me, it was a giant pinball machine, a maze that I was forced to get through while eluding those who wanted me dead.

In short, it was a nightmare.

I had to be grateful for the pandemonium, though, at least a little. Without it providing cover, I wouldn't have a chance at escaping, and I would've been caught a long time ago. It was a price I had paid for months now: get swallowed by chaos to keep from getting eaten by monsters. It didn't always work—I found myself in the clutches of demons way too often—and sometimes I was afraid that one time I'd let the chaos swallow me and lose myself completely.

Stop, I ordered myself, bringing my attention back to the present: to the soles of my ragged tennis shoes against the harsh pavement and the stench of too many humans pushed together. *Stay focused.*

I knew the monsters that were chasing me were close behind, but that didn't stop me from scanning every face I passed, doing so nonchalantly while keeping my head partway down. It seemed that half of the city had decided to show up to the pier today. It was a nice day considering it was late November in Chicago, but there was a definite chill in the air. Tonight was going to be cold. I shivered at the thought, the chill penetrating my secondhand black hoodie. My thrift store outfit was complete with worn skinny jeans and white knock off sneakers, allowing me to remain inconspicuous. My face, while well known by my pursuers, was plain and unremarkable, and my greasy brown hair was in a hasty ponytail. I was the definition of forgettable, and my survival counted on that.

I took an unsteady breath as I surveyed the area around me. People. People everywhere. No exit, no entrance, no fence to jump over or ditch to hide in.

They're coming. They're behind you. They're going to catch you.

I whipped my head around, scanning the crowd. My height allowed me to see over a lot of heads, but the advantage only brought more panic. There were people *everywhere* and any one of them could pop up and surprise me. Any one of them could be against me. In fact, *every* one of them would be against me, probably, if they knew the secret I was hiding and protecting with my life.

The thought threatened to suffocate me in a mass of strangers, but I forced myself onward. Step after step, person after person. I couldn't see an exit but that didn't mean there wasn't one. There *had* to be one. I would make one.

A family in front of me passed by, the two young boys running for the shooting game booth, allowing a break in the crowd. Through it, I saw a parking lot.

Jackpot.

Stuffing my hands in my hoodie pocket, I started for the exit. A familiar man entered my line of sight several yards away, blocking my path to the parking lot, and I skidded to a stop. Felix saw me in the same second. Our eyes locked for a moment, then he smiled and headed for me, and I twisted myself around and bolted the other direction. It took me further into the crowd, but at that moment I didn't care. I weaved in and out of people, putting as many bodies as possible between Felix and me.

Get away, get away, get away, I have to get away.

Through the carnival music and toddler wails, I heard an employee calling for a single rider on the Ferris Wheel. Panic had overtaken every thought, the need to hide consuming everything, and I dashed ahead to take the spot. I didn't even wait for the worker; I just scampered past the line and sat myself in the empty seat, locking the bar over me and the stranger next to me. The pimple-ridden worker shot me an annoyed look before pressing a button on his console, and then I was drifting up into the sky.

My new vantage point allowed me to see everything, and my eyes automatically searched the ocean of people for faces I recognized. A small triumphant smile played on my face when I caught sight of Felix making it to the spot where he'd seen me moments earlier. He was rifling through the crowd, his own smile fading into frustration when it seemed I had disappeared.

Take that, Felix.

The guy sitting next to me cleared his throat, snapping my attention to him. I gave him a quick once over, analyzing what I was up against. While successful so far, any escape plan that forced me to talk to strangers lost points in my book. I was supposed to be forgettable, after all.

The rider next me wasn't all that memorable himself. He looked about nineteen, short and stocky, with dark buzzed hair, chocolate brown skin, and a diamond in each ear. He glanced at me, then the crowd I'd been anxiously scanning, like he was trying to see what I saw.

I stole another look at the scene below us, to make sure I didn't lose Felix. With any luck, he would think I got away, and they'd leave the pier.

"Nice day, huh?"

With a start, I turned back to the stranger. "What?"

He didn't betray any emotion in his expression, though there was a hint of something in his eyes. Amusement, maybe? "I said, nice day, huh?"

"Uh, yeah." I finally caught my breath from my escape. "I guess."

The guy sat back in the seat, sprawling like he were making himself comfortable, though it was impossible to be comfortable in the hard plastic bench. He spread his arm halfway out on the back of the bench, and I instantly sat up straighter, inching away from him. If he got any closer…

"Funny," he said, watching the people again, oblivious to my discomfort. "You don't seem to be enjoying it."

My eyebrows pulled down in distaste as I eyed his arm. "Enjoying what?"

"The day."

A brief recap of the day played in my head—a day full of found hiding places and frantic running—and snorted.

He glanced at me again, in question. I didn't offer anything else, and after a second he returned to watching the scenery. I stared at his arm for a minute, as if willing it to stay put, before I decided it wasn't moving for the time being. I had other problems, anyway.

My hands fidgeted in my lap as I searched the crowd again. We were higher up now, and the people on the ground had gotten smaller, but I could still make out specifics if I stared long enough. It took me a moment, but eventually I found Felix again, stalking his way through the crowd. People tended to part for him once they saw him, since his brawny build and malicious eyes weren't exactly friendly. Those people were smart to move for him; I knew exactly how nasty he could get.

I watched Felix cut through the throng once, then twice, circling the area. When he came up empty a fourth time, he met up with two other men—Vega and Zed from the looks of it—and the three of them went to go break the news of my escape to their boss.

My toes curled as I saw them make their way to the parking lot and converse with a fourth man. Though they were farther away now, just larger than specks on the asphalt, I'd recognize him anywhere: immaculate bronze hair, icy blue eyes full of disdain, arrogance oozing from every molecule. He held himself well, powerful and proud like an accomplished adult, but he wasn't that much older than me. His face was all angles, harsh and cold and completely unforgiving.

Sark.

Sark used to not care about me. He used to not even know I existed, and I lived my peaceful, mundane life as an average person. But then, one day someone gives you an experimental formula, moderately changing your biology, and all of a sudden you're a freak show hunted by everyone— most notably, a guy named Mr. Sark.

At least, that was my experience.

Felix, Vega, and Zed all made their way to their boss, but since Felix was the second-hand man, he was the one that broke the news to Sark. I could almost feel his frigid fury from here.

I shivered in spite of myself. Even though I hated Felix, it was hard for me not to feel bad for anyone caught on the wrong side of Sark's wrath.

"Why are you a single rider?" the guy sitting next to me asked suddenly, making me jump. He glanced at the silver bracelet around my wrist; I pulled my sleeve over it. "You single?"

As much as I didn't want to be stuck up here for another five minutes with this stranger, it was better than the alternative. Although, sometimes, I'd almost prefer the torture to social situations.

I made a face without looking at him, disgusted. "You really that desperate?"

The guy snickered and extended his hand. "I'm Charlie."

One of my hands clenched into a fist at the pang that went through my heart. Of course, Charlie was just a name, a name of thousands of people in the world. Just because I knew one too once didn't mean I had to get all weepy about it. At least, that's what I told myself.

I appraised him with a raised eyebrow. "I'm not impressed."

Charlie raised his hands in mocking surrender, and I was glad his arm moved farther away from me. "Just seeing what I'm up against. You're not like a lot of the girls I've met today."

I couldn't help an eye roll. What a stupid line. I turned my focus back to Sark and his crew, willing them to leave. "Gee, thanks."

He shrugged coolly. "I know a runaway when I see one."

Every nerve in my body snapped to attention. I angled myself to face him, annoyed when a small smirk played on his mouth, like I'd done exactly what he wanted. I didn't care. Random girls at the carnival were forgettable. Single rider runaways were not.

"You got a name, Runaway?"

I wrinkled my nose. I couldn't stand him calling me that, even for the next four minutes of the ride.

"Erin," I answered, using my go-to fake name. "Care to elaborate on your observation?"

The corner of his mouth pulled up. "I'm right, aren't I?"

"Not necessarily. But I can't say I'm flattered someone would think I'm homeless."

"Ducked head, second-hand outfit, jumpy eyes. I know the drill."

I snorted again. Nothing about my life fit into any *drill*, at least not anymore. I looked over his baggy jeans, white tank, and thick black jacket.

"I'm no runaway," he went on when I didn't. "If that's what you were thinking. Sorry to disappoint."

I rolled my eyes. "You're breaking my heart."

"My little brother got busted in a drug deal awhile back. Only made it two months before the police caught up to him." I couldn't tell if his snide tone was for me or his brother. "Looks like you could've given him some tips."

"I'm not a druggie," I muttered, annoyed I took the bait.

We began our descent and I lost sight of Sark. The sun glinted off the top of a strip of cars, momentarily blinding me, and I had to squint. When I got back to the top of the wheel, I would plan my escape. I would get out.

I have to get out.

"Do I get a couple of guesses then?" Charlie asked me. "We've still got another circle on this thing, you know."

"My boyfriend was making out with some other girl behind the dart booth," I said, unable to keep the sarcasm out of my voice. "I ran to the Ferris Wheel to drown my sorrows. Not that exciting."

Charlie clicked his tongue in disappointment. "Nah, I'm thinking something else. Robbery?"

"No."

"Vandalism?"

"No."

"International art thief?"

"Creative, but no."

"Oh, I know. You're one of those mobster's girlfriends."

"You got me."

"Knew it."

Our bench dipped down low, then paused for a second to let someone else on. I automatically ducked my head, turning my face away from the crowd and holding my breath. Sure, Sark had been in the parking lot just moments earlier, but he could've decided to check the area one more time.

Go away, go away, go away, leave me alone.

Charlie smirked at me, like I'd proven his point. I rolled my eyes again, like it was the best comeback and not a pathetic cop out.

"Okay, next guess," he said once we had rounded the bend and were drifting up again, the pandemonium below fading into a distant humming.

I wasn't listening. I scanned the hordes of people again while tracing my best route of escape. I could do this. I could make it. Sark wouldn't get me today.

"I think I got it: it's your family, right? Your parents?"

Again, my spine straightened like I'd been electrocuted, and the back of my neck prickled.

Charlie nodded, gaining enthusiasm from my reaction. "Your dad?"

I pursed my lips and analyzed him again, warning bells going off in my head. It wasn't *the* secret, but it was definitely personal information. Either Charlie wasn't as innocent as he seemed or he was really good at guessing games. Was he a new hire of Sark's? A new plan, a new trick, a new trap?

Finally, I said, "That's very specific."

He shrugged, but his casual posture didn't match the hard glint in his eyes. "Yeah, well, those of us who know that life can sense when someone else is in the same mud."

I raised an eyebrow. "And you know that life?"

His expression darkened. "My little brother didn't get into drugs for nothing."

"Ah." I nodded once.

We both turned and watched the sky, and I caught myself distracted, wondering what Charlie was thinking about. I wondered what his dad was like. Certainly not anything like mine, though the idea set off a pained kind of comfort in my chest.

"How did you stay clean if your brother couldn't?" I knew it was more of a personal question, but if he had any tips on staying sane, I would gladly take them.

Charlie just shrugged again, but he wouldn't meet my eyes anymore. "Somebody has to."

I nodded again with a new respect for him. I knew that life. Most days I wanted nothing more than to just give up the fight, but doing that would mean turning myself in and giving up the secret I'd abandoned everything to protect—a secret that could kill millions. I had to keep that secret safe.

Somebody has to.

Our bench had passed the top of the wheel and we were descending back into the lively carnival atmosphere. I tapped my hands against my legs with anticipation, my eyes darting everywhere, looking for an enemy. I was going to run, I was going to hide, and I was going to be fine.

Calm down. Stay focused.

"Here," Charlie said. I turned to see him holding a twenty dollar bill out to me. "For a cab ride outta here."

I stared at the money a moment, uncertainty tightening in my gut. Nobody gave money to forgettable people. Nobody forgot the people that owed them a debt.

Charlie pushed it closer to me. "I don't need it. My friend'll feel so guilty that he didn't come with me on the Ferris Wheel and I had to sit next to this girl that wouldn't stop sobbing over her cheating boy. He'll owe me dinner."

I grinned and took the money as our ride came to a halt. "Thanks."

"We screw-ups gotta stick together."

The second the worker lifted our restraint bar, I was up and out of there.

"Good luck, Runaway," I heard Charlie mutter before I let myself get swallowed by the crowd.

~~~

I managed to make my way to the entrance of the pier, holding my breath nearly the whole time, so I was almost wheezing when I finally broke free of the last group of people. The constant thrum of voices and carnival rides melted into the background, replaced by the squealing and honking that came with Chicago traffic. I wrinkled my nose as I walked over to the crosswalk where a pack of tourists and couple joggers were waiting for a red light. I hated big cities, especially downtown anywhere, but it was so much easier to get lost in. Plus, Sark hated spectacles. It was easier to cause a
~~~

scene, therefore forcing Sark into the shadows, when there were a million people everywhere.

Glancing at the people next to me to assess any threats, I took a deep breath and longed for a secluded house on a beach in the middle of nowhere.

Someday.

The crosswalk beeped at us, and I forced myself to keep a casual pace as I crossed the street: behind the joggers but just in front of the tourists. Average and forgettable.

The back of my neck prickled either from my nerves or because someone was staring at me. Swallowing my budding terror, I looked behind me without stopping, surveying the scene I was leaving behind. There wasn't anyone I recognized stuffed in the crowd.

Stay calm. Stay focused. You're going to make it out. Not that the disgusting hotel room I had for the night was anything to look forward to.

Oh well. We can't have everything. At least it wasn't a park bench.

I turned to face forward again, almost to the other side of the street now. My eyes scanned the sidewalk up and down to check for any hostiles. I missed him on my first pass, but caught him on the second.

Felix. A half block down to my left and headed for me.

My heart skipped a beat, then started pounding erratically. I wasn't to the sidewalk yet, but I turned right anyway, prepared to make a run for it.

I stopped dead in my tracks. Vega was a half block down on my right, heading for me.

Biting my lip so hard it bled, I whipped back around. Sure enough, Zed was watching me from across the street, carnival goers bustling around him. He caught my eye and waved.

I was surrounded.

Panic threatened to overwhelm me, to surge over my head and down my throat and drown me. The streetlight had turned green now, and traffic was whizzing by like a rocket, painfully close. I looked around wildly for any kind of escape, any kind of ticket out of here.

I found it parked on the curb: a yellow cab. The driver was closing the trunk, getting ready to go.

It was stupid to involve other people, but I was desperate. Before I'd really decided to go for it, I had scampered to the vehicle, yanked open the door, and stuffed myself in the backseat.

There was already someone back there. She was a young woman wearing an apron from the diner across the street—early twenties, strikingly beautiful, with long curly black hair pulled back in a ponytail, alabaster skin, and bright green eyes.

Those green eyes widened in annoyed surprised when I slid in next to her. "This cab is already taken," she told me, blandly polite.

"We're going to the same place," I said, my gaze locked on Felix fast approaching.

The cab driver—Sal, according to his ID hanging from the rearview mirror—had started ducking into the driver's seat, but something had stopped him, and he was standing next to the vehicle instead.

Come on! I wanted to scream, but I settled for slapping my palm against the passenger seat headrest over and over. *Come on, come on, come on, come on.*

"Look, I don't know what's wrong with you," the young woman went on, "but I need you to get out."

I barely even heard her. My eyes were locked on Felix, just yards away, closing in. What was taking the stupid driver so long?

This was an awful idea.

Finally, I turned my head back to see Vega was almost to the cab, but his eyes weren't on me and he was talking. To the cab driver.

I'd basically gift wrapped myself for them.

Heart lurching in my throat, I made a hasty decision: I jumped in the front seat, yanked the door shut, jerked the car into drive, and slammed on the gas. Felix shouted and Sal spewed profanities and the young woman screamed. Felix's fingers brushed against the edge of the cab just as I pulled away from the curb.

"I'm sorry," I whispered, like the enraged cab driver could hear me. I hated stealing, especially a whole freaking car, but my guilt had been overtaken by my panic monster.

"What are you doing?" the young woman demanded, her tone an explosive hybrid of authoritative and terrified. "Stop the car!"

Why hadn't I made her get out first? I gritted my teeth at the stupid mistake.

"Stop, now!"

I was afraid she was going to fight me for the wheel, so I shouted back, "I can't!" The burst of emotion threw off my focus, and I nearly overcorrected into an accident.

"Do you even know how to drive?" the woman asked me.

I almost laughed—the question was so absurd, given the circumstances. The short answer was 'no' but I wasn't going to tell her that.

"What's your name?" I asked instead, trying to stay calm. On TV, the people who were good at staying in control always asked the scared people what their name was.

The woman hesitated, answering slowly. "Erika. What's yours?"

"Arie." The response came impulsively, and I slammed on the brakes too late at a red light. Why had I told her my real name?

Once the vehicle had stopped and I'd suffered a good amount of whiplash, I turned around to face her. "Get out. Get out now and get as far away as you can."

Erika raised a perfectly plucked eyebrow, her curiosity creeping out from underneath her rug of fear.

Her response was drowned out by my raging pulse. In the lane next to us, two cars down, Vega was sitting in the passenger seat of a black SUV with Felix at the wheel.

With a gasp, I wrenched myself back around and signaled to turn right, taking the first opening I could and ignoring the honks I received. In the rearview mirror, I saw Felix trying to do the same.

Just then, something dinged. I glanced across the dashboard to find the low fuel warning blaring at me. I was going to run out of gas.

"Arie, where are we going?" Erika asked me. She sounded like she was talking to a wounded animal, and even in the messy conflict, I found myself hating it.

My eyes focused on the buildings we were passing, street signs whizzing by. Where *were* we going? I'd only been in Chicago for a week, and I had no idea where we were. I (mostly) knew how to get back to the motel I was staying in, but there was no way I was headed there now, with Felix right on my tail.

Where can I go?

"Arie?" she asked again. "Are you running from someone?"

No duh.

I grimaced, knowing this experience would be etched in her mind forever. So much for forgettable.

Erika tried again. "Do you need help?"

"Look, this doesn't concern you," I responded, my voice harsher with fear, though I didn't mean to be. "As soon as I get far enough away, I'm going to pull over and run, and you are going to forget you ever saw me. Deal?"

She didn't respond, but I didn't care. I couldn't let her get mixed up in this. She probably wouldn't want to help me anyway, if she knew what I was.

Get out and get lost.

I drove until I hadn't caught a glimpse of Felix in a solid five minutes. My fingers tingled with nerves as I hesitantly pulled the cab to the curb and put it in park.

"Take it wherever you want to go," I told Erika without looking at her. No need to let her see my face again. "Just get out of here."

Erika started to say something, but I jumped out of the cab and yanked my hood over my head.

Stuffing my trembling hands in my sweatshirt pocket, I scurried down the sidewalk for a block before ducking into the nearest alleyway, prepared to disappear.

I hadn't gone eight steps before a wall appeared out of nowhere, and I slammed into it face first. The wall caught me by the shoulders as I stumbled back; I glanced up to see Felix grinning down at me.

He shoved me backward and I crashed into a real brick wall, my head smacking too hard against the surface and making everything really dizzy. I sucked in a sharp breath at the shock of the pain— that was a mistake. Right as I breathed in, a damp cloth was at my mouth.

A half scream escaped me as my nails scraped at Felix's hand on my face, but it was too late. The chemicals stole into my body, shutting it down, and I slipped into unconsciousness.

2

The panic always came first.

It was the first thing I tasted on my tongue, the first sound that thudded in my ears, the first sensation that coursed its way through me and locked up my nerves, sent my pulse racing, and set my teeth on edge. Every time I woke up in the last year, I always remembered the panic before I remembered my own name.

Coaching myself through the wave of fear, I forced my body to stay still, my breaths to remain even, and my eyes not to flutter open. Feigning prolonged unconsciousness was the best way to gather information unnoticed.

Where am I?

The floor underneath me was hard but warm, and the air around me was quiet—I was inside. My hands were fastened tightly behind my back, but my legs were free and there was nothing around my mouth, which probably meant I was somewhere Sark deemed relatively secure and too far away for me to successfully scream for help.

My fear bubbled up in my throat anyway, threatening to break loose. I shoved it down. I had to stay calm and focused if I wanted to get out.

Keep your eyes closed. You can get out. You have to get out.

Memories played across my eyelids like scenes from horror movies, images of a helpless girl tortured, starved, and beaten by a monster named Sark. That monster was searching for something, something he believed the girl might have. That was his job, sickeningly enough. He got paid ridiculous amounts of money to perform experiments on me and report back to his boss, Donovan Alexis, with the hope that the information he gained would lead them to what they wanted. And Sark was one of many. Alexis had lists of employees who sought out kids like me (called 'infecteds') that had been given the formula and might give Alexis the power he craved. Sark had been assigned to me about a year ago, and he spent every waking moment trying to prove that I was the infected they were looking for.

No matter what awful things he did to me, I would die before I told him he was right.

You can't give him anything, I reminded myself, gearing up for whatever Sark had decided to inflict on me today. *No matter what happens, you have to keep the secret.* Charlie's voice on the Ferris Wheel echoed my thoughts: *somebody has to.*

Suddenly, someone kicked me between the shoulder blades and my eyes flew open, a gasp escaping through my teeth. Felix smirked down at me. With another harsh prod from his foot, I rolled onto my back and used my hands to push myself up into a sitting position while Felix backed up.

My wary gaze followed him to see where he would go. He stopped at the entry to my right, blocking my exit, and I gritted my teeth. Getting through him was never easy.

I glanced around, taking in my surroundings. I was in a medium-sized room with hardwood flooring, no furniture, and really high ceilings. Right across from me stood a giant glass box. It was maybe six feet tall and about three feet wide, and the glass was several inches thick. It was connected to a wide tube that came from the wall.

I shivered in spite of myself. I'd never seen the freaky box before, and something in my gut told me I didn't want to know what it was for.

Sark leaned against the wall to my left, watching as I surveyed the scene. His face was expressionless besides the faint smug pull of his mouth and the glint of hatred in his eyes that emerged whenever I was in his presence.

I forced myself not to flinch at that hatred. I forced myself to be brave, or at least indifferent, when up against that icy glare. In some ways it was pathetic how hard I tried to pretend like I wasn't scared of him—everyone knew that I was—but I just despised the fact that I cringed every time he lifted his pinky finger.

Sark stared at me. I made myself meet his stare evenly. His eyes seemed to reach inside me, and I couldn't stand it. He always studied me with such measured hatred and calculation—as if with just one look he knew everything about me. As if he knew my secret.

No, of course he doesn't know. If he did, life would've been a lot worse. *He doesn't know and you are going to keep it that way.*

After a minute of us staring at each other in a silent challenge, he said, "I heard you made a scene at the pier today." His voice was always low and soft, his slight British accent adding a captivating effect. That was another thing about him that scared me: his voice was inviting, like a devil in disguise beckoning you to follow. I'd learned not to follow.

I shook my head slowly. I hadn't made a scene, not really. At least, not compared to a lot of the other disasters I'd found myself in before.

His eyes narrowed. "Hm," was all he said.

The disapproving skepticism in his tone automatically made me question what I'd said. Looking back, I *had* made a little bit of a scene: stealing a cab with a screaming woman in the back probably wasn't the most inconspicuous thing in the world to do. What had happened to her?

A pit formed in my stomach and I shrunk in on myself, desperately trying to become smaller under his gaze, though I managed to keep from dropping my eyes. I wished that there was something— *anything*—that would keep me from being the center of Sark's incensed attention for the next hours or days or however long I would be stuck here until I could escape.

My wish was granted. Suddenly, Vega came barreling through the door, dragging a flailing body along with him. I caught a glimpse of curly black hair and nearly threw up. It was the girl from the cab. *Erika.*

My eyes widened in horror when I recognized her, and Sark nodded to himself once, like he was reaffirming it was my fault.

"Let me go!" she was shouting, throwing her fists every which way. Vega dodged the blows with ease despite having a difficult time keeping a hold on her. "Let me go now!"

Felix stepped forward and grabbed her other arm, then helped Vega toss her roughly to the floor next to me. She bolted up straight, blowing a piece of rogue hair out of her face and running a hand over her ruined ponytail, like she was more embarrassed about her rumpled state than the fact she'd just been kidnapped by psychos.

"What is going *on*?" She aimed the words at Felix and Vega, but they just glared at her and went back to guarding the door. Then her green eyes found me and they narrowed. "What are you doing here? Why am *I* here?"

Sark stepped forward then, one eyebrow raised like he was half amused, half annoyed. I wanted to tell her to shut up—I tried to convey it in my expression—but Erika just turned her wrath on him instead.

"I'm going to call the police. Explain yourself and let me go before..." Suddenly, she lost steam, her eyes widening as they really took in Sark, his authoritative aura pulsing uncomfortably in the air as he stood over the two of us. The scarlet in her flushed cheeks drained out of her until she was paler than the moon rising through the window. Her mouth hung open without words and she became very, very quiet.

I couldn't breathe. I just bit my lip and flicked my eyes back and forth between Sark and Erika, too petrified to move.

He appraised the girl for a moment before addressing her. "What's your name?"

Though his voice was barely at regular volume, Erika shivered, and I felt a slight sense of satisfaction that she was at least starting to understand the severity of the situation.

Again, her mouth opened, but for a second nothing came out. She just stared at him as if she were in some horrified daze. Then something in her throat cracked and she finally managed to say, "Erika."

"Hm." Sark shifted his eyes to me, and my blood went icy in my veins. "What did you tell her?"

"No-nothing," I said hoarsely, shaking my head. "I didn't."

He rubbed his jaw without looking away, and his glare bore into me.

My stomach sank. He didn't believe me.

"I swear, I didn't," I added, like it could help. If Erika was here, Sark had already planned on killing her in the first place—he didn't tolerate witnesses, which was part of the reason why I'd sworn myself to a life of solitude.

"She was in the vehicle, I'm told," Sark said, still talking like Erika wasn't there. "She was waiting for you by the curb."

I shook my head again, confused for a moment, before shooting a glare at Felix. He just smirked at me in a mocking challenge.

Forcing myself to look at Sark again, I blew a harsh breath through my teeth. "I stole the cab and I didn't know she was in there. I don't know her. She wanted to know what I was doing, but I got out a few blocks later and ran without telling her anything." I left out the part where I made it less than five seconds before Felix caught up to me. I hated that guy so much. "That's it."

He seemed bored with my explanation. "Hm." Then he gestured to the glass box. "Let's get on with it then."

My mouth went dry. I managed to keep my nerves from fraying and unravelling the rest of me. "You're not getting me in there."

Sark raised an eyebrow, almost amused but not quite. "Well, I'd imagine it would be considerably easier if you got in yourself."

I actually snorted. "And why would I…"

Oh. It was an effort to keep my eyes from straying to Erika. How much did I care about this stranger?

She's still a person, I reasoned with myself, hating how quickly I jumped to self-preserving callousness. *But is she worth whatever is going to happen to me in that box?*

Erika gasped quietly to herself, finally understanding the conflict that was surely splayed across my face. I couldn't bring myself to look at her.

What do I do?

Naturally, Felix forced my hand. Each of his steps seemed to taunt me as he stepped up behind Erika and held a gun to her head. A dry sob escaped her mouth and she trembled underneath his vicious scrutiny. The force of the sound drilled into my chest.

My heart spoke to my legs before my brain stopped it all. I got to my feet. I kept my gaze on the box as I took slow, deliberate steps toward it.

Stay calm. Stay calm. Just stay calm.

I stopped in front of the box, next to Sark. His eyes scalded my skin, looking everywhere, seeing too much, and I felt hideously exposed despite my large hoodie, like my guts were all strewn out for him to see and assess. He stepped toward me; I flinched. He reached behind me and freed my hands; I rubbed my wrists and rolled my shoulders. He placed something in my palm; I looked down to see a bundle of cords.

My stomach dropped. I glanced at Sark. He stared right back at me, gauging something, and Erika whimpered from behind when Felix cocked the gun.

"Fine!" I hissed, an explosion of desperation. Hating myself nearly as much as I hated Felix, I unwound the bundle of cords. There was a tiny chip at one end, and the other end broke off into five different cords, each complete some kind of sensor.

Bile rose in my throat and I had to swallow it down. Hands shaking, I pressed the sticky side of the sensors to my head, chest, and one around my finger—I was all too familiar with this sadistic drill.

I hoped my face was expressionless as Felix helped boost me up. Swinging my legs over the side, I sat on the edge of the box, peering at the bottom. This couldn't end well.

Sark cleared his throat and I made myself drop without thinking. Felix pressed a button on the base and something slid over the top of the box—a slate of metal—effectively trapping me inside.

The second I was secure, a rushing sound came from under my feet. I looked down to see a puddle of water. Within six seconds it'd climbed over my shoes and seeped into my socks.

Terror crashed into me so hard that my knees buckled. I collapsed against the side of the box, shaking my head in denial.

"No," I whispered, verging on hyperventilation. "No, no, no, no, no, no, no." The water hit my shins and my eyes snapped up to look at Sark, who was as impassive as ever.

Demon.

"I'll drown," I said. "I will. I'm not *that* indestructible. This can't...I won't..."

"Yes," Sark muttered dryly, actually rolling his eyes. "I'm sure you will survive this endeavor, much to all our dismay."

I shook my head. "I'll drown."

"We'll see."

Instinct overruled my better judgement. I banged my fists against the sides of the box, then tried to climb up through the top, though the slate barred my exit. The glass was too thick and slick. All too soon the water was surging steadily over my shoulders, neither warm nor cold, and I thought my heart would burst out of my chest. When I realized there was no getting out, I filled my lungs and closed my eyes just as my head went under.

Time seemed suspended in space. My limbs still flailed desperately, but the movements were sluggish in the water. My heart thudded, my mind raced, and I held it for as long as I could. Eventually, though, I couldn't take it anymore. I didn't consciously decide to break, but suddenly there was water down my throat and in my lungs. My movements slowed and my racing mind went numb.

Reality slammed into me with a vengeance. When I came to, I found myself crumpled against the glass wall, coughing up gallons of water. I noticed the chip on the end of the cord was blinking, recording information. Once I caught enough oxygen to live, the chip beeped and the water started rising again.

My shoulders shuddered with a panicked sob. I kicked the box savagely, but I only hurt my ankle. The water hit my neck and I scrambled to my feet, tipping my head back to glean as much air as I could until it sucked me under again.

The third time I didn't bother getting up. I slumped back, spluttering, every cell in my body weighing thousands of pounds. The liquid drained out of my ears, and incensed screaming took its place. Confused, I managed to crack my eyes open to find Felix and Vega gone. Sark was across the room, frozen as a statue, his back to me. Erika had been screaming at him; now she turned and scampered to the box, frenzied eyes on me.

Sensing I'd come to myself again, the chip beeped and the water started rising. Erika's hands fluttered around desperately before she slammed the button on the base. The metal slate over my head slid away. Erika stood straight up, solid and silent, watching the water now with hopeful anticipation.

It wasn't until the water reached my shoulders that I understood. Standing up, I used the water to help me half float, half climb to the top of the box. Without the slate I was able to pull myself out. Erika tried to catch me, but she was so thin, and we both fell to the floor in a heap. Once I was free, I realized my mistake.

My head snapped up, my eyes searching for him, my insides curling inward and ready to flinch against his punishing blow. But I found Sark exactly where he had been: across the room, his back to us, so still I wondered if he was actually breathing. The muscles in his shoulders were tense and brittle, like with one gust of wind he would break.

Erika pulled me to my feet. I glanced at her, but she was also watching Sark. He gave no indication we were even in the room.

What did she say to him?

To my utter shock, Erika linked her arm in mine and jerked me out of the room. Banking a hard right in the hallway, we went out what looked like the front door of a house, and stepped outside without any problem.

I looked back. No Sark. No Felix or Vega or Zed. We ran and ran and not once did anyone stop us or chase us.

The frigid air bit into my wet skin, and within seconds I felt frozen to my bones, each movement bringing a roaring pain. But I kept up with Erika. I drank in our crazy freedom greedily, like a dog lapping up water so quickly it nearly choked.

The moment came, as I knew it would, when she skidded to a stop. A choked sound came from her mouth, and for a second I thought she would collapse with the weight of what she'd just seen. She jolted away from me like I'd electrocuted her. I stepped back, shivering, and wrapped my arms around myself. A dozen questions were ready to pour out of my mouth regarding the suspicious and miraculous escape, but before I could voice any of them, she raked her gaze over me and darted down the street.

Ripping the cords off me, I threw them on the ground and watched her go until she disappeared from my sight. My breaths shuddered. I surveyed the snowy night, waiting for someone—anyone—to jump out and grab me.

Nothing happened.

Hesitantly, I started trudging down the street, knowing someone would follow.

Nobody did.

I tried to focus through my soggy headache to find my way back to the hotel, certain that someone would take advantage of my state and apprehend me.

Nobody came.

I walked into the grubby hotel I'd chosen two days earlier, finding little shelter inside the thin and slanted walls. The pathetic excuse for a lobby smelled like sweat and spoiled milk, and was barely bigger than a closet. An ancient lady sat behind the cracked desk—I'd never once walked in, no matter the hour, to find she wasn't there. Per usual, she didn't react at the sight of me, even when I was sopping wet in the middle of the night. She just gave me a glassy stare as I walked through her lobby and down the hall toward my room. Shutting the door behind me, I used the rest of my energy to inspect the place. There wasn't any ambush set up or any tracker on me—that I could tell anyway. I pulled up my sleeve and took off the metal bracelet I always wore, setting it on the rickety nightstand so it wouldn't freeze to my skin. Then, when no attack had come, I collapsed onto the bed, finally allowing myself to think the insane truth I'd been too afraid to hope.

Sark let me go.

3

Water coursed over me, under me, around me. It crashed into my mouth and down my throat, forcing its way into my lungs. Darkness threatened to yank me under, but I rushed up instead, desperately darting for the surface before I succumbed to the numb blackness.

And then my eyes opened. Breathing hard—but breathing *air*, thankfully, not water—I tipped my head back and deflated. I was still in the motel room. It was stuffy, damp, and freezing, but it wasn't a glass box filling with water.

Oh well. We can't have everything.

Groaning, I slowly pushed myself up, shoulders sagging as I rubbed the crusted goop out of my eyes. Then I did an inspection. My body was shivering, and had been all night, as my clothes were still slightly clammy and the cold had settled into my bones. My lungs burned like I'd just run a race, and a construction crew had set up shop in my head. Purple splotches dotted my hands and wrists that hurt to touch.

I held my head in my palms and took a breath. I was lucky.

Heaving myself off the concrete slab the motel pretended was a bed, I headed straight into the box of a bathroom. I barely had enough room to move without hitting my elbows on the walls, but I managed to peel my stiff clothes off. Against my better judgment, I stepped into the shower, which had broken fake tile and something that suspiciously looked like mold in the corners. The water only got lukewarm at best, but I relished in any degree of heat I could find.

When I got out, I dried myself off with a scratchy towel and pulled on my dry pair of thrift store jeans and hoodie, leaving the damp ones on the towel rack to finish drying. I'd have to ditch these clothes and get new ones soon, especially since Sark had now seen both outfits.

But, for once, Sark would have to wait. I had one other order of business this morning.

The sun was bright in the sky, a deceptive ploy, since it did nearly nothing to warm up the air. My shoulders hunched as I ducked out of the hotel, stepping lightly on the snowy sidewalk and hoping

I knew where I was going. I did a perimeter check every block; I never found any threats.

Hopefully it lasts.

It took awhile to find it, but eventually I made it back to the pier. The carnival was just opening for the day. I found myself wondering about Ferris Wheel Charlie—what had happened to him?—but then I thought about Charlie at home and dropped the thought. Instead, I searched along the streets until I found the cafe name I'd seen printed on Erika's apron last night in the cab.

She'd likely taken off, since what she saw last night probably scared the daylights out of her, and there was only a small chance she would come to work today. But it was the only lead I had, and I hoped I would overhear something that would point me in the right direction. Sark had never once let me go—I didn't know why he did it, but it had something to do with Erika, and checking up on her to see if she was okay before I skipped town was the very least I could do.

I watched the front of the cafe from across the street for a few minutes, noting the people who entered and exited. A couple went in, then a woman in a suit. A girl with a purple jacket came out, then two girls giggling and holding coffee cups, and then a man in a long gray trench coat, with swept up hair that looked just like…

Sark.

My jaw snapped shut and every muscle went rigid. I fought the urge to run as I watched him look around before sliding into his car and driving away. My eyes traced his car until it disappeared, and then

I glanced around wildly for Felix or Vega. No sign of any of them.

What was he doing here alone? Sark didn't just 'go out' for food, unless his boss was in town. No, he came here because he knew *she* could be here.

Suddenly terrified of what bloody mess he'd left behind in the cafe, I raced across the street and jerked the door open. A bell rang as I entered, making me jump, and my eyes scanned the area. There wasn't any carnage or even a trace of any threat. Just regular people enjoying their regular breakfast before a regular day.

Instead of leaving, I sat in the corner booth, surveying the quaint restaurant. Chatter buzzed through the scent of sizzling bacon and fresh coffee, but the lively atmosphere just further bristled my nerves. I'd been late. I'd been *too late*. My fingers tapped erratically against the table as I gritted my teeth. He'd had the same idea as me—only with much more sinister motivations behind it—and I'd missed him. Did he already kill her? Could he somehow get away with it in public to make it look like an accident?

I hoped I was right: I hoped she hadn't come into work today. I hoped he came here looking for her and didn't snuff out a single clue as to where she was.

As if the universe heard my plea only to blatantly ignore it, Erika walked out from the back. My jaw fell open when I saw her.

She was *laughing*. Laughing and smiling and talking with her coworkers like everything was normal. Like she hadn't been kidnapped and witnessed an almost-murder the night before.

I watched her run the cash register until she disappeared into the kitchen. I couldn't believe it. Did I make all of last night up? Did she not get the danger of the situation? Especially since she *was* here, and Sark was just here, and he would want her dead.

What is happening?

Then she came back out of the kitchen, carrying a plate full of scrambled eggs, pancakes, and bacon. I jolted in my seat when she walked right up to my booth and sat across from me.

"Hey, Arie," she said cheerfully, as if greeting a friend she'd planned on meeting for breakfast. With a smile, she set the plate of food in front of me. "How are you?"

I drew back in shock, though my mouth started watering as the aroma of fresh food wafted into my nose, and my stomach grumbled. I was so floored from all sides that I just said, "What?"

"I asked how you were." The smile on her face wasn't the same one I saw the night before. This smile was a little too fixed. "Rough night, huh?"

"I...I don't...um...what?"

The fixed smile grew and she pushed the plate of food to me. My eyebrows furrowed, the hunger monster in my stomach growling at me to eat, which was a major distraction.

"Go ahead," Erika said when I hesitated. "I brought it out for you."

My eyes narrowed and I straightened up. "Why?"

She waved her hand at me like it was obvious. "You're way too skinny. Looks like you've skipped one too many breakfasts."

I further narrowed my eyes. This wasn't the interaction I'd been anticipating.

"Come on." She gave the plate another nudge, which made me want to push it back. "Eat."

The hunger monster snarled at me. I bit my lip, weighing the pros and cons, before snatching up my fork and shoveling the food in my mouth. An actual moan of relief escaped me when I swallowed the first bite of hot food. I couldn't remember the last hot meal I'd had.

Erika gave a knowing grin—a *real* one, and it made me want to spit the food right back out—before leaning her elbows on the table and resting her chin in her hands, watching me. I didn't like the sensation that she saw a lot more than I wanted her to.

"So," she started, "how are you?"

I stopped scarfing for a moment to stare at her. Finally, I managed to get my head screwed on straight, and my priorities shifted back into place. "I came here to see how *you* were. And..." I considered telling her about Sark, but I didn't want to scare her even more. "Yeah."

"Well thanks for checking up on me," she said. "Plus, you saved me a trip. I was going to find you after my shift."

"Me?" My forehead creased and I paused mid-bite. "Why?"

The fixed smile came back on, but it didn't match the expression in her eyes. "I was hoping you'd come with me somewhere."

About fifty warning bells went off in my head. Slowly, I lowered my hand and set the fork on my plate, leaving my bite of pancake in a pile of berry syrup. "I can't," I said simply. It was better I shut this down fast. "But thanks."

"Because of Sark?"

I hated the slight challenge to her tone, like Sark was just a nuisance and if I just tried hard enough then he wouldn't be a problem.

Pushing the plate away, I sat back in the booth, half glaring. "You wouldn't understand, okay? He could kill you."

"He hasn't killed me yet."

"He was just here. I saw him leaving when I walked in. He knows where you work."

That terrifying fact did not have the effect I wanted: Erika's fixed smile just grew.

"I know, silly girl. I talked to him."

My blood went cold. "You *what*?"

"I talked to him." She said it like we were discussing the weather, not a heartless murderer. "He was here for awhile. Beat you by quite a bit. Couldn't wake up this morning? I know you're stronger than me for whatever reason—you're infected, right?—but that still doesn't sound like a fun awakening."

I just sat there staring, dumbfounded, nearly getting crushed underneath the weight of the billions of questions I had for her: like why Sark behaved that way last night, or why she was so chipper, or how she had even heard of infecteds in the first place.

But before I could begin, she went on to say the craziest thing I'd ever, ever, ever heard:

"I have a date with him."

I blinked. My mouth started to curve up, as if to laugh at her joke, because part of me knew that she had to be kidding—it was some insane joke—but the laugh froze in my throat because the other part of me registered she was totally serious.

"What did he do to you?" I finally asked. Because that was it. Blackmail. She'd been dragged into the game. "What did he threaten?"

Erika shrugged. "Nothing. I was the one that asked him."

I blinked again. Erika just watched me. I glanced around the restaurant, searching for cameras or Felix or something that would give me a clue as to whether this was another trick or I was on TV. There were only couples laughing, forks clinking, and teenagers typing.

Shaking my head to clear it, I looked back at Erika, splaying my hands on the counter. "Okay, look, I'm only going to say this once, so pay attention: you are in over your head. I don't know if you're attracted to the whole 'British-bad-boy-I-can-save' thing, but this isn't like a TV show, okay? Sark will use you for whatever cruel intentions he has, and then he'll get rid of you, and it'll probably be awfully painful. He'll get Felix to dispose of your body, and nobody will even recognize you're gone until he's vanished."

Erika just smiled that smile at me all throughout my speech, not fazed at all. "It's okay, Arie, that won't happen. It's just a date."

My mind could not compute that. "Stay away from him. If you want to live, stay away from him."

She shook her head. "Oh no, I'm going. I'm excited, actually. He's really attractive, in that whole mysterious way."

My mouth fell open. I shut it again. There was no way I was hearing this.

I moved to stand up and leave, but she held out her hand to stop me. "Where are you going?"

I shrugged and held my hands up. "It's your funeral, not mine. I've warned you and that's as far as I can go. I'm leaving. Have a nice life—hopefully he doesn't beat it out of you before the wedding."

"But I want you to come."

That line sent me reeling, falling back into the booth. "*What*?"

She brushed a piece of her curly hair out of her face. "Well I *need* you to come," she said with a little giggle, like she'd made an embarrassing mistake. "I know he's got a dark side, and I feel like if you're there then he'll be less likely to hurt me. You know how to deal with him, after all."

My body actually curled in slightly at the blow. "You're crazy."

Her eyes narrowed just a tiny bit, which was the most normal response she'd had this whole conversation, but that stupid smile was still on her face. "I am not crazy. I'm asking for your help."

I shook my head before she was finished. "You're not getting it. Good luck."

Once again, she stopped me in my tracks. "Don't you want your bracelet back?"

Instantly, my hand clamped over my right wrist. Even through my sleeve, I could tell my wrist was missing a band of metal, and I frantically patted down my pockets. Nothing. Had I not put it on this morning? Why did I even take it off in the first place?

Erika's smile morphed into a triumphant smirk when I came up short. "Missing something, huh."

Gritting my teeth, I shot a glare at her. "Who do you think you are?"

"I think I'm the girl that followed you home last night. I'm the girl that has your bracelet, and I'm the one you're going to meet up with tonight for her date with Sark."

"Over my dead body."

She actually had the nerve to roll her eyes. "Now that's a little dramatic, don't you think?"

"No," I retorted icily, "because it almost happened last night. Because he's a *psycho*."

"To each their own." She shrugged. "So it goes without saying that you'll show up if you want your bracelet back, right?"

"Why do you think I'd care so much about a stupid bracelet?" I gestured to my hobo self. "Do I look like the jewelry type to you?"

"Because you're a girl living with nothing and you have that," she answered. "Because you obviously hate this conversation, but you're still here having it because you want the bracelet back. So, tonight—"

"I have to work," I cut in flatly, detesting that she called me out on my bluff. "But thanks."

"Where do you work?"

"Why would I tell you?"

"Tomorrow night, then." Erika pulled out her waitress notepad and wrote something down on it. "Meet us here. I'll have your bracelet."

I only paused a moment to consider it; I was too furious to really think anything through. Growling under my breath, I snatched the paper from her and stalked toward the door.

Erika called after me like we were the best of friends. "See you later, Arie!"

I just clenched my fist tighter, smashing her note in my hand, and kept walking.

~~~

So, Erika, the supposed innocent bystander, was actually insane. I had to admit that I hadn't seen that coming. A *date* with Sark? Was that...was that even possible? No, it couldn't be. It was some new plan of his and he'd dragged her into it...but Sark would never concoct a *date*.

Maybe I was dreaming. I had to be, right? The whole diner encounter was probably some hazy episode straight out of my waterlogged brain. It wasn't real.

I went straight back to the motel and ransacked my own room. Since I didn't have anything besides a change of clothes I'd managed to nab out of a goodwill bin, the search went fast and, of course, was useless. My bracelet was gone.

Pulling on my hair, I collapsed onto the rock hard bed with an undignified sigh. Why did it have to be my bracelet? Why did it have to be *that* bracelet? Why couldn't she have taken something—anything—other than my most prized (and only) possession on the planet?

I hate her.

I had to get out. I had to leave Chicago now, especially if Sark was going to be distracted for a night. It was the perfect opportunity to disappear without him right behind me.

And yet…
~~~

Suddenly, I snapped upright, particles of an idea beginning to form in my mind. Digging into my pocket, I yanked out the rumpled note Erika had given me and smoothed it out against my leg. I could still read her faint, loopy writing.

Sucking a sharp breath, I made a hasty decision: I was going. I was going to meet up with Erika—and even Sark—and I was going to get my bracelet back.

But first, I had to make a phone call. Because there was no way in this universe I was going to show up to just hang out with the murderer that'd been tracking me for months and a new lunatic that wanted to be my best friend. If they were going to pull crazy plans then I was going to create one of my own. Sark would hate it, but, if it worked, then I'd never have to deal with his wrath again.

A few weeks into my living-on-the-run-while-being-hunted-by-a-psychopath situation, after getting some police officers severely injured when I naively called them on Sark, I decided I needed real, major, specialized help. I spent a day in a library doing research on any help for infecteds (which is sparse, considering we're pretty unknown) and came across a branch of the government called the Office of Cultist Intelligence. They'd been after Alexis and his crew for a while, and Sark was on their most-wanted list. So I called. I explained that I was an infected that needed help getting away from my handler and had to talk to someone immediately (refusing protective custody after the first and only time I'd taken the offer, when I sat down in the 'safe house' and Felix walked in ten minutes later). For better or worse, they patched me through to Richard Dalton. I'd like to say that changed my life, but it really only minorly inconvenienced it.

Dalton became assigned to my case, which really meant he was assigned to putting Sark behind bars—he couldn't care less about me. The problem was...Dalton could kind of be an idiot. And Sark was always a brilliant genius. So Dalton was about as helpful as a bowl of soggy mashed potatoes.

I kept trying, though. I kept calling him. I kept attempting to set traps for Sark so I could finally be rid of him. It usually just ended with two frustrated guys that took out that frustration on me. Sark *hated* Dalton and got extra mad at me every time I called him. Dalton *hated* Sark and got extra mad at me every time he got away. I figured maybe the universe would take pity on me one time and somehow let everything work out—it was worth a shot, right?

Ducking out of my room, I walked down the slanted, narrow hallway to the pathetic excuse for a lobby. Sure enough, the ancient lady was sitting behind the desk. I hesitantly went up to her and asked if I could use the phone on the counter. She stared at me, beady eyes imbedded in a mess of wrinkles that were probably etched out by cavemen. Despite the weather, my palms started to get sticky with sweat, until eventually she shifted her head up, revealing a neck twice as thick as my arm. Taking that as a nod, I mumbled a thanks and grabbed the phone, going to the opposite corner. Then, taking a deep breath and ignoring the ancient lady's eyes on my back, I dialed the cell number I'd memorized months ago.

He answered halfway through the first ring, his familiar voice terse and brimming with misplaced self-confidence. "Dalton."

"Hi." I managed to keep my voice from shaking, though it was much smaller and quieter than I'd hoped. "It's me. Arie."

He stifled a sigh, breathing just hard enough that I still caught it. "Well, Arie, what do you have for me today?"

I gritted my teeth at his patronizing tone. It wasn't like I really liked him either. "It's Sark. I—"

"You saw him again, now did you?" I could imagine the way his thin mouth would pull down as the corners turned up in a mocking smirk. "Interesting, since nobody else has. Tell me, Arie, why does he care so much about you in the first place?"

Biting my lip, I forced myself to stay cool. Lately Dalton had been pelting me with questions— questions about *me*—more than he ever had before. It freaked me out, like he was catching onto something he couldn't know. Despite the fact he was supposedly on my side, I'd never trust him with my secret in ten thousand years.

I opened my mouth to give the same answer I always had, but he beat me to it. "Yes, I know: he has an affinity for your kind, doesn't he? Disgusting, if you ask me. Still seems strange, though, since you're just a teenage girl. You can't really be *that* valuable to someone like him, can you?"

My hands tightened on the phone. Willing myself to stay calm, my tone hardened slightly. "Dalton, I called you—"

"For a reason, yes," he cut in, puffing himself up like he was in charge of this whole thing. "What is it?"

"I need you in Chicago. Tomorrow."

Dalton laughed once, a fake, airy sound meant to make me feel two feet tall. "I'm a very busy man, Arie," he said, even though I knew he wasn't. "What do you need?"

"I know where he's going to be."

He tried to hide it, but a touch of surprise colored his tone. "Sark?"

"Yes." I smiled in spite of myself. Usually I called Dalton after escaping Sark, and Sark was usually long gone by the time Dalton caught up. "Tomorrow night."

"Tell me."

So I did. I gave him all the details I had, besides Erika's name—despite everything, I didn't want her to get in trouble if Sark was just using her to get to me.

"I think we could do it," I finished. "I really think we could."

I just want Sark gone.

Taking a breath, I waited in anticipation, hoping he'd agree to my plan. He had to. I'd probably never get this opportunity again—surely he had to at least know that.

A beat of silence passed. Then two. Three. I thought I was going to combust when his voice finally came through.

"I'll be on the next plane."

4

The anticipation of waiting for Dalton was agonizing, and reduced me to a nervous wreck. Besides a trip to the thrift store to sneak some new clothes out of the donations bin (people donated for others in need, right? I was in need, I just...took without anyone knowing), I spent the majority of the afternoon secluded in my nasty hotel room. Sleep was fitful and tiring, and the next day was miserably slow and terrifyingly fast at the same time. It seemed I'd only blinked and aged ten years when I finally walked out the door to go meet Erika.

The oversized maroon sweatshirt I'd managed to grab fell halfway down my thighs, which probably made me look like a washed out munchkin, but it helped protect me from the cold evening air. Snow crunched underneath the gray sneakers I'd been wearing for months—the soles had worn so thin that the snow threatened to push through, and my toes were always frigid. My hands were shaking, but not from the cold. I stuffed them into my hoodie pocket as I trekked down the blocks.

Soon, it would all be over. For better or worse.

My face was frozen by the time I made it to the place Erika had described, and I took a shuddering breath when I saw what it was: a club. A club full of people partying on this...was it the weekend? Or did people just flock to this place regardless of what they had in the morning?

Steeling myself, I took a breath and went through the front door, having to push through three groups of people just to get inside.

Here goes everything.

I'd never been to a club before, but I instantly hated it. The expansive space was swarming with crowds, mostly young adults, and shadows twirled under the dim lights. The air was smoky, thick, and smelled like a mix of sweat and alcohol. A bar took up the wall to the right; a stage took up the far wall where a girl was singing a pop song people were dancing along to. It all gave me a headache.

This is not my kind of place.

Gritting my teeth, I forced my way through the hordes until I got to the bar, but it was too crowded. The whole place was too crowded. Bodies pressed in on me from all sides, and I felt too hot and too out of place in my sweatshirt, and I found myself heading blindly for the back corner, where supposedly there was a back door. I had to get out. I needed real air.

I literally ran into her, which was more convenient than having to track her down in this zoo. Erika fit right in with her designer jeans, stylish jacket, and flawless hair. She flashed me a dazzling smile and I almost winced at her brightness.

"Hey Arie!" she shouted over the music.

I cut her greeting off. "I'm here," I said flatly and held out my hand. "Give it back."

She countered with some excuse—my attention got snatched up by the guy walking toward us. I'd never seen Sark look so out of place. He was too sharp and harsh, too real, for the hazy club atmosphere. His face was expressionless as his eyes darted around, surveying the area, before they found Erika. I almost gagged at the slightest glint of interest in his gaze...like he actually cared where Erika was more than just keeping tabs on her.

Then his eyes landed on me and his face instantly hardened into a barely contained scowl. It was an effort not to flinch at his glare.

Just a few more minutes, I reminded myself. *Just a few more minutes and Dalton will grab him and this will all be over.*

I forced myself to look at Erika. "I came, I saw, we're done. Give me my bracelet back and you guys can go back to your lovely evening."

She pretended like she didn't hear me and—to my horror—grabbed my arm. "Come on!" Her smile was too big for her face. "You *have* to meet this guy!"

Thankfully, she continued yanking me toward the back, which was where I wanted to end up. Dalton said he'd be set up in the alleyway that ran behind the club. I was supposed to get Sark out there at some point and Dalton would take care of the rest. Supposedly.

This has to work.

Erika pulled me through the masses with much more skill that I had, and stopped at a door. With a smile, she said something to the security guy watching over everyone; I found myself leaning closer to her when I sensed Sark following a pace behind us.

Stay calm. You can do this. You have to do this.

Whatever Erika said to the security guard must've been the right thing, because he let us through. Instantly the chaos of the club melted into faint, muffled sound as we stepped into a back room and the door shut behind us.

The room was about a quarter of the size of the club area, and served as a backstage. Instruments, speakers, and boxes of cords littered the floor, and a card table was pushed into the corner with water, a bowl of fruit, and a giant container of licorice.

A shorter, balding man walked in, forehead glinting with sweat. Erika perked up at his entrance and I used her distraction to jerk my arm from her grasp.

Just keep her occupied. Just a little longer.

"Hey Neil!" she exclaimed with a wave. "How are you?"

Neil jumped at her voice but smiled when he saw her, and some of the age faded from his face.

"Erika! Nice to see you. What brings you around here?"

She shrugged and gestured to me. "Just showing my friends around town. Had to bring them to the best club, right?" She winked. "Plus, knowing the owner has so many perks."

Neil nodded at me, then behind me (I assumed at Sark and fought the urge to turn around). "I'm glad you stopped by. How's the internship treating you?"

"It's good." Her answer was a little too quick. "The diner is still good too."

Neil chuckled at the slight dip in her tone. "Yeah, well, one thing at a time, Erika. You'll go from pouring coffee to fame and fortune eventually."

She smiled. "Just not soon enough."

A girl sauntered in from the left, which I assumed was where the stage was, and gave us a passing glance before turning her platinum blonde whine on Neil.

"Where's Liam?" she demanded, her sugary voice too high.

Neil barely contained a sigh. "I think he's—"

A group of teenagers barreled in from the right entrance, all chattering at the same time. One of them groaned and made an exaggerated gagging expression when he saw the blonde girl, but she just glared at him before turning her smile to another boy with brown hair and easy smile.

"Liam!" she sang, but Neil cut her off.

"Guys, Erika brought some new people in tonight," he said, "so make sure we show them a good time." Then he glanced at Erika. "Sorry, I've got to get back. Don't be a stranger, all right?" With that, he was gone. I wanted to run after him. I wanted to scream that Sark was standing four steps behind me, and his friend Erika was either in huge trouble or crazy, and that I just wanted to get out of here.

Stay calm, stay calm, stay calm.

The second Neil was gone, the fake gagging boy glanced over us, sizing us up. "Newbies, huh? Don't know if they'll survive around here."

Erika rolled her eyes. "Mark, right?" When the boy nodded, trying to hide a smile she remembered his name, she went on. "This is Arie—" she turned slightly to point, "—and that's Sark."

"Liam," the dark haired boy said, ignoring the incessant attention the blonde girl gave him. He nodded to the two other girls and one other boy in turn. "This is Mara, Chelsie, and Andrew."

"We're the band here," Mark said, puffing his chest out a bit, like that should impress me.

"And they're actually not bad," Erika added.

"Not bad?" Mark repeated in offense. "We're—"

"The best." The blonde girl cut in front of Mark to shake Erika's hand. "I'm Claire. I'm the lead of the show here." Mark scoffed at that, but she ignored him. Instead she surveyed me with a sneer, clearly unimpressed with my hoodie hobo look I had going on, before glancing at Sark. One look at him and her sneer quickly lifted into a blinding smile. "So are you visiting or are you from here?"

I bit my lip to keep from screaming. She had *no idea* who she stood across from. Though part of me was itching to turn around just a little to see Sark's reaction to getting hit on by a high school brat.

"Visiting," Erika answered for us, a slight edge to her tone, as if she noticed Claire's interest from ten miles away. "We're just out for the night."

Claire's smile remained plastered to her face, but her eyes narrowed with venom on Erika. "Well, then, you better show him a good time." She then went on to detail the inside track at the club like she was queen of the whole place, talking to all of us, but really focused on Sark, glaring at Erika, and completely ignoring me.

Then, Claire actually took Sark's arm and started leading him away, and I couldn't help but snicker at the annoyed disbelief written all over his face. He shot me a death glare when he heard me laugh, and yanked himself free, but Claire pretended like she didn't notice and kept on talking. Erika glanced between Sark and me, torn who to watch over most, but in the end she went to Sark's side. Probably to make sure he didn't murder Claire and leave her in a pile of hair bleach and orange spray tan.

That left me totally vulnerable out in the open. I froze with uncertainty, mind racing with terrible ideas on how I could possibly get Sark to go outside.

"So, Arie, right?"

I jumped at the sound of my name in a stranger's voice, and turned to see Liam watching me with the warmest brown eyes I'd ever seen.

"Uh, yeah," I responded, a little late. Brushing a piece of hair behind my ear, I rocked on my heels, glancing around the room.

Is Dalton here? Is he ready? My fists tightened in my hoodie pocket. *How am I going to do this?*

"Hey, um, are you okay?"

My eyes snapped back to Liam, whose eyebrows were furrowed with concern. The other band members were bustling around him, all except for Mark, who was watching me skeptically like I was some kind of intruder.

I took a breath. "What? Sorry, I'm…all over the place tonight."

Mark started to say something, but Liam elbowed him and cut in instead. "Do you need some air?" He gestured to the door behind him. "This heads out back. It's secluded in an alley type thing—you can totally have some space."

My eyes widened. "That door goes to the back alley?"

"Yeah." He turned uncertainly. "You, uh, okay, then? Or—"

"I'm okay. I might head out in a minute, though." I glanced across the room to where Claire was still talking a mile a minute to Sark and Erika.

"Don't worry about Claire," Liam said, and Mark raised an eyebrow at him.

I laughed once, a nervous sound. "Yeah, I don't think she likes me much."

Mark snorted. "She doesn't like *anyone* much. She's got a Queen Bee complex."

"Yeah I kinda got that vibe."

"Was it the crazy long nails that gave it away? She could claw out someone's heart with them."

"No, actually, it was the orange spray tan."

Both Mark and Liam cracked a smile, then one of the girls shouted at them, "We gotta warm up, guys. Show's almost starting."

"Right," Liam said, looking from me to Mark, then to me. "Do you, um…do you…"

"Can I hang out here for a minute?" I asked. "Just until they—" I motioned toward Erika, "—are finished?"

Mark opened his mouth to say something, but once again, Liam beat him to it. "Yeah, sure. We're just gonna tune up. Take a seat."

I sat on the very edge of a big speaker and bounced my leg with anticipation, stealing looks at Sark every few seconds to make sure he didn't disappear or hurt anyone. He typed a few things into his phone, but that was it. The band members took to exercises on their respective instruments. I kept having to remind myself to breathe and not to stare at the door too much in case someone noticed.

Stay calm, stay calm, stay calm. Just a few more minutes. This will work. This will work.

"That's a beautiful guitar," I said, more to myself.

Liam looked up from tuning his instrument, sweeping his hand over his guitar. "It is, huh?" He leaned forward slightly and lowered his voice dramatically. "Don't tell her, but my best girl is hidden away in my room. I wouldn't risk leaving my actual favorite guitar lying out around here, especially with people like him stomping around." He jerked a thumb at Mark, who was busy tuning his own guitar, and Mark promptly threw a guitar pick at him.

"Do you play?" Mark asked me.

The corners of my mouth pulled into a fond smile. "I used to."

Then one of the girls started yanking them onto the stage. Mark left me with a smirk as Liam said something about talking to me later, but I hardly paid them any mind. It was time. If I waited any longer, I could blow my chance. I had to believe Dalton was out there.

I have to believe this will work.

Taking a deep breath, I filled up my lungs with as much air as I could, then blew it all out. I watched Erika, waiting until she was sufficiently distracted by Claire's babbling and noting how Sark was barely containing an eye roll at the girl's aggravating attention. Aiming for blatantly fake nonchalance, I stood up, hands stuffed in my pockets, and wandered too quickly over to the back door Liam had so kindly pointed out. I turned the handle painfully slowly, so as not to make a sound, and cracked it open. Frigid air slapped my face. Bracing myself, I glanced back into the room one more time. Sark had noticed me; Erika hadn't. I knew the alarm that splayed in my expression wasn't fake as we stared at each other for a half second before I slid out the door.

The sun had just set, and there were no street lights back behind the building. Dying light from the sky was all I had to work off as I scanned the scene. The alleyway went several yards to my right before ending with a couple dumpsters and a chain link fence. To my left, the back street stretched on and disappeared around a corner.

Where are you, Dalton?

I knew I only had seconds though, so I broke right just as the door opened and ducked behind a dumpster. Just as I planned, Sark stepped outside. Snow seeped into my kneecaps as I leaned to the left to watch him through the crack between the wall and dumpster. He did a quick sweep of the area with his eyes before stepping toward the corner, away from me. He was perfectly silent—the only hint he wasn't a figment of my imagination was his breath fogging in the winter air.

I waited for the ambush. Sark looked back my way before continuing to walk away from me. He assumed I ran. Which, I would probably have to anyway, if Dalton didn't show up soon.

Where are you?

Sark saw something on the ground and stopped, giving a death glare at what looked like an old cigarette, then smashed it with his foot. As quickly as his anger came, it disappeared. Suddenly he was looking for me again.

What was that about?

Then I caught it: a glint of metal. I only had a moment to register the detail before Sark had rounded the corner and there was an eruption of shouting, ordering Sark to put his hands up.

That was my cue. Heart thumping wildly in my chest, I jumped out from behind the dumpster and beelined it for the door. Sark and I locked eyes for a second—he could've frozen me to the core, frosting over every muscle on the way, with the glare he gave me—before I jerked open the door and rushed back inside the club. The second I slammed the door, shooting sounded from the alleyway.

"What's going on?" Erika asked, appearing out of nowhere and touching my hand still on the doorknob with concern. Claire was gone now; we were alone.

I flinched away from her touch. She backed off an inch and glanced uncertainly between my face and my hand clamped around the doorknob.

Muffled yelling sounded, but it was drowned out by the uproar coming from the stage entrance.

Erika tried again. "What's going—"

The doorknob rattled, making us both jump. I held on as tight as I could, hoping my shaky hands wouldn't go slick with sweat. Jerking my chin, I nodded to one of the bulky speakers on the ground. Erika didn't question me; she started pushing it with all her might toward the door.

"What's happening?" she asked me, her voice strained with exertion. "Are you okay?"

The doorknob rattled again. More shots sounded. I thought I would throw up. "I called someone," I finally admitted.

"What?" She managed to push the speaker the rest of the way so it barricaded the door.

"His name is Richard Dalton." I hesitantly took my hand off the knob. "He's going to lock Sark up. We won't have to deal with this anymore."

Erika's mouth nearly fell to the floor. "You did *what*?" she demanded, a hybrid of horrified and outraged.

My eyebrows furrowed, and I stepped away from her in spite of myself. Wouldn't she be happy about this? "I called—"

"They're out there right now?" she cut in, exasperated, and jerked her thumb at the door.

Confused (and kind of nervous) I pursed my lips and nodded. Her eyes just grew bigger, and she raked her hands over her face and through her hair, rumpling her pristine look. Suddenly she went from supermodel to disheveled raccoon.

"No, Arie, no…" she trailed off, glancing around wildly as if anticipating an attack on us right there. "No, no, no, no."

Rocking on my heels, I took a step back. I didn't have time for whatever episode she was having—I'd done everything I could do. Now it was time to get lost.

I turned and darted for the door across the room, ignoring when my name was called by Erika and someone else. The pandemonium of the club punched me in the face when I opened the door, but I flung myself into the crowd without much hesitation, letting it swallow me up.

I'd barely taken three steps into the masses when someone grabbed my arm. Heart lurching in my throat, I whipped around, prepared to go down kicking and screaming. But it wasn't Sark or Erika. It was Liam.

"Where you going so fast?" he asked with a timid smile, his cocoa eyes warming up the tips of my frozen fingers. "You just got here."

For a second I stood there speechless, a total idiot. When was the last time someone normal had asked me that? Then I shook my head. "Oh, um…I have a thing I've got to get to. I'll see you later."

Or never.

His forehead creased. "Really? Because we—" A burst of cheers from the crowd overwhelmed his voice, and I heard Claire's sugary tone come over the speakers. Liam gave an apologetic grin and repeated himself. I stopped paying attention when I saw Erika dart out of the back room and make a break for the front door without even acknowledging me. All her swaggering confidence and dazzling smiles were gone; now she looked like a wounded deer running from the roaring lion.

"I have to go." I said the words to myself and Liam, a reminder for both of us. Turning, I fought my way halfway to the entrance when Liam caught me again.

Go away please, nice boy.

"Arie, will you—"

Just then, I caught sight of the back door opening again and I literally felt him come into the room. I didn't wait for pleasantries anymore. I ran.

Smashing into people and ignoring the slurred curses they shouted after me, I forced my way through the crowd and through the entrance, finally stumbling onto the icy sidewalk. Cars whizzed past me, and headlights strobed in the darkness. I spun around, momentarily disoriented, then took off. The thin soles of my sneakers slid against the dangerous ice, but I didn't slow down.

I can't get caught, I can't get caught, I won't get caught.

I didn't know where to go—where *could* I go? It was too much to hope that Dalton actually caught up to Sark and apprehended him, which meant he was going to be angry at me that the plan didn't work. He'd likely track the phone line I'd called him from, so going back to the hotel was out. Not that I couldn't handle Dalton's frustration, but…

Sark. I had to stay focused on the real threat. I forced the bitter disappointment I felt to the bottom of my stomach to be dealt with later.

But, really, how stupid did Dalton really have to be? I'd practically *handed* Sark to him, and he couldn't manage to apprehend one single, solitary, unsuspecting criminal?

I gritted my teeth, furious at the tears that sprung in my eyes.

Later, I reprimanded myself harshly. *Disappointment later. Escape now.*

I'd made it about six blocks (getting too worked up always distracted me from counting) when I caught sight of a man walking toward me in the shadows. Breaths shuddering, I slowed down to a fast walk, balling my hands into fists. He looked just like Felix. Well, he could've been Felix, but also the nose didn't seem quite right, and had he always been that short…?

I couldn't tell if it was him. And that was bad.

So I turned, just to be safe. I broke left and crossed the street, attempting to look like a normal girl walking around, and glanced back when I'd safely reached the other corner. The man walked right on, oblivious to me.

Not Felix. I breathed a sigh of relief. *You're okay.*

I turned around too late, and crashed into someone else, smacking my nose against their collarbone. Their hands automatically caught me by the shoulders.

"Sorry," I mumbled, rubbing my nose and looking up.

The hands on me tightened. I yelped in spite of myself.

It was Zed.

"Going somewhere?" he asked with a lazy grin. "It's cold out to just be walking, don't you think?"

I tried to shake his hold off and back away, but he just used my momentum to push me between two office buildings. Sure enough, a black sedan was parked there, engine still running.

Zed pulled a gun from his waistband, then gestured mockingly to the car. "Want a ride?"

"No thanks." Somehow, thankfully, my voice didn't tremble like my hands were. "I've got somewhere to be."

"I'll say. Boss needs to talk to you."

I couldn't help a wince. Dalton really did completely fail.

How did this happen?

I forced my expression to stay calm. I had to get out of this. "He didn't appreciate my gift then, huh?"

"Appreciate?" Zed barked a laugh. "If by 'appreciate' you mean 'become sadistically pissed off' then yes. In fact—" he twirled his gun dramatically in the air, "—he even gave me permission to shoot you, if I needed to. Or felt like it."

I swallowed my scream, but my tone was still too high. "But not kill me?"

He smirked wryly at me. "You're not *that* lucky, kid. So, what'll it be: the car or your kneecap?"

Heart hammering in my chest, I scanned through my options—the likelihood of me striking him and getting safely away before he managed to fire off a shot…

Zed's grin grew as I considered the tight space. My chances were slim.

Hanging my head, my shoulders sagged as I sighed, accepting bullet-free defeat. He gripped my arm and yanked me toward the car.

"That's what I—"

I threw my elbow into his ribs, then backhanded him across the jaw, making sure to smack his hand holding the gun. Then I took off.

Zed snatched my hood in his fingertips. I jerked back as the collar of my hoodie bit into my neck and I flailed backwards, slipping on the ice. He caught me from behind, the frigid barrel of his gun pressed into my chin.

I closed my eyes, waiting for the shot and surely blinding pain. Instead, Zed just started hauling me to the car.

"Big talker," I muttered because Zed let me get away with snarky conversation, which I appreciated in a weird, messed up way.

He shrugged, flashing me a malicious smile. "I'll save the honors for Boss."

~~~

I tried to escape again when we arrived at Sark's house. Zed forced me through the garage, and I turned on him in a burst of desperation. The struggle lasted longer than it used to, but still not enough— while stronger than I'd ever been, I wasn't trained for any kind of fighting, and since I'd spent all my pre-infection days in libraries and movie theaters, I had zero experience. I did manage to make Zed's nose bleed. A rare flash of anger glinted in his eyes, but it passed after he clocked me with the butt of his gun.

Frustration quickly morphed into panic when he towed me into Sark's house, through a dark kitchen and living room, then pushed me down a flight of
~~~

hard stairs. My head pounded, palms sweaty, as he dragged me through a door and left me on cold cement floor.

Alone.

The door clicked shut behind me, and I jerked my sore chin up to see where I was: an unfinished basement. Three bare lightbulbs were screwed into the framed ceiling, beaded silver strings hanging from them, but they were all off. The only light came from the half window on the far side, shadowed from the night sky and window well. There was a square table and a couple chairs, and silver cabinets lined the back wall. A few metal hooks stuck out randomly near the floor in the corner. That was it.

Already shivering, I jumped to my feet, only to hear the door open behind me and get knocked right back down to the floor. His presence alone weighed me down, making my body feel like it was ten thousand pounds. For a second, I relished in the freezing cement floor. Then Sark flipped me onto my back and drove his fist right into my face.

Another scary thing I'd learned about Sark: he seemed perpetually angry, or at least indifferent, but whenever he got *really* earth-shattering, world-ending, hide-under-a-rock angry, he was silent. Like he was too angry to even speak.

Like now.

Any of his coworkers—any villain on TV even—might make a show out of it. Drive me to my knees, make me apologize and beg for my life. Any of them enjoyed that power. Sark never cared for that. His rage pulsed in the air around him, and that alone was enough to make me retreat.

He punched me twice more before wrapping his hand around my throat. I coughed and dug my nails into his hand, but he just choked me tighter. My eyes finally adjusted to the light to see his face: twisted with rage, battered with two noticeable bruises, and bleeding. *Bleeding.* I'd only seen that red piece of evidence he was actually human twice in my life, but there it was, trickling down from a wound underneath his eye.

I'm dead.

Sark reached backward and I heard the slick sound of metal, then felt a cool blade at my neck. I flinched back, grinding my scalp into the ground. As the knife grazed the skin below my jaw, I wondered if this would be the night Sark actually lost his careful control and finally killed me, burying my secret with my cold body.

"Stop!"

The shadows parted and Erika was there, her beautiful face distorted with smudged makeup and sheer terror. She fell to her knees next to us, wide, green eyes, on the blade pressing down on my throat.

"You're going to kill her!" she somehow screamed and whispered at the same time. "Stop now!"

I felt Sark freeze. Erika's brief moment of desperate bravery drained out of her as she timidly glanced up to see him staring at her like she was someone else he'd met a long time ago. The moment stretched on for an eternity, their eyes locked—his distant and hers paralyzed—and my quiet wheezing the only sound in the chilly air.

Then his hand was gone. I gasped, drinking in the oxygen as carefully as I could since he didn't move the knife.

Erika was still immobile, but taking deep breaths. I tried to match mine with hers. One. Two. Three. Four.

"Can I…" she started, still daring to hold Sark's gaze. "Can I talk to you?"

Her voice snapped him out of whatever fleeting daze he was in. He blinked and glanced around for a second, as if needing to return to the moment. When he looked back at me his face hardened into a disgusted scowl, like it was somehow my fault that we'd found ourselves in this situation—whatever the heck this crazy situation was.

Then, even crazier: he let me go.

Not completely. But instead of carving me up while he choked the life out of me, he took me by my hair and dragged me across the ground to the corner, grabbing something from a cabinet on our way. Making sure my head hit the concrete roughly, he secured my hands behind me, then zip tied them to one of the hooks sticking out of the wall. He didn't spare me another glance before he stalked out of the basement. Erika gave me one last look, as if to remind herself I was there, before following him. I heard two sets of footsteps going up the stairs, and I was alone.

I didn't realize there were built up tears in my eyes until they started spilling out. My hands shook violently against their restraints, and I yanked my arms until my shoulders hurt so badly that I couldn't keep going. My head fell back against the wall in defeat when I realized I was truly trapped down here until he came back to finish the job. I cried harder when I thought of Erika upstairs, alone with him, and what he could do to her beautiful face.

This is a disaster.

My tears didn't last very long; I was too tired to keep up the crying. I tried stretching myself out to reach something—anything—in the cabinets but they were too far away. I tried again to break or loosen the zip tie. Nothing. Eventually, I got so cold that I huddled into a tiny little ball to conserve heat, shuddering against the frigid air and trembling with fearful anticipation. I'd screwed up. Erika would likely die. Sark would come back.

Sark will come back.

Sark will come back.

Sark will come back.

Eventually I nearly started crying again, but I couldn't muster up the energy to let it out. My body was stiff, frozen into the side of the building like a permanent ice sculpture as a fitting monument to the last moments of my pathetic life.

It seemed four winters had passed when I heard footsteps on the stairs again. My sluggish heart started sprinting and I managed to tilt my head up to look at the door. It was here. He was back. For a second I wondered if I'd be so numb that I wouldn't feel any of his retribution.

He's here he's here he's here he's here he's here.

The door opened and a shadow entered, a wraith in the dead of this awful night. It stopped in the doorway. I felt its eyes on me. My teeth chattered like a jackhammer. The shadow walked toward me slowly, and every step was like an ice pick to my chest. I imagined a knife cutting into me, my warm blood flowing over my wintry skin, just as I…

It's Erika.

The shock of seeing her instead of Sark nearly knocked me unconscious. She was haggard and wrinkled in appearance and demeanor, a wilting blossom trying desperately to cling to life in such a harsh and cruel winter.

Like a wraith, she was silent. Afraid of waking the real monster. Her lips pursed as she looked me over once. Then, without a word, she cut my hands free and helped me ease to my deadened feet. I stumbled. She held me up against her narrow frame. I shivered. She wrapped her thin arms around me. I decided I was either dreaming or dead as the angelic wraith helped me up the stairs.

The house was dark. It passed by me in a blur as we went through a living room, then a kitchen, into another hallway that went on for ages. Erika picked the last door on the right and went inside.

It was a bedroom. The normalcy of such a thing in Sark's house was appalling to me, and one of my knees buckled. Erika nearly got crushed under my weight but soldiered on, gently setting me on the bed. It was a warm feather duster, and my aching body sunk into it like it was an endless pile of fresh laundry. A soft sigh escaped me. Erika wrapped three of the blankets around my shaking form, then squeezed my arm gently before walking out the door, shutting it softly behind her.

I was delirious with disbelief and cold. It took ages for me to really understand that I was alone in Sark's house—that I was in a huge, soft, comfortable *bed*. I wasn't dead. Neither was Erika. Nothing was making sense.

While allowing myself to bask in the wonderful mattress, I stayed alert, jumping at every tiny sound. Nothing happened. Nobody came.

Once the clock struck two thirty and I could feel my toes again, I hesitantly got out of the bed, body aching and whining in protest. I paid it no mind. I had to get out of here before Sark broke through whatever crazy spell Erika had put on him.

I leaned against the door and strained my ears. All was silent. Taking a deep breath, I inched the door open and peeked my head out. All was dark.

You can do this. Stay calm and stay quiet.

Creeping soundlessly, I went down the black hallway without incident, feeling my hand along the wall. I marked six other doors, including the bathroom, as well as another hallway, but I went left, the way I'd come from.

Eventually I hit the kitchen, which was a little easier to navigate thanks to the single light on above the sink in the far corner. Both the kitchen and the living room were empty. I checked the back door going out to the deck, but it was locked and I couldn't find any kind of bolt or latch.

This house is freaking creepy.

I forged onward, jumping when the house creaked and settled into itself. The hardwood floor didn't make a sound underneath my feet, though, which I was grateful for. Turning into the next hallway, I found another slew of doors. The first one on the right had light seeping out from underneath it, which automatically ruled it off my list of doors to try. Instead, I opened the next one and slowly poked my head inside.

It was the ballroom-esque room from the other night, where Sark had the terrible box that tried to drown me. The moon gleamed through the giant overhead window, illuminating the empty space and making the floor shine. I quickly stepped out and shut the door. I didn't want to relive any of that.

The hallway ended with a small foyer, the front door straight ahead, and a half bathroom to the left. I breathed a silent sigh of relief—I was getting out of here.

Of course, the front door was locked, but I slid a bobby pin from out of my hair and kneeled on the ground, prepared to pick the lock and get out of here. Feeling along the smooth wood, I found the doorknob and went farther up. There was a square panel, but no lock. I felt underneath the doorknob. Nothing.

What the heck?

My heart started pounding as I kept searching the door, then tried to pry away the square panel with my fingernails. Nothing gave. I twisted the handle but it didn't budge at all, not even the slight turn a doorknob does when it was locked.

He sealed everything off, I realized, hyperventilation threatening to settle in. *He trapped me in here.*

Unwilling to accept that, I felt over the door again and around the edges, desperately searching for anything that could help me. There had to be a way out. If this door wasn't it, then there had to be another.

Suddenly, something creaked behind me. I turned to see the first door in the hallway—the one I hadn't tried—opening. Heart lurching in my throat, I jumped to my feet and darted into the bathroom, pressing my back against the far wall and watching the mirror.

Don't come down here, don't come down here, don't come down here.

As if my pounding heart and sweaty palms were a beacon for danger, footsteps sounded toward me. I clenched my teeth and forced every muscle into immobility. The footsteps got louder until they were right by the front door. I saw a shadow of a reflection pass in the mirror as they went by the bathroom. Then they paused.

Go away go away go away go away go away go away.

My ears strained to hear something, anything, but all was quiet. Two footsteps sounded. Silence. I held my breath. Three more footsteps and I saw the shadow in the mirror again. It stopped there. I bit my lip to keep from making a sound. My gaze stayed glued on the shadow, my eyes playing around with the hazy reflection until it slowly became more defined. Two pairs of eyes stared back at me and my blood went cold.

Sark was standing in the hallway, facing the mirror, and I could've sworn his icy glare was on me.

A scream built in my throat and I choked on it, fighting to keep it down. I felt the daggers in his glower from here, and they burrowed into me, but he made no other indication that he saw me. He didn't call me out. He didn't threaten. He didn't head me off or corner me or grab me to lock in the basement again. He just stood there, paralyzing me with his scowl, and let out a long breath. Then he turned and walked away.

He walked away.

Sark *walked away.*

It was a trick. I knew it. I didn't relax or move or hardly breathe, knowing the second I admitted my presence or walked out the door, he would pounce.

Seconds passed. Minutes. Eons, it felt like. My body got sore from standing perfectly still for so long.

What are you doing, Sark?

Finally, I built up some courage and leaned outside the door just enough for my left eye to scour the hallway. It was empty.

What game are you playing now?

Biting my lip so hard I tasted blood, I took a timid step out of the bathroom, then froze. Waited four seconds. Nothing happened. I took another step. Waited. Nothing. Step. Wait. Nothing.

Somehow, I made it to the living room. It was just how I'd left it.

Okay, Sark, now you're freaking me out.

Continuing at my deliberate pace, I finally got back to the bedroom Erika had left me in. My hands trembled violently as I shut the door behind me and let out my breath all in a rush.

Where are you, Sark? What are you doing?

Overrun by paranoid fear, I shoved all the blankets off the mattress, checked underneath the bed, and opened the closet. It was all clear. Nobody was hiding.

My whole body was trembling now, and my throat stung like I'd been screaming. Every nerve on edge, I picked up the comforter from off the floor and wrapped it around my shoulders, then curled into a ball on the floor in the farthest corner from the door.

He wouldn't just leave me alone.

I knew that. I'd tried to escape. That never *ever* went unpunished. Ever.

I waited for my judgment, terrified anticipation rattling my bones, until I couldn't take it anymore. My eyelids got heavy as the adrenaline drained out of my system, dragging me down. It was almost five when I finally fell asleep.

He never came for me.

5

A knock on the door woke me up.

"Arie?" Erika called, opening up the door right after knocking, so it didn't really matter what I did.

Groggy, I lifted my head to find myself still huddled in the corner. Light streamed in from behind the curtains, making the room seem much less sinister than it had last night.

Erika stopped momentarily when she saw my position, but then she blinked it away and her mouth pulled into a superficial smile that was too big, like she'd had plastic surgery to put it on and would never be able to get rid of it. "Good morning, lazy bones. It's after nine thirty. Do you always sleep this late?"

If there had been any doubt in my mind that something absolutely insane was happening, it was gone now. I shot to my feet and yanked Erika inside the room, shutting the door behind us. She yelped in protest, but I motioned for her to be quiet.

"You have to help me," I whispered in a rush. "We have to get out of here. I tried but all the doors are locked and the windows are sealed, but there has to be a way."

The smile on her face didn't change, but something shifted in her eyes. "I know, silly girl. I watched him lock them."

I blinked in shock, taking that in. "Wait, you knew that…" I blew out a breath and shook my head. "Look, it doesn't matter now. We have to get out. I don't know what he has on you or what he's promised you, but it's not worth it, I swear."

"He doesn't have anything on me," she said, still in that infuriatingly cheerful tone. "We just have to stay here, for now. We'll be okay."

"No." I gripped her arms and stared into her eyes like I could force her to understand. "He will *kill us*. Do you understand that? This isn't a game or a joke or a dream. It's real."

"I know, silly—"

"No you don't!" I felt like I could rip my hair out. "I've seen him shoot people. I've seen him walk behind a man and slit his throat with a razor. And take out what he's done to me—I've seen him torture innocent kids in the name of crazy science that can't actually be real." I huffed in exasperation, pulling on her arms. "You saw him try to drown me, for crying out loud! He's insane and dangerous and we *cannot* stay here. Do you understand me?"

Erika's eyes narrowed and she jerked her arms from my grasp, the slightest edge to her voice despite the smile plastered to her face. "I understand just fine."

I shook my head, drowning in bewilderment. Who was this girl? "Do you hear me? I'm telling you that it is not safe to stay in this house."

"And *I'm* telling you to trust me." The charade recovered. "Besides, I talked to him. You need a place to stay, I need something to do, and this house needs people to live in it. So here we are."

My mouth fell open, sarcasm filling it up. "Oh, okay, so you *talked* to the psychopathic murderer and he's going to play nice now? Do you hear yourself? You don't know—"

"I know enough." That edge slipped back into her tone for just a second. Then she beamed again and touched my greasy hair; I nearly hissed and ducked away, but she didn't miss a beat. "Anyways, you must be starving and you probably want a shower. The bathroom across the hall has anything you need, plus—" She leaned in as if sharing trade secrets. "The towels are the softest things I've ever felt in my life." Then she patted my head like a dog. "If you're going to shower first, then hurry up. I'd hate for your breakfast to go bad." And with that, she turned and practically skipped out of the room.

I stood there frozen in infuriated disbelief for a moment before shutting the door and collapsing on the bed. Our conversation played again and again in my mind as I analyzed it. Finally, I decided there were only two plausible explanations: one, she was crazy. Completely, totally, astoundingly crazy. Two, she worked for Sark. He'd traded in Felix for a dazzling smile, killer hair, and conflicting personality.

Actually, three explanations: she could be both.

I wasn't sure which of the options was scariest.

I didn't leave the bedroom for the rest of the day, besides my two emergency faster-than-lightning trips to the bathroom across the hall. Desperate for a way out, I inspected every square inch of the room, from the window to the floorboards to the ceiling of the empty closet. I didn't find anything besides a whole lot of dust—nothing to help me escape.

Erika brought me breakfast and lunch. Since I didn't have any more information other than her weird behavior, I had to assume she was working for Sark or at least against me, which meant I couldn't trust anything she touched, even food. It took every ounce of my willpower to not break down and eat it, and finally I had to set the plates in the hallway to eliminate the temptation. She asked me over and over again to come out and hang out with her, why I wasn't eating, or if there was anything I needed. I managed to bite back all my irate remarks and largely ignore her. She'd deflate like a little puppy, but, just like a dog playing fetch, she always came back. I could not understand her.

Even weirder: I didn't see Sark once that whole day. Here I was, living in his freaking house like an unwilling hotel guest, and *nothing happened.* My brain went in circles trying to anticipate what he was up to, and it just left me with a headache.

That night when Erika brought me a bowl of chicken stir fry for dinner, I broke. It was only half as good as it looked, but my stomach didn't care one bit. Erika watched me with mild amusement as I scarfed down everything, even the broccoli, which my mom had never been able to get me to eat.

"I *knew* you were hungry," she said in triumph when I handed her my empty bowl five minutes after she'd given it to me. "Want any more?"

I couldn't stop my stomach from taking control. Watching her for a moment, I nodded. At first I was afraid she'd make me go out and get it myself, but she just smiled at me and left, reappearing a minute later with a full bowl and a cup of water. While I'd gulped water from the sink the two times I'd gone to the bathroom, I downed half the cup in three swigs before digging into my food again.

Erika perched herself lightly on the edge of the bed, glancing around the room like she was seeing it for the first time. "So," she started, all conversational. "How long have you been like this?"

I stopped chewing and glanced up at her. We stared at each other. I almost spit my chicken out. Then she gestured to me.

"You know," she said, as though motioning to my whole body was explanation enough. "Like that."

I swallowed hard. Sark already knew this. Why spend time fishing out needless information?

When our heavy silence stretched too long, Erika sighed and threw her hands up, like I was a toddler that had thrown too many tantrums. "Fine, don't talk. I just thought I'd make this more bearable for the both of us." She pointed to the bathroom before wrinkling her nose. "I'll find some other clothes for you so you can shower. You really need it." And then she was gone again.

Yep, I decided as I stabbed another piece of chicken with my fork. *She's definitely crazy.*

She came back once more that night, to drop off the clothes she promised: a pair of old black sweatpants, two brown socks, and a gray thermal shirt a few sizes too big. Dropping them on the foot of the bed, she eyed them with distaste.

"These are temporary," she told me in apology, like I didn't look like a dirty, matted badger every day of my life. "I'll get you real clothes soon, but for now you can shower."

I didn't say anything. I just stared at her until she huffed in annoyance and walked out.

The next day started off exactly the same as the first: Erika barged in with breakfast to find me asleep in the corner in a failed attempt at guard duty. I ate a few bites to appease her, then started another in depth inspection of the bedroom. When I still came up fruitless an hour later, I made a brave decision. Scooping up my new clothes, I sprinted for the bathroom and locked the door behind me.

The bathroom was nearly as big as the bedroom, so it took a few minutes to search for anything—or any*one*—dangerous. After a fifteen minute inspection, I turned on the shower and let it run for awhile as I stood in front of the door with the plunger held up, ready to use as a weapon. Nobody came in to surprise me. Finally, I shed my disgusting clothes and stepped into the shower. The relief of running water and soap overwhelmed me, but it quickly melted into anxiety that had me peeking around the curtain at every imagined noise.

I ended up rushing through the shower, slamming the water off with bits of conditioner still in my hair.

Yanking on the clothes, I stared at the door, sure someone would bust in the second the shower was off. Nobody did. Water dripped from my hair as I sighed and cautiously opened the door, prepared to dash back into the bedroom for the rest of the day.

I walked right into Erika and choked on a scream.

"Hey!" she exclaimed, beaming at me. "You're up and clean! That's great!" Then, to my horror, she grabbed my arm and started pulling me down the hallway, the opposite direction of my room. "Come on, I need your help with something."

I dug my heels into the ground, but the new socks were slippery and her grip was like a vise. She literally dragged me down the hallway and into the kitchen.

I felt him before I saw him. Suddenly I was standing in Sark's kitchen and he was sitting on the leather chair in the living room reading a newspaper. The second he saw me, the room ballooned to twelve thousand degrees, and his glare pierced me, paralyzing me. I knew it then, without a doubt, that I'd seen him in the hallway the other night when I was trying to escape. He knew. He knew and he was pissed about it.

Somewhere in my frozen terror, the thought echoed how strange it was that he was reading an actual newspaper when he had so much technology at his disposal.

Erika had been babbling at eighty miles an hour for five minutes before she realized I was still frozen in the entryway. I knew she knew what was happening, but she just waltzed over and grabbed my hand, pretending not to notice the demon of death in the next room. She just pulled me in and put me to work. Feeling Sark's eyes burning holes in my back down to the spine, I pulled my hair into a thick, wet bun and followed Erika's directions, not even paying attention to what we were cooking. I tried to make myself as small as possible. I kept moving just to keep my hands busy, but I didn't make a sound. I didn't respond to any of Erika's millions of questions or comments. I hardly even breathed.

It got worse—yes, it got *worse*—when we finished cooking (it was egg salad sandwiches and pasta salad). Erika dished up two plates and dragged me into the living room. It took everything in me not to throw up as she sat on the couch, pulling me down with her.

She turned on the TV while she ate. I wasn't sure why, since she never stopped talking, choosing to comment on an actress's hair or the commercial slogans rather than actually watch it. Somehow, she managed to eat half her plate. It took a solid thirty minutes before I was able to force myself to nibble on the end of a sandwich, and even then it was only because Erika commented on wasting food.

To her slight credit, she never left my side. I waited in absolute terror for the moment one of her conversations would lead to her going to grab something, but she only got back up to make dinner, and she asked me for my help. Cue more hesitant cooking and another four hours trapped on Sark's couch with only the TV and Erika's voice to fend off Sark's heated glare.

Somehow, I survived the night and Erika dropped me back in my room like a taxi driver. The tense day had left me exhausted. For the first time, I slept in the bed, and despite the fact I didn't sleep all that much, it was amazing. Three hours later, I got up and snuck back into the living room, which was now empty. Just like I did in my bedroom, I inspected every square inch, including the kitchen and foyer. Any door that led outside, even the garage door I found in the mud room off the kitchen, was mysteriously locked from the inside without anything but a square panel that wouldn't *do* anything. My bones were heavy with dread and disappointment when the sun started rising and I snuck back into my room.

That day, I was slightly more prepared. As I expected—and feared—Erika didn't bring me breakfast. Instead she came to wake me up and dragged me into the kitchen again to make French toast. Like yesterday, Sark was reading a newspaper, but unlike yesterday, he was sitting at the kitchen counter.

My stomach dropped. I couldn't do this. I couldn't.

Erika made me. She babbled incessantly about everything from the Grand Canyon to different brands of paint (seriously, the girl *never* shut up) as I helped and tried not to pass out. Eventually, I couldn't pour anything because my hands were shaking so hard, and I spilled a drop of milk on the counter. Sark hissed under his breath without looking up; Erika quickly took the cup from me and gracefully added the milk herself without missing a beat.

The fatal moment came, and I knew it would, when we were separated momentarily. It was so fast, it shouldn't have been a problem, but if life had taught me anything, it was that it didn't like me.

I was trying to cut butter into cubes for the syrup Erika wanted to make, but my shaky hands made it difficult. Sark got up and went to the coffee maker next to the fridge. Erika started washing her hands before saying something about needing more soap. I rarely paid attention to what she was actually saying, so I didn't realize she'd gone into the supply closet until she was already gone. Panic seized my throat and I whipped around, but I was too slow. Sark was already there.

In one second, he had me pinned backward against the counter, one hand around my neck and the other around my wrist holding the knife. My spine nearly snapped in half against the granite edge as he plowed my head onto the countertop and held my wrist hostage there.

"Drop it," he seethed under his breath. When I didn't immediately obey—or understand—he tightened his grip on my throat. "Now."

I released the knife. It clattered to the floor, and the sound made me realize what he'd seen: he thought I was going to attack him with it. I was partly annoyed I hadn't thought of that, and partly annoyed that he thought it had been my plan and I'd failed so miserably.

Sark released me and scooped up the knife in one quick motion, the whole ordeal lasting under a minute. When Erika walked back in, Sark was back at the coffee machine, and I was pulling apart butter with my trembling fingers.

The rest of the day went exactly like the day before: I was trapped on the couch with Erika and the TV, only breaking to make food that we hardly even ate. If I hadn't been so terrified, I would've called everyone out on their superficial BS.

That night, I waited for a few hours before sneaking out to search the place once more. Again, I found nothing, and again, I trudged back to my room knowing I was stuck here.

The realization sent my heart racing, and I barely made it back to my room in time. Tripping over my own feet, I snatched the comforter off the bed and wrapped it around my shoulders, then sunk into the corner just as my breath caught and my body rocked with a dry sob.

I was stuck here. I was stuck here, in Sark's house, with him watching me and only crazy Erika to keep me company. I was stuck here, slowly going crazy myself, as I tried to anticipate every single threat that could come my way.

I shuddered, stuffing the edge of the blanket in my mouth to keep me quiet, because the real, horrible truth of the situation would make me scream until my throat cracked open and I bled out.

I'm stuck here and Sark's going to figure out what I am.

Sark knew I was infected. He knew that I came from a town in New York that I ran from after I became infected. He knew that I was uncomfortable talking to people, that my brainwaves were significantly different than anyone else, and that I could run about four seconds faster per mile than the average Olympian when I was pushing the absolute limit.

But he did not know that I was the key. He didn't know that I was the one Alexis had employed him and all his coworkers to find. He didn't know that I could wipe out half the population someday, if the wrong people got their hands on me.

He could not know that. But I knew that the longer I stayed locked in his house, the easier it would be for me to slip. Sark was smart. He was resourceful. He'd figure me out.

And then it would all be over.

I bit down on the comforter as the tears I didn't know were there finally spilled over, threatening to fill up the empty cavern inside my heart and drown me.

6

I woke up in the bed, feeling more rested than I had in months. Stretching my arms out, I sat up to find a huge plate of scrambled eggs and toast on the edge of the bed, waiting for me. I grinned at the food. It was so nice to have regular meals again.

Leaning forward, I reached for a piece of toast glistening with butter when a sound shattered the stillness of the eerie house: a scream. Erika's scream.

My blood went cold but I jumped out of bed anyway, flinging the door open and running down the hallway. The living room was empty. I searched around wildly, looking for Erika, but I couldn't find her, or anyone. Had I imagined it? Was I really losing my mind *that* fast?

"Hey, Arie."

I spun around to find familiar faces, which was such a relief after being locked up in this house. First, Charlie, my best friend from high school (tied with Erin, of course) with dimples and shaggy black hair that was always hiding his eyes. Second, Kieran, my older brother and best friend in life, with arms burly enough to tackle other people for a football and blond hair always cut short so he could look people right in the eyes.

"Hey, guys," I said, unable to smile in excitement at seeing them. Something was bothering me. "Have either of you seen Erika? I can't find her."

Charlie just shrugged while Kieran said, "I'm sure she's fine."

I *wasn't* sure she was fine, but I decided to take his word for it because I'd trust Kieran with the used iPod I'd saved up for seven and a half months to buy.

I invited them into the kitchen and offered them food. Charlie gave a quiet thanks and nibbled on a piece of toast. Kieran grinned at me and put enough eggs on his plate for three people. Something tugged in my gut. I'd missed his grin. How long had it been since I'd seen it?

Something clattered to the ground. I looked at my feet and saw a knife on the floor. I wasn't sure how it got there, but I leaned down to pick it up, and when I stood again, Charlie was gone from his seat and Connor was standing next to Kieran.

"Where'd Charlie go?" I asked. Kieran shrugged, clearly invested in his breakfast.

Connor—who could've been Kieran's younger, less buff (but I'd never tell him) twin with stronger cheekbones and straighter teeth—just waved me off.

"Come sit with me?" he asked, gesturing for the couch. Kieran gave him a warning glare since he didn't like Connor much, and I glared back at him. Kieran was just prejudiced because all brothers were prejudiced against their sisters' boyfriends. It was nothing, really. I knew what I was doing. Right?

Where is Erika?

Connor sat on the couch and pulled me down next to him, much closer than I would've chosen, and he put his arm around me, running his finger along my forearm. My skin prickled with discomfort when he touched me, a pit forming in my stomach like it knew something bad was coming from him. But that was crazy. Connor was my boyfriend. He was supposed to sit next to me and touch me and I was supposed to be okay with it.

He brushed a piece of hair behind my ear; I forced myself not to shudder in revulsion. He leaned in to whisper in my ear, warm breath on my skin; I made myself smile and lean in, like I actually wanted to hear what he had to tell me.

"I know what you are."

I jerked away from him like he'd electrocuted me. He smirked, tightening his grip around my wrist, his fingers like metal. My bracelet. The room got darker, as if a cloud had wandered over the sun and blocked out every last ray. I blinked. It wasn't Connor anymore; it was Kieran. He took the metal band off my wrist and fastened it around my neck.

Tight. Too tight. I started choking and reached to take it off. I blinked and it was Connor again. He shoved me onto my back and pinned me down.

"I know what you are," he said, stroking my face. Except it wasn't his voice. The voice was like the smooth purr of a jaguar before it ate you, and it scared the devil out of me. It was Sark's.

Then the face shifted and it was Kieran's face again, then Connor's, and it kept flipping faster than I could keep track—Kieran, Connor, Sark, Connor, Sark, Kieran, Sark, Connor, Sark—and they kept chanting "I know what you are" while Erika screamed in the distance and Charlie shouted "Monster!" The shackles around my neck got tighter and tighter, until I couldn't breathe, and I clawed at it but it wouldn't come off. I used the last of my air to scream. Then the couch opened up underneath me, and I fell into a pit of blackness with the Kieran-Connor-Sark zombie still reaching for me.

Arie.
Monster.
Arie.
Kieran.
"Arie!"

My eyes jolted open, hands at my throat, gasping for breath. I found myself on the floor of my bedroom, my legs twisted up in the comforter and rogue hair from my bun sticking to my sweaty neck. Erika was kneeling in front of me, her pale face screwed up in panic. Sark was in the doorway, utterly expressionless and staring at me.

I shook my head and braced my arms against the wall, trying to stabilize myself after such a fall. I had been falling, I'd been...it was...

"A dream," I breathed, my shoulders relaxing when I came to the realization. "It was a dream."

Erika's perfect eyebrows shot up. "A dream? That was not...that was like...a hallucination. It was...you, you were screaming and, and you..." She gestured to my shaking hands and I glanced down to see my fingers spotted in blood. My neck stung, like I needed a reminder that I'd tried to claw off a make-believe metal band closing around my throat.

I slumped forward and she gasped, but I ignored her hovering hands and put my head between my legs, forcing myself to breathe in and out. In and out. In and out.

It was a dream.

A dream.

Just a dream.

Not real.

The falling sensation wouldn't go away, though, and I couldn't get my body to stop shaking. It had happened again. *Again.* Before infection, I'd dream every couple weeks, but nothing like that. Nothing that made me thrash around screaming while making myself bleed as I truly believed I was dying. Those dreams had come with infection. And while I was horrible at keeping track, I knew they were becoming more frequent, especially when I was under extra pressure.

"Arie, can you hear me?"

It took me a moment to realize Erika had been talking to me for a few minutes. Still shuddering, I forced my head up to look at her.

"Leave," I said, harsher than I meant to, but I was too freaked out to really care. "I'm fine now. Thank you for waking me up."

Erika's eyes narrowed and I knew she wasn't going to leave me alone. She looked me up and down and asked, "Water?"

My throat ached from screaming. I nodded.

She stood and headed for the kitchen. I caught another glimpse of Sark watching me from the doorframe, and it made me jump to my feet and trail after her, holding my breath when I walked past him.

Once in the kitchen, I gulped down the water Erika gave me. It was gone too soon, though. It wasn't enough. I turned on the sink and flipped the water on as hot as it would go, then scrubbed my hands three times until the skin was pink and blood-free. But they still shook.

It was a dream.

I know what you are.

It was just a dream.

Monster.

"I need air," I told Erika, because I knew I was going to combust any second. "I need real air."

My expression must've convinced her I wasn't kidding. She bit her lip, thinking for a moment, then turned to Sark, who had noiselessly come into the kitchen and had his terrible eyes on me again.

"The backyard should be fine, right?" she asked him, like a toddler asking for a cookie before dinner when she knows she's not supposed to have it. I fought every muscle in my body to keep from shaking her by the shoulders and screaming in her face that she had no idea what she was doing.

Sark glanced at her before staring at me again. I didn't get it. What was he trying to figure out? I had creepy realistic nightmares that often caused me bodily harm—so what?

I knew it wasn't actually that simple, and he'd probably gleaned all sorts of new information about infecteds through this whole ordeal, but I forced myself not to think about that at the moment. I had to deal with one thing at a time.

After an eternity of him staring and Erika waiting and me realizing that I was actually hoping he said yes, he walked up to the back door. My mouth nearly dropped to the ground when I saw him slide the square panel aside to reveal a keypad, which he used to enter a code and unlock the door. I stepped closer to get a better look, but by then it was too late. He opened the door and gestured to the freezing air that rolled in. I gritted my teeth. How humiliating.

"Letting the dog out?" I muttered to him.

"Don't make me get the leash," he muttered back. I didn't miss the warning, and I wasn't going to find out if he was just matching what I said or if he really did have some creepy infected-death-wish collar somewhere.

Erika procured slippers for me from out of nowhere, and I slid them on before trudging out onto the snowy deck like I carried the storm cloud on my shoulders, hearing the door shut behind me. The cold was shocking to my system, and it helped me focus a little. I took deep breaths, basking in the fresh air—it'd been ages since I'd gone so many days without setting foot outside.

Once I'd finally collected myself, I took inventory of my surroundings. A large deck connected to the house led to a backyard half the size of a soccer field. The property was surrounded by giant stone walls a head taller than me and twice as thick.

I rolled my eyes, annoyed. How archaic.

Feeling two gazes boring into my back—one scalding compared to the other—I made a brave decision and clomped through the backyard, walking right up to the wall. To the left of the house I found a gate. It was also locked from the inside, and clad with a square panel.

Stupid Sark.

His warning glare from the window made my bones shake inside me, but I pressed on anyway, studying every square inch of the wall and backyard. Of course, I found nothing. For a second I considered trying to jump up and pull myself over the wall, but even if I could somehow manage it, Sark would be on my heels in four seconds flat and yank me back down. Somehow I didn't think Erika could save me from his wrath then.

Eventually my face was stinging from the cold and I ran out of steam. Unwilling to go back into prison, I pushed some snow aside and sat down on the stairs of the deck, resting my chin in my hands and thinking that life was the stupidest thing I'd ever done.

Only a few minutes passed before I heard the door open and close. I tensed, expecting the worst, but it was just Erika—who was annoying and certifiably insane, but wasn't the *worst* thing that could happen to me.

Clad in a fashionable maroon coat and black boots, she walked up to me and kicked some of the snow away, her nose wrinkling with distaste. I was surprised when she actually sat down. We both stared into space for a moment before she inevitably broke the silence.

"Are you okay?"

I actually snorted. What a dumb question. Her voice was different now, though. Softer. More real somehow. The plastic surgery smile had been replaced with a thoughtful expression, showing the creases in her face and making her seem years older than the twenty-something she actually was.

"Yeah," I lied. "I'm fine."

She pursed her lips, still staring straight ahead, so I did too. "How long have you been like this?"

I sighed and the defeat shone through my tone. "A year and a half."

She broke for a second. Her gaze flicked to me. "You've been running for that long?"

"No. I left home about a year ago."

"Oh." A beat of silence. "That's a long time."

"I guess."

"Did...did Sark do this to you? Infect you?"

I shook my head, words like gravel in my mouth. "No. My dad did."

Another beat of silence. Two. Three.

"Oh." She crossed her legs and her boot crunched further into the snow. "Does it...does it mean anything? Why would...why—"

"Would my dad do something like that to me?" I supplied bitterly. "Million dollar question. He got into the cult mentality. Thought he was 'chosen' to do something. Some guy hundreds of years ago wanted to make a formula to create the perfect human. They try it out on people, then study us in an attempt to figure out how to fix it. It's all crap."

And I'm the key to fixing it.

Erika ignored the bite in my tone. "I just don't understand. If...if someone wanted your...I know they're not abilities necessarily, but...why not infect themselves?"

"Because the formula is broken. Incomplete. It doesn't work like it's supposed to. All infecteds are just faster, stronger, more durable mistakes."

"If you're a mistake then why does Sark chase you?" She straightened up with self-importance. "I know there are more than you."

I rolled my eyes. "Everyone has their reasons. Power. Money. I've heard some people collect infecteds, like statues or bobble heads. Some sell them as glorified slaves, as if we still live in the Stone Age. Like we aren't still people or something."

"So you're..." For once, Erika deflated, a balloon slowly sinking into itself. "You can be valuable? Infecteds?"

"Yeah, I guess." I shrugged and my voice dropped into a whisper. "It's awful, isn't it?"

She took that in with quiet contemplation, her aura emanating disappointment, though I didn't know why. I didn't care. Now it was my turn.

"Is he blackmailing you?"

Erika blinked and drew back. "No. No, he's not."

"Then why are you keeping me here?"

Now she sighed, her shoulders slumping out of their perpetual perfect posture. "I know. I'm...I'm trying to help."

Fury at her ignorance bubbled in my stomach, but I forced it to simmer rather than boil over. Instead, I scoffed. "Yeah, well you have a funny way of helping people."

I thought I saw her flinch at that, but the moment passed. "Do you dream like that a lot?"

My shrug was noncommittal. "Sometimes."

"Does anything specific bring them on?"

"Infection," I answered flatly, watching my breath in the air. "Stress."

"Look, I know this is stressful for you, but—"

"You don't know the half of it."

Erika glanced sideways at me. "You're shivering," she commented.

I didn't answer. Denying it would be stupid anyway.

"Do you want to go back inside now?"

I laughed once, scornful. "Oh yes, because Sark's house is just my favorite place to be."

Her tone hardened slightly, and I found myself curious at her irritation because it made her seem a tad more normal. "It's a roof over your head."

"It's a prison and a death sentence, and I'm sorry, but you thinking anything otherwise is just idiotic."

Erika took a measured breath, reaching for patience, and I stared at a crack in the stone wall, willing it to all come crashing down. My toes were numb and the bitter cold had frozen my muscles, and for a moment I wondered if I would just freeze into a statue like that forever.

She fractured that plan with another sigh. "I want to be your friend, Arie."

I couldn't help it. I laughed out loud and turned to look at her. "Why on earth would you want to be my friend?"

The tip of her nose was pink, highlighting how pale her skin was. Her eyebrows furrowed. "I do. But I need you to let me."

I shook my head and laughed again. "You don't want to be my friend, I promise you."

"You don't seem like you have that many."

"Yeah, well there's a reason for that."

We didn't talk again for a few minutes. When she suggested going inside again, I grudgingly agreed, mostly because I felt I was made of ice. I watched the ground as I walked, purposely ignoring Sark's stare. He let us back in, and stepping into the house was like crossing over a magical barrier: instantly Erika went from semi-normal-friend-seeker to unstable-stranger-with-a-freaky-smile. She practically shoved me into the bathroom for a shower, and since I was nearly frozen through, I went with it.

As the hot water ran down my face, I made a new escape plan: I would fake another nightmare and ask to go outside again, moping around like I'd accepted my fate as a prisoner. When Sark unlocked the door, I'd make sure I was closer so I could watch the code he typed in. Then that night after they'd gone to bed, I'd sneak out and bring a kitchen chair with me so I could climb over the stone wall and get out.

I mulled over the idea as I dried myself off and wrapped up in a fluffy robe Erika had left out for me. When I got back to my room, I found her there, rummaging through my closet, which was now full of new clothes that had just been freshly washed. She'd ordered them for me off the internet. When I mumbled a thanks, she gave me a meaningful look—a *real* one, not the plastic surgery one—and it left me more confused than ever about her. The Erika I met in the cab only to drown myself for later that night was vastly different than the one sitting in the living room.

It didn't matter, though. I was going to get out and I'd never think about her again.

I commenced my plan that afternoon. It wasn't a perfect plan, but it was a plan, and I refused to let myself consider the consequences of failure. The first step was feigning defeat.

Since I'd been at Sark's for three days without a nightmare, I had to wait for at least three more—probably four—before I faked another, otherwise it could raise suspicion and I didn't want to press my luck. Sark was watching me like a hawk, and he knew me much better than I'd ever admit. Forcing patience in this terrible house would kill me, but it was patience I had to have if I had any hope of pulling this off.

So I pretended to give up, like I was accepting the fact I was here to stay. I got up in the mornings, getting dressed and ready for when Erika came to my door, still unwilling to go out on my own. I helped her cook all the meals, and spent all my other time trapped on the couch with the TV on and Erika's voice floating through the stiff air. I made sure my shoulders always sagged and I rarely looked at the doors.

As the days wore on, I fell into a routine. I knew where everything was in the kitchen, and had washed each dish twice. I knew where the supplies were kept, how to adjust the water pressure in the shower, and what TV channels Erika liked best. Sark watched me less; I relaxed ever so slightly. Things were insane but they were manageable.

Despite the weird calmness to everything, there was one aspect of the situation that I hadn't anticipated, and it was nearly killing me: boredom. When my mind wasn't going twelve thousand miles an hour trying to anticipate the next attack, it got very, miserably, fatally bored. Maybe that was Sark's new plan. He'd never tried to torture me with that before, and it was proving overly effective. I never thought it would be so numbing to have nothing to do.

The TV—which had once seemed like a staple, then luxury, of life—was now a shackle that I could not stand. Restlessness shone through when Erika turned it on after breakfast *again*, and I stifled a sigh.

Does anyone know how to do anything else?

After just an hour, I thought I would really lose my mind. I tapped my fingers against my bouncing leg, then played with the ends of my hair, fidgeting and readjusting and holding in more sighs.

Finally, I twisted around so my legs hung over the back of the couch and I was looking at the TV upside down.

Erika huffed with irritation. "You really can't sit still, can you?"

"Nope." I popped my mouth with the word and she huffed again. Like usual, I didn't look at Sark.

The remote was sitting in between me and Erika. I glanced at it, then picked it up and twirled it around in my hands, effectively losing my grip and smacking myself in the chin with it. Erika snorted. I rolled my eyes. I was the only one providing decent entertainment around here.

I played with the remote, pulling apart the battery compartment and anything else that would come loose. Then I put it all back and prepared to do it all over again.

"Stop torturing my remote."

That was the first time I'd heard his voice all day. Strangely, it wasn't full of the kind of livid hatred dark enough to suffocate someone on the spot— more like annoyed resignation.

Still, I set the remote back on the couch, then let out the longest, loudest, most dramatic sigh I could muster. If I was going to suffer through this monotony, then someone was going to suffer with me.

Sark leaned forward in his chair, eyes on me. "Why are you still sitting here? Go downstairs, rifle through things that aren't yours, or come up with anything else infuriating. Surely you can find *something* to do."

Noting his behavior—his 'lack of violent response in front of Erika' behavior—I shrugged. "I'm locked in your house. I thought you'd want to keep an eye on me."

He glared at me, reminding me that at any time I could lose the privileges I'd somehow earned through Erika, like a bed and clothes and food and no bodily harm. Instead of threaten though, he just said, "Yes, well in this case I believe the less you're in my sight, the better this will be for the both of us. You'd like it better down there anyway."

Surprised he acknowledged the oddity of the situation, I wanted to press him on that, but thought better of it. Instead, I took him up on his offer and went downstairs.

Rather than go through the locked door on the left, shuddering at the memories of my first night here after the Dalton fiasco, I turned right. A gasp escaped me when I went through the door into a library.

It was *beautiful*.

The room was open and spacious, the far wall lined with shelves full of tons of books. Sunlight streamed through the windows, showing aesthetic stone window wells that matched the counter of a desk next to the last shelf. There was one door next to the desk, and two more on the far end of the room.

I didn't care about any of that, though. I went straight for the books. Pulling the first one off the shelf, I plopped on the ground and started reading, my eyes so grateful to soak in printed words on a page rather than moving pictures on a screen.

I stayed in the library for the rest of the day, only coming upstairs for lunch and dinner. Erika came down with me after lunch to see what all the fuss was about, since I'd basically swooned over it while we ate, probably using more words in one conversation than I had the entire week. Sark didn't comment, of course, but the corners of his mouth turned into a faint, smug smile that just made me roll my eyes. I hated giving him a win for anything, even gorgeous libraries hidden in the basement.

Going to bed that night, I felt a new sense of renewal. I'd been here a week and it had been three days since my nightmare. Tomorrow night, I'd make my move. I'd fake a meltdown, Erika cluelessly comforting me while I pretended to be too shaky and terrorized. Sark would never guess it would all be a ruse to get the code.

It would work. It had to. Soon I'd be stealing through the snow in the backyard, frigid air whistling in my ears as I climbed over the stone wall meant to keep me in.

And then I'll finally be out of here.

7

The next day, I tried not to be too chipper at breakfast. It was difficult, though, because after such a terrible week in Sark Prison, I was still on a high from discovering the library, and I could practically taste freedom sprinkled in my scrambled eggs. I actually smiled at Erika. She looked at me like I was actively sprouting another head, then beamed back at me.

I wolfed down my breakfast, the food settling comfortably in my stomach and fueling my veins, which made me stop and think for the first time.

How much *had* I been eating? Definitely more than I'd had in the last month combined. Maybe even longer than that. I couldn't remember a time in the last few days when the hunger monster had growled incessantly from the back of my head.

That thought made me uncomfortable, so I pushed it from my mind. Instead, I rushed through dishes and practically ran downstairs, answering the call of books before I got trapped in a blanket of awkwardness by brainless television.

Once downstairs, I turned on all the lights despite the sunlight coming in from the three windows, before scanning the shelves. How did Sark keep track of all of these books? I'd always thought he was like a shadow in the night, disappearing and reappearing just when I needed it least. Now, though, I had an image of Felix and Zed trying to move all these books when Sark decided to leave, and I had to put my hand to my mouth to muffle my snort.

After a quick scan of the shelves, I wandered to the desk with a computer. Intrigued, I sat in the chair and wiggled the mouse. The monitor glowed to life, displaying a traditional waterfall picture for the desktop. It wasn't locked with a password, which seemed uncharacteristic to me, so it probably wasn't Sark's main computer. Still, I pulled up the browser and went to the search history, out of curiosity. My insides squelched together at the first thing in the history queue.

Stockholm Syndrome.

The two words were like a sucker punch to the gut. Suddenly struggling to breathe, I sat back, mind reeling, then clicked on the words and glanced over the information that came up.

"When a victim of kidnapping or a hostage-situation forms feelings of trust, affection, or sympathy for their captor as a means of coping or surviving."

My head started shaking before I was even done with the page, denying the pit in my stomach. No, this wasn't me. This wasn't *going* to be me. I wouldn't let it. I was getting out of here.

Why was someone looking at this in the first place?

Hastily closing the browser window, I rose from the chair and looked around, eager to find something else to occupy my wandering mind. A wide double door was to the right of the desk. I tried it, but had no luck. Locked.

Both disappointed and a little relieved I couldn't see what was inside, I turned back to the shelves, walking along them and running my fingers over the endless spines. The collection didn't surprise me a ton, when I thought about it—they were nearly all nonfiction, types of history books or discourses on scientific theories. I didn't expect the small collection of classics in the top left corner, though. Stretching on my tiptoes, I glanced over the titles, an excited smile breaking on my face when I saw an old volume of Sherlock Holmes stories. I didn't know Sark liked those too.

No, stop.

My smile quickly turned to a frown and I rocked back on my heels. Humanizing Sark would get me nowhere but in more trouble, and there was no way it would help me get out of here.

You're not Stockholm-ing me, Sark. Sorry.

My eyes caught sight of a box above the classics, shoved hastily on top of the shelf. I dragged over the chair from the desk and stood on it, then pulled the box down and coughed through all the dust. Settling on the floor, I dug my fingernails under the packing tape and opened it up.

The cardboard held some kind of makeshift time capsule. There was a musty, pink plaid collared shirt, fabric worn and soft, and a small candle with a half inch of wax left and no wick. A little red box held a couple bracelets, two pairs of stud earrings, and a modest diamond ring. Underneath the box was a small stack of scuffed books with yellowed, dog eared pages. Each title page had the name Kristen inscribed with a nearly dried out marker. And lastly, smashed between the books and the side of the box, was a wad of envelopes. Mail. Some of them were handwritten notes, while others were just bills or junk mail, but they were all addressed to either Kristen McCoy or Kristen Reynolds in Los Angeles.

Curious, I opened one of the letters, wincing when it nearly fell apart. The paper didn't seem very old, but it had been folded and unfolded so many times that the creases were wearing thin. The modern language used in the letter confirmed my timeframe, and it was full of such love and admiration that I melted a little. They were signed by someone named Aiden, and I assumed they were meant for Kristen. It wasn't intimate enough to be for lovers, I thought, but the two of them were definitely close.

Who were these people and how did Sark know them? Did he used to work with Aiden? Maybe before that? I couldn't imagine Sark as a child or having friends, so it was weird to consider the possibility Aiden was a childhood friend. Especially since the letters were addressed to California while Sark had his stupid British accent. There had to be some kind of connection, though, for Sark to preserve this stuff, even if it was forgotten on a shelf.

Maybe it's a victory box. The thought made me drop the letter, and suddenly my hands felt dirty. Box of mementos from an old friend—not Sark. Box of souvenirs of someone he murdered...now that sounded much more plausible.

Poor Aiden and Kristen. What had Sark done to them?

Handling everything carefully, I packed it all back up and nestled the box on top of the shelf again. Then, with a renewed sense of purpose, I sat back on the floor and started with the farthest corner of the shelf, pulling out the first three books. If Sark was going to keep me prisoner, then I was going to learn everything I could while I was here. It was too much to hope that one of these books would hold any information about infection or Alexis' organization, but I'd scour every page just in case, and I'd make mental notes of what I learned about Sark in the process.

I sprawled out on the floor, studying interesting paragraphs and skimming boring pages. Quite a bit of time passed—I was on book number four, and they weren't small—when I heard footsteps coming down the stairs.

Erika. I held back a sigh. What was she up to now? I still hadn't been able to pinpoint what the heck she was doing here, and that continued to unnerve me. At least she was trying to entertain me, though. I would have never guessed boredom would be the worst way to die.

When the door opened and shut, I didn't look up, hoping to finish the page I was on before she stole my attention. When I made it to the end without interruption, I got suspicious. When was Erika ever *not* talking?

Confused, I glanced up at her and froze. It wasn't Erika.

It was Felix.

Time sped up and slowed down. My heart started pounding, hands shaking, as we stared at each other. I hated the surprise that I knew was laced in my expression, admitting that I'd totally let my guard down. He looked at me like a starved predator that had finally found meat.

This had been such a stupid idea, coming down here alone. Did Erika know he was here? Was she a part of it?

You're such an idiot.

Slowly, I got to my feet without breaking eye contact, willing my head to stay clear. He grinned at me, shifting his weight to emphasize the fact he was blocking the shut door. I measured the distance between us, the chances of me somehow getting around him and up the stairs, where I could get my hands on a knife. Those chances did not look good.

I just waited, knowing he'd become impatient with the showdown eventually and make the first move. I was right. Felix surged forward with a blow to my head. I ducked and punched him in the gut, then dashed around him. Fingers reaching for the doorknob, I barely made it three steps before he snagged my wrist and yanked me back hard, throwing me into the shelves.

My head rattled as I staggered, books falling to the ground around me. Then I squeaked out an ugly sound when the shelf shuddered and fell on top of me, pinning me to the floor, face first. Groaning in a mix of pain, panic, and frustration, I glanced around wildly for Felix, my chin scraping across the carpet, as I struggled to squirm free. I was finally able to crawl out, but before I could get to my feet, a blow to my chest knocked the wind out of me.

I heard the door open just as Felix closed his hands around my throat, then a scream sounded. It snatched both of our attention, and I craned my head to see Erika standing in the doorway, hand covering her mouth in horror. I used Felix's slight distraction to punch him across the face, then kneed him in the stomach. Scrambling to my feet, I turned to Erika—prepared to tell her to get the heck out of here—but stopped in my tracks when I saw Sark appear behind her.

Giving them a second of my attention proved to be a fatal mistake. Felix grabbed me and hurled me into the window. Glass shattered around me, slicing at my skin, and I screamed when I automatically braced my arms to catch myself and my elbow buckled.

Icy air and snow spilled into the room, and it seemed to freeze the scene. Erika was still paralyzed in the doorway. Sark was beginning to push past her. Felix was glaring at me, hateful fury on his bruised face. Despite everything, only one thought echoed in my head.

I can't get caught.

Immediately, I made the only escape I could find: I stepped through the broken window and clambered out of the window well. Erika shouted my name, but I didn't stop. I raced across the front yard and down the street, too scared to look back and see who was chasing me. I just cradled my hurt arm to my chest and kept running. It seemed I'd left my mind back at the house—I couldn't think, I could only go.

Eventually the cold got to me despite my fast pace. I slowed down and looked around, trying to make sense of where I was. While I didn't know what direction I'd been running or how long I'd been going, I wasn't near downtown, which wasn't necessarily helpful information but it wasn't *un*helpful either. Really, the only thing that mattered was that I didn't go back the way I'd come. I didn't understand what Sark and Erika's purpose had been in keeping me locked up, but now that I was out, I was never going back.

A solid, sharp rock formed in my stomach at the thought of living on the run again—no more constant food, heat, bed, bathroom. I stifled a sigh and forced myself to keep walking. It had been stupid to get comfortable there. Nothing in the universe ever lasted, despite all the pleas and wishes of deserving people.

Focus, I commanded myself, taking inventory of my surroundings. It seemed I was on the edge of Chicago, or maybe even outside it. The sidewalk was uneven and half finished, and the land next to it was empty except for lumpy snow. An abandoned gas station stood about a block and a half down. I was pleased there wasn't anyone around, but it also made me uneasy to be so out in the open. Maybe I'd hide out in the empty gas station until dark and formulate a new plan.

I looked behind me to try and judge my distance, and I thought I caught a glimpse of the rooftops of the secluded subdivision Sark lived in. I hadn't gone as far as I'd hoped, but it was a start. I'd never set foot there again.

Turning back around, I shifted my attention to my hands and began pulling out the few pieces of glass stuck in my skin. I tried not to look too closely at my elbow—even out of the corner of my eye, I could tell it was swollen and not quite the right shape. It also hurt like crazy, but I was trying to take it all one thing at a time.

I was about to cross the street and duck into the gas station when I heard a gravelly sound behind me. My pulse stuttered when a car pulled up next to me, appearing out of nowhere, and Sark stepped out of the driver's seat, eyes on me.

Hands shaking, I automatically backed away from him, trying to gauge how far I could sprint before he ran me over with his car. My chances didn't look good.

To my surprise, Sark lifted his hands in placating surrender.

Fake. It had to be.

"Arie," he started slowly, quietly. "Get in the car."

A retort bubbled up in my mouth, but I choked on it when I stumbled over a hard lump of snow. It wasn't nearly as deep as it looked, and the surface underneath was uneven and rocky.

Sark tried again, and edge of impatience in his tone. "He's not coming back." Movements laden with caution, he took another step forward. I matched with two back.

"Get away from me." My voice trembled violently—I told myself it was because I was freezing—and the combination of shivering body and shaking hands jostled my hurt elbow. I nearly tripped backward again, and barely caught my footing, refusing to take my eyes off of Sark.

I can't get caught. I won't. I'm not going back.

Sark stopped and dropped his hands, and I was struck with the hesitant doubt in his expression. He seemed to be debating with himself for a moment— I edged myself farther and farther away—then sighed through his teeth. Irritated. That was more like the Sark I knew. "Listen, I'll call Erika and she can come get you. She's driving around as well, looking for you. It won't take long for her to get here."

I didn't believe a word of that. How convenient for him, finding me alone after Felix just happened to show up and drive me out. Any phone call he made would be to Felix, or maybe even Jefferson, Alexis' second in command. Regardless, I wasn't going to stick around to find out.

Sark pulled his phone out of his pocket, and I hesitated for just a moment until I thought he was sufficiently distracted. Then I turned to run.

I dashed halfway across the lot, nearly sprawling into the snow when my foot collided with a rock, and caught myself in time just to skid to a stop. Ten feet away, Felix was racing for me. I whipped back around to find Sark behind me. Cornered.

Taking an unsteady breath, I broke left in an effort to evade them both. Felix barked something at me, Sark right after him, and then I felt a hand close around my wrist. I half screamed when the hand yanked me back, pulling on my dislocated elbow. Then Felix had his arms around me and Sark was shouting and I kicked my legs wildly, refusing to be thrown in the back of a car.

I can't get caught I can't get caught I can't get caught.

I managed to drill my heel into Felix's kneecap. He swore at me and I kept kicking, but instead of gripping me tighter—like I'd expected—he picked me up and hurled me as hard as he could. Limbs flailing, I flew back several feet before crashing into the snow. Pain exploded as my ankle, head, and ribs connected with jagged rocks, splitting skin, flesh, and bone.

Tears sprung in my eyes, hopelessness crashing in. I tried to drag myself away, but any movement, especially crawling, just brought on bursts of fire from my ribs. Liquid flowed down my neck, hot and sticky. I pressed my good arm against my side, frantically trying to dull the burning.

I. Can't. Get. Caught.

I didn't know why nobody had grabbed me yet, but I welcomed every free second and kept trying to squirm my way forward, away. Realizing my eyes were closed, I forced my eyelids open and squinted at the bright light reflecting off the snow. I looked up to see Sark and Felix facing each other. My ears were ringing, but I could tell they were shouting, each of them angry at...each other.

What is happening? I gritted my teeth and shimmied a little farther. *Doesn't matter. Get out.*

Something gleamed in Sark's hand: a gun. I froze, waiting for him to turn it on me and force me into the car. Instead, he waved it at Felix, almost like a threat. More shouting ensued. The ringing in my ears got louder, my head cloudier. Unable to hold myself up any longer, I dropped my head onto the ground just in time to watch Felix turn and stalk off in the opposite direction of the car. My cheek pressed into the snow as my eyes tracked his movements, until he disappeared.

Where is he going? He had to be coming back. Felix never just *left* unless I was completely secure and Sark needed something else.

A figure knelt in front of me, obstructing my vision. My gaze trailed up and rested on Sark's face. I shuddered, the movement killing me, and I shoved my hand against my mouth to muffle the sounds that escaped me.

"Try not to move," Sark instructed, voice lacking all the hateful anger I expected but still laced with frustration.

"Get away from me!" I spat at him. The words were a little distorted, but I think he got the message. I continued my pathetic attempt to get up despite the uselessness of the gesture.

Where can I go?

Sark sighed with exasperation. "If you move, you'll make it worse."

I didn't dignify that stupidity with a response. I kicked him instead. Gasping at the spasms that shot across my side, I groaned and started crawling again while Sark was trying to pick himself up.

With one hand at my ribs, I used the other to drag myself along. I only went about a foot before my ankle caught on a rock and my elbow gave out. Another cry went through my teeth, a mix of pain and frustration.

"Calm down." The words were harsher but still not violent. What was wrong with him? Erika wasn't here to keep him from being his awful self. "You're just going to hurt yourself further."

He grabbed my arm to prevent me from crawling again. I screamed hysterically in response, trying to kick him again.

"Get away from me!" I glanced around wildly, wondering what the chances were that somebody would hear me. "Help! Help me!"

Then Sark's hand was at my mouth—the first normal response he'd had all day. "Arie, stop!" he snapped. "Be quiet and stop moving."

"No!" I bit his hand and twisted my arm out of his grip. Tears started to fall down my face as I started crawling again. "Get away from me!"

Suddenly, I was in the air. I turned my head to see that Sark had picked me up and was carrying me to his car.

"Stop!" I kicked my legs in a frenzy, screaming at the top of my lungs, begging the universe to let someone hear, to force Sark's hand somehow. "Stop, let me go! Now!" Sark only tightened his grip on me, making all my agonizing squirming pointless, but I kept trying. I couldn't go back. I couldn't get caught.

He's going to figure it out.

The thought broke the rest of my determination, and my tears gave way to sobbing.

"I'm not going!" I screeched. "Get away from me!"

Sark didn't say anything else. We got to the car, and he somehow managed to open the passenger door without putting me down. He slid me into the seat and shut the door before I could scramble out. My hands fumbled for the handle, but they were slippery. I inhaled sharply when I saw they were red. The breath killed my ribs and I doubled over, gasping. Then the car was moving.

Frantic with panic, I pounded my fists on the window, painting the glass crimson while screaming. My words ran together, making my screams a mess of sounds.

Sark seized my wrist as I went to hit the window again. Another shriek sounded, and my vision started to go blurry at the edges.

"Arie!" Sark tried to yell over me. "Arie, calm down!"

I tried to yank my arm away, but it just hurt my elbow. Everything hurt. Everything hurt and everything was too bright and blurry. I just screamed back at him.

Sark groaned in frustration, and the car came to a stop. I didn't care enough to see what the problem was. He released my wrist, bringing his other hand toward me, and I cringed away. Cowering back, I hid my face in the seat and waited for the silencing blow. Instead, I felt gentle fingers on the back of my head. I cried out when they touched a sensitive spot, and the pressure disappeared.

The voice that came was so different than anything I'd ever heard Sark use, and for a second I thought I'd been knocked unconscious.

He was afraid.

"Just give me three minutes," he said as the car started to move again. "Three more minutes and we'll be back at the house."

He said something else, but he sounded distant, getting farther and farther away. Were we in different cars? Was I somehow getting away from him?

Spent, I collapsed back, one fist still sliding on the window. "Let...let me...go," I demanded weakly. "I can't. Can't...get caught. Can't."

"Arie?" Sark was yelling again now, but it sounded muffled, like there was cotton in my ears. "Arie, you stay with me."

My eyelids slid closed just as my hand fell into my lap, fingers sticky and hot like the back of my neck.

"Can you hear me?"

Let...me...

"Arie? Arie!"

Go.

Then everything was gone.

~~~

My head hurt.

No, wait. *Everything* hurt.

My brain was full of muddled images, a mix of memories or dreams tainted and warped beyond recognition.

Where am I?
~~~

"Arie?" someone asked, despair coloring their voice. "Arie, can you hear me?"

My breath caught at the familiar noise, and my ribs exploded. I moaned in response, urgently trying to open my eyes, while my hands felt along for some clue as to where I was. Only one hand moved; the other was trapped across my stomach. A sling? Why would my arm be in a sling?

My elbow ached in response, as if reminding me what happened to it, and the memories hit me like a freight train. I knew exactly where I was.

"Sark!" Erika called. "Sark, she's waking up!"

My heart skipped a beat at the name and I wanted to scream.

Not him. Not now.

I shot upright, my eyes sliding halfway open. The living room seemed to melt, bile rose in my throat, and my arm buckled. My head hit the arm of the couch on the way down and I cried out at the impact. I felt hands try to restrain me, but that only induced more panic, and I thrashed around until I slipped from their grasp and fell onto the hard floor. My head smacked against the surface and everything disappeared as I blacked out.

When I came to again, I couldn't move. I opened my eyes to see Sark kneeling over me, holding me down against the floor. Erika was beside him, crying, gaze on me. Verging on hyperventilating, I squirmed and tried to get free. Sark just reaffirmed his hold.

"Let me go." I wanted to scream, but my voice was hoarse and spent, and instead it cracked into brittle pieces. "Please, just let me go."

Erika just cried. Sark met my eyes cautiously.

"Arie, I need you to calm down."

I cowered away from his voice, trying to turn myself away from him, then whimpered. Everything hurt. The pain was only amplified by the knowledge that I'd never get out of here. Not like this.

"Arie, listen," Sark went on. His muted tone was so different than what I was used to from him, and the shock of the difference made me start crying again. "I'll let you go. I will. If you will calm down and stay still, then I will let you go."

I didn't understand why that was such a big deal or why he was even offering in the first place—why hadn't he just locked me up already? Because of Erika?

My breath caught at another stab from my side. "What did you do to me? What did you—" Another moan of pain. I wasn't going to last.

I was caught and I'd never be free again.

"You're hurt, Arie," Erika said, drying her own tears at the sight of mine. "You're hurt, but you're safe now, and you need to let us help you."

I shook my head, which was a mistake. I hadn't been safe in a long time. I knew I wasn't now.

Overwhelmed with desperation, I let out a broken scream. Erika said something else, too quiet for me to hear, and Sark's expression clouded over with conflict. Somewhere in my chaos, the thought echoed that I'd never seen him so unsure of himself.

"He's, uh...he's not here." Sark's eyebrows furrowed, like he was concentrating really hard on forming words. "He's gone now. There wasn't...he shouldn't have been here in the first place. Now...that won't...he won't come back."

I barely paused my struggle for freedom to listen what he had to say. He was lying. He had to be.

When his words didn't have any effect on me, he tried again. "Arie, he's—"

"Why?" I shouted, borderline sobbing again. "Why would I *ever* listen to you ever? You *hate* me. Why would I believe you?"

"I don't know!" Sark snapped suddenly. I recoiled and half shrieked, sure I had just woken the real monster that had been sleeping the last few days. Scrunching my shoulders, I shut my eyes and tried to shield myself from his fury.

When nothing happened, I cracked one eye open. To my disbelief, Sark had his eyes closed, and Erika had his head cradled in her arms, both of them at a slightly awkward angle since Sark was still holding me down. They stayed like that for a moment until Sark sighed and pulled his head up, avoiding my gaze.

Erika leaned forward, talking softly to me and forcing a light tone. "You split your head open, crazy girl, and you lost a lot of blood. We really need you to stay still, okay? If you show us you can do that, then Sark will let you go."

Exhausted, I crumbled at her voice, losing myself to silent tears. "Let me go," I whispered, hating how pitiful I sounded, but the floor was hard and everything hurt. "Please."

Sark nodded at me without looking at me. "If you calm down, I will."

Never before had he offered me anything like that, and I realized I didn't have another choice. Even if he was lying, calming down would help me think more rationally, and maybe clear the clouds in my head. Slowly, I nodded.

Erika gave me an encouraging smile, made tragic by the rogue tears in her red eyes, and she turned around momentarily only to come back with a wet washcloth. It was stained with blood, but she rubbed it softly against my forehead. It was warm, and I automatically relaxed slightly when it touched me.

"There you go," she said. "Just relax."

Closing my eyes, I took as deep of breaths as my hurt ribs would let me, trying to match them with Erika's strokes with the cloth. Gradually I stopped fidgeting, my tears drying. The sounds of pain from my mouth quieted until they were hushed gasps. I tried to stay as still as possible.

Please let me go.

After what seemed like years to me, Sark broke the silence.

"Okay," was all he said. Then he slowly loosened his grip on me until I was free. The urge to run was a violent itch that demanded to be scratched, and I fought it with everything I had left.

I wouldn't make it an inch. He would hold me down again. My breath shuddered at the thought, and I quickly reached for control again when I felt hands hovering over me.

"So," Sark started, words still quiet and calm and laden with discomfort. "I imagine...with the floor, that's...being on the floor is hurting you further, isn't it?"

I just whimpered slightly in response.

"Then I'll move—can I move you to the couch? Erika will sit next to you. You'll be...you'll be fine.

You just have to be cautious with your head, all right?"

I didn't answer, unsure of what I thought. Sark waited for a few seconds before picking me up. I panicked at his touch, feeling his grip tighten as I tried to start kicking and thrashing. My pathetic attempts didn't do anything, though I don't know what I was trying to accomplish. I closed my eyes, too afraid to see where he was actually taking me, so I was surprised when I felt the leather couch underneath me and he gently set me down. True to his word, he leaned me up against Erika, who smelled like jasmine perfume. For some reason her presence helped calm me.

"I want to leave," I said, trying to sound stronger than I felt. It didn't work. "You can't just keep me here forever."

There were a few beats of silence before Erika answered. "Arie, you can't. You're really hurt. You need help."

"No. I need to leave."

"You're not safe out there."

"I'm not safe anywhere."

Nobody argued with that. I opened my eyes and straightened up, which was a mistake. The room started spinning, bringing me dangerously close to throwing up again, and something was squishing my brain. Another moan of pain escaped me, and I collapsed back into Erika as my eyes slid shut. This was impossible.

"Do you have any more of that medicine?" Erika asked.

My attention perked up. That did not sound good.

I heard footsteps go around the couch, into the kitchen, then come back to me. Forcing my eyes open, I found Sark standing over me with a syringe full of liquid.

"No!" I gasped, then cried at the eruption from my ribs. I tried to scramble away from him—over Erika—but both of them held me back. "No! Stop! Let me go!"

"It's just medicine, Arie," Erika assured me like I was five years old.

I shook my head vehemently despite the pain it brought. "That's what you want me to think."

The fight only lasted a few seconds, and with one arm in a sling and the rest of me beat up against the two of them, I lost bitterly. It didn't take much time for Sark to grab my good arm and push my sleeve up. I nearly choked on the panic rising in my throat.

"Please don't!" I begged, crying again, trying to jerk my arm from his grip. "Please please please don't."

Keeping a hold on my arm, Sark bent down so he was eye level with me. "Arie, it's okay. It's medicine, I promise you." I'd never heard him use such a gentle tone, and it caught me so off guard that I stopped struggling. "Like Erika said, you are severely injured. This will help with some of your pain and, hopefully, help you to heal faster. You will be okay."

Then he brought the syringe to my arm. I yelped and squeezed my eyes shut. My skin pinched and I waited, a few last tears rolling down my cheek as I expected the worst. After a few seconds, the pain miraculously started retreating. Everything went

soft and gray and numb, slowly wrapping me up and
lulling me into unconsciousness.

8

This time, waking up was slower. Grogginess clung to my mind like a dryer sheet in a bundle of warm clothes, and I had a hard time shaking it off. Groaning, I swiped my hands around to feel where I was, but only one hand would move. Then I remembered.

Frantically, I opened my eyes and squinted against the dizziness that came on, forcing myself to breathe through it. Finally my head cleared enough that I could see straight and I found myself in the bed I'd been sleeping in for nearly two weeks now. The lamp on the nightstand was on, the curtains drawn against the night sky. My breath caught when I looked up and found the door open, lights from the distant hallway spilling across the doorframe. I strained my ears but couldn't hear anything; the house was still.

Despite the silence, my fear kept me frozen in place for too long. Finally I decided that if Felix were really waiting for me in the hallway, he wouldn't be this patient, and he wouldn't have brought me to a massive, cozy bed to rest my injuries in. And if I really wanted to get out of here—for good this time—I'd have to actually get *out* of the bed.

It took a few tries, but I managed to sit myself up and lean against the headboard, catching a glimpse of myself in the mirror. It was not a pretty sight. My face was streaked pink and red, the colors stemming from the back of my neck; a thick bandage had been wrapped around my head; and my clothes were stiff, stained with blood and mud.

How am I going to survive out there like this?

I started to shake the hopeless thought out of my head, but stopped when it felt like a drill bit was going through my brain. I couldn't think like that. I had to get out of here.

Going as carefully and quietly as I could, I stood up and removed the bandage from my head. It was caked with dried blood, so I threw it in the garbage can next to the dresser. My ankle was secured in a brace and whined under my weight when I stood up. My ribs ached, my head was buzzing, my foot was swollen, and my arm was in a sling.

This is going to be interesting.

Limping to the door, I winced at the scratching sound my brace made against the hardwood floor, but when I peeked into the hallway, nobody was there.

Stay calm. You can do this.

I had to steady myself against the wall with my good hand while I went down the hallway as fast as I dared. Turned the corner. Passed the closed doors. I couldn't pass the bathroom though—my heart was racing, which just made it harder to work with one arm—but when I unlocked the door and poked my head out, the place was still empty.

Where is everyone?

Once I got to the also-empty kitchen, I came to my biggest problem: the doors were probably still locked. The locked back door confirmed this, and I was sure the front door would be the same. How on earth was I going to get out of here?

My memories were murky, but I had a sudden flash of climbing through the window in the basement after Felix broke it. How long ago was that? Was it too much to hope it hadn't been fixed yet?

Though every step was painful, I checked the front door, just in case. Locked. I ran my hand over the parts of the doorframe I could reach, searching for anything that could help me open it. No luck. I was too afraid to try typing a code into the keypad: the wrong one would likely trigger an alarm, and then all hope would be lost.

With a throbbing, frustrated sigh, I headed back toward the kitchen, knowing any second my luck in being alone would run out.

Three scraping steps later, that luck ran out. The door to the front room opened—the front room I almost drowned in over a week ago—and Sark stepped out. There was a half second suspended in time where our eyes met and the situation registered in each of our minds. Then I turned to run as fast as I could, and Sark swore under his breath before calling my name, footsteps behind me. Knowing the living room was a trap, I made a panicked decision and turned for the stairs, slamming the door behind me to slow him down for a moment.

I limped down the stairs in my brace, each step a stab of pain, barely able to keep myself from tripping. Spilling into the library, I found that the window I'd crawled through was already fixed and the fallen shelf back up, but books were still scattered everywhere. Sark hit the staircase and I surged forward, stumbling over debris with no idea where to go. The door that was locked earlier was now open, but I saw a corner of a desk and knew it would be a dead end, so I went for the closed door straight ahead on the far wall, begging the stars to let it be some kind of back door or secret staircase. A scream caught in my throat when the door opened to the furnace room.

Sark called my name again—just a few feet behind me—and the sound of his voice made me shoot forward. The room was more like a closet and most of the space was full, so there wasn't really anywhere to go. I felt Sark's fingertips barely miss my shoulder as I dove to the floor and wedged myself in between the water heater and pipes. Sark grabbed my good ankle, but I kicked my leg and he lost his grip, and I wriggled backward as far as I could go. It wasn't far, but it was enough. When he reached for me, his fingertips brushed the air an inch from my toe.

Panting, I watched Sark appraise me with a raised eyebrow, kneeling on the ground in front of the closet. Instead of yelling at me—like I expected—his mouth twisted with something that wasn't a smile but wasn't a frown either.

"Well, now," he said, nearly mocking but not quite. His voice sounded off to me. "That can't be comfortable."

I didn't answer. My pained gasping was evidence enough.

Sark sighed at my silent stubbornness, shaking his head and rocking on his heels. "Fine. I don't care. Shout when you come to your senses and need help getting out of there." Then he stood and walked away.

My mouth fell open—well, it tried to. My head was tipped forward thanks to a pipe behind me, making my chin dig into my chest and pulling at something on the base of my skull. My legs were all tangled in each other, my braced ankle bent underneath a pipe, and all kinds of sharp corners were digging into my back at just the wrong angles. Between my scrunched posture and deep gasping, my hurt ribs were dying. *I* was dying. I didn't think I'd be able to last another thirty seconds in here, let alone until Sark miraculously left.

I watched him walk away from me, my eyes tracking him as he disappeared into what I assumed was his office. He returned less than a minute later carrying a few books and a tall bottle half full of alcohol.

He was *drinking*. That's what was wrong with his voice: it was a little too slurred. While I'd seen him drink from time to time among his coworkers, that was all recreational, and he never had enough for me to tell a real difference in him.

A pit formed in my stomach. I couldn't even handle a sober Sark. What was drunk Sark like? Did I even want to find out?

Taking another long swig, he sat down on the floor and settled the books into a box. I recognized the box as the one that had been on the top shelf, full of things about Aiden and Kristen. It had seemed forgotten when I'd found it, but Sark must've remembered it, because he left the floor littered with other books and focused solely on rummaging around the box. Watching him interact with it ruled out my 'victim box' theory: he was handling it like it was full of ten thousand-year-old porcelain relics.

My curiosity could only pacify me for so long, and soon I found my position unbearable. Eyes watering, I bit my lip and refused to cry, but I didn't know how much longer I could last. There wasn't any way I'd be able to get out—or move at all, really—without catching Sark's attention, distracted and drunk as he was, and I became panicked at the thought that he was right and I wouldn't be able to do it on my own.

Stay calm, I told myself. *You can do this. You have to do this.*

Taking a deep breath and doing my best to avoid angering my ribs, I straightened up and leaned forward, using my free hand to balance myself against the water heater. Then I slid myself an inch forward. My hurt elbow hit against the wall in the cramped space, and a mangled cry of pain went through my teeth.

"That was fast," Sark muttered without sparing me a glance. He just took another drink, clearly not concerned about my escape attempt.

What is with *him?*

Gritting my teeth, I started to maneuver myself around a pipe, holding my breath and begging my ribs to stay calm for a second. I got halfway around it when I lost my balance on my hand. My arm buckled, and I instantly put my hand at my side to protect my ribs, though it was no use. My head bumped against a pipe as I fell onto my injured side, landing on my useful arm and pinning it underneath me while my legs remained tangled and caught in a separate pipe. I choked on a scream from the agony that shot across my body, and another built in my throat from the panic of being stuck.

Stay calm, stay calm, stay calm, stay calm.

A shadow loomed over me and Sark's voice was at the doorway. "Stop squirming. You'll only make it worse."

I wanted to bite back with something tough and brave, but my voice crumbled and broke. "I can't move. I can't—" My breath caught, another scream in my throat. It hurt too much, *everything* hurt too much, and this was how I was going to die, bent in half in a furnace room in Sark's basement. What a terribly stupid way to go.

"Stay calm." His voice was still that slurred hybrid of harsh and smooth. "Is your head bleeding?"

I crunched my teeth together as a tear escaped my eye and rolled down my face and onto the cold cement floor.

Stay calm stay calm stay calm stay calm.

"Arie, this is important. Is your head bleeding?"

Forcing myself to pause, I tried to focus on what my head felt like. It was dizzy and cloudy and pounding, but not wet. "I don't—I don't think so."

"Good." I felt a hand on my good ankle, gently pushing it back and then pulling my leg out of the pipe. "Can you push yourself back up?"

Shifting my weight as best I could, I pushed myself up on my good elbow, but it stretched my side too far. I fell back down, gasping. "I...I can't. Ribs...I can't."

"Okay, then try to slide yourself toward me."

"There's a pipe in the way."

"I know." He patted my ankle once, like I needed the reminder he was still holding it. "I'm going to help guide you out."

I absolutely hated everything that statement stood for, but my body wasn't going to let me waste another second. Gritting my teeth, I inched myself out, obeying Sark's frequent instructions while trying not to cry out too loudly when something caught wrong or bumped something hard.

The worst part was the end. I had gone over the last pipe rather than squeezing myself under it, which worked well until I found my spine bent in half over it, my legs spilling into the room and my head hanging back with the blood rushing to it. I was twisted the wrong way and using my good hand to keep me from falling backward on my head, and my ribs were shrieking at me from being stretched so far. I didn't have the free arm or core strength to pull myself up. Sark literally had to lean in over me and hang on like he was giving me a hug, nearly falling in himself. He braced his palm at the base of my neck to keep my head from flopping around and slowly extracted me. It was a long, painful, and awkward moment, but finally he set me down on the carpeted floor. I was free.

I crumpled onto the ground in relief, gasping with pain and exertion. Sark didn't make any move toward me or announce any threat or get angry that I tried to evade him. He just took a moment to catch his own breath before glancing over me.

"You're bleeding again."

I assumed he meant my head, but he nodded toward me while looking at my shoulder. Glancing down, I saw red seeping through the collar of my shirt, a cut at my collarbone bursting out of its stitches.

Stitches? Sark stitched me up?

Instead of responding to that, I jerked my chin toward Aiden's box. "Who is that for?"

"You found it." I wondered if he'd be mad or even surprised by that, but the statement came without expression. "The seal was broken. I assumed it was you."

I watched him, cautious of and curious about this stranger in front of me. "Do you know Aiden?"

Sark actually flinched at the name—it was minimal, but it was there—and averted his gaze from mine. Reaching behind him, he snagged his bottle of alcohol. "A long time ago," he answered before tipping his head back and swallowing a mouthful. Somehow the action made him look younger. Then he gestured at me with the bottle. "The cut was dirty. You need to keep it clean and stitched so it doesn't get infected."

I was so surprised by that, I laughed. My ribs weren't happy with that decision, and the laugh was quickly replaced with a moan as I curled in a ball.

"I'm serious," Sark added, which only made my headache worse because I could not understand his behavior at all.

"I know," I said even though I didn't. "It just doesn't seem...like my biggest...problem right now."

Sark pursed his lips and took that in for a moment, then got to his feet and walked around me. I braced myself when he kneeled down behind me and moved my hair aside.

Don't hurt me don't hurt me don't hurt me.

I sucked in a sharp breath when I felt his fingers at my neck, softly probing up the back of my head. Nausea bubbled in my stomach as he pressed against ridges in my skull.

"It really split open?" I asked, nearly a whisper.

"Yes."

"How...how did you…"

"Staples."

The nausea in my stomach rolled and I nearly threw up right there. I closed my eyes instead. "Oh."

"It hasn't reopened. How does it feel now?"

How does it feel? Why do you care?

"Hurts," I managed. "It's cloudy and...dizzy. Pounding hard."

"I can imagine."

Neither of us said anything else for a moment, and I decided I must've been dreaming. That was the only possible explanation for everything that had happened since I'd woken up: I hadn't really woken up at all. What state would I be in when I finally did? How was I going to get out of here?

I heard the sloshing of liquid in a bottle—he was drinking *more*?—then Sark spoke again. "You really need to take care of that cut."

I just scoffed. "Yeah, well I'll make sure...my doc looks at it next...next time I'm in."

There was a beat of silence and more sloshing, then suddenly I was in the air. I squeaked in shock and my eyes flew open to find Sark carrying me.

"What are you—" I pushed against him, then stopped when my ribs got mad. "Put me down."

Sark's face remained passive, though I detected a hint of discomfort shining through. "Erika made me swear to take care of you while she was gone. Not ideal for either of us, believe me."

He carried me into the next room, which I realized was his office, and stopped at a table against the wall. Using his elbow, he pushed aside stacks of books and files, then stretched me out on it with a pile of packets as a pillow. Once I was secure, he turned and procured a first aid kit from the bottom drawer of his massive and overflowing desk and brought it over to me. Objections got stuck in my throat as he moved the collar of my shirt just enough to expose the cut and wiped it with a wet square, before giving a small injection to numb it. My stomach clenched when he picked up a needle and thread.

"Um, you're drunk," I said, doing nothing to hide my fearful skepticism.

Sark didn't even look at me. He just worked on threading the needle. "I'm not drunk. I've just had enough to take the edge off the real world."

An image of the half drained alcohol bottle filled my mind. "Yeah, well that's a real needle through my real skin."

He successfully threaded the needle, then turned his gaze on me and held out his hand, palm down. I stared at it, unsure what I was supposed to do.

"I'm steady," he explained, which was true.

I wasn't convinced. "I don't…"

"I'm fully capable." With that insistence, he began working. "I've stitched myself up many times, in much worse shape than this."

Holding my breath, I squeezed my eyes shut and my hands into fists, expecting the worst. I felt the needle, but not the pain. The tugging wasn't comfortable by any means, but it was bearable.

Waiting a few minutes to see if Sark would somehow morph back into a monster, I asked, "Where is Erika?"

"The grocery store," he answered, his tone a little more rigid with concentration. "She claimed you would need to eat when you woke up, despite the pantry still being stocked. I imagine she needed a sense of normalcy for an hour."

Normalcy. What a strange thing for such a strange girl to go after. I did feel a little relief, though, at the idea that Erika didn't know about Felix coming after me. Of course, she left me in the hands of Sark, so her judgment was still highly questionable.

"Was she...she was crying." My head got fuzzy the harder I concentrated, memories slipping out of reach just as I caught them.

I detected a hint of surprise in Sark's voice. "You remember that?"

"I think so. Unless it was a dream."

"What else do you remember?"

The tugging continued, so I tried to focus on his question instead. "Um, I was down here reading and...Felix, um, came in." My hands shook slightly but Sark didn't comment on it or Felix. "The shelf fell and the window broke, so I ran. You all followed—no, just you two followed me. In the snow. You had a gun, I think, and then Felix left and I...got in a car? We went...well I guess we came back here because I fell off the couch. Erika was crying and said something about my head. Then you gave me...something. I thought it would hurt but it didn't. It was medicine?"

Sark didn't respond to that, so I garnered up bravery and opened my eyes. He still had the impassive expression he'd been sporting since I woke up, but now his eyebrows were furrowed in concentration and his mouth was twitching like he wanted to yell but couldn't. Even though he was stitching me up, he was trying *really* hard to not look at me.

"Why is it hard for me to remember that?" I asked. I felt like he owed me that much.

His tone was as methodical as his hands, like reading a doctor order, stumbling here and there with uncertainty. "I assumed you had hit your head when you fell, but I did not realize the extent. After getting you into the car...there was blood everywhere. Much more than there should have been, even with your injuries. I've known infecteds under Alexis that have died from severe blood loss, so I...I brought you back here and was finally able to stop the bleeding, but at that point...I didn't know.

Erika demanded a transfusion, but I wasn't sure if you being infected would cause your body to reject anything foreign like that. You were still breathing, so we waited until you finally woke up. I thought you were going to kill yourself when your head hit the floor."

He finished up the stitching, then traded his needle for a bandage. "You'll feel the effects of both the head trauma and blood loss for awhile. We'll have to be cautious." Securing the bandage to my cut, he moved my shirt back in place, then started packing up his supplies.

My eyebrows furrowed. "Why? Why would you even think of helping me—or saving my life?"

I could be valuable to him. That's why. I always got the sense that Sark would never actually kill me, though I never thought we'd get the chance to really prove that theory.

Sark sighed but wouldn't meet my eyes. No answer.

"So you really didn't know about Felix? He just got bored or mad and decided to take it out on me?"

"That's how he usually handles his frustrations, isn't it?"

"You know what I meant."

Sark stopped suddenly and met my gaze, and it was so penetrating, full of so much other than the icy hatred it had always held, that I nearly drowned in it. "No. I didn't know. It won't happen again."

A few seconds passed before he continued cleaning up, releasing me from his stare and allowing me to breathe again. Once he was done, he offered his hand to me and helped ease me into a sitting position. The room spun and I had to lean against him for a minute, but the second I was stable enough on my own, I shied away from his touch. He pretended not to notice and let me go.

"You can go back upstairs, if you want," he told me, gesturing to the doorway where the messy library was waiting. "It'll take me some time to clean up down here."

I just stared at him, dumbfounded.

Who is this guy and what did he do with Sark?

His eyebrows pulled down when I didn't answer. He nodded at my ankle. "Do you need help up the stairs?"

Help? Like the good kind?

"Um, no," I said before he took my hand again. "I just...I…"

"Just what?"

I took a deep breath. "I just didn't think I had an option."

Sark dropped his eyes again, and awkward tension pulsed in the air around us. Desperate to make it end—since when was *awkwardness* the worst thing about being with Sark?—I scanned his office and said the first thing I could think of.

"Why is there an elevator?"

He put the first aid kit back in the bottom drawer of the desk. "To transport people and things from one floor to another."

I rolled my eyes, though it did not help my headache. "It's kinda flashy. You could just take the stairs."

He smirked at me. "Now where's the fun in that?"

Going slowly, I stood up and wandered through the luxurious office—clad with flat screen TVs, leather couches, and three monitors—limping until I got to the silver door in the back corner. I pressed the up button and the door slid open immediately, so I stepped inside, inspecting the buttons.

"There are two options," I said. "Where else does it go?" I couldn't remember ever seeing another one around the house, not that I'd really thought to look for one.

Sark appeared at the door, stepping easily inside while putting as much distance as possible between us. "I'll show you," he said, pressing the top button.

The door slid shut, and suddenly I was struck with fear: this could lead anywhere, and I'd just walked right in without trouble. Just because a Sark from another dimension was visiting didn't mean I had clearance to make stupid mistakes.

I glanced at him. He didn't look at me. We went up without an issue.

Different dimension for sure.

My brief moment of fear ended when the elevator stopped and the door slid open again. Amazement overwhelmed me, and I forgot my precarious situation as I stepped out into the night, a gasp escaping me.

We were on the roof of the house, but it seemed we were so much higher, perched in the heavens. Bright lights sparkled from the distant skyline of Chicago, and stars dotted the black sky, both twinkling with a kind of pure beauty I hadn't seen in ages. I gawked with my mouth open in awe, taking in the view.

"Wow," I murmured to myself. "This is...wow." Then a thought occurred to me. I tore my gaze away from the scene to look at Sark. "Why isn't it cold?"

There was a slight chilly breeze, but it didn't match the thick snow on the neighboring rooftop.

"There's a heating system built in the ceiling underneath us. It drives away most of the cold air."

I raised an eyebrow, surveying the view again. "Well it's beautiful."

"Yeah." He glanced around too, like suddenly remembering the sky was there. "It is."

My ankle whined at me, but I didn't want to leave, so I was excited to find a lounging area on the roof, complete with a couch, table, and loveseat. I eased myself onto the couch without looking away from the sky. It was so pretty, I could've cried.

Sark hesitated before sitting into the loveseat next to me. We were silent for a while, just taking in the surroundings, and for once I appreciated Sark for letting me see this. Maybe it was just the beginning of some evil plot where he used awkward politeness to confuse me to death, but, for now, I was basking in the peace of the night.

A good chunk of time passed before Sark broke that peace. "I found something."

I stiffened at his voice, unsure if I was relieved or nervous that his tone still held that uncomfortable reluctance. This new Sark was messing with my head.

Turning to look at him, I braced myself for whatever test this would be. "What?"

"I found something. Don't tell Erika—I imagine she won't be thrilled to find it missing from its hiding place—but it's yours."

Now he definitely had my attention. "*Mine*?"

He didn't elaborate. Instead, he reached into his pocket and pulled out a simple silver band with the light inscription *Team AK*. My bracelet.

For the billionth time since I arrived at Sark's house two weeks ago, my mouth fell open in shock. I gasped and held my hand over my mouth, blinking fast, waiting for the mirage to disappear because it was a trick. It had to be a trick. I thought I'd never see that again. I thought I'd lost him—*it*—I thought I'd lost it forever.

"It *is* yours," Sark went on, watching my reaction. "Isn't it?"

Relief flooded through me and grief sunk me down, threatening to drown me. I bit my lip and nodded slowly. Then I threw on my emergency brakes, eyes darting away from the bracelet to him.

"Why?" I asked, though it sounded more like an accusation. He wouldn't offer me this unless he got something back. I knew that. "What do you want for it?"

Sark let out a long breath, sitting back in his chair, and I fought the urge to lunge forward and tear the bracelet out of his grip before making a run for it. Something kept me in place, though, and I knew it wasn't Sark's presence or my temporary disabilities.

"As you've so acutely observed," he said with a wry grin, "I've been drowning my old demons in a bottle all night. I want to hear about yours now."

I closed up instantly, hearing the figurative deadbolt in me slide into place. Sark had been following me for a year now. He'd done research on me for who knows how long before that. He had thick files on my history, countless notes on experiment results, and a scary ability to anticipate what I would do next. He had so much on me—except this. What he was asking for was information only I could give, information he could never find in a file. If he wanted it, he'd have to get it from me. Or, in this case, he'd have to barter for it with the only thing I had left from my older brother.

Sark wasn't getting anything about Kieran. I could barely think about Kieran in my head, alone, and I couldn't imagine telling Sark of all people about him.

No. We were not going down this road.

My eyes must've given away my resolve, because Sark just smirked at me and twirled the bracelet in his hand. "I figured as much."

I lifted my head higher. I'd play the game. "It's just a bracelet. I got it as a present a few years ago. That's pretty much it."

"Then why did Erika steal it from you?"

"Does anyone actually know why Erika does *anything*?"

He nodded, as if validating my point, which was weird. "Still. There's a story here."

"Not really." I did my best shrug. "I don't really even care about it. I was just wearing it when I first ran away from home."

His eyes narrowed as he analyzed me, and I forced myself not to shift uncomfortably. "Uh huh."

I took a breath. "Sorry to disappoint."

"I don't believe you."

"I don't care."

"I might, had you not made that expression when I pulled it out. I now believe you're bluffing."

I opened my mouth, then shut it, stunned at his behavior. "Why do you care?"

He stretched his legs out. "I told you: I'm bored. I want to hear about someone else's pathetic life sorrows."

"So you chose mine?"

He spread his arms around. "Do you see anyone else?"

"Yeah, well, I don't have any."

Sark laughed once—actually laughed—but it was a derisive sound. "Now, even I know that's not true."

I ignored that. Turning my head, I pretended I was still admiring the sky.

"Fine," Sark said after a moment. "If you really don't care, I'll just put it back where I found it."

A deep, thudding ache settled in my gut. "Fine."

The next seconds ticked away loudly in my head. I was tense, waiting for the moment Sark would leave, taking my bracelet with him. The thirst for it was drying me up, as if I'd been stranded in the desert for days, but I knew if I drank too much then I would drown.

Sark's foot shifted, and I panicked, thinking he was getting up to go.

"Who is Aiden?"

He hadn't really been moving, but I still felt him freeze. I turned back to look at him, to analyze him the way he'd been analyzing me, and watched his face reassemble into an expressionless mask. It was amazing, though, how when he was drunk his eyes totally gave him away.

"Why do you care?" he finally asked. Slow. Calculated.

And a little afraid.

I shrugged again. "You asked me for a story. Shouldn't I get one too?"

"You didn't give me a story," he pointed out.

"Your terms were unreasonable."

"I'd say I'm being very reasonable. Usually if I wanted something from you, I would've tried to beat it out of you by now."

My eyebrows shot up. So we were talking about that now? "Then pick one. Either you explain this weird ceasefire thing you've got going on—and what the heck Erika has to do with it—or you tell me about Aiden."

For the first time in probably forever, I rendered him speechless. He opened his mouth to answer, then thought better of it and closed it again, eyes narrowing. I enjoyed his discomfort more than I thought I would.

Sark finally settled with, "I don't see why you care about it."

"Because you obviously do."

"I don't...I..." He pursed his lips. "He's not worth talking about."

My eyebrows creased. "Why? Is he dead?"

Sark's eyes flashed, his tone gaining a little edge. "Might as well be."

"How do you know?"

"Because I was the one that buried him."

"Oh." I lost my voice for a moment, unsure what to do. It felt like I should be comforting him for some reason, but how does someone say 'I'm sorry you murdered someone'? Unless he hadn't.

The thought startled me. I'd always seen Sark as immovable and unshakable—a statue carved out of ice. I never would've imagined he could be upset by losing someone. Or that he'd even have someone to lose.

"And…" I continued, wanting to know but not wanting to ask. "And Kristen?"

At the name, Sark's jaw went slack, and he closed his eyes, as though some horror was playing out before him and he couldn't bear to look. Then he lowered his head into his hand—the one holding my bracelet—and ran the other hand through his hair.

It was terrifying. What had *happened* to him?

"I'm—I'm sorry," I stammered, unnerved by his reaction. "I didn't mean to…I don't…I can leave now."

Sark looked up at me, his eyes swelling with a kind of torment I'd never known. "She...she was his mother. She…"

I got caught up in the emotion, unable to bring my voice above a whisper, but unable to stay quiet either. "What happened to her?"

He stuttered through something I couldn't make out, but then I caught the word 'alcohol' and he moved to stand.

"No!" I blurted, then clamped my mouth shut. My response had the desired effect though: Sark froze. He froze with those terrible eyes on me, and I felt I would drown in all these ghosts that weren't even mine.

"Did you kill her?" I breathed. I didn't know why I cared so much about this stranger, but I had to. His reaction made me *need* to know her, for some reason, and somehow I felt that he wanted me to on some level, even if he didn't realize it.

"No." He shook his head in fervent denial, breaking the spell. "No, I—I didn't. No."

I remembered the letters in the box, the unconditional love and admiration in the handwritten words, and my heart ached. "Did Aiden?"

The answer came faster, more adamant. "No, of course not. He...no."

"Then who did?"

Another change overcame him, and *this* Sark I was familiar with. His expression twisted with loathing, a deep, scalding hatred that he'd never even aimed at me before. He had to try three times before he was able to force the name through his teeth.

"Bryce Reynolds."

I recognized the last name from the pile of mail that had been in the box. Some envelopes had been addressed to Kristen McCoy, but there were a few to Kristen Reynolds.

I felt my face crease with the sadness that coursed through me. "Her husband?"

Sark nodded and looked out into the sky, as if the answers to every problem were written on the horizon. "He...he was the most revolting, heinous excuse for a human being I have ever met. I still don't understand how—what she saw in him. He was charismatic when he wanted to be but...she was smarter. Smarter than that." He flinched with every word, the syllables sounding broken in his usually glossy accent, like the sentences were nails scratching up his throat but he had to spit them out. "They got married, but he took off once she got pregnant. He was in and out for a few years after that, but he largely left them alone, and they figured out how to get by on their own. Barely, but it worked."

"Aiden," I murmured.

Sark nodded, still not looking at me, slowly getting sucked into the story. "He knew of his father, but she never talked about details. She focused on raising him right, which was difficult to do in the slums of LA, but she tried. They were dirt poor, but every Thursday she'd give these two homeless men two carrots and a half a loaf of bread—they used to call her LA's angel."

I smiled in spite of myself, ignoring my throbbing body and readjusting my position on the couch so the back was supporting my neck and I could look at Sark head on. I didn't want to miss any of this.

The delicate care in his words about Kristen quickly hardened into sharp steel. "Aiden was thirteen when he—when Bryce came back to stay. He was always drunk and always smoking, so Aiden avoided the house for the first few months, giving them space to work out their problems. But…" He had to stop and start over, clenching his jaw so tight that I thought his teeth would shatter. "One night she had a black eye. The next day she limped. She still smiled, but it was forced, and the light in her eyes went dark. After that...Aiden never left her side."

"Did...did he...did Bryce…?"

"Beat him?" For the first time, Sark shifted his gaze to me, but, again, it was full of things I didn't know how to hold. He gave another derisive laugh, a hollow sound. "Senseless. All the time. And of course they couldn't afford a doctor, so he and Kristen would take turns patching each other up—assuming they could both still function."

My breath caught, and I felt tears coming on. A poor little kid, living with a monster, trying to protect his mom. "That's...that's so awful. Did they...they got him in trouble, right?"

Another laugh. He averted his gaze from me again, twirling my bracelet around. "No, Bryce already had her trained. Too much damage done in the early years of their marriage before the baby. Aiden tried once, but Bryce threatened to kill her if anyone ever found out."

A lump formed in my throat. I had to work to swallow it down. My dad had done terrible things to me, made me afraid of my own house, but I knew he wouldn't have hurt my mom. I'd spent all my time lately taking care of my own bruises—which was horrible enough—and I couldn't imagine trying to save someone else too. In that moment, I wanted nothing more than to pick up Aiden and Kristen in my arms and run away with them, so far away that their sad ending couldn't find them.

But Sark was quiet. I knew that meant the end was here.

He didn't put a lot into it, which let me know how hard it was for him to say it. His voice was rough but robotic, sounding off, and he stared into space in a daze.

"They lived that way for years. One day Aiden finally got fed up and made plans to run. A week before they were supposed to leave, Kristen got sick. We thought it would blow over. It didn't. A month later she was diagnosed with lung cancer. Caused by secondhand smoke. Bryce took off—didn't want to be implicated or pay for anything. She...she died six months later.

"The funeral was small. The homeless men showed up. A handful of others. I think they all knew, on some level, and all harbored guilt. Someone...someone should've saved her. Out of...out of everyone on this miserable planet, she was the last that deserved a life like that."

I gave a moment of silence for Kristen before whispering, "What happened to Aiden?"

"His grief swallowed him whole. There is nothing as painful as watching the one you love most suffer so horrifically, and be unable to do anything about it. Two days after she died, he robbed a bank and flew to London—a place she always wanted to go. He lived on the streets there, and slowly reinvented himself. He got in a lot of fights too. Too many punches meant for Bryce that never got used. One day, after a brawl in an alley, a man walked up to him once the others had gone. Introduced himself as Donovan Alexis and asked if he wanted a new life. He said yes and never looked back."

My insides shriveled up on themselves. Aiden worked for *Alexis*? No, that...that was so *wrong*.

Oblivious to my reaction, Sark sat back in his chair, seeming to relax a bit now that the worst part of the story was over. I wasn't done with it yet though.

"Where is he now?" I asked, with a little too much fervor, because I really wanted to ask what job Alexis gave him and if he'd ever made a living torturing infecteds.

Sark just leaned back, poker face back on, though there were traces of guilt hidden in the corners of his eyes. "I told you: I buried him."

"But why?"

His answer sounded like he was talking to himself more than me. "You spend your life running from demons, refusing to look back, until the day you realize you became one instead." He leaned down to reach for something on the ground, but it wasn't there, and he groaned under his breath when he remembered he left his alcohol inside next to the Aiden box.

And then I realized.

Oh.

Oh.

My eyes widened as I murmured, "You're Aiden."

Sark stiffened, then blew out a long breath. "I heard the name Sark on a TV show once. I started using it when I got to London."

I forced my jaw not to drop as my mind reeled. That was why his voice sounded so different, besides the amount of alcohol: it was fake. Drinking shook the charade, inhibited him from keeping it up as perfectly as when he was sober. The accent was fake, the name was fake, everything…

"The books?" I asked, thinking of the battered books in the box, pages crinkled with loving use.

Sark's mouth twitched in a ghost of a fond smile that quickly vanished. "I used to save money on the side and buy them for her. I loved her face, the way it would light up. They were some of the only times she ever got something for herself. Something good.

She was so selfless, always giving so much of herself. Too much."

For a half a second, I saw him. I saw a little kid, bruised up, taught that violence was life and fighting was the only way to protect who he loved most. A little kid turned into a young adult, forever running. How could anyone survive that?

Then I blinked, and Sark was there again, sitting in the chair. My head got even dizzier than it already was.

He sighed. "I haven't thought about any of that for a long time. I wouldn't have, if not for Erika's appearance, your breakdown, and the box falling onto the floor. Some things are best left on the top shelf," he added bitterly.

My forehead creased and my mouth pulled down. "My breakdown?"

Sark's eyes flicked to mine, a new level of caution in them. "I've seen you do a lot of things, but I've never seen you that hysterical. You're usually so composed, despite everything. I didn't know you were capable of something like that."

I shook my head slowly. "So that's it then? Erika...she isn't actually part of this at all. You didn't know her before?"

He shrugged. "Met her the same day you did."

"And she...she was the one that…" I stopped myself. Sark had been vastly different in the last hour, but accusing him of being just like his father was a tough blow that I was too afraid to deliver.

His eyes narrowed; he understood where I was going, probably because he'd been wallowing in it all night. "She was the one that opened my eyes to possibilities outside working for Alexis. I left you alone because she asked me to."

I still couldn't believe that. Sark actually *liked* her, for real. How did that even work?

"That can't be it." I found bravery underneath my curiosity. "You wouldn't give that up—give *me* up—for a pretty girl. Even I know that."

His tone was clipped. "The compromise was difficult, to say the least. It was nearly unbearable in the beginning. But then I started noticing...similarities." He grimaced, obviously still annoyed by this fact. "The way you tiptoed around me, always looked over your shoulder, always suspicious...or how you flinched every single time I lifted my hand..." He shook his head, disgusted, but I couldn't tell if it was with me or himself.

"I did?" The revelation made me feel like an idiot. So much for being tough.

"Most of the time, it seemed like an automatic reaction. You didn't even realize you did it. Just like..."

Just like her.

The thought stole the air from my lungs. Suddenly, my body was too sore and the air too sharp and the sky too big, and I felt like I would be overwhelmed by everything that had just been unloaded onto my shoulders. I didn't ask for Sark's pain. I didn't want it. I had enough of my own. But somehow I knew I wouldn't set down the knowledge I'd gained tonight for a long, long time.

As if sensing my shifting thoughts, Sark took a long breath and twirled my bracelet one last time before offering it to me. "I believe you owe me a story now."

My mouth went dry as I stared at the silver band, my first thought to say 'I don't owe you anything' and walk out. But his confessions clung to the dark, their aura magnetizing, gradually pulling out my shadows too.

"It was from my brother," I started, voice low and raspy. Slowly, as if approaching a snake, I reached out and took the bracelet from him, then winced. It almost stung my skin to touch. "*My* best friend in the world."

At least, he used to be.

"Kieran?" Sark asked, matching my volume.

I flinched at hearing the name out loud. It had been *so long*. "Yes." Then I shook my head and looked up at him. This was a bad idea, for about a million reasons, and not knowing how he would react scared me. "I'm sure you don't really want to hear this."

Sark just sprawled back lazily in his chair—drunk Sark was *weird*—and gave a shrug. "And I'm sure you didn't want to hear mine. Here we are."

I held his gaze, performing my own experiment. "My dad is obsessive. Always has been."

Then I stopped, giving Sark time to realize where I was headed, the backstory I'd have to give for the ending to make sense. Just like his story.

One of his eyebrows arched for a split second, understanding. Then he pursed his lips and nodded.

I took a deep breath, picked a star in the sky, and stared at it as I launched into the story I'd never completely told to anyone.

"There was always something to do, something new to try, a new place to go. Skydiving, geocaching, art collecting...he was everywhere, always. And eccentric. Made it hard for him to hold a job or for other people to really tolerate him. My mom loved him though. She'd always say he was a really old painting: weird for his time, would be appreciated later, frantically trying to include all the colors in the rainbow before he dried."

My lips almost quirked into a smile at that, but I stopped it. The only happy things about this story were gone now anyways. "When he got on something new—which was every few months or so—he'd ramble about things...usually I'd just smile and nod, listen to him for awhile and look at the pictures he'd show me. But this time...it was different. He was manic. When he rambled, it didn't make sense, and he'd talk about Norse mythology and old scientific formulas. It scared me. It scared...it scared Kieran too." Saying his name scratched my throat and burned my tongue. "We got scared enough that we started saving money. He was a senior and I was a sophomore. He was going to move out once he graduated, and I was going to go with him. We tried to talk to my mom about it too, but she...her dad had just died, and sometimes she'd go days without speaking or acknowledging anyone. She wasn't any help."

I paused for a moment, for Grandpa, since my bones still ached with grief over his loss. He would've never allowed my life to become what it was.

Scoffing, I closed my eyes and shook my head. "We should've left. We should've left right then." For the billionth time in the last year, I begged the universe to take me back to that time so I could shout at myself to start running and never look back.

The silence stretched on for a second, then five, then too long. I didn't know if the next part was the worst, but it was definitely on the list, and I wondered if I should just skip it. Sark knew what happened, anyway. Generally.

Unsure if I could say the words out loud, Sark finally had to break our thick silence. "Because he infected you." When I shot him a look, he eased back, as if surrendering. "It was in your file," he added quietly.

I gave a lifeless laugh. "Really? Was my math test in there too?"

His eyebrows furrowed. "What?"

"My math test," I insisted. "That day I had a math test last period. I got a C minus. Kieran had football practice that day, so I took the bus home, and I had to pull my hood up over my head to hide the fact that I was crying because I knew that if I didn't get good enough grades for a scholarship then I'd never be able to go to college, which I wanted more than anything. I had the test clenched in my fist when I walked through the front door of our house."

My head dropped. I couldn't keep it up. I watched the bracelet in my hand, using it as a distraction as I muttered the rest. "He was waiting for me. The lights were off. He tried to come up behind me and I saw the syringe and...we wrestled but I was normal then, he was bigger than me, and he had surprised me. I called for help and cried and begged and begged him, but he...he didn't even flinch. He said it had to happen and shoved the needle in my arm, and then...and then..."

I took several ragged breaths and closed my eyes, desperately trying to keep myself in the present and out of the harrowing memory. "I didn't know pain like that existed. I didn't...I couldn't do anything. I just laid there and burned and screamed. Mom got home when Kieran did and they...freaked out. Kieran punched Dad. Mom broke them up before they fought. Kieran demanded Dad do something, but he said it was too late and not to do anything or it would be worse. So Kieran just cried and held me and I screamed. So much. So loud. Sometimes in my nightmares I still hear it: the first time I heard myself really scream." I took another shuddering breath. "Was any of that in your file?"

Sark didn't answer. I soaked in the quiet stillness of the night, letting the slight breeze touch my face and remind me where I was. After a minute, I opened my eyes and peeked over at him, just to gauge his reaction. His expression was smooth, revealing nothing, but his eyes bled out all over him. I realized drunk Sark must be more like Aiden used to be. How long had it taken him to master his mannerisms and countenance to become someone totally different?

Sensing his next question, I pressed on with my story. "It took a few days before the pain went away. I knew something was different. *I* felt different. Not a ton, but enough to be different, for people to notice. My reflexes were faster, I was more durable and stronger and...it was weird. Everyone thought I was weird. My few friends just like...ignored it all and wouldn't really acknowledge it. Kieran pretended like he wasn't freaked out but I could tell he was.

That weekend he and I snuck into my dad's office and spent hours going through everything."

Again, I left out the really important details, like all the horror stories my dad had about the monster key, or the blue marks that enveloped my body during infection and had since faded, marking me as that monster.

"Infection." I spat out the word like it was bile. "I was fifteen. I was fifteen, and I was just...I was so scared." The band felt heavier in my fingers, slowly dragging me down. "It was April then, and Kieran graduated in June. He said we'd leave right after the ceremony whether Mom would come with us or not. Then he gave me the bracelet. He told me to always wear it so even when I was alone I would know that he was on my side. He would get me out. No matter what."

My voice caught. I went rigid, keeping myself locked still. I was *not* going to cry. The universe would not get another drop from me over this.

That resolution made it hard to keep going, so I didn't. My body ached, and I readjusted, bringing my good leg up and stretching out the other, content to just sit there underneath the night sky until the stars finally came for me.

Clearly, though, my story wasn't over, because when Sark had first found me I was obviously and painfully alone, without my older brother. The denial ate at me, keeping my mouth shut. If I said it out loud then I was admitting it was real and not some kind of extravagant nightmare I would soon wake up from.

Sark gave me a couple minutes of quiet before asking, "Where is he now?"

Usually that question sent me into a nosedive of despair, but I just laughed bitterly at the stinging in my chest. "Oh he followed the plan, all right. Took off right after graduation. Joined the army and left me in the hands of our crazy father."

Now it was Sark's turn to be surprised. His eyebrows shot up, and the response made the cracks in my heart deepen, because even someone like him understood the heartbreak of the situation. "He *left* you?"

To rot.

I squeezed the bracelet in my hand, nearly bending the malleable metal. "I went to graduation. During the ceremony he told me to meet him at home. By the time I got there, he was all packed and someone was there to pick him up. My dad was shouting profanities at him—my parents hadn't known either—and my mom just sat in the corner, so still. Like a ghost.

"Kieran ignored them, though. He came to me. He said sorry and he didn't think we would make it on our own. He told me he needed a better chance than what 'my kind' would give him. He said that. *My kind.* Like I was some kind of monster all of a sudden rather than his little sister." I left out the part where he said he couldn't live with me being the key, and he didn't want to be around for whatever happened to me in the end. That part I would take to my grave, which was fitting, considering it pretty much murdered me.

Sark leaned forward and rested his elbows on his knees, looking at the bracelet now with distaste. Ironic, from the murderer. "Have you tried to contact him since?"

I sighed and tipped my head back, closing my eyes and letting the breeze wash over my face, hoping it would blow away all the sad things inside me. "I used to write letters. The garbage can in my room is full of them. I could never bring myself to send one. He wrote at first, but it tapered off pretty fast. Six months later, we get a letter out of the blue."

My tone went bland and robotic, but rough too, like Sark's had when he told me Kristen's harsh fate. "They were driving...they didn't...they didn't see the bomb. They all...they all...no survivors." The bracelet felt scalding in my hands now, and I was suddenly revolted by it. "Three days later, I found my 'boyfriend' Connor actually worked for Alexis. He brought you in. I ran. I put the bracelet back on the day Kieran...the day he...I shouldn't have brought it. I thought somehow it would protect me, but I'm still all alone. He promised. And he's not here."

In a rush of raging emotion, I clambered to my feet, settled the bracelet in both my hands and snapped it in half. Then I chucked the pieces as hard as I could off the roof. They flipped around a couple times in the air before disappearing into the darkness.

Wiping away any rogue tears that may have fallen when I was engrossed in the memories, I exhaled and turned to face Sark. "And here we are. Have I successfully drowned you in my sorrows?"

Sark's eyes were wide, watching the spot where my bracelet had vanished. As if in slow motion, he let out a long breath and gradually sat back. A solid minute passed before he said, "That's not quite what I was expecting."

I barked a harsh laugh, gesturing over myself with my good hand. "What *were* you expecting? I mean, look at me. I'm a walking disaster."

"You're sixteen?"

"Seventeen." Not that I'd really celebrated when the day came a few weeks ago.

Sark looked me over as he took in that information. "You seem older than that."

I blinked, momentarily caught off guard. "Well you seem older than you are."

"It's a side effect of survival."

"Yeah, well, it's a miracle I've survived this long. If that's even the word for it." I blew a rogue piece of hair out of my face. "It feels more like surviving on...a whisper or ghost of who I was before all this. It's not substantial enough to actually keep me going."

"It has so far."

"Barely."

He shrugged. "Sometimes surviving is all you can do."

I mulled that over for a second before sitting back on the couch, catching a moan in my mouth before it escaped. This whole 'injury pain' thing was getting really old. Going carefully, I lied down on my back and stretched out, pulling gently on my sore muscles and aching bones, then sighed and collapsed back into myself, exhausted. What a strange night.

Biting my lip, I tilted my head up so I could look at Sark. "I'm sorry about Kristen."

Even with the odd angle, I could see him scowl, not directly at me but in my general direction, like he wasn't sure if he was more mad at me for saying that or the universe for making it happen in the first place. "I didn't tell you so you could say that."

"I didn't say it for you. I said it for her. She seems like she was a wonderful person."

Sark blinked slowly once, then twice. The scowl melted into grief and regret, making him look younger, softer. "She was."

After that, we settled into our own silence, which was surprisingly comfortable, given the circumstances.

It wasn't until my stomach grumbled that Sark spoke again. "You hungry?"

Giving a lazy shrug, I mumbled. "Mm hm."

"Do you need more medicine?"

"Yes," I answered with clear intentions I wasn't moving.

His tone laced with uncertainty again. "We can go in now."

Going in would shatter the odd sense of sad calm I felt, and I hesitated despite my body's needs. I didn't know what I was going to do about my injuries or the fact that I'd wake up tomorrow with the same cold ache in my heart that I'd carried for a year. I didn't know what Sark was going to be like tomorrow or what horrors were in store for me now that I'd seen so many of his skeletons while he wasn't himself. I didn't know how I was going to get out of this house again, or where I would run to next, or how I could possibly keep myself from the fate my dad had damned me to. I only knew that the sky was a gorgeous blanket and the stars twinkled with empathy. They were imploding, crumbling, and collapsing, and yet the world loved them for it.

"Okay," I said. "In a minute."

Sark nodded, and we sat there in our mess of haunting memories and fragile peace, just watching the sky.

9

I was only dimly aware of the fact that Erika walked into the living room. It was too difficult to open my eyes, so I just stayed on the couch, resting in a mess of pillows and blankets set to keep my ribs from protesting and my head protected. It wasn't until she spoke that I knew she was actually there.

"Is she okay?" Even in a hushed murmur, her voice was colored with worry.

"Yeah," Sark answered softly from his chair. We'd made a deal earlier that I'd let him keep an eye on me if he didn't start on another bottle of alcohol. He had grudgingly agreed. "She had more medicine a while ago. She's a little out of it."

"What was wrong with her?"

"What *isn't* wrong with her?"

I could imagine her face, the way her thin eyebrows would scrunch up in light scolding. "You know what I meant."

"She's okay. Her head didn't reopen, and she was talking better than I anticipated. She remembers more too. She was just in a lot of pain, so she asked for some."

"She *asked* for some? You didn't..."

Sark scoffed. "Force it on her? No. We both donned the white flags of truce this evening."

Erika's voice softened, and I heard her steps get closer until fabric slid against leather. The couch didn't move though, so she must've been sitting on the arm of his chair or something. "That's not what I meant either. But you're drunk and under a lot of stress, and I know she tends to try your patience."

He laughed once, and it was the most tired sound I'd ever heard him make. "Yes, well, after a rough start, we managed to remain civil while you were gone. I also made sure she ate something, so I wasn't completely ineffective."

Her gentle smile reflected in her tone. "I knew you could do it. I'm...I'm sorry I left you. I didn't mean to...I didn't mean that. I just needed to breathe for a second."

"I know. I understand. Are you...are you all right now?"

"Yes, but I shouldn't have left. Really. Are *you* okay?"

Sark let out a long sigh, stalling. "I believe I'm too drunk to tell."

"That means not at all."

"It means I've prolonged it slightly."

"Lucky you."

They went on to talk about other things, like how the store was busy because Thanksgiving was this week, and everything had been so crazy that she completely forgot the holiday existed, and what would he think about getting a Christmas tree, and things that seemed more like the Erika I was used too but was still too soft than the one in my memories. Eventually I couldn't tell what was real and what wasn't, and I didn't catch the end of the conversation before I fell asleep.

When I woke up the next afternoon, I was still in my spot on the couch, and I felt about twelve times worse than I had the night before.

"Hey," Erika said when I finally got my eyes open. I was surprised to find her sitting on the floor next to me with the TV off. I couldn't remember the last time she'd been in here without it on. "Are you with me?"

I groaned and tried to nod, my tongue like sandpaper. A tornado was raging in my head, destroying everything in its path, but the toxicity building up in my core took precedence.

"Er—Erika," I stammered breathlessly. "I...I need…" I clutched my stomach to illustrate, and her eyes widened in alarm.

"Oh, okay, um…" She waved her hands over me in a panic. "Um, let me get…"

Too late. I turned on my shoulder and threw up over the side of the couch. Erika was nice enough to hold my hair back as well as keep me from falling to the floor. When it was over, I opened my eyes to find Erika stabilizing me on the couch, and Sark holding my hair back. My vomit had all landed in a big bowl on the floor that seemed to have appeared out of nowhere.

Erika helped ease me back into my pillows, and I let out a harsh breath through my teeth. Sark wordlessly checked my head before disappearing again.

"I'm...I'm sorry," I said, wrinkling my nose at the stench.

Erika waved her hand. "No, don't worry about it. Not at all." She was softer than I remembered, not as tense and oddly perky. She seemed more...normal. The plastic surgery was all gone. "How are you?"

"I'm...I'm fine. Just…"

"In pain?"

"Yeah."

The rest of the day went by in a haze that melted into another one. Erika stayed in the living room with me, giving me space but on call for anything I needed. It was actually kind of nice, if it weren't for me feeling like roadkill.

I rarely saw Sark, and we never spoke. He checked over my injuries when I was asleep (and when he *thought* I was asleep) but we never made eye contact or interacted. After our heavy conversation, I wasn't sure what he thought of me—or what I thought of him—but we didn't have the chance to really go into it.

The third day I got up to go to the bathroom, and ended up vomiting in the sink after I washed my hands. Head spinning, I collapsed to the floor, half draped over the bathtub so I wouldn't have to move when I threw up. Sark was the one that found me, about twenty minutes later. He only asked me the bare minimum of essential questions before carrying me back out to the couch, where I promptly faked sleeping until Erika came back in, relieving him of his guard duty. She had already told me she wouldn't be leaving me alone for a bit, just to make sure my head trauma didn't cause any further issues. After the adventure in the bathroom, I didn't have any more internal complaints about that decision.

Day four was better. I kept down my food and took the brace off of my ankle. Day five I took my arm out of the sling, and was walking around on my own and eating normally again. Erika felt like she could leave for a few hours—Sark stayed downstairs while I dug into my roots and watched old cartoons and colored—and when she came back I helped her decorate the Christmas tree she bought and she helped me wash my hair. Day six I felt like a new person besides some lethargy I hadn't shaken off yet.

Day seven was the best, in that I felt pretty much myself again. It was the worst, in that Sark told me my head was healed enough to get the staples taken out. I was a shaky, sweaty, nervous mess, clutching Erika's hand as I sat on Sark's desk downstairs. He rarely looked at me and never made anything close to eye contact, not talking unless he absolutely had to, but he was oddly gentle and patient, and getting the staples out wasn't comfortable but it didn't hurt. Once the deed was done, Sark cleaned up and prepared to disappear again, I assumed, when Erika interrupted to talk about my driving. I thought it was a bizarre way to hit my pride, but quickly saw through her when she suggested Sark take me for driving lessons.

Both of us were shell shocked, and managed to wave her off. The next day, though, she was pushing it to the point where I agreed just to get her off my back, thinking I'd have some time to get out of the situation. I should've known better. A half hour later I was sitting in the passenger seat of Sark's smallest car. We didn't speak a word as he drove us to the parking lot of a restaurant closed for renovations. I kept my eyes straight forward, hands clasped in my lap, breathing in the thick awkward dust between us and trying not to cough on it. We switched places without a word. My stomach flipped when my hands gripped the steering wheel.

Once Sark had settled in the passenger seat, he sighed and broke our silence.

"You have the basics already, correct?"

"Basics?" I asked, my voice nearly squeaking. I cleared my throat. "Like, you press one pedal to go, one to stop, and turn the wheel to steer?"

He pursed his lips and nodded. "More or less." Then he gestured to the road, which wasn't a crazy stuffed downtown road, but it wasn't deserted either. "Go ahead."

My eyebrows shot up so fast they almost cracked my forehead. "What? On a real street?"

Sark shrugged. "Sure. It isn't your first time. You'll be fine."

"Um, I...I'm not...I'm not sure."

"Go ahead."

I took a deep breath and faced forward again, finding the street to be a lot more narrow and harrowing than it had just a moment earlier. "Um, okay." Gritting my teeth, I put the car in drive, counted to ten, then tapped the gas. We lurched into the road, spiking my nerves.

"Slow down," Sark said, voice tight with nerves he was trying to hide. "You don't need to—"

I pressed the brake—a little harder than I should've, admittedly—nearly sending Sark through the windshield. When the car behind me honked, I hit the gas again and we shot forward. Sark yelled something at me and I jerked the wheel to the right, screeching into a parking lot. A car was coming out, and I had to swerve again to miss it, making the tires screech and me lose control for a second. Sark swore under his breath as I stomped on the brakes. We slid sideways into the cement pillar of a light pole and it finally brought us to a stop. I winced when I heard the crunch of my door.

Throwing the car in park, I leaned back, breathing hard and yanking my hands off the wheel, like just touching it would make it go again. Sark leaned back in his seat and took a few breaths before ducking out of the car. My stomach knotted itself when I watched him walk around to inspect. Wanting to just get out and run, I tried my door, but the cement pillar was in the way. It wouldn't budge.

I just crashed Sark's car. My hands started shaking. *I just crashed his car.*

He's going to kill me.

Heart pounding, hands shaking, I stayed frozen in my seat, barely able to breathe. Sark walked around the vehicle twice, appraising the damage, then slid back in his seat.

I swallowed hard before whispering, "I'm sorry," to the steering wheel, sure they would be the last words I'd ever say.

And then, in a completely calm-and-devoid-of-all-furious-rage voice, he said, "It's okay."

I blinked, not moving. I'd heard him wrong. I'd made that up in my head, a symptom of desperation.

When I didn't move, Sark leaned forward slightly, as if making sure I knew he was talking to me. "It's all right. I crashed my first time too. Much worse than this."

Reaching for any bravery I had left in my system, I glanced timidly at him. "But I...I just..."

"It's a car. I have four of them. I'm sure I'll manage." He gestured to the dashboard. "Let's go again—just in the parking lot this time."

"I don't..." I shook my head, leaning farther away from the steering wheel. "I don't think that's a good idea."

"*You're* giving up?"

The challenge in his tone caused me to turn and look at him. "What's that supposed to mean?"

He shrugged, but there was too much meaning in it to be casual. "Well, you're usually infuriatingly stubborn. It's surprising."

I shot him a glare, defensive. "I'm not giving up. I'm just..." I let out a shaky breath, glancing at the wheel again. "I'm just nervous."

"That's to be expected." With a cautionary look, he reached over and put the car in drive, causing me to hurry and slam on the brake in time. "If you stop now, though, then you'll never learn."

"And *you* want me to know how to drive."

"Not particularly, but we're here."

So we went again. It took ten minutes for my hands to stop shaking. I know he noticed but he pretended he didn't. When I wasn't under the pressure of real traffic, I did better, and eventually I relaxed enough to drive around the lot like a normal person.

After nearly a half hour with no other incidents, I posed a nonchalant question. "Who taught you to drive?"

Sark blinked, taking a second to recover himself. I was surprised he answered. "My tenth grade English Literature teacher."

"Huh. Were they nice to you?"

He gave a small smile, the slightest curve of half of his mouth. "Nicer than I deserved."

We tried a real street again, and despite a questionable start, I did okay. By Sark's suggestion and permission, I went deeper into Chicago, turning around before I hit the real downtown area. I gradually got comfortable enough to relax my shoulders and command the radio. After some searching, I found a nineties station and crowed in excitement when one of my old high school favorites came on. Sark just pursed his lips without saying anything.

An hour later I drove back to his house, pulling into the garage like an expert. Turning off the car, I sat back and beamed at the windshield, unable to contain my excited pride. I practically skipped up the steps and into the house, and Sark just pursed his lips again. I realized he might've been hiding a smile—secretly making fun of me—but I found I didn't care.

"Erika!" I called. "Erika, guess what?"

I walked into the kitchen to find the living room decked out in Christmas decorations, the walls drenched in red, green, and white that all came straight from a catalogue full of pretty things my mom could never afford to buy. My feet slid to a stop when I saw part of the mirror wall was hanging open somehow, like...like a door.

There's been a secret door there this whole time?

"What…?"

Sark had been hanging up his jacket, and he stopped next to me when he saw the scene. His eyes seemed to glaze over the decorations and rest on the hanging piece of mirror, and they widened as his face drained of color.

Just then, Erika poked her head out from behind the door, grinning at us. "Hey guys. Glad to see you both survived."

"What is that?" I asked, gesturing to the door.

Her grin grew. "It's a surprise."

"A surprise?" I started walking forward, curious, especially since Sark stayed glued to the ground.

"Yeah, for you."

I skidded to a halt. "For me?"

Erika nodded, still beaming. "Yeah, from Sark."

My mouth fell open. "What?"

She nodded at me, as if I needed the confirmation, and I turned on the balls of my feet to look at Sark. He was still pale and rigid, aiming a harsh look at Erika full of alarmed accusation. When he realized I was staring at him, he hesitantly shifted his gaze to me. It took him a couple tries to get out a coherent sentence.

"It's not...it wasn't really…on the…" He shook his head, running a hand through his hair. "I was drunk. I hardly knew what I was doing. I forgot I'd done it until they delivered it."

"You knew enough," Erika chimed in before clapping her hands together. "Come on, Arie! Come take a look."

I shook my head once and took a step back, movements laced with uncertainty. "I don't...I don't need anything. I'm okay."

"Oh come *on*!" Erika exclaimed, her face creasing with disbelief. "You can't really pass this up. It's a present!"

"I know," I said with a forced smile. I didn't want to make her feel bad. "I just...I have something I have to take care of, you know, so—"

"Yeah?" She folded her arms across her chest. "And what important business do you have?"

"I...um, I have to…"

Sark piped up then, still brimming with discomfort as he tried to backpedal the whole situation. "If she doesn't want it—"

"Of course she would want it," Erika cut in. "It's beautiful. You're both being ridiculous."

Curiosity was itching in the back of my mind, but preset caution overwhelmed it. I didn't really see a way out of it, though. Erika would bug me until I took a look, and I couldn't deny my interest in what made Sark so uncomfortable. Or what he bought in the first place.

For me.

This is weird.

Erika threw her hands up in the air in exasperation. "You can't be paranoid about everything, Arie! Please just trust me on this? You'll love it and, no offense, right now you're kind of killing it."

"Um...okay?" It sounded more like a question than anything, but once I took the first step, I found it was easier to keep moving, my curiosity propelling me forward. Sark sucked in a sharp breath through his teeth, and that made me go faster.

Erika backed up out of the way, and I touched the smooth glass, which was when I saw a small door handle nearly hidden in the reflective surface. How had I not noticed it before?

"Go ahead," Erika said again, nearly bursting with excitement. Steeling myself, I stepped around the door and looked inside.

The light was on already—Erika had been in here—and the bulbs from the small chandelier sparkled. The two walls on the side were painted white, while the back wall and front wall were windows, looking out into the backyard and the living room. The floor was slick, speckled white tile, as immaculate as the walls. And set perfectly in the center of the surreal room was a white baby grand piano.

My hand nearly slapped against my mouth as I gasped at the gorgeous instrument, speechless.

It was a piano.

A *piano*.

Seconds passed, and Erika bounced on the balls of her feet. "So? What do you think?"

What do I think? I shook my head slowly, still disbelieving. "You...you bought me a piano?"

Sark had braved coming to the living room, but had stopped at the edge. Out of the corner of my eye, I saw him run his hand through his hair again. "You don't have to use it. It's just there if you...if you need it, I guess."

Erika scoffed and waved her hand at him before turning to me. "Do you play?"

Numbly, I nodded. "I took lessons as a kid, but I...I hated my teacher. My mom let me drop out and taught me instead." A wave of homesickness came over me at the thought of those shared afternoons on the piano bench, and I found my fingers aching for the keys just for a sense of normalcy. Of home.

"So you *do* play," Erika said thoughtfully. "I figured you probably could if you wanted, but I didn't know if you really liked to or not."

"I love it. It's one of the things I did...before."

Erika nodded. "Well now you can do it again. The piano isn't even the coolest part of this place: the mirrors are one sided, as you've probably noticed, so you can see out but nobody can see in. They're soundproof too, so you can play as long as you want and nobody can hear you, if the door is closed. Even if they're sitting on the couch."

"Wow," I breathed. "That's..."

"Cool, right?"

"Yeah."

Erika gushed for a little while longer, showing me the minute details of the piano room, then of the decorations she bought. Then she headed for the garage, claiming she left some wreaths in the car that she needed my opinion on.

Sark was standing in the kitchen, looking so out of place in his own festive house. He had picked up a roll of Erika's red ribbon, studying it. Stealing another glance at the piano, I counted to ten, then wandered over to where he was standing.

"How did you know?" I asked. "That I loved the piano, I mean."

He focused on the ribbon as though it was ancient Egyptian papyrus. "I told you: I was very drunk that night. I suppose I just guessed."

"That's a pretty good guess."

"Yes, well…" He blew out a long breath, his shoulders slumping ever so slightly. "My…my mother used to play the piano. It was one of her favorite things to do. She used to say that it was the only time she felt truly at peace with the world."

"Oh." I took that in slowly, sponging up each word and letting it fill my whole being. Of course I had no real tie to Kristen, but I felt like I did. "Well, she was right."

Sark cleared his throat, still not meeting my gaze. "I'll admit, you're an excellent pianist. I've only heard you play once and it was remarkable. I didn't…I was drunk and somehow decided you wouldn't want to give it up, if…" He shook his head, backpedaling, his shoulders tensing back up. "Again, it was a mistake. I can return it."

"No, don't…" I strived for nonchalance, knowing a big deal was the last thing he wanted, and I wasn't about to let the piano slip from my grasp. "Don't worry about it. I'll try it out if I get bored."

He nodded and set the ribbon down on the table before disappearing into the hallway, and that was that.

10

The next morning, I woke up earlier than usual and made myself get out of bed despite the chill to the air. My feet padded softly against the hardwood floor as I crept down the hallway and into the living room. Like I'd hoped, it was empty.

Sunlight was peeking through the curtains and glinting off the mirrored wall. I held my breath as my eyes searched, and my heart stuttered when I caught sight of the tiny handle. Timidly, I turned the knob and pushed the door open.

I couldn't help the small gasp that went through my teeth at the sight of the gorgeous piano, made even more stunning when I turned the light on. I hadn't been dreaming after all.

I closed the door behind me and sat myself on the bench, brushing my fingers up and down the keys. Though this piano was much newer and nicer, the smooth feel of it reminded me of my mom's piano at my house or my grandma's piano in her old condo, and the comforting familiarity warmed my core. Music had always had a way of bringing me home, no matter how dark my world had become.

It took a few minutes for me to work up the courage, but eventually I made myself press down on one key. Then another. And another. I built a melody out of them, solidified a tempo, and then my fingers were flying. I couldn't help the smile that broke across my face.

I played until my neck was stiff and my fingers were sore. Then I kept going.

I didn't stop until a movement in the corner of my eye caught my attention. It was Erika, up and dressed for the day, rummaging around the kitchen. Biting my lip, I waved my hands frantically at her. I said her name. Then I yelled it. Not once did Erika acknowledge me.

I smiled. I loved being invisible.

Stretching out my arms, I went back to the piano and played every song I could remember, making up measures I'd forgotten. I kept an eye on Erika as she made breakfast—some kind of egg casserole thing—but she didn't really capture my attention until Sark came in.

Intrigued, I watched as he strode into the kitchen and poured himself a cup of coffee. Up to her elbows in cooking, Erika smiled and kissed him on the cheek. I wrinkled my nose. I was more than glad they saved *that* for when they thought I was still sleeping.

They spoke softly to each other, and while I could only make out a few words here and there, their tones and postures told me it was a very casual conversation. It was weird to watch. It was so *normal*.

The scene got even weirder when Erika put her creation in the oven, then started washing dishes. My jaw dropped to the floor when Sark abandoned his cup of coffee and took the position of dryer, toweling off the wet dishes she handed him.

I blinked at the odd picture. Sark was working. Not just working, but doing *dishes*. I didn't even know he knew how to do that.

They continued like two very normal people until Erika flicked some water in Sark's face. My mouth fell open in shock all over again, and it tripled when Sark smirked and flicked water back at her. She let out a mix between a shriek and a laugh, and they went back and forth a few times before she stretched up on her toes and kissed him. Dishes clearly forgotten, he wrapped his arms around her waist and she wound her arms around his neck. I blanched and jerked my gaze away.

The back of my neck felt hot, and my skin prickled with embarrassment that I'd spied on a moment like that. Despite wanting to burn the image out of my memory, I couldn't help analyzing it.

So it *was* true. Their whole...relationship, or whatever it was, wasn't some kind of ruse or prank or contrived plan. In fact, I'd never seen either of them so relaxed and carefree.

What is the world coming to?

I shook the thoughts out of my head and turned back to the piano, unwilling to look back into the kitchen in case they were still all over each other. Suddenly, breakfast sounded a lot less appetizing.

Closing my eyes, I forced myself to forget and start playing again, humming along to myself as well to make sure I only heard music. Eventually, the humming turned to words, and then I was singing along to the melodies I played. My muscles loosened up and I felt the calmest I had in what seemed like forever.

That stretch of calm ended, though, when I sensed someone behind me. Gasping, I wrenched myself around only to see the door open and Erika leaning against the doorframe.

"Don't stop!" she exclaimed. "You're so good, Arie, it's crazy."

For the second time that day, my skin heated with embarrassment. "Um...thanks," I stammered. "How did you know I was in here?"

Erika smirked. "You haven't come out looking for food yet. I figured there was only one thing that could keep you from breakfast. I wish I would've caught you earlier. Whatever you were playing was amazing."

I ducked my head underneath the compliments and shut the lid on the piano, unwilling to play with an audience. My stomach growled as I stood up, and Erika laughed.

"Knew it."

I rolled my eyes at her and we both left the room, turning off the light and shutting the door behind us.

Sark was sitting at the counter, cup of coffee refilled and newspaper spread out before him. He gave me a small nod in greeting; I nodded back. I took the chair two spots away from him—not the farthest, but not the closest either. He was either too absorbed in his newspaper to notice, or just didn't care.

Erika checked on her food in the oven, then poured herself a cup of coffee, all while going on about the recipe she'd found online the day before. If either of them were aware I'd witnessed their whole morning, they didn't show it.

The sight of the coffee cup reminded me of something. "Erika?" I asked. "What did you do about your job? You haven't been in...forever?" I couldn't think of when she would've had time in the past weeks to sneak out for a shift.

She beamed triumphantly. "I quit. Isn't that great? I hated being a waitress anyway. It's so much more fun to hang around you guys."

My eyebrows furrowed, but she didn't give me the chance to ask any of my follow up questions. She set her cup down on the counter so she could safely sweep her arms in excitement.

"Speaking of, I know what we're doing today," she announced. "We're going to the park."

At that, Sark glanced up from reading. "The park? You do realize it's been below freezing all week, right?"

"Yes, but it's going to be a little warmer today, and Lincoln Park is absolutely gorgeous in the winter." She took a sip of coffee, then added more sugar. "I go every year, but I haven't made it yet, and I figured it would be so fun to go with you two." Then she turned, pulled her creation out of the oven, and set it on two hot pads on the counter in front of us.

I opened my mouth to say something, but nothing came out, no words adequately describing what I thought. My gut told me no. Spending unnecessary time outside was a dangerous risk that wasn't worth taking for a walk around the park. On the other hand, I was dying to get out of the house—never before had they offered such freedom—and I couldn't help a little bit of curious excitement. I never just got to walk around and look at pretty places for fun.

Erika set a plate and fork in front of me and Sark, then leaned her elbows on the counter and looked at both of us. "Will you come with me? Please?"

Sark thought it over, then stole a quick glance at me before shrugging. "All right."

Erika grinned, then turned on me. "Will you please come, Arie? You'll love it. Please?"

Biting my lip, I let out a long breath. "Um...yeah, sure. I guess."

"Yes!" She squeezed my hand before grabbing a serving spoon. Scooping a generous amount of egg, potato, and ham hash on my plate, then on Sark's, she settled for eating out of the pan. "Eat up, then go put something warm on. This will be so much fun!"

~~~
~~~

It had seemed like a great idea earlier.

Okay, I'd never really been sold that the park was a good idea. But once Sark parked the car and I stepped out into the frigid air all bundled up, and I saw the crowds of people in the expanse of unfamiliar territory, I decided it was all such an awful idea.

It was beautiful. I couldn't deny that. The barren trees glistened, and the snowy ground sparkled under the sun, like diamond stars in a white sky. I loved it. And I probably would've loved it more if I wasn't so afraid of being vulnerable. What was the objective here? It felt weird to just walk down a street without any motive but to enjoy myself. There was usually always something ahead of me to run to, or something behind me to run from. Could I remember how to be a normal human for five seconds?

Stuffing my gloved hands in my coat pockets, I forced myself to trail after Sark and Erika, only half listening to Erika gushing about the park and stories from past years. Sark had to have been cold in his European-style black trench coat, and he stuck out, a too formal character for such a laid back scene. Erika, on the other hand, was stunning in her stylish white coat, a thick scarf with matching gloves, and knee-high boots. With her dazzling smile and curled ponytail, she looked like she was posing for an advertisement. Walking with the two near models made me feel like a bundled up sloth.

I tried to pull some of my earlier excitement from somewhere, to enjoy the fresh air and beautiful scenery. I couldn't stop myself from glancing at the strangers around us more than the trees. I'd always loved to people-watch, but with too much paranoia the game quickly loses its fun.

Most of the people were families, parents trying to keep up with their kids. Several couples walked hand in hand, some crazy joggers were getting their exercise in, and a few groups of teenagers passed us, loud with boisterous laughter.

I was so busy trying to be excited, relaxed, and enjoy myself while twisting my gloves in my hands with anxiety, that I didn't notice Sark had fallen in step next to me until I almost tripped over him.

I started a mumbled apology, but Sark just waved me off. Erika walked ahead of us, still talking and thinking we were paying attention, unaware that Sark was watching me now instead.

I shrunk in on myself, trying to ward off the cold and his gaze. "What?"

"This makes you nervous," he stated. His tone was casual, and it didn't match the cavernous depth in his eyes.

"No." The response was automatic, stifling my surprise. "No, it doesn't. I'm just cold. That's all."

Sark must've either detected the slightest false note to my voice or was just really good at reading me—both of which were infuriating for me. He gave me a faint smile, his voice a hybrid of light joking and sincere honesty. "I'm here with you, Arie, so there's nobody else to be afraid of or watch out for. You can relax."

I didn't know how to respond to that. I didn't like that he noticed my discomfort, nor was I thrilled about him acknowledging it. It was naive thinking too, on his part—there were so many people to be afraid of, especially if they knew what I was. I couldn't help a small smile, though, at his effort. It was weirdly nice of him to try.

Opening my mouth, I closed it again, then secured my hair behind my ear even though it was already in a ponytail. "Uh...okay. I guess...okay?"

Erika turned around then, noticing we were both behind her. Thankfully, she remained oblivious to my nerves.

"You guys coming?"

Willing some of the tension away from my limbs, I nodded. "Yeah."

After that, I tried harder to enjoy myself, though now Sark kept watching me, like it was his job to make sure I had a good time or something. It was weird. But I went with it. I listened to Erika's stories as we walked, and it was nice to laugh with her and stretch my legs. We stopped every once in awhile to admire a fountain or so she could show me the exact spot she slipped and fell one time and never went running outside again.

This is life, I reminded myself as I caught sight of a group of kids throwing around a football. *This is what it looks like. You're forgetting.*

The thought hit me so hard that I stopped walking. Erika continued on, not paying attention, and Sark went with her, giving me space. I just stood in the snow watching the kids, the simple image framed by majestic trees and twinkling snow. It was truly beautiful.

This is what life looks like, and you're missing it.

Suddenly, something crashed into my legs, nearly knocking me off balance. I looked down to see a mound of pink. It shifted and looked up at me, and I realized it was a little girl. Her giant pink puff coat swallowed her tiny body, so I could only see a pair of big brown eyes and strands of white blonde hair poking out from under her hood in every direction.

I mumbled an apology and almost kept walking, but something about her made me pause. I recognized the nervous shift in her eyes.

Kneeling down so I was eye-level with her, I offered her a smile. "Hi."

She gave me a small smile back. "Hi. My name is Savannah."

"I'm Arie. Are you...are you lost? Is your mom here?"

Savannah's eye welled with tears. "I don't know where she is." Her lower lip quivered and she started crying. "I'm lonely and scared."

"Hey, it's okay." I reached out and took her little gloved hand. "Thanks for telling me. Can I tell you a secret now?"

"A secret?" she asked, hiccupping, curiosity highlighting her trill voice.

"Yep."

She considered that a moment, and her tears momentarily stopped. She pursed her lips, nodding.

I leaned in closer to her. "I'm lonely and scared too."

Her mouth fell open in delighted shock. "You're like me!"

"Yeah." I couldn't help another smile. She was just so cute. "Maybe we can help each other?"

"Okay," she said. "But you have to give me a piggyback ride."

"Deal."

Squealing with excitement, Savannah climbed up on my back, her puffy coat arms tight on my neck. She squirmed for a moment, trying to get comfortable, then tugged on a strand of my ponytail. "Go!"

With a grin, I stood and twirled her in a circle, her giggles loud in my ear. Then I caught sight of Erika and Sark a ways down the sidewalk from us, both staring at me. Sark's face betrayed no expression, but Erika eyes were wide with shock, as if watching a stranger.

"She lost her mom," I explained to Erika once I'd caught up. "Is there someone we can call to help find her?"

She just stared at me. "Um, I…I don't know."

"Snow!" Savannah yelled in my ear, tugging on my hair again and pointing to a giant mound of snow ahead of us. "Go!"

Walking forward, I swung Savannah around so I was holding her in my arms, then dropped her in the pile of snow. She shrieked with laughter and sifted her fingers through the white powder all around her.

I walked back to Erika, who had her eyes on Savannah. We both watched as she threw handfuls of snow into the air and tried to catch some in her mouth, but only got hit in the face.

"She's cute," Erika admitted, unable to keep the corners of her mouth from turning up at Savannah's antics.

"Yeah, she is." I laughed when a clump of snow finally fell in Savannah's mouth, and her eyes widened as she screamed through the fluff. "We need to find her mom. I'll play with her until then."

Erika gave me a sidelong glance. "I didn't know you were a kid person."

I shrugged, smiling at Savannah. "I never wanted to share my brother with another girl ever, but I was always so excited for him to have kids. I had all these leftover games and stuff from old babysitting kits I was saving in my closet—I could not wait to be an aunt."

"You'll make a great aunt!" Erika told me. "When's that going to happen?"

"Um…" My smile faded. "In another life, I guess."

Erika's face fell, her eyes glinting with sorrow. "Oh, right. I totally for—"

"It's okay." I cleared my throat. "Anyways, how can we find her mom?"

"Arie!" Savannah waddled over and took my hand in hers, yanking on my arm. "Come on! I have to show you."

I let her pull me over to the snow mound, glancing back to see Erika pulling out her phone with exasperation. Savannah tugged my hand when she realized I wasn't paying attention.

"Arie, look. It's my castle."

I surveyed her 'castle' in the snow, which was basically a little dug out hole for her to sit in.

"Wow!" I exclaimed, appraising her work. "This is such a beautiful castle."

Savannah beamed. "I know. I worked extra hard. It's the best castle in the whole kingdom." She pointed to different spots of snow as she went through her list. "It has a washer and a microwave and a big TV and a cup for sour candies."

"Well that's everything a castle needs."

I watched her play in her castle while keeping an eye on Sark and Erika several yards away. Erika scrolled on her phone as she muttered to Sark, while he glanced over at me every few minutes. Focusing on the three of them, I was unprepared when someone bumped into me roughly, a streak of crimson going across my vision.

"Hey!" they barked at me. "Watch it—"

I turned to see a girl about a year older than me, dressed like a shabby punk rocker. She was thin as a rail, with harsh black eyes and fiery red hair. Recognition dawned in her sharp face the same time it hit me.

"Alaina?" I gasped.

"Arie?" Her eyes lit up with incredulous excitement. "Arie!" She threw her arms around me, and I hugged her back tightly. It had been nearly a month now since I'd seen her—much too long a time for me to go without seeing my infected best friend.

I pulled away from her, as if needing to double check it was really her. "What...how did...what are you doing here?"

She flipped her hair in annoyance, like the psychos working for Alexis were just flies that were constantly buzzing her ear. "Oh, you know, just living on the run and all that jazz. Nowhere to go for the likes of us, really, but my brother actually lives here so I was gonna go—"

Alaina choked off, stiffening as her eyes locked on something over my shoulder. At the same time, I heard Erika's voice behind me, a mix of cautious and excited, as she walked up next to us.

"Arie, who's this?"

I glanced over to see Erika standing there, distrusting eyes on Alaina, with her hand clamped down on Sark's arm. He was about a foot behind her, stone faced and angled like he was going to bolt any second. If it weren't for Erika's fingernails digging into his arm, I knew he would be gone.

Alaina hissed and snatched my wrist, starting to run and expecting me to follow. I pulled back and braced myself.

This is going to be difficult.

"It's not what you think," I told her, which probably wasn't the best way to start out. "I know what this seems like, but—"

Alaina didn't say anything. Her eyes narrowed and she yanked on my arm again. When I didn't budge, she glanced over me, suspicion clouding her expression, and let go of my wrist, taking a step backward.

"Arie," she said slowly, gaze rolling over the three of us. "What are you doing?"

"It's me, I promise. If you'll let me explain, I…"

Explain…how can I explain this?

"Are you insane?" Flames of fury danced in her eyes, and she stepped around me, shoving Sark hard. "What did you do to her?" she demanded. "What did you *do*?"

Sark's face didn't betray any emotion, but Erika flipped out. Before she could get in Alaina's face, I stepped in between them, facing my friend.

She ignored me, hateful eyes still on Sark. "What did you do to her?"

"Alaina! Alaina, listen to me. Look at me, Alaina."

Finally, her gaze snapped to me. "Arie, whatever he's doing, whatever he has on you, just drop it. It's not worth it."

I took a breath. "It's not what you think, okay, I promise. I'm still me, and I can...I can kind of explain, but—"

"But what?" she exploded. "What could he possibly…" She trailed off, scanning me, as if searching for a threat, and my heart sank when she took another step away from me. "No. No, you wouldn't do that. Other people, maybe, but not you."

I shook my head fervently, grateful she had doubts about my capabilities for betrayal. "Please trust me. It's a long story." I glanced at Savannah and several other park goers who were staring intently at us. "And this really isn't the place for it."

She opened her mouth, just gaining steam. "You don't—"

A ringing sound cut her off. At first I thought it was Erika's phone, but then I realized it wasn't coming from Erika's pocket. It was coming from Alaina's boot.

Alaina doesn't have a phone.

"What the…" she muttered, pulling the small cellphone out of her scuffed boot. Her eyes flicked to me in question before she pressed a button. The ringing stopped and a voice came over the speaker instead.

Not any voice. Of course, it couldn't be some hobo on the street.

Alaina and I both froze, while Erika gritted her teeth in annoyance and Sark blinked with surprise.

"Alaina," the voice on the phone taunted. "Alaina, I know you're out there."

Savannah abandoned her castle and hugged my leg, skittish at the threatening voice on the phone. "Arie, who is that? It's scary."

Instantly, my eyes went to Sark, the gaze an accusation as much as a question. He shook his head. "I didn't know. I had nothing to do with it, I swear."

Understanding passed in Erika's face, and she stiffened too. "Is that Alexis?" she murmured.

"No," I whispered, fear taking my voice. "It's Lennon. He works for Alexis. He's assigned to Alaina."

Lennon finding Alaina is like Sark finding me.

"This could've been any time," Alaina said, trying to be brave though her voice was shaky. "He could've recorded this any time today and stuck it with me. It doesn't mean—"

"Alaina, I know you're here," Lennon's voice went on. "I know you're here in the park, I know you stopped by that food cart on the corner, and I know Arie is here too."

Alaina's eyes widened, and I put my hand over my mouth to keep from throwing up. Erika gasped at my name, while Savannah just hugged me tighter.

No, not Lennon. Not here, not now.

"You're not getting away this time. Either of you. I'll have you both—"

Suddenly, Alaina threw the phone on the ground and stomped on it until it broke into pieces. This time when she went to run, I automatically started to go with her.

Erika snatched me back. "What are you *doing*?" she demanded, and for a split second I almost felt guilty that I'd considered leaving her.

"We have to go," I said breathlessly, then risked a glance at Savannah. My insides twisted painfully at the thought of what would happen to the little girl if Lennon saw me with her. Maybe he already had.

Then I looked at Sark. If Lennon had seen me with him and some strange girl...I doubted Sark had reported Erika to Alexis. If Lennon saw him with Erika without explanation and me without punishment, we were all screwed.

"He doesn't know." Sark was adamant. "If he'd seen me, especially with you, he would've called me by now."

Erika's gaze was still locked on me. "Go where?" she insisted. "Why can't you come with us?"

Alaina huffed and rolled her eyes. "Oh, right, sure. I'd bet you'd just *love* to help us out. You've got 'accomplice' written all over that stupid scarf of yours."

I ignored her. "Lennon is dangerous. He can't find us, and he can't see you with us." My gaze flicked to Sark for a moment, and I knew he was thinking the same thing.

And you shouldn't be seen with him, either.

"If he's dangerous, then you should come with us, Arie," Erika said, slipping back and forth from authoritative to pleading.

My voice was harsher than I meant. "I can't be seen with you."

"I don't care!"

"Yeah? Remember what happened last time?" I gestured to her and Sark. "It won't work out this well for you again, let me tell you."

Erika turned to Sark now, as if seeking backup, but he was watching me and Alaina with conflicted eyes and a tight jaw. He was angry. But, for once, not at me.

"Savannah?"

The new voice sliced right through our tense encounter. I turned to see a middle-aged woman walking toward us, puffy eyes wide with relief. "Savannah!"

"Mommy!" Savannah released my leg and ran to her mother, who scooped up the blob of pink in her arms. The mom called a thank you to me before turning away.

The break made me take a look at our surroundings. People were staring at us. That was bad. We were making a scene.

And scenes are memorable.

"I'm leaving," I told Erika, ignoring the pain in my heart when her expression seemed to break. "I'm leaving now, and I need you to get out. Please."

I don't want you to die too.

Erika opened her mouth to argue, but Sark cut her off.

"Be careful," he told me, eyes boring into mine. They almost seemed regretful, but that emotion was lost in stone cold graveness and a flash of understanding. "You can come back. I'll help you. But regardless, you can't let him catch you."

Like I don't know that.

Erika's mouth dropped open when she realized he was letting me go. "No! She can't—"

"Erika, no." Sark nodded solemnly at me. "Be careful." Then, he took her hand and walked briskly away, slow enough to be casual but too fast to be comfortable. He ducked his head slightly too, quieting Erika's streaming demands and questions.

I watched them go for a second, a pit in my stomach. Sark would protect her. I had to believe that.

Alaina closed her mouth—it had dropped open when Sark willingly let us go. "Well that was insane," she remarked, her voice steely. She turned her mild glare on me. "I hope you know I have about four thousand questions and I will demand answers for each one."

I sucked in a breath. "Yeah. I know."

"Good." Alaina's eyes scanned the area around us, and I felt her shifting into survival mode, everything non-vital taking a backseat. I did the same. "Then let's get lost." This time when she took off, I was right behind her.

11

I scrunched my knees closer to my chest in an effort to make myself smaller. There wasn't a whole lot of space between the dumpster and the wall, especially when both Alaina and I were trying to squish into the hiding place. A swarm of flies buzzed overhead, and the stench made me wonder if there was a rotting corpse in the dumpster, but it would have to do. It had been hours since we left the park, and we were hiding in an alley. Four of Lennon's guys had been on our heels all afternoon. While some situations had been too close for comfort, we'd somehow managed to evade capture and lose them. For now, at least. It was hard to ever feel safe these days.

Taking a deep breath, I nearly choked on the rancid smell. It would taint my hair for sure. I stiffened at the thought—it'd been so long since I had the means to care about what my hair smelled like.

As if sensing my thoughts, Alaina cleared her throat. "Arie, can I ask you a question?"

"Well you said you had four thousand of them, so we better get started."

"Do you enjoy pain?"

I looked at her curiously. "What kind of question is that?"

"I'm trying to find an explanation for you waltzing around the park with Sark, besides a memory wipe or alien inhabitation or whatever."

I sighed. *Here we go.*

She continued. "The last person on this whole entire planet who would ever even remotely trust Sark on any level is you. The fact that you *do* leads me to believe either Sark has dirt on you, he actually managed to create some form of mind control, or you made a really crappy deal."

I shook my head. "It's not like that. Any of that. It's...it's crazy and impossible to explain. I wouldn't believe it if I hadn't seen it for myself—I *have* seen it and I still don't understand it. But...I think...Sark doesn't really want to hurt me...anymore. I think."

"He doesn't *want* to hurt you anymore? So, what, he just woke up one day and saw the light? Hallelujah, the heavens opened, and the angels started singing?" She scoffed. "That's the stupidest thing I've ever heard. Please tell me you didn't actually buy into that crap."

I bit my lip. "I know what it sounds like, I do. But...you'd just have to see it. I mean, you *saw* him today, just walking around like a normal person, and he let us go—"

"He could be tracking us right now," Alaina pointed out. "That doesn't mean anything." She breathed on her hands and rubbed them together, trying to keep warm. I peeled off my gloves and gave them to her.

"Yeah, maybe, but...I don't know." I rested my head back against the wall. "It's so different, so different from anything...he's usually so sure of himself. So confident and stiff and empty except for...hatred. Now, though, it's like it's too awkward to be anything but real."

Alaina snorted. "So the torture is awkward now?" She tried for her best male British impression. "I'm, uh, sorry if this is uncomfortable, ma'am, but I'm a deranged psycho interested in formula freaks."

"It's not like that," I said, unamused. "It's all stopped. He just lets me live there. Gives me clothes and food and then leaves me alone unless I need help."

"Why in the world would you stay there?"

"The doors were locked. I couldn't..." I trailed off. She had me there. "But the feeling of it all—"

"Do you hear yourself?" she exploded, exasperated. "This is Sark we are talking about. *Sark.* Your mortal enemy, the bane of your existence, the demon sent from the underworld to make your life a living hell. We hate this guy. *You* hate this guy. Remember?"

Irritation seeped into my voice. "Of course I remember."

"Yeah, well with the amnesia you've got going on, I wasn't so sure." She twisted a strand of hair around her finger. "And what's with that chick that was with him? She's new. Maybe Sark's latest plan is to annoy us to death. She would've fit—"

"He saved my life."

Alaina did a double take, raising her eyebrows in disbelief. "What?"

"He saved my life."

"No, that doesn't…" She trailed off and started again, frustration getting the best of her. "Sark wouldn't do that, Arie? Don't you get it? This isn't what you think it is. He's playing you. Can't you see it? He's—"

"Felix bashed my head in." I kept my voice neutral, focusing on a smudge on the green dumpster to keep me calm while reflecting on the harrowing memory. "I should have died. I *would* have if it weren't for Sark. I know he really wouldn't let me die, but this time it was different. He panicked. It was mostly because of Erika, I think, but still. I've never seen him like that. Especially about me. I owe them both my life."

For a half a second, I froze, realizing what I'd said: I knew Sark would never let me die because he believed I might be the key to the formula. Thankfully, Alaina was too fired up to notice my mistake.

"You *owe* them your life?" she repeated in disgust. "You don't owe Sark anything besides a bullet in the chest. People like him don't change."

She shook her head. "I can't believe we're even having this conversation."

"I can't either," I muttered. "But he acts differently. I can tell it's difficult for him sometimes, but he does it. And we've...talked. About things. He was drunk—and sober Sark is scary enough, so I was terrified—but he was drunk and he helped patch me up. He told me about his childhood. And he asked me about Kieran and...I told him." Mentioning Kieran sobered Alaina up. She knew I wouldn't mention Kieran to anyone, let alone talk about him, unless I was completely serious. "I don't know why I did. It just felt different. And I can't...I can't decide because I am still afraid of him. It's not that. It's just the person I'm afraid of doesn't come out as much anymore."

Alaina took that in. "So...despite having locked you up and tortured you on multiple occasions in the last year, you've decided he's an okay guy after a drunken conversation and two weeks without incident? Aren't there, like, disorders for that kind of thing?"

Stockholm syndrome.

"Yeah," I admitted. "But it just…"

"Doesn't feel like that," Alaina finished. "Right, yeah, I get it. Well, not really, but you have piqued my interest." She made a show of stretching out in the two inches of space she had. "I've got time to burn. I'll listen to whatever he sold you."

I rolled my eyes. "Your faith in me is inspiring."

She gestured for me to go on, so I told her everything that had happened since the pier. I kind of skimmed over the details about Kristen since I didn't feel like it was my place to share. Alaina seemed to understand, though, at least a little. She had lost her mom too.

When I finished with bumping into her in the park, she whistled. "Wow. That's…"

"Crazy." I sighed. "Yeah, I know." Then I closed my eyes, bracing myself for her reaction. "If Lennon…if Lennon catches up to us, I think we should go back. To…to Sark's house."

Alaina exploded with a stream of expletives, and I had to remind her that we were trying to *hide*.

"Are you serious?" she hissed, her voice quieter now but with no less venom.

"You know what happens to us when Lennon finds us." I cringed at the memories, but they paled in comparison to the nasty black hole in my gut at the thought of living on the run again. "Sark could help us hide, while we're—"

"Okay get this into your head: Sark isn't helping us. He isn't capable of that. The only things he's capable of is hurting innocent people and turning your brain into zombified jello."

"He'll help us," I argued. I didn't know why I was so stuck on this. "Erika will make sure of it."

"The unstable stranger who helped your nemesis put you on house arrest?"

I gritted my teeth. I didn't have anything for that. "It's just—"

"Different." Alaina rolled her eyes. "Yeah, you said that. Good thing I ran into you or who knows what else you might've gotten yourself mixed up in." She stood up then, extracting herself out from behind the dumpster and stretching. "It's almost dark now, buttercup. Let's go."

Annoyed at Alaina for her condescending remarks and myself for my idiotic feelings that made no sense, I stood up too. I would follow Alaina for now, and she would follow me. But I couldn't shake the feeling that going off too far from Erika—and, by extension, Sark—was a bad idea.

Which, yes, I told myself bitterly, *is insane.*

Maybe Alaina was right. Maybe I should take off with her while I had the chance. It wasn't like Erika was about to just let me go, though her motives in all of this remained a mystery to me, and Sark wasn't either.

Except he did. In the park. None of this made any sense.

I brushed the dirt off my pants while Alaina pulled her hood over her dark crimson hair. Despite her life, she refused to dye it something average—it was a part of her. While it would make her so much less conspicuous, she said she didn't want Lennon to take another thing from her. I understood that logic completely, but I couldn't say I really agreed with it. Of course, that only highlighted the huge difference between Alaina and me, one that she wasn't aware of. The more Sark caught me, the more chances he had to figure out I was the key. I had everything to lose, where Alaina was just another infected kid running to save her own skin. Another failed science experiment.

We walked slowly out of the alley, surveying the area for any suspicious men or vehicles. We were out of the main part of the city; these streets were much quieter. When neither of us found any threats, we stepped hesitantly into the open and started down the sidewalk. Alaina didn't know it, but we were within forty minutes or so of Sark's house. I kept a mental tab on where we were in relation to it; I couldn't help it.

Something is wrong with your brain. Hopefully Alaina would keep me from doing anything else stupid.

The moon wasn't out, and the only light across the pavement came from the streetlights. Tiny dots of snow began to fall from the black sky, bringing a stillness to the night and making our footsteps seem too loud. It could have been peaceful, but it only felt sinister. The calm before the storm.

There weren't many people out. We were in the suburbs now, and with the dark and the cold, nearly everyone was inside. I shivered despite the thick coat I was bundled in—a coat I never would've been able to get on my own. I caught my thoughts wandering to Erika. Had she made it out safely? I hoped she did. Erika was often too loud, bright, and nosy—not to mention borderline crazy—but I still hoped she made it out of the park without incident.

I caught myself wondering if she was wondering about me. While she'd only brought me closer to Sark, and therefore closer to danger, her concern for me always seemed genuine. Was she worrying about me right now? Something in my gut told me yes. And if everything went well tonight, I'd never see her again to placate her worries.

Oh well. I tried to shrug off the sadness I felt. *We can't have everything.*

Suddenly, Alaina tripped, barely catching herself before she splattered onto the snowy pavement.

"Stupid knee," she muttered to me. "Eudrico would've never let that go."

Instantly, my muscles stiffened at the codename. I forced myself to maintain a casual posture while I paid more attention to what was around me. Sure enough, my ears strained and heard the sound of a third pair of footsteps about a half block or so behind us.

I gritted my teeth at my carelessness. Getting distracted always caused problems.

We took the next left. The second we rounded the corner, we broke into a run, dashing down the slick sidewalk and banking right at the next chance. My heart sprinted with me when I heard the footsteps behind us clomp on the pavement, chasing us.

We ran. There was nothing else to do. The icy air burned my throat as I gasped in exertion and fear. Always fear.

We can't get caught, we can't get caught, we can't get caught.

We shook him off, just to get cut off by another. Within five minutes, two men were chasing us down the street, which meant there were probably many more close by. We had walked into a trap.

I can't get caught I can't get caught I can't get caught I can't get caught.

Nearly choking on terror, I took a hard right at the next corner, Alaina following. It was the worst move I could've made. Ten steps later and we were at the edge of an orchard. The length of the fence went about two blocks down, leading me to believe the orchard wasn't very big, and the trees twice my height, having lost half their leaves due to the

November season. It was the perfect place to hide and disappear in; it was also the perfect place to kill someone quietly without anyone finding out.

They herded us here. It couldn't be a coincidence.

I turned on my heels, ready to beeline it out of there, but the two men caught up to us, blocking our exit and pulling out their guns. I glanced to my right, prepared to try and jump the chain link fence. Two SUVs and a small trailer were parked in my way.

My hands started shaking. With guards on one side, cars on the other, and an orchard to our backs, we were cornered.

Alaina huffed, acknowledging our situation. When the two men aimed their guns at her, she just glared back, the stare as heated as her hair. She didn't attack, though. I was grateful for that. Now was not the time for either of us to get shot.

One of the car doors opened and a man stepped out. Immediately, the already cold temperature of the air plummeted to unbearably freezing.

Lennon.

Lennon was a long guy. Long legs, long torso, long face. He was even wearing a long black trench coat. It made it easier for him to stand over you, to look down on you with a sneer as he crushed you underneath his foot and smeared you on the pavement. A sly grin spread on his face when he saw us, the lust for blood clear in his blazing eyes.

"Hello girls," he said, charisma dripping from his words. I fought the urge to vomit at his slimy voice and Alaina's hands clenched into fists. His gaze went from her, to his men, then rested on me.

His smile grew. "Arie, it's been awhile. It's nice to see you."

I tasted bile in my mouth now, but I forced a wry grin. "Can't say the same. Sorry."

His face fell in mocking disappointment. "I suppose I expected as much. Regardless, I'm happy you're here to play with us this evening. I have something truly spectacular." He motioned with his hand, and a couple of his guards stalked over to the white trailer.

"Spectacularly insane, likely," Alaina muttered, just loud enough for him to hear. When that caught his attention, she feigned pity, her thin eyebrows pulling down. "Did you forget to take your meds again? The nurses say you can't do that if you leave the padded cell, remember?"

Ignoring their verbal fight, my eyes scanned the area, searching for an escape. Snow fell in tiny dots around us, perfectly framing the air, but now it felt suffocating, like Lennon had planned it. I would almost believe it, if it were possible. While just as ruthless, Lennon had always been much more dramatic than Sark. Theatrical. Sark had no patience for any extra frills—it all just was what it was—but Lennon seemed to thrive off of it. A lot of Alexis' men did, except for Sark.

Does that make me lucky or not?

My gaze followed the men by the trailer, which was when I realized something was off. The trailer was moving. Ever so slowly, but it was, rocking back and forth subtly but viciously. Like it were alive. One guard lowered the door, and a roaring sound echoed through the night. Lennon cocked his head toward the sound and smiled.

My blood went cold. *This can't be good.*

The men pulled on thick ropes, yanking out what was inside: four huge dogs. At least, I *thought* they were dogs. They had a canine form, but their skin was jet black and scaly, like a snake, and their jagged fangs glinted like steel as they snarled. Thrashing against the men's hold on their leashes, their small eyes remained locked on Alaina and me.

The sight of the dogs shut Alaina up. We exchanged a glance. Lennon grinned wickedly at our expressions. "What do you think?"

My shaking hands clenched to fists in my coat pockets as I watched the dogs. They struggled against their restraints, snapping their teeth, and one collar crackled with electricity. The dog didn't even flinch; the spark didn't touch it.

The shocks are meant for us. My stomach dropped. *We're going to get eaten alive.*

"What do I think?" Alaina repeated, rebounding part of her fatal sass. "I think you must've missed a lot of pills. Does the mental ward know you're missing?"

Biting my lip, I glanced around again, willing Alaina not to dig our hole any deeper than it was. How could we get out? Surrounded by men with guns was one thing, but if Lennon let those dogs loose on us...we had no chance. And if they didn't kill us, Lennon would still have us. And any extra second spent with him was another second he could find out I was the one they were looking for.

I can't get caught. We can't get caught. My heart stuttered when one of the dogs snapped its teeth and its collar crackled again. *We can't go out like this.*

We'd have to run into the orchard. It was the only way to go. It was also the way Lennon *wanted* us to go, but we didn't have anything else to work with.

Lennon smirked at me, as if sensing my thoughts. "Now, nobody can ever say I wasn't fond of you, Arie. I'll give you a head start, if you'd like."

Gritting my teeth, I glared at him—never before had I hated someone so much, except Sark. "I'm not playing your game."

Lennon laughed at me, a puffy, fake sound. "It looks to me like your life is my game." He nodded, and the men behind us shot the pavement at our feet and the air over our head, getting closer with each bullet. "Tick tock, girls."

I nearly felt the air of the next bullet whiz past me, and I couldn't make myself stay still any longer. I ran. Alaina ran too, and my insides curled at the eager laugh of excitement Lennon gave behind us. It was only a matter of seconds before I heard the snarling of the dogs coming up on us.

We can't get caught. We have to get out.

There was no out, though. We hadn't been running for more than a minute, and we were already lost. Everything looked the same in the stupid orchard, branches reaching out, clawing at us, threatening to hold us prisoner until our grisly execution. I was barely able to make out the shadows of the trees enough to duck, though the limbs still scratched my face and pulled at my hair.

"Where do we go?" Alaina yelled to me, panic tainting her voice. We were lost.

"I have no idea!"

We can't get caught, we can't get caught, we can't get caught.

"Do you have anything?" It was supposed to be a question, but it came off as more of a plea.

"I have my knife," she answered without hope.

We ran wildly through the endless trees, heart thudding in my chest. I didn't stop until I heard Alaina scream and she dropped out of my sight. I skidded and went back, horrified to see her on the ground with a dog on top of her, teeth inches from her face as she pushed against its huge muzzle.

I started for her, unsure what I was actually going to do, when a force shoved me to the ground. The air in my lungs all left in a *whoosh*. Paws held me down, the weight of the dog crushing me into the earth, and it snapped its teeth, nearly taking my nose off. I struggled underneath it, pushing its mouth away from my face without letting it eat one of my fingers. It wouldn't budge. Then its collar went off, sending a burst of electricity through me, and the dog swiped its claw across my face.

I crumpled instantly. I couldn't fight this thing.

Alaina cried out and I heard something clatter to the ground. In a split second, I craned my neck to see her knife and then snatched it up, nearly popping my shoulder out of place in my haste. The dog lunged for my throat but I dug the blade into its neck instead. It gave a garbled howl, stumbling off of me. Baring my own teeth, I managed to dislodge the weapon and slice its throat. The monster collapsed onto the ground.

I barely paused for a breath before I was up. I took two giant steps and plunged the knife into the other dog's back. It snarled and reared back, slamming me into a tree, but then Alaina was there, and she finished the job with her blade.

Both panting and bleeding, we glanced at each other before taking off again.

We can't get caught. We can make it.

I ran as fast as the trees would let me, blindly feeling my way through the orchard. I couldn't see anything and was running so fast that I didn't notice the tripwire until I had already tripped. Sprawling into the snow, I yelped when my head hit something hard and tried to scramble back to my feet.

I smelled him before I saw him. He could kill people with the bottles of nasty cologne he wore all at one time. One second I was picking myself up; the next second Lennon had his hands around my throat. He pulled me up so I was sitting, then slammed me back against a tree trunk, staying behind me so none of my flailing limbs hit him.

"Oh, Arie," he said much too close to my ear, his tone animated like he were watching a good show on TV. Revulsion coursed through me but I couldn't get away. "Why do you even keep trying? Don't you think it's high time you gave up already?"

I could only gasp in response, clawing at his hands on my throat and fighting for oxygen. He just laughed at me. Even when dying for air, I recoiled away from his breath on my face. I didn't get very far, though. Lennon whistled loudly and within seconds two hulking shadows were coming at me through the trees.

Terror took hold of me and I thrashed harder, striking my fist out behind me and hearing a satisfying thud when I caught his jaw. His grip on me slackened just enough for me to lean forward and gulp in precious air. My clothes were soaked through and my skin felt frozen as I elbowed Lennon in the ribs and crawled forward. My freedom was short lived. The dogs lunged at me, pinning me against the tree. The wind got knocked out of me again, claws raking across my skin. One dog snatched my arm in its jaws, its teeth sinking into my flesh.

I can't get caught I can't get caught I can't get caught I can't get caught.

Both collars went off, and I screamed through the searing shocks. Then again. I saw stars at the third shock.

I'm going to die.

A gunshot sounded, then another, and two more. The dog holding my arm captive dropped to the ground in a pile of blood. I jerked my arm out of its grasp and smacked the other dog in the nose. It snarled at me, but backed off slightly when another bullet almost got its shoulder.

Alaina.

Her crimson hair was wet and matted as she came through the shadows, carrying a bloodstained gun. Eyes narrowed, she shot at something behind my head—Lennon, probably—then aimed at the dog still on me. Growling at it, she fired.

Nothing happened.

She tried again. Empty.

The dog snarled and lunged forward, munching on her ankle. She cried out, falling to the ground, and the empty gun dropped into the snow. Alaina kicked and thrashed, but the dog wouldn't let go, its collar sparking again.

The electricity gave me an idea. Grimacing, I reached over and unlatched the collar on the dead dog next to me. The other dog noticed me messing with his brother, and came at me again, tearing up my leg and shooting another nasty current through me, which set the one in my hand off. Shrieking, I forced my hand to unlatch the dog's collar, then I turned it on the monster. It jumped back away from the electricity, still baring its teeth at me.

Holding the collar out in front of me to keep the dog at bay, I scraped the other against the tree next to me. It took a couple tries, but eventually the spark hit the wood right, igniting a flame. I used the other collar too. Within seconds, the tree was on fire, and the three next to it were catching.

The temperature ballooned and the dog scampered back from the inferno. I dragged myself to Alaina, groaning in frustration when I saw she'd hit her head on a rock. She was dazed, but I was able to get her up.

"We have to go," I said hoarsely, already coughing over the smoke. "Now." She nodded in somewhat understanding and, both limping, we stood and took the first pocket of trees that hadn't yet caught flame. Smoke burned my lungs while my fried hands throbbed and dizzy head ached, but we kept going. We had to.

I didn't pause once we got out of the orchard. I didn't really even remember making the conscious decision to go to Sark's house until we were almost halfway there. I knew Lennon would follow us, and I knew in our condition he'd catch up to us. He'd be furious we managed to ruin his dogs. Alaina would be lucky to last the night.

We. Can't. Get. Caught.

If Alaina recognized I was running with a destination in mind, she didn't argue or fight. She only sighed in resignation. She knew we didn't really have another option. She would do it, because she had to. Amazing what you can do when you have to. It was how we became friends in the first place, really—the need to team up and do what was necessary to survive.

We were so close—so painfully close—when one of Lennon's guys, the bald one, caught up to us. Thankfully, I saw him before he saw me. The moonlight glinted off his shiny head, giving me a split second to yank Alaina behind a small, aesthetic fence before he turned around.

Breaths stuttering with fear, I looked at Alaina. "Four more blocks," I told her in a desperate whisper. "Four blocks down and turn left. Cut through the cul de sac and it's on the opposite side of the next street. You'll know it by the huge, stone walls around it. Stone not cement. Do you got all that?"

Alaina managed to glare back at me through her fluttering eyelids, blood dripping down her temple. She knew it was no use arguing now, though. Survival came first, and her head was too banged up for her to be much help. "Four blocks, left. Stone walls."

I nodded. "Yes."

When I moved to stand up again, my body screaming at me in protest, Alaina snatched my arm, digging her fingernails into my coat. Her black eyes burned bright as she pressed her bloody knife into my hand. "Be there."

I nodded again. "Promise."

Then we separated. She snuck along the fence toward Sark's house while I darted the other direction. Every limb hurt so badly, but I forced myself to keep going, used my all-consuming fear to stay afloat. When I thought Alaina was far enough away, I let myself be seen by Baldie. He thought he had the jump on me. I pretended I didn't notice him following me down the block, feeding his growing ego at the idea he'd be the one to catch me.

Not tonight, pal.

The neighborhood was much different than the ones I was used to hiding in: the houses were ginormous, some of them taking up a whole block, and each were surrounded by thick gates or fences. There were no alleys to hide in. No zipping traffic to use as a distraction. I was a wounded gazelle, stuck out in the open as perfect prey for the manic hunter.

I can't get caught. I won't get caught. We'll all be okay.

I didn't mean for Baldie to corner me so quickly, but my head was pounding and I was having a difficult time keeping everything straight. Suddenly, he was grabbing me by my shoulders and yanking me back, closing a hand around my mouth. I launched myself backward, using his momentum as well to slam him into the cement wall guarding the estate next to us. Then I slid Alaina's knife from my sleeve and lodged it in his thigh. With a twist of the blade, Baldie was on the ground. I kicked his head against the wall twice, and he was out.

Slumping against the wall, I saw double of everything. I breathed through the pain. Baldie was down. I was free to get to Sark's house without him seeing or following.

I'm not getting caught.

My vision came into focus again just as a shadow came down on me. A fist came out of nowhere, striking my face and sending me to the pavement. Then a hand took me by the back of my neck and dragged me deeper into the gap between two cement walls. It was darker back there without moonlight or street lights, but I still recognized the face of my attacker in the shadows. Another one of Lennon's guys Alaina and I called Toothless after an unfortunate accident.

Toothless slammed me against the cement wall, hatred in his bug eyes. "Well, well, look what I found." He bared his teeth at me—what teeth he had, anyway. He was missing a few, thanks to me. It was too much to hope he wouldn't remember that. "Managed to wander a far ways, didn't you? Where's the redhead?"

I glared back and spat in his face. He punched me in the gut, then brought a blade to my neck. He looked over me, then, noticing the gash in my arm from the dogs, dug his knife into my wound. I clamped my mouth shut, but still whimpered.

Toothless ran his tongue along his remaining teeth, and I shuddered in revulsion in spite of myself. "You're pretty banged up already," he acutely observed. "Don't think Lennon'll notice any extra blood, don't you?"

He twisted the knife in my wound until I couldn't take it anymore and cried out in pain. Then he used his other hand to reach for my mouth. I shook my head furiously, trying to keep him from getting a hold on me. It didn't work. He snatched my jaw in his hand, then pried my mouth open with his knife. My own blood dripped onto my tongue as he held the blade against the gum of my front tooth.

"You owe me a couple pearly whites," he noted with disdain. "I think I'll take them back now."

Before I could scream, Toothless collapsed to the ground, and I went with him. Sprawled in the snow next to his unconscious form, I glanced up to see a new shadow looming over both of us.

Sark.

And he was *pissed*.

Self-preservation took over. I scrambled back against the wall and braced myself for his fury, putting my throbbing hands up in front of my face and stifling a sob.

I was going to get caught.

Sark reached down and grabbed my elbow, yanking me to my feet. "What were you *thinking*?" he hissed at me, enraged. When I just stared at him, he shook me hard, and I whimpered. "Are you insane? You can't pull these kind of brainless stunts, especially when you're in this shape…" He trailed off, too angry to keep going. Then he pulled me out of the little alley, surveying the scene for threats before leading me down the sidewalk, his hold tight on my elbow.

I stumbled after him, struggling to keep up. "Alaina. She's really hurt. She—"

"She's fine," Sark snapped back. "By the time she got to the house, she was nearly hysterical and screaming that you were still out there." He shook his head, muttering something along the lines of 'so incredibly stupid.'

"They couldn't find you," I insisted. "Any of you. They were following us. I had to shake them off or they'd kill us all."

"You know, there's such a thing as too altruistic, Arie. What you did was reckless and dangerous, and you *have* to take care of yourself better."

Despite my pain and fear, I found myself annoyed. "Since when do you care?"

He actually stumbled a step, his anger stopping in place before melting away. He straightened up, like he remembered himself.

"I don't," he muttered. "Erika was worried."

I rolled my eyes but my head only shrieked in response, and the world started spinning. I staggered a step, slowly losing the ability to push through my injuries. Sark grabbed my hand to stabilize me, and I gave a choked scream at the stab of fire that emanated from the touch.

Panting, I thought I'd sink into the snow and just die. My knees buckled. This time, Sark caught me by my uninjured arm, while being careful to avoid touching my aching hands. Rather than get irritated and jerk me along—like he used to—he strengthened his hold on me and tried to take more of my weight without hurting me.

"We're almost there," he said quietly. "You're so close."

Unable to do anything but put one foot in front of the other, I closed my eyes and sagged against Sark's shoulder, letting him lead me. After years of walking, Sark stopped. I cracked my eyes open to see him entering the code on the gate of his house.

Once he got it open, his gaze went over me, a hint of his anger heating up his eyes again.

He frowned. "Can I carry you?"

I blinked. For a moment, I thought I heard him wrong. Then I nodded. In one motion, he picked me up and stepped through the gate, locking it behind us. My vision glazed over as he trekked through his snowy backyard, up the few stairs to the deck, and into the house. I couldn't help a sigh of relief at the blast of warm air; it wasn't until then I realized I was wet and shivering.

Somewhere, I heard Erika gasp my name, and I relaxed slightly at her voice. Sark walked over to the couch, where I saw Alaina sprawled out, her ankle wrapped up and wide eyes on me.

I breathed a sigh of relief. *We're okay.*

Then the doorbell rang.

We all froze.

My heart stuttered. My mouth went dry.

It rang again.

Alaina whimpered. Sark swore.

Then he turned and threw the mirror door open, all but dropping me on the ground of the piano room. Panic pulsed in my ears, in my veins. Erika protested, but Sark shoved her and Alaina in the room too, throwing a few bloodied rags after us, and shut us all inside.

The doorbell rang again. Sark smoothed his shirt and took a breath, then disappeared to go answer it. The three of us huddled on the floor in the corner—Alaina on my right, Erika on my left—trembling with terror. Erika was pale and frozen. Alaina was sobbing silently. We knew who would be at the door.

And we're trapped in here.

We wouldn't be seen or heard, but we were sitting ducks, and completely at Sark's mercy.

There's nothing we can do.

Voices echoed down the entry corridor, then footsteps down the hallway. Lennon entered the living room first with Sark right on his heels. Alaina cowered into my shoulder when she saw them, and I fought to keep from screaming.

"...and I assumed you were in the area if she was," Lennon was saying. His coat was filthy, smudged with dirt and ash, and a bruise was forming on one side of his jaw. He stopped when he saw the room. Sark's living room, decked to the nines with Erika's Christmas stuff.

My stomach dropped. We were screwed.

"Well..." he finally said, eyeing the decorations suspiciously. "You've been busy." He turned to see Sark's stone face, perfectly composed in a cool mask.

Sark just shrugged. "Arie hates Christmas. I figured I'd try your approach."

"I see." He raised his eyebrows at the blood smeared on Sark's nice shirt. My blood.

"She was here earlier," Sark said, irritation seeping into his tone. "She escaped this morning."

"Unfortunate." He looked like he was going to say more, but the TV caught his attention. I glanced over to see the news was on, showcasing the fire burning in the orchard.

Lennon scowled at the screen. "She ruins everything, doesn't she? One would *think* she would've learned her lesson by now."

Even I caught the challenge in his words, but Sark didn't take the bait. His silence caused Lennon's mouth to twitch with annoyance.

"She got a taste of what she deserves," Lennon went on, watching the TV again. "I brought out the animals Alexis bred. They're beautiful creatures. Horrifying. The orchard was enclosed and out of the way. It was perfect."

"It's burning to the ground," Sark noted.

Lennon glared at him. "Yes, well *your* infected managed to kill three dogs and use the shock collars to set the trees on fire. I don't know how she did it, honestly. The voltage was fairly high to begin with, and she held two of them with her bare hands." He gave a tiny smile. "I imagine she's dealing with some serious repercussions about now. Perhaps her brain will never recover from the electricity." Then his tone was hard. "One can hope, anyway. She cost me the chance to grab Alaina before we left."

"Unfortunate," Sark echoed. I didn't know how he could stand there so blandly without giving a hint away to Lennon.

"They're getting better at this," Lennon admitted, chagrin coloring his words. "I was able to chase and corner them, but they evaded any capture. That doesn't—*shouldn't*—happen." He walked over to examine the giant Christmas tree. Alaina, Erika, and I all cringed when he passed the mirror door. Sark just tracked the movements will his harsh eyes.

"Alaina gets in your face," Lennon went on, as if rehashing a conversation they'd had a million times before, "but it's all talk. Hit the right buttons, and she'll fall right back in her place." He pinched a red ornament between his finger and thumb. "Arie is...different. Stories are spreading. Some of the other infecteds are taking after her: they're fighting harder and they're starting to win."

Releasing the ornament, his eyes scanned the mirror, pausing at the handle. My heart leapt in my throat and Alaina squeezed my arm.

His eyebrows furrowed with interest and he came closer. "This can't continue. That fight, that drive...we have to beat it out of her. Before this spreads further."

"What do you suggest we do?" Sark asked, a little too quickly.

Lennon stopped and turned to face him. "I *suggest* you put her in her place: in the ground. Make an example of her, torture her until she dies, then move on."

I half expected Sark to get excited about that idea. He didn't. His eyes narrowed slightly, but otherwise his expression didn't change. I'd never seen the two of them at odds with each other like this.

Lennon laughed once, a derisive sound. "Oh, right, I forgot: you won't kill her, will you? You still believe she could be the key."

I flinched, the pit in my stomach morphing into a black hole.

"Whether or not the key actually exists," Lennon went on, clearly loving the role of scolding Sark, "you must do your job, and you must realize how this works. You feel special because Alexis took you under his wing and handed you everything we've all had to work for, but let me assure you, you're not. Deluding yourself into thinking Arie

Nolan is the key just so you can impress Alexis and remain his favorite is an idiotic and rather pathetic move. It just shows how naive and desperate you are."

My mouth fell open. I couldn't help it. Nobody would *ever* dare say anything like that to Sark.

Despite the rage building in his eyes, Sark remained cool. He just regarded Lennon with those icy blue eyes, freezing him out with bitter wrath. The glare was frosty enough to make Lennon pause.

When Lennon spoke again, his tone still had an edge of steel, but the attacking nature was gone. Smart guy. "I hope you realize that this reflects badly on both of us. Arie may be your assignment, but she's my problem too. She's turning into *everyone's* problem. And it can't be ignored any longer." He took a step toward Sark. "Jefferson is still seething over the incident in March—we *all* are. And if you won't do anything about it, somebody else will have to."

Again, Sark stared at Lennon with cold calculation, which only seemed to annoy Lennon further. He wanted a reaction, and Sark wasn't going to give him the satisfaction of an explosive one.

"Do you have a point, here, Lennon?" Sark finally asked, words as frigid as his eyes. "Because it looks to me like you lost. Badly. And instead of trying to fix your mistakes, you're hiding behind insults while lecturing me on how to do my job—a job you obviously can't do much better. If you're doubting my intentions, let me assure you they are greater than yours in that I'm willing to keep working after a defeat rather than parade around complaining to everyone else."

Lennon's silence stretched a second too long for normal conversation, swallowing how thoroughly Sark had beaten him in this confrontation. "I don't doubt you," he finally said, straightening his shoulders and jerking his chin out with arrogance. "I've seen you with her. Nobody hates her as much as you do. Even Jefferson would agree. Still…" He stole a glance at the knob on the mirror again.

"I'll deal with her," Sark said with resolve. "Like I've always planned. Anything else you have for me this evening?"

Lennon muttered something under his breath before answering. "I'm going after Alaina in the morning. If you find Arie, let me know."

Sark nodded and Lennon let out a breath.

"Well, then, Mr. Sark, until next time." And with that, Lennon strode down the hallway. I heard the front door slam as he let himself out.

Alaina burst into tears next to me, and Erika shuddered. I didn't realize I'd been holding my breath until I let it all out. A tension I'd been clutching inside of me loosened, and I lost some of my control. A few tears dripped down my cheek while the pain of everything attacked me all at once, ravaging freely now that I didn't have a barrier of adrenaline and survival instincts protecting me.

Erika jumped to her feet and shoved the door open, colliding into Sark. With a dry sob, she hurled herself at him, flinging her arms around his neck and crying into his shoulder. He hugged her back, kissing her temple softly and whispering in her ear.

Drying her spell of tears, Alaina turned to me. "Arie?"

My eyelids fluttered and I winced. It felt like someone was taking a cheese grater to my brain.

When I didn't respond, Alaina shook me by my shoulders. I whimpered in pain, but couldn't find any words to speak, or make myself move. I just hurt. Hurt everywhere.

"Arie? Arie, talk to me. Please." Her voice became panicked. "Arie, can you hear me? Please, Arie, say something. You look like—"

She cut herself off as Sark kneeled down in front of us. When he reached for me, Alaina swatted his hand away.

"Don't touch her!" she spat at him, her voice shaking with fear. "Don't you dare."

"Alaina," Sark said evenly. "I need to help her."

Then Erika was there next to Sark, pulling Alaina away from me. Alaina shoved her aside, and wrapped her arms around me.

"No! Get off me! You'll hurt her, I know it!" She took a ragged breath. "I don't know why she brought us here, I don't know what…" Her voice broke. "Just leave us alone."

Erika opened her mouth to argue, but Sark put a hand on her knee, his eyes on Alaina. "Do you trust Arie?"

The answer came through Alaina's teeth. "Yes."

"She brought you here, Alaina, so we could help you. I know you can't trust me or Erika. That's okay. But you can trust Arie. You do trust her."

Alaina just stared at him through the new tears that were sneaking down her face. "Lennon said she could be really hurt."

Sark nodded, the slightest strain showing through in his expression. "I know."

When Alaina didn't say anything else, Sark moved toward me again. Alaina just screamed at him and held me tighter, acting as a shield for me, and I cried out when the movement jostled me and set off my smarting nerves. I lost the rest of my control, and my body started convulsing while mangled sounds of pain escaped my lips.

Sark pried Alaina off me as she screamed profanities at him. Without any support, I slumped into a ball on the floor. Sark took my face in his hands, forcing me to look at him, and I saw traces of alarm in his eyes.

"Arie?" he asked over Alaina's protests, now aimed at Erika for holding her back. "Arie, if you can hear me, I need you to tell me somehow."

I opened my mouth, but the movement hurt—every muscle hurt—and I could only manage one word. "Here."

The sound of my voice silenced Alaina. She stopped fighting Erika, both of them staring intently at me.

Sark nodded at me. "Good. Can you tell me what hurts the worst?"

I took a shuddering breath, and my voice cracked. "Everywhere."

He pursed his lips, then quickly examined me. Motioning for Erika to get him supplies, he wrapped up the bite wound on my arm, and cleaned the wounds on my face and leg. When Alaina saw he wasn't seriously hurting me for the time being, she let Erika finish patching up her injuries too.

Sark paused when he got to my hands. They were covered in angry red splotches and black burn marks, and it hurt for even the air to touch them.

Everything got progressively hazier. Voices sounded, but I only caught words here and there. Eventually, I felt Sark pick me up and carry me down the hallway, and I closed my eyes, willing unconsciousness to take me so I could be rid of this pain.

I must've drifted off right then. In my dream, everything was exactly the same: same pain, same hallway, same Sark. When we got to my room, he said something so quietly I almost didn't hear it.

"I'm sorry. I'm sorry for every time you were trying to live for once and I got in your way."

Then I drifted off again, and it felt more like sleeping. The pain slowly ebbed and I found myself falling into dreams that made more sense: dreams of wild dogs, red snow, and a mirror that hid me from the monsters and saved my life.

12

When I finally woke up, it took me a moment to figure out how to open my eyes. The simple movement was a chore, and it seemed to remind the rest of my muscles that they were really sore too and wanted me to know. I groaned in response.

"Arie?"

The sound of Alaina's whisper helped me to force my eyelids to work. I found myself in the room I'd been staying in at Sark's house. The windows were dark; the clock said it was just after four in the morning. Alaina was lying on the pillow next to me, and even in the shadows I could see the cuts on her cheek and dark circles under her eyes.

"Arie," Alaina whispered again. "Say something."

I cleared my throat, and it felt like it'd been rubbed raw. I winced. "You look like crap."

Alaina laughed. With a sigh of relief, she relaxed further into the bed. "You don't look so hot either, buttercup. I was afraid your brain would still be soup when you woke up."

I rubbed my temple and winced again. "Feels like pretty nasty soup or something up in there."

"Yeah, because someone was an idiot and grabbed two live electric collars."

"Saved your butt, didn't it?"

"Yeah. Thanks for that, by the way."

I cracked a smile through my stiff face. "It was a joint effort."

Alaina burrowed further into the pillow, taking deep breaths. "Well, you're talking like normal now, so that ought to count for something. You were pretty fried last night." She paused for the slightest second and stole a glance at the door. "Sark said it should wear off eventually. He said he *hoped* so, anyway. Didn't sound too confident about it, but here you are."

I opened my mouth, prepared to apologize for bringing her here, but the words died in my mouth. Alaina watched me. Not expectantly. She just stared at me, studying my face. I was starting to feel self-conscious when she finally said, "He didn't give us up."

I stared back for a moment. "I know."

"He lied to Lennon."

"I was there."

"He could get killed for that. Murdered. They'll hack him to nasty pieces if anyone ever found out."

I sighed. "Yeah."

She shook her head and let out a long breath. "This is insane. There has to be something else going on here."

I tried to shrug, then thought better of it. "Maybe, but for now, I'm taking what I can get."

Alaina's hand trailed along the sheets. "It's the nicest bed I've had in awhile. If anything, Sark has good taste."

My forehead creased. "Have you even slept?"

"I nodded off for a couple hours," she admitted, "and woke back up around one. I've been up since."

"You go back to sleep now. I'll take the watch." It was what we would've done if we were on our own, and, I guess to Alaina, we were.

"You sure?" Her dark eyes softened, giving me a glimpse of the scared, caring little girl that hid behind a rough exterior and vibrant hair. "You really don't look too good."

I nodded. "I'm sure. Get some sleep while you can."

"Okay." She didn't think twice. It was barely a minute after she closed her eyes that she started snoring softly.

I smiled, but it hurt, so I stopped. Then I started to take inventory of myself. My feet were numb and prickly, still asleep, and my calves and thighs were sore, as if I'd run a marathon yesterday. My stomach was queasy, which only added to the enormous headache I had going on. Every muscle in my body seemed to twitch, especially in my arms, shoulders, and neck. My left upper arm was wrapped in bandages, spots of blood soaked through, and my hands were wrapped in similar red stained gauze. Though the dressings were the softest I'd ever felt, the contact burned my hands and made them throb.

I blew out a long breath. I was a wreck. A wreck very lucky to be alive.

While still exhausted, my body ached enough to help keep me awake and watch over Alaina like I'd promised. Memories of last night played like horror movies on the dark walls, and when I couldn't remember much of Lennon coming to the house, I decided it all had to just go away. Instead, I focused on breathing and worrying about what to do when everyone woke up.

Alaina had barely been asleep two hours when the door cracked open. I held my breath, heart stuttering, but sank in relief when Erika poked her head in. When she realized I was awake, she stepped soundlessly into the room and sat on the edge of my side of the bed. The streak of light streaming in from the hallway allowed me to get a good look at her, even in the dark. Her curly hair was falling out of her lopsided ponytail, and her makeup smeared all down her face. She was still in her clothes from yesterday, though they were wrinkled and stained with blood, and her eyes were red and puffy.

Those eyes watched Alaina for a moment, like the sleeping girl was a rabid animal about to spring to life and attack. When thirty seconds passed without incident, Erika turned her gaze back on me, and flinched.

"Are you…" she started in a hesitant whisper, eyes flicking to Alaina again for a half second. "Are you, um…"

"Talking?" I supplied. "Yeah."

She sighed in relief, loosening up slightly. "Sark said it should start to wear off after you slept some, but…I mean, we didn't know. I didn't…" Her voice caught and she took an unsteady breath, suddenly glaring at me. "Don't you ever, ever, *ever* do that to me again, okay? You can't just leave and then turn up hours later nearly…nearly…"

Touched at her concern, I automatically reached out to take her hand, then thought better of it once I saw the bandages. Instead, I rested the top of my hand on top of hers.

A small, dry sob shook her, and any anger gave way to mourning. "Arie, I am so so sorry."

"I know," I said. "It wasn't your fault."

She laughed once darkly, rubbing her face with her hand, and suddenly she looked like she had the weight of the world on her shoulders. "You wouldn't have even been there if it weren't for me. I should be protecting you. Not making this worse."

I couldn't really argue with that, so I didn't. "Have you slept?"

Erika shook her head. "Can't. Every time I close my eyes I…I just can't. I don't want to be in there alone either, but Sark won't come to bed. I think I might've fallen asleep on the couch for an hour or so, but…"

"How, um…what's…is he…" I couldn't figure out how to say my question, or what I even really meant to ask.

She dropped her hand from her face. "I don't know. He won't talk, really. I tried at first, but now...just the way he's pacing is scary enough. I know to leave him be."

I nodded. It sounded like the smartest plan she'd ever had.

"Can I ask you something?" Erika asked. "It's not important, really, but I'm just...trying to understand."

I internally braced myself. "Sure."

"How does Sark know Alaina? Did he chase her before he chased you?"

The tension in me relaxed. That was an easy one. "No, Lennon has always been her handler. We ran into each other on accident. We both got caught, then escaped together, and have been friends ever since. Alexis assigned Lennon and Sark to work together from time to time. I don't really know why. Maybe trade notes or see if our relationship somehow affects the data."

"Oh. I guess that makes sense."

"None of this really makes sense."

"Yeah, but it's..." She looked up at the ceiling, searching for words. "It's just different than I thought. Bigger. More real. Hearing about it is one thing, but experiencing it? Watching you two be so horribly..." She took a breath. "I guess I never realized how real it is. How real you all are. More than just numbers on a screen."

Suddenly, Erika looked at me, as if realizing I was still there. "Sorry, that's a stupid thing for me to say."

"No, I don't think so. After being alone so long...it's weirdly satisfying to have my pain validated, you know? It all sounds like a load of BS until you're a part of it. Now you know why I don't have any friends."

That won me a faint smile and a half laugh. "Yeah, I guess so." She bit her lip and searched my eyes. "Do you ever get used to it?"

"Um…" I mulled that over for a second. "In some ways, yes. You have to shift your normal or else you can't function at all. But in other ways, no, and I don't think I ever will. Sometimes it all just hits, sometimes out of nowhere, and you just drown in this awful, overwhelming knowledge that this...this is your life now. And swallowing that...I choke on it all the time."

Then I took a breath, uncomfortable by my own sudden vulnerability. I never talked like that to anyone.

"I'm going to try and sleep some more," I lied. "You try too."

"Okay." She gave one last glance over me, her expression evidence enough that I looked awful. "I'll see you soon. Yell if you need anything at all." With another wary look at Alaina, she left, silently closing the door behind her.

~~~

By the time Alaina had woken up a few hours later, I'd successfully come up with zero plans that would work out for everyone involved.

"So we're both still here," she mused, yawning. "And I imagine you're about to ask me to leave the safety of this magical room where nobody bothered

241
~~~

us for some reason despite the fact we are literally sleeping in the belly of the beast."

I rolled my eyes. "There's no way out on this side. Can't get through the windows. Or the locks on the front door. Everything is locked up tight."

"And that doesn't bother you?"

"Of course it does. But right now, all I know is that the soft bed is in here and food is out there."

As if hearing me, Alaina's stomach growled like a ravenous monster. She held the back of her hand against her head as though she were fainting. "Eat and die or don't eat and die." She sighed dramatically. "I guess we all know if I'm dying then I'm going out full." She sat up, but words caught in my throat held me down.

Finally, I just closed my eyes and spat them out. "I'm sorry I brought you here. I didn't know what else to do."

Alaina snorted. "Don't say sorry until I get a taste for what kind of food is around here."

I cracked my eyes open. "I'm serious, Alaina."

"Fine." She turned to look at me. "I'm not thrilled to be here, obviously, but this place possibly saved our lives. I still plan on killing Sark if I get the chance, of course. I'm not mad at you, though—I'm here because I trust your judgment."

I gave a small grin. "Thanks."

"It's not really a compliment, buttercup." She smirked. "We're both completely nuts."

The procession down the hallway was quite the ordeal, and probably would've been funny to watch if I wasn't one of the ones hobbling in pain. We walked side by side, me dragging myself along the wall for support while Alaina's eyes darted everywhere for threats as she limped along. By the time we made it to the kitchen, I was dizzy and exhausted.

Alaina swore under her breath when we found the kitchen wasn't empty. Erika was there, with fresh hair, fresh clothes, and a fresh, strained smile. She and Alaina exchanged a glare in some unspoken challenge, while I sank into a chair at the counter and gestured to the ingredients spread out on the counter.

"I'll sell you my soul if we can have whatever you're making," I told her.

That broke the spell. Alaina snickered, and Erika turned her attention to me, a little too perky. "Well, I was making it for you anyway. German pancakes and scrambled eggs."

"Perfect."

After surveying the room several times, Alaina finally sat on the chair next to me, still at attention. My head was heavy; I automatically rested it in my hands, then flinched and jerked upright again. This whole 'injured hands' thing was going to get old really fast.

The awkward tension in the room was thick enough to use as a baseball bat. Too tired to try and merge the gap between parties, I just sat there in a daze while Erika and Alaina glared at each other in between food preparation and threat checks. Though my imprisonment here had gotten better over time—it could hardly be called imprisonment at this point, besides the 'can't leave when I want' issue—I couldn't escape the sinking feeling that leading Alaina here was a bad idea.

It saved our lives, I reminded myself. *Just take one thing at a time.*

Some of the sinking feeling dissipated when Erika produced two cups of orange juice and two cups of water, each with a straw. Alaina and I both sighed in contentment when the liquid reached our tongues. Erika finally started talking, the kind of hyper babbling she used to grace me with back during our first days at Sark's house, and the kind I knew I didn't really have to respond to. I was grateful that she filled the silence, even if Alaina just seemed annoyed.

As breakfast got closer, my body got more impatient, and finally I couldn't stand the bandages against my hands anymore. When Erika turned her back to stir something on the stove, I started to work on pulling them off.

"Don't do that."

The soft voice came from behind. Startled, Alaina and I both jumped and turned to see Sark entering from the other hallway, probably coming up from the basement.

How long has he been watching us?

Alaina hissed under her breath at him, eyes narrowed with suspicion. He gave her a glance—a bland, non-threatening acknowledgement—before walking a little too slowly up to me. He looked from me to my fingers gripping the bandages, and suddenly I felt like a little girl caught trying to cut her doll's hair.

"It hurts," I finally said, though even to me the excuse sounded lame. "I want them off."

Sark didn't budge. "They're keeping your hands together, and protecting you from infection."

I snorted, and out of the corner of my eye I saw Alaina raise an eyebrow. Sark just stared at me.

"It's funny," I said, "because I'm already—"

"Yes, I see," Sark interrupted, unamused. "The irony isn't lost on me."

When my stupid comments didn't drive him off, I sighed. "Please? Can't my hands just breathe for a moment? They need to do that, don't they?"

Sark just pursed his lips. I took his silence as permission. Starting with my left hand, I pinched the edge of the gauze at my wrist between the very tips of my right pointer finger and thumb, then pulled it off. Unprepared for the searing sting, a cry of pain escaped through my teeth.

"Be careful," Sark told me. "You can't just rip them off."

To my—and Alaina's, based on the way her jaw dropped—surprise, Sark cupped my left hand in his and slowly started to peel the rest of the bandage off. The gauze stuck to my skin, and I winced and gritted my teeth, instantly unsure of the decision. My resolve continued to weaken when I caught a glimpse of the red nastiness underneath the bandage, and the *smell*...the smell was a rotten mix of burnt flesh, dried blood, and sterile ointments.

My hand got a little fuzzy, but I couldn't rip my eyes from it, even as the rest of the bandage came off and I saw it in all its disgustingly fried glory.

"Hey." Sark's voice caused me to look up at him, though his face was kind of fuzzy too. "Arie, breathe. You're really pale. Just breathe."

I did what he said, and slowly he came back into focus. His forehead creased as he looked me over.

"Have you fainted since you got here last night?" he asked me, as if going through a checklist in his mind.

I shook my head, which my head didn't like very much, so I settled for talking. "No. I mean, not that I know of, I guess."

"Has your vision been impaired at all?"

"Um, just a second ago it got fuzzy but I think I was just too dizzy."

"So you are dizzy."

"Yes. It won't stop."

"Headache?"

"A nasty one."

"Any convulsions?"

"My muscles hurt like they're sore and twitch every few minutes but that's all."

When he didn't immediately follow up with another question, Erika popped in with one of her own, her voice a little more subdued now than earlier. "Is she going to be okay?"

"You're talking," he told me, answering her. "Much better than you were last night. I'm assuming the effects will continue to wear off with time."

Erika breathed a sigh of relief and went back to her cooking. Alaina didn't take her skeptical eyes off of Sark.

"And this?" I asked, holding up my unbandaged hand.

Sark looked at the angry red flesh, gently pulling my hand up closer to his face to examine it. "They're second-degree burns, easily, possibly third in some areas. While miserable to deal with, the fact you feel pain is a good indicator that your nerves remain largely unaffected. The main concerns now involve making sure it doesn't sink into further layers of skin or cause any infection. Keeping your hands wrapped and protected will help with that, as well as keeping salves on them. If it worsens, we may have to try a more extreme treatment or skin graft."

My stomach dropped and twisted painfully. "I'm—"

"Relax. I don't believe it's necessary at this stage. Just a possible avenue, if we need to take it." His eyes flicked up to mine for a moment, almost as if asking permission. "Based on your...history that I'm aware of, I'd imagine they'll heal to the point of usability in the next few days. It's too soon to predict possible scarring, though."

"Oh." I took a breath and slowly pulled my hand away, aware of Alaina glaring darkly at Sark now. Had this whole thing been some elaborate experiment? A way for him to get data from me willingly? "Okay."

At that, Sark gave a muttered, "Make sure you eat something," before leaving the room. Erika deflated in disappointment, but caught herself when she saw me watching her. She gave me a not very believable grin before turning to dish up our plates.

The second Sark was gone, Alaina let out a long breath. She gave me a pointed glance, but I was too tired for it—yes, I already knew coming here could be a huge mistake.

Our misery was quickly forgotten when Erika set out two plates in front of us, each brimming with fluffy scrambled eggs and syrup-soaked pancakes. I almost cried. I think Alaina might've for a second

247

before she scooped up her fork and started wolfing food down at an alarming rate. It was probably the first real meal she'd had in awhile. She'd already finished more than half her plate by the time I realized I couldn't cut my pancake. I scowled at the fork and my injured hands, one wrapped and one bare. What a cruel thing for the universe to do.

Prepared to just lean in and lap up my food like a dog, I was both mortified and grateful when Erika took my plate and cut up my breakfast for me.

"Thank you," I murmured.

She gave me another strained smile. "You're welcome."

I managed to pinch my fork between two fingers with minimal pain, and it was worth it for the food. Some of my headache cleared as I swallowed the pancake, allowing me to think a little more clearly.

Erika watched us eat. It would've been weirder, if Alaina and I weren't so wrapped up in our food. She served Alaina a second plate—the crimson crusader showed no sign of slowing down—while I was verging on full with just half my plate eaten.

Finally, I met Erika's eyes. "I can tell you have questions. Just ask."

"I don't want to bother you..." she trailed off, clearly hoping I would let her anyway.

I did. She'd fed us after all. With another bite of scrambled egg, I gestured to her. "Go ahead. We got nothing else to do."

She leaned her elbows on the counter and settled her chin in her palms. Alaina leaned away from her; she pretended not to notice.

"Why does Lennon chase Alaina?" Erika asked.

Alaina rolled her eyes and snapped something back, but her mouth was too full for the words to be intelligible.

I answered for her. "It's his job. Alexis assigns handlers to infecteds to track them—"

"And experiment on them like lab rats," Alaina cut in.

"—to try and get more information about us."

Erika nodded. "So he thinks one of you is this key thing? The key to solving the formula?"

My insides shriveled, but I forced my face to stay the same. "Alexis does. He believes he'll find the key in one of the failed infecteds, like us. Lennon doesn't care much about that."

Erika's eyebrows furrowed. "He doesn't?"

I shrugged. "They're all in it for different reasons. Alexis and others—" *Like Sark*, I added to myself, "—have a dedication to the formula's creator, Philo Castor, and a devotion to bringing his work to life. For others like Lennon, though, they don't really believe in it."

"It's a devotion to his cash," Alaina added. "His cash flow and excuse to hurt other people. Nothing else."

"Then why does he hate you guys so much?"

Alaina snorted, but I answered. "I don't know. A lot of people think of infecteds as second class people—failed experiments and all that."

"Then what was that incident Lennon was talking about?" Erika asked, pushing the syrup bottle to Alaina as she reached for it. "He seemed pretty upset at you for it."

My forehead creased, unsure what she was talking about, but Alaina tapped my elbow with hers, swallowing another huge bite of pancake through a smirk. "He was talking about the Jefferson incident."

I glanced at her, confused. "He was?"

"You don't remember? Come on, Arie, that was golden stuff."

"No."

Her smirk grew. "Well that's too bad because he basically admitted we totally beat them that day."

"What day?" Erika asked, verging on annoyed that she wasn't in the loop. "What's with this Jefferson guy?"

I bit my lip. "Well...Jefferson is Alexis' right-hand man. And...once...I kinda...broke his leg."

Alaina cackled in delight. Erika's mouth fell open.

"You did *what*?"

"I broke Jefferson's leg," I repeated, swirling a pile of syrup on my plate with my fork.

"On purpose?"

"Um...mostly."

"Mostly?"

"I wasn't *planning* on breaking his leg. It just kind of happened."

"How?"

"Can I tell the story?" Alaina begged, bits of food falling from her full mouth. "Please? It's my absolute favorite."

At that, Erika narrowed her eyes on Alaina. "You were there?"

Alaina pressed a hand to her chest, pretending to be appalled. "This has the potential to be the single most important event in the history of our pathetic lives and the entire human race as we know it. *Of course* I was there."

Erika didn't seem thrilled with that, but she pressed on. "Well? What happened?"

Alaina sat up straighter, her third plate of food now forgotten, getting animated as she fell into storytelling mode. "It was a cold, dreary day in March, walking the abandoned streets by the border of Pennsylvania and New Jersey, and struggling to decide where to go—runaways, outcasts, nobodies without a home. Brennan, being the—"

"Who's Brennan?" Erika interrupted. Alaina huffed in irritation. I suppressed a smile and took another bite of eggs.

"Brennan and Lucy are two other infecteds Arie and I actually get along with."

"You know other kids like you?"

Alaina blew a piece of hair out of her face. "A few. Me more than Arie. We're a paranoid bunch. We don't like crowds." She waited to make sure Erika was done, then continued. "Anyways, Brennan decided we should take this back road, which was an idiotic idea. Within five minutes we were completely surrounded on every side." She used her hands to paint a picture in the air. "Lennon and Baldie, and Sark and Felix, and Alexis and Jefferson were *all* there, plus Brennan and Lucy's assigned psycho Blaine. Our hope was setting with the sun."

She paused dramatically for effect. "But my friend Arie here just won't take no for an answer. Brennan, the little loser, always keeps these homemade smoke bombs on him, and Arie signaled for him to let them all loose. Amidst the blindness and confusion, Arie ran to the closest car, Felix's, and fought him for it. By the time the smoke had

251

cleared, Felix was beat up on the ground like a little sissy and we were speeding down the street."

Alaina was sitting on the edge of her chair now, bouncing up and down, and nearly getting her hair in leftover syrup. I pushed her plate away from her as she kept going. "It was only moments before they were chasing us down, and the most epic car chase was born. There we were, speeding down the streets of Philadelphia, when I pulled out my gun and leaned out the window and started shoo—"

"What?" I cut in.

Alaina grimaced. "Arie, I'm the one telling—"

"You didn't have a gun," I said, an amused grin on my face, "and the car chase lasted all of five minutes. We never made it within thirty miles of Philadelphia."

"Will you just let me tell the story?"

I raised an eyebrow, barely holding in a laugh. "You didn't have a gun."

Alaina rolled her eyes, annoyed I ruined her fun. "Fine. I didn't have a gun. And thanks to Arie's amazing driving skills, we lasted maybe four and a half minutes. Yay Arie!" She clapped her hands ostentatiously before glaring at me. "Way to go."

Erika actually giggled. "Yeah, I know about Arie's driving skills."

"Hey!" I protested.

Alaina pressed on without me. "So there we were, captured and taken prisoner. They were furious with us, obviously, so they got a kick out of knocking us around. Arie got the brunt of it all 'cause she was dubbed our 'ringleader' or something stupid like that. Anyways, Arie was standing there and Jefferson was getting all in her face with a...what was it again?"

I winced. "A crowbar."

Erika gasped. Alaina wrinkled her nose. "Oh yeah. Those things suck. Anyways, Jefferson was getting all in her face with a crowbar, and she was getting mad, but Arie's always way too calm to actually do anything. He was getting angry that he couldn't get a good reaction out of her—she just took it like our martyr, keeping the rest of us out of the line of fire."

I opened my mouth to protest that, since she made me sound way better than the wreck I'd been, but Alaina didn't give me the chance to ruin her story again.

"Then, for the finale of his 'we are better than you scum' speech, Jefferson spat in her face. A big, disgusting wad of saliva."

"Ew!" Erika cried.

"It was disgusting," I agreed.

Alaina's smile could've split her face in half. "That was it! Jefferson turned to walk away, the rage boiling in Arie's eyes, and she kicked him as hard as she could. He must've been standing on it just the wrong way because we heard the bone snap and he started screaming." She pumped her fist in the air. "It was amazing!"

Erika looked at me now. "Didn't you get in trouble?"

I nodded, swirling my fork in the syrup again. "So much. Everyone was livid, and Sark…" I trailed off, stealing a glance at the empty hallway. "I've never seen him that angry before. They locked me up and...well, it wasn't nice." I grinned. "But it was totally worth it."

Alaina put her hand over her heart in a reverent manner. "That, Arie Nolan, was quite possibly the best, most amazing, most inspiring, most freaking awesome thing I have ever witnessed you—no, scratch that—I have ever witnessed *anyone* do in my entire life. You have my undying respect forever."

I shook my head at her and rolled my eyes, then looked at Erika. "So, yeah. Now Jefferson limps and hates my guts. Alexis, Lennon, Blaine...none of them like me much."

Her eyes were wide with astonishment and she smiled. "I can't imagine why."

"And that's the event that inspired every other infected to fight back against the barbarians that hunt them," Alaina concluded. She settled back into her chair, then pulled her plate of food closer and started eating again.

"Oh please," I muttered. "That's not true. You just like the story."

"How could anyone *not* like the story?" Alaina demanded, spitting a piece of chewed something as Erika flinched away in disgust. "It's the best thing ever! Talk about scoring points for the losers. It's going to go down in history as the start of our revolution."

I raised an eyebrow. "Our revolution?"

She just nodded smugly, her cheeks full of food like a chipmunk.

"Whatever, Alaina."

"It is a good story, Arie," Erika told me, beginning to gather dirty dishes. "It says a lot about who you are."

I wrinkled my nose. I didn't like the sound of that. "Why?"

She shrugged. "It just matches what I've already learned about you. I like it. It's a good story."

"Um, thanks?"

"You should do that more often," she suggested, turning toward the sink. "Maybe you'll finally scare them off."

I rolled my eyes, though she didn't see. *Yeah, wishful thinking.*

Alaina looked at me, then motioned at Erika and made a gagging gesture. Instead of insulting her, though—thankfully—Alaina swallowed and said, "Yeah, last night you should've busted out some moves and snapped Lennon's femur. I hear that's the most painful bone to break."

"Yeah, I'll keep that in mind for next time," I retorted.

Alaina just grinned. "With you, buttercup, I never really know what's gonna happen."

~~~

It all went wrong when I went to the bathroom. Which is really stupid, considering we went hours without incident in a house full of people wired to blow each other up, and is just a further demonstration of my rancid, rotten luck.

Going to the bathroom was a chore enough. Walking there was tiring, and trying to figure out how to maneuver with my hands...well, it wasn't
~~~

easy. I was feeling rather proud of myself, honestly, until I got back into the living room and collapsed on the couch.

It was empty. That should've been my first clue. Especially since I had to convince Alaina to let me go to the bathroom alone. Maybe I shouldn't have, after all.

Right then, two steps of footsteps registered in my ears: smooth, lithe ones from the entryway and quick, panicked ones from the hallway near the bedrooms. Both of them coming for me.

I sat up, a pit forming in my gut, unsure what was going on. Where was Alaina? Erika?

The footsteps from the hallway came out first, and Sark appeared in the kitchen. When his eyes fell on me, they widened with something I'd rarely ever seen in his expression.

Fear. Ice cold, genuine fear.

Then his eyes flicked to the approaching footsteps, and he was racing for me, somehow keeping his own steps silent. I stood and started to ask what the heck was going on, but he slammed his hand over my mouth and whipped me around, pushing me backward toward the mirror door.

It was too late. The footsteps entered the room with Sark's hand inches away from the handle. Three things happened in that moment:

First, I saw Lennon come in, gaze trained on Sark's back like a sniper rifle.

Second, I saw Sark's face twist with frustrated panic, then harden with resolve, his eyes meeting mine.

Third, I returned the gaze with my own resolve, showing my understanding and—albeit hesitant—permission. This was going to be ugly.

But I knew the stakes as much as he did. He saved our lives last night, and now it was my turn to keep the charade and save his.

We were going to have to fake it.

"Well, well," Lennon said from behind Sark, his face lighting up with excitement. "Now this is more like it."

In seconds, Sark transformed before me. The sorrow and fear in his eyes were replaced with calculation and hatred, while his jaw set with a cruel angle and his hands on me went from protective to threatening. All at once, he was scary Sark again, and my insides curled in response, automatically flinching away, while some rational thought echoed that I hadn't actually seen scary Sark in a long time.

When he turned to look at Lennon, dragging me with him, his change was complete. Even I would never guess a Sark existed that rescued me in an alley last night or helped me with my hands this morning.

I wrenched myself out of Sark's grip and collapsed to the ground, scrambling back until I was pressed into Erika's Christmas tree. Sark barely spared me a glance, as if acknowledging an unruly dog in his charge.

"What are you doing here?" he asked Lennon, voice acidic.

Lennon smirked with all the ego built up in his air head. "I was just in the neighborhood. Thought I'd drop by."

Sark glowered at him, and I shivered in spite of myself. "You're investigating me."

"I just happened to mention your odd behavior to Jefferson last night. He asked me to check in. Harmless, really." His viper smile hinted that it was anything but harmless. "Seems that everything is in order."

Sark had no patience for it. "Good. Then get out."

Lennon ignored that. "Where's Felix? He's usually here, isn't he?"

Sark's jaw worked with irritated impatience—an expression I knew well since I often caused it. He answered grudgingly. "On a personal errand. I trust that won't be reported."

"Again, I regret my suspicions, Mr. Sark," Lennon said, with all the superficial grace he could muster, before resting his eyes on me. "Now I'm just here to do my job." He began walking toward me, but Sark's voice cut him off.

"I've already done it. Alaina is going to New Orleans."

At that, Lennon's eyes widened in surprise, eyebrows shooting up his forehead. He glanced at me, as if in confirmation, since I was the only one that would have that kind of information on Alaina.

Where *was* Alaina? Erika? Sark must've had a second to hide them.

If we're pretending I gave up Alaina, then I have to freak out.

"No!" I croaked, hands shaking. "No, she's not."

Sark glared at me, a look meant to shut me up. That wasn't enough to be believable, though. Sark was pulling his punches.

And we can't afford that.

I glared back at him, a small act of defiance that couldn't go unchallenged, especially in front of Lennon. I knew there was nothing fake about the scowl Sark dished back to me. Which was stupid. Not that I wanted him to beat me up, but passive anger was not going to work here, especially when Lennon was already suspicious.

Come on, Sark, work with me.

Forced by my hand, he stalked up to me and yanked me to my feet, then dragged me over and made me look at Lennon.

"Why don't *you* tell him," he said coldly in my ear, his hand around my throat, though I hardly felt the pressure. "Tell him what you told me."

"I didn't!" I shrieked, letting real panic take over and faking a struggle against Sark's pathetically soft hold. "I just said that so you'd leave me alone! It's not real!" I stamped as hard as I could on Sark's foot, then kicked him in the shin, knocking him off balance so he automatically tightened his grip on my throat, effectively choking me off.

It was better, but it still wasn't enough.

What's wrong with you, Sark? Now was a bad time for his newly grown conscious to start acting up.

"Really?" Lennon asked. "How did you get that information out of her?"

I threw my elbow backward, drilling Sark in the gut. He let go of me, and I lurched forward, surprising Lennon with a backhand to the face, then started for the front door. Lennon caught me by my injured arm and dug his fingers into the wound, then kicked my legs out from under me. With an undignified cry, I fell to the ground. He smashed his foot in my jaw for good measure, and I rolled over to protect my face, seeing stars.

Sark huffed in annoyance. "*Look* at her."

My chin ached—my whole body ached—and I remembered how terrible I'd looked in the mirror this morning. That was our best defense right now: the idea that Sark had already beaten me to a pulp.

"If you're done here," Sark went on, not hiding his disdain, "then I believe your infected is on her way to Louisiana about now. You're free to go." The permission was more a demand than anything. He seized me by my hair and started dragging me toward the basement stairs.

"I'd like to talk to Arie for a moment, actually."

I heard Sark's teeth snap together. Thankfully, Lennon seemed to take it as irritation derived from a wounded ego.

"You can't be bitter forever, Mr. Sark. It's just the business we're in."

"Yes," Sark muttered. "I suppose the business doesn't allow much room for trust, now does it?"

"Trust is for people desperate enough to afford it."

Lennon fell in step behind Sark, but there wasn't much else we could do about that. My stomach dropped at the thought of what was coming: a real interrogation without Sark's newfound protective tendencies and with Lennon's very real hatred for me.

The stairs were brutal. I could only barely keep my footing, and instead ended up nearly falling down the stairs if not for Sark's hold on my hair. When a whimper of pain escaped me, he adjusted his hold so it wasn't as harsh, and I mentally kicked him in annoyance that apparently I was more dedicated to this show than he was.

They would kill you! I wanted to shout at him. If Lennon found out, Sark was a dead man, Erika would be shot without a thought, while I'd be subjected to who knows what Lennon could come up with until I died. *Make this believable.*

We got to the bottom of the stairs, but instead of turning right into the library, Sark took me through the door on the left, into the unfinished area. A chill ran down my spine, both from the deep cold and the memories of the last time I'd been in here—back when Erika was just a random stranger and Dalton had been my only hope. That felt like lifetimes ago, rather than weeks.

Sark dropped me in the metal chair bolted into the ground. Lennon scooted the table over, then took a chair and sat right in front of me. Behind him, Sark walked to the other end of the room, leaning up against the counter, hard eyes on me.

I took a breath, sure the cloud of cologne would kill me before anything else could, then braved meeting Lennon's gaze. He punched me in response, and the room spun as my head snapped backward.

Just get through this, I told myself. *Just get through this, and he'll leave, and it'll be over. No escaping or running or hiding. Just over.*

Gritting my teeth, I felt blood drip out of my nose as I stared at Lennon. He pulled what looked like a hunting knife out of his pocket, twirling it in his hand.

"So, Arie," he started, all casual, like we were talking over dinner. "I feel as though we didn't really get the opportunity to talk last night." His eyes wandered over me to my hands. My instinct was to clench them into fists, but it hurt too much to try.

Lennon snatched my right hand, the one still wrapped up. I pulled back, but he just yanked harder, and finally clasped my hand tightly in his. A half cry escaped through my teeth. I fought it down and relented, terror building inside me.

"Too bad about your hands," Lennon said. He unwrapped the gauze slowly, methodically, but still rough enough to pull at my skin and hurt like crazy. "Losing real use of them is probably a huge vulnerability for you, isn't it? Makes sense then, how you were able to get caught so quickly."

I watched as the rest of the bandage came off and fell onto the floor. My palm seemed to pulse with varying degrees of red, some areas barely beginning to form whispers of a scab. He started with those first. I worked to keep myself perfectly still as he positioned the tip of his knife at the pad of my thumb, refusing to react to the pain, though the sudden wave of nausea I felt was nearly more overpowering.

"I wonder, though," he went on, "where Alaina is, considering she wouldn't leave you this defenseless, I imagine. If she had to leave—to New Orleans, as you said—she must've told you why. I imagine she told you her entire plan, now didn't she?"

When I didn't immediately answer, he started digging the knife under the scab on my hand. My jaw clamped shut in response, but the resolve in me only grew stronger: the resolve I'd first found months ago when I realized I had one friend in this big, angry world, and I would protect that redhead at all costs.

The knife went deeper, edging around the scab and pulling up filmy skin. My stomach rolled and squelched.

"Talk to me, Arie," Lennon said, a warning note in his tone. "What's Alaina doing? If you'll just tell me, I'll leave these crispy hands of yours alone."

I tore my gaze from my hand, now beginning to dribble blood, to Lennon's steely expression, a hint of excitement amid his hateful determination, then looked at Sark. Harsh loathing sharpened his expression, but for once, it wasn't aimed at me. When our eyes met, I could almost feeling him shouting at me amongst profanities to just *make something up*, and for a second I wondered how far he would let this go.

I settled my gaze on Lennon, decision made.

"She didn't tell me."

I felt the daggers from Sark's eyes sharper than Lennon's knife in my palm. Lennon's mouth pulled into a frown, daring me to stick with my answer. I stared back.

Don't give him anything. I never had, and I never would.

Lennon wasn't convinced. "Really? I find that hard to believe."

"She didn't tell me," I insisted, real desperation leaking into my stubborn tone. "So believe it. I don't have anything for you."

Face twisting into a scowl, Lennon yanked my hand down to the floor, then crushed it under his shoe. I gasped—both in surprise and pain—and he held me there, digging his soles into my burnt flesh and leaning over my half bent form.

"Let's try this again," he seethed in my ear. I shuddered at his breath on my face, and he took my other hand. "Every second of my time you waste will be another layer of skin off your hand."

Then his blade was at my palm. I squeezed my eyes shut and clenched my teeth, unsure if I wanted to succumb to my nausea and pass out or not.

Don't give him anything.

"One."

Silence.

Cut.

You can do this.

"Two."

Silence.

Cut.

Grimace.

You have to do this.

"Three."

Whimper.

Cut.

Whimper.

I can't do this.

"You're pathetic," Lennon spat at me, losing patience. "If this won't get through to you, then maybe losing a few fingers will."

"Lennon." Sark's voice echoed a quiet warning.

Lennon ignored him, and I felt the tip of the knife digging into the base of my pointer finger.

"She didn't tell me!" I shouted at him. "She didn't tell me anything!"

He gripped my chin roughly, yanking me up while still trapping my hand under his foot, stretching me too far. Then he cut into the dog bite wound on my arm until I choked out a half shriek and opened my eyes.

"Well, you've said enough, haven't you?" He gave me a cruel smile. "Uncharacteristic of you, Arie. Imagine Alaina's expression when I tell her how I found her."

That won't happen. It can't.

"She'll be surprised, of course," he went on, dragging the knife across my face and smearing blood along my cheek. "And she'll refuse to believe me. After all, Arie *never* gives anyone up, let alone Alaina."

This isn't real. Alaina is fine. She's okay.

"Not surprisingly, she'll deny it at first. 'Arie is too brave, too loyal, too selfless,' she'll tell me, over and over, while her mind works to realize the truth: that you were the only one with knowledge of her destination, and that you must have given it to me."

It's not real, it's not real, she's okay.

His words painted an awful picture I couldn't help but see. "Can you imagine her face? As I give her what I have ready for her—what you all deserve— and she'll see your face behind her eyelids when she closes her eyes to scream."

"No," I breathed.

"And it will all be your faul—"

"No!" I snapped my head up, connecting hard with his jaw, dazing both of us. I barely felt his knife slash across my cheek as he lost his hold on me. Ripping my hand out from under his shoe, I clasped his fist in my bloody hand and drove his knife into his shoulder. He howled in pain and I pushed him

265

off the chair. Noticing Sark coming for me, I picked up the chair and threw it at him. Then I ran.

I was halfway up the stairs when Lennon's hand caught my ankle. Sprawling, my chin smashed into a stair, and I saw stars for a second, tasting blood. I kicked my feet wildly, trying to shake him off. He slashed his knife across my thigh, wide eyes manic and desperate for blood.

Whipping myself around, his arm got twisted and I used his momentary distraction to kick him square in the face. His grip went limp and he fell down the stairs. I barely paused to breathe before I took off again.

Half limping, half crawling, I finally got upstairs. The front door held no exit for me, so I chose the back. Leaving a trail of blood, I dashed out to the back deck and down the stairs, heading for the gate.

Then I remembered: the gate was locked from the inside too.

My heart thumped wildly in my chest as I ran into the wall. Desperation driving me into a frenzy, I tried the gate anyway.

It opened. Unlocked.

I wasted a precious second marveling over how that could be. Then I started to make a run for it.

A thought skidded me to a stop. Lennon would run after me. He'd expect Sark to too. One of them would find me, in my condition—what were the odds Sark would find me first, after he managed to convince Lennon they should hunt me separately?

The decision was rash, but I stuck with it. Smearing my blood all over the gate, I left it hanging open. Then I turned, hoping against hope

Lennon wasn't already upstairs, and limped to the other side of the yard, farthest from the gate. Steeling myself, I dropped into the snow and crawled underneath the deck.

There was barely enough space for me to fit, but I wormed myself as far as I could go before my body gave up. I heard approaching voices heading for the back door. I went completely still and held my breath as Lennon's shouts crystallized above me, footsteps pounding on the deck. My ears tracked his movements, going down the stairs and crunching through the snow to the gate.

Keep going, I begged the universe. *Please keep going.*

Bile rose in my throat when I thought I heard him pause. Slow footsteps now, snow crunching back and forth, back and forth.

Please please please please please please.

Another set of footsteps pounding on the deck. They stopped. The wood groaned softly as someone shifted their weight. Then the footsteps in the snow trudged back to the deck.

"She got out," Lennon said, clearly loathing the defeat in his tone. "She's gone."

"Well, then." Even hidden under the deck, I cringed away from the cold fury in Sark's voice. "I suggest you be on your way, Lennon. Trust I'll be very selective in what I harmlessly let Jefferson know about your efforts today."

Both steps of footsteps retreated into the house, taking the rest of their conversation with them. My heart started beating normally again when I heard the door close.

My body screamed at me, but I refused to come out of my hiding place, just in case. I had to do something, though. I couldn't stand this. Going as slowly and silently as I could, I turned myself so I was lying on my side, facing the yard. My breath caught when I was finally brave enough to look over myself. The snow underneath the deck was sparse, and it mixed with dirt to create a slushy kind of mud, which was now tainted red. My thigh was bleeding all over the place, crusting my skin and pants, so I couldn't tell how deep the wound actually was. My left hand was also a smeared, bloody mess, while rock and various debris from Lennon's shoe were embedded in the flesh of my vulnerable right palm. Blood also crusted from the bite wound on my arm, but I didn't know if it was still bleeding or if it had stopped and dried.

As softly as I could, I cupped some dirty snow in my throbbing hands, and pressed it against my leg. The biting cold stung my hands, but also numbed them slightly. Then I closed my eyes and forced myself to breathe through my nose. Breathe through the pain. Breathe through the panic.

How long will I have to stay under here? The thought made me want to cry. How was I supposed to know it was safe?

Suddenly, the space seemed a lot smaller, and I felt claustrophobia creeping up on me. My body shivered, my clothes soaked and much too thin for hanging out in the snow. Clenching my teeth, I forced myself to concentrate on breathing.

Seconds felt like eternities. I stayed there for what seemed like forever, slowly bleeding out and freezing over and losing rationality.

Suddenly, the back door opened again. My frostbitten heart leapt in my throat, and I bit my tongue to keep from screaming.

I can't get caught I can't get caught I can't get caught I can't get caught.

Slow footsteps went across the deck and down the stairs, then crunched in the snow. They faded for a moment—going back over to the gate or something, I guessed—then came back to the stairs. Passed the stairs. Panic thudded in my ears when shoes entered my line of sight. They walked along the deck to the edge of the yard. Then came back. That's when I realized the spot of snow where I'd crawled under the deck was smeared pink with blood.

Before I could even begin to wonder what to do, the footsteps stopped in front of me. Whoever it was knelt down, tracing a finger along the pink streak. Then they ducked their head underneath the deck. Even though he likely came looking for me, disbelief still flicked across Sark's face when he found me scrunched in a bloody, frozen ball.

"He's gone," Sark said quietly. "He left for Louisiana."

I tried to take a deep breath, but I only got half the air I needed, and I choked on nothing. He reached his arm toward me; I flinched and cowered back. The reaction seemed to strike him across the face. He exhaled and glanced around the yard, as if looking for someone else to help. When he didn't find anyone, his gaze landed on me again, eyes glinting with conflict.

"Okay, look, I know…" he started, then trailed off with a curse word under his breath. "I know, all right? Just...can I help you get out of there?"

I studied him for a moment, my frosted brain understanding the clear distinction: scary Sark was in the house an hour ago when I got hurt. This Sark was the other Sark. He was different. Scary Sark would've never asked me that.

Meeting his gaze, I nodded. He glanced at my bleeding leg covered in red snow.

"Can you move?"

I just stared at him, words moving sluggishly from my brain to my mouth and coming out in pieces through my chattering teeth. "I...I don't...don't...thi-ink so."

"Okay." Sark nodded, then looked around and nodded again. Taking a breath to steel himself, he shocked me by taking off his jacket and placing it on the deck, then getting down in the snow and crawling in after me.

If I had more presence of mind, the ordeal might've been awkward, but I was too done to care. Sark asked to move my hands to look at my leg, then moved them for me when I couldn't. The second his hand touched mine, he cringed away.

"You're freezing," he murmured. That revelation just made him work faster. After checking on the gash in my leg, he wound his arm around my shoulders and slowly, painfully, dragged me out. I tried to help, but I couldn't move much. Every part of me was frozen and throbbing.

Once we were out, Sark sat me upright, which was a mistake. I felt the blood drain out of my face, and I nearly passed out right there. He let me lean against his shoulder while he wrapped his jacket around me, then scooped me up. It wasn't until then that I realized how violently I was shaking.

He carried me into the house and set me softly on the couch, apparently unconcerned with all the blood, snow, and mud I smeared all over it. Then he momentarily disappeared from my line of sight.

"I found her." It took me a moment to realize he wasn't talking to me. He was on the phone. "She's here."

For a second, panic registered. He'd just told them where I was. He was turning me in. I struggled to sit upright, to get out, when Sark reappeared, carrying first aid supplies and four huge blankets.

"Hey," he said when he saw my expression. "You're okay. He's gone."

At his insistence, I settled back down. A woozy feeling came over me, and my eyelids fluttered, struggling to stay open.

"Arie?" Sark asked after a few minutes, concern coloring his tone. "Can you hear me?"

In trying to answer, I fell into a coughing fit before finally stammering, "Yes. Cold."

"Yes, I know. Just give me one more minute."

A minute passed, and he wrapped me up in the blankets, pulling one over my head so I was cocooned inside with an opening for my face.

I heard the garage door open. Footsteps rushed inside. Erika appeared, Alaina right after her, both of their faces screwed up in panic, and both of them relaxing in relief when they saw me.

"What did you do to her?" Alaina demanded, sitting on the floor next to me like a guard dog.

Erika pressed her hand against my forehead, flinching slightly and ignoring Alaina. "Why was he here?"

Sark sighed, the most tired sound I'd ever heard him make, which only added to the image of him in wet, rumpled clothes stained with bloody mud. "He reported me to Jefferson."

Alaina's eyebrows shot up. Erika sucked in a sharp breath. "They won't...will they…"

"No, they'll leave us alone, for now anyway. Lennon cleared me—it was more about his pride than my behavior anyway."

"So he's really going to Louisiana?" Alaina asked, skepticism on clear display. "Why would he do that?"

"Because I told him you're going there."

"But how would you know...oh." Her eyes flicked to me. "I get it. I'll bet he loved that."

Sark shook his head. "It was the first thing I thought of, but I didn't think it through well enough. He only wanted more information."

"What did she tell him?"

"Nothing." Sark laughed once, a dark sound. "Stupid, stubborn girl."

"And he believed it?" Erika asked.

"Yes. He's headed there now, and I imagine it'll be quite some time before he figures it out." He looked at Alaina. "You should find at least a little freedom from him in the next month or so. You can stay here as long as you'd like and leave whenever you want."

Alaina just stared at him, expression torn between accepting the amazing gift and tossing it to the side because it was too good to be true.

"You lied to Lennon," she stated.

Sark stared back, as if waiting for a punchline.

"He could kill you for that," Alaina added.

"Yes," Sark answered, rubbing his jaw with his hand. "I'm aware."

"Why? Why do this for us?"

"Does it matter?" Erika asked, narrowed eyes on Alaina. Alaina ignored her and waited for an answer.

Sark let out a long breath, his shoulders beginning to sag from their constant perfect posture. "A shift in priorities."

Alaina's forehead creased as she mulled that over, while Erika's eyes flicked to me, then back to Sark, her hand the only speck of warmth on my face.

"She's freezing," Erika said. "She might have hypothermia."

"I know. I took care of her injuries, so she should be okay to lay like that for some time." Sark gestured to something in the kitchen I couldn't see. "Warm that up and have her drink it. Watch her temperature carefully. When she can move again, get her fresh clothes and—"

"Where are you going?" Erika cut in, face taut with nerves.

"Um…" He ran a hand through his hair, eyes searching the room for something he couldn't find. "I'll be downstairs. Call me if she gets worse." With a last glance to me, he was gone.

We all watched him go—Erika with sorrow, Alaina with disbelief, and me with a kind of dread.

Shaking herself out of it, Erika turned to me. "I'm going to warm that soup up for you, okay?"

Once she was gone, Alaina scooted closer to me, expression trying to downplay the emotion in her eyes. "Are you okay? Really? Sark didn't do anything to you?"

I gave the best head shake I could muster.

Her gaze flicked to the hallway Sark disappeared into, and she lowered her voice. "He did it again. I can't believe it. Not just again but...he sent Lennon off my trail. For, like, a long time. Sark...he wouldn't do that. This is...this is insane."

Using the very last bit of energy, I lifted my head to look right at her. "Told you."

She glared at me, but it cracked when she rolled her eyes and fell into a grateful smile. "You're a stupid idiot, Arie Nolan. Next time, you have my full permission to fake give me up."

13

The next few days were really quiet. Well, quiet as in nobody showed up at the house, there was no immediate danger, and we were left in peace. It wasn't very quiet, though, because Erika and Alaina were constantly trying to talk over each other whenever they were in the same room together. Each competed for my attention and validation, which got old really fast. Alaina had a year of friendship and memories on her side, while Erika had home court advantage. If Erika was warm water,

Alaina was thick oil, and by the laws of nature the two of them would just not mix.

Besides their incessant competition to be my best friend, everything was mostly okay. Alaina and I continued to get better from the orchard incident. My left hand was still a bit of a mess thanks to Lennon, but my right hand had scabbed over and, while gross, was healing. The improvement was much quicker than usual; usually we found ourselves huddled in an alleyway, surviving on what we could scavenge, furthering our injuries by pushing our bodies. Here, though, we had food, shelter, and a relatively stress-free environment. It was crazy, in the best way.

Alaina struggled to keep up full skepticism as the days wore on without further problems. Sark left us alone. Lennon never came back. Never had we ever gotten the chance to just sit and hang out with each other without something dangerously wrong. It was hard to let go of, even with survival instincts, and I was both surprised and glad every morning I woke up and found she'd decided to stay.

I could sense she was in the weird daze that I was in—this whole situation just had that effect. Like standing on the edge of the cliff, knowing any moment you could plummet, but the breeze and view are so refreshing, you just can't bring yourself to step back. To leave. It was like being constantly aware of possible disaster without really believing it will ever come. At least, you hoped it wouldn't. Hope was such a tricky thing.

While slowly accepting the situation as I had, Alaina never swallowed things easily, and it wasn't long before she started pushing it. They began as small things—brushing crumbs on the floor, leaving garbage around, being too loud—and slowly got bigger. She ran her own kind of experiment, waiting for the moment Sark would finally break. He never did. He stayed on the outskirts of everything, quietly enduring behavior Alaina would've been slapped for a month ago. As he passed each test, she got more and more comfortable until she was lounging around the place as if she owned it.

When she wasn't arguing with Erika or testing Sark's new unfathomable patience, we hung out, and—when we were alone—talked about what to do in case we were somehow wrong about this whole thing. We both agreed getting Sark caught by Lennon or Alexis was a stupid idea, and would only make him seem suspicious or get him killed, and we would just wind up in major trouble or back on the run anyway.

I halfheartedly mentioned Dalton, knowing before she scoffed that Alaina would adamantly disagree. She thought Dalton was a grown-up idiot with a government badge, and she'd long-since been telling me to stay away from him. We considered turning Sark in to someone else that would lock him up, like the FBI, but our plans never made it past the brainstorming stage. Truthfully, we just wanted Sark's new behavior to be real so we didn't have to deal with anything else.

The days morphed into each other, and we found we'd been there a week without another incident. To celebrate, Alaina announced we were having a party, runaway infected style.

Turns out, 'runaway infected style' translated to a movie marathon with food. Erika said Sark gave us permission to get whatever we wanted, and Alaina was too happy to write out a list for Erika to get at the store. She returned with an obscene amount a food—I'm pretty sure Alaina accounted for nearly every time running from Sark had left us starving—and he also said we could order pizza. Once everything was there, Alaina spread it all out over the coffee table and queued up the first film in a long line of cult classic films I'd never heard of. We settled into the couch: Alaina sprawled out in the corner she'd deemed her own, Erika perched on the opposite edge, and me plopped in the middle in a mess of blankets. Despite the slight tension between the two girls, it was the funnest night I'd had in a long time.

We were all surprised when halfway through the second movie, Sark appeared with his laptop and sat quietly on the chair, taking a moment to watch the screen with a raised eyebrow before snagging a bag of licorice and turning his attention to his computer. If he was surprised or annoyed with how much food we'd bought with his credit card, he didn't show it.

Half-filled cups, empty boxes, and ripped packages littered the coffee table, the enormous amount of food strewn every which way. Alaina and I each ate half a pizza, and I downed a whole bag of gummy worms by myself, not to mention the three bags of popcorn we ate and two liters of soda we drained. Alaina kept burping—Erika eyeing her with distaste—and we kept laughing over nothing, our voices tainted with euphoria, like we were drunk on food and safety and fun. It had been so long since I'd felt so airy, light, and just okay.

The laughing subsided as the night wore on. As each film melted into the next, Alaina and I settled back into the couch, in a daze from all the food. I felt sick to my stomach but I didn't care, and I broke into another giggle fit when Alaina groaned about a stomachache herself, only to then reach for another package of chocolate chip cookies.

"We could die tomorrow," she explained as she shoved two of them in her mouth at once. I snorted in response.

Eventually, Erika left, running out of patience for the movies Alaina chose. She disappeared for chunks at a time, and came back in to whisper to Sark cryptically before leaving again. He just stayed in his chair and typed on his laptop, the glow of the screen the only other light in the room besides the TV. I never caught their conversation, but Erika seemed to get more irritated every time it happened. Since I was busy pretending not to notice what she was up to, I had a hard time trying to figure it out.

My eyelids grew heavy; it wasn't long before I couldn't keep them from closing. The credits for our fourth (or fifth?) movie started rolling when I allowed my eyes to shut for a minute before blinking them open again.

It was dark now. The TV was off. Sark and Alaina must've went to bed, because they were both gone. My eyes struggled for a moment to make out the shadows of the couch, coffee table, and food I knew was there. I couldn't find anything.

How'd I get on the floor?

A spark of light flashed in the corner of my eye, like a giant match trying to be lit. Confused, I turned to the noise, my nerves beginning to tingle with agitation. Something was wrong.

The light flashed again, much closer to me, illuminating one of Lennon's monstrous dogs, and a scream got caught in my throat. I scrambled backward, only to run into a wet snout. The other dog snarled into my hair and a terrified cry escaped my mouth.

Several collars sparked now: five, ten, fifteen, twenty-five dogs, surrounding me in the absolute darkness. I had nowhere to go. I curled into a ball in the center of them, shaking and waiting for one of them to lash out. They drew closer and closer, pressing in on me, breathing rotten breath and smearing snot on my skin.

I reached up and wiped some slobber off my cheek. Three collars sparked, giving me enough light to see my fingers were tinted red. Sucking in a sharp breath, I studied the dogs closer, and suddenly found their mouths were covered in blood. Blood that wasn't mine—not yet.

A putrid stench assaulted my nose, and I flinched away from it, nearly into the snapping jaws of a dog. Somehow my eyes knew where to look, where the body would be. The collars all flashed at the same time, giving me just enough light to see the mangled corpse of my brother Kieran on the ground behind the dogs, nearly eaten beyond recognition.

I opened my mouth to scream, but a dog pounced on me, slamming me onto my back and knocking the wind out of me. Then the ground started moving against my skin. Slow, slippery, slimy, like I was lying on a bed of wet snakes. The snakes encircled around my wrists, ankles, and neck, holding me down, then two of them slithered over my face, their scales electric blue. A half shriek escaped me before they barreled into my mouth and down my throat, choking me off. They sent a scorching fire through me, coursing through my veins and burning me to ash.

My limbs thrashed in their shackles. My screams echoed underneath the weight of the snakes in my throat. Blue spots danced across my vision as I fought to stay conscious, fought to die, fought to make it stop, to keep it from happening again, to get them off, to get it out, to keep that despicable formula out of my body, even though I knew there was nothing I could do.

"Arie!"

I jolted when my eyes snapped open, and my aching body whined in protest. Oxygen rushed into my lungs, and I wheezed in terror, turning over to gag again and again at the ghosts of the snakes still caught in my throat. I was folded in half at an odd angle, aggravating my healing injuries. A gentle but firm hand took my jaw and opened my mouth, the other pulling me by my shoulders into a halfway sitting position. My airway cleared almost instantly, and I gulped in the air while my eyes darted around in a frenzy.

I was in the living room. I hadn't moved from my spot and my blankets were twisted around my legs. A movie was still playing on the TV, though the volume was turned low now. Our food was still all over the coffee table, and Alaina was sprawled out in the corner of the couch, head tipped back as she snored softly. Sark was sitting in front of me, holding me up and looking into my mouth. My breath caught and tears stung my eyes, my heart pounding with horror and adrenaline.

"It was a dream," Sark said quietly as he finished his inspection and let my mouth go, satisfied I wasn't actually choking on anything. "Just a dream. It's over now."

Trembling, I shook my head, clenching my hands into fists that turned my knuckles white and burned my palms. "They're here," I whispered hoarsely, glancing wildly around the room. "They found me. They found me. They're here."

"Nobody is here." Sark kept his voice soft but firm. "You fell asleep, and now you're awake. You're safe."

I surveyed the dark room, looking for any evidence of scary dogs, or slithering snakes, or bleeding brothers. I couldn't find anything.

"Dream," I muttered to myself. "It was a dream. Just a dream."

Sark nodded. "Just a dream."

Blowing out a long breath, I collapsed back against the couch, and Sark released his supportive hold on me. Reality started becoming sharper in my hazy mind as my senses came back to me, highlighting the pain I felt everywhere. My hands throbbed, and I glanced over them to find several of my scabs had been torn off and little bits of blood dotted my sleeves and the couch. I remembered whose blood *had* been on my hands, just moments before, and shuddered. The harsh movement jerked my injuries wrong, and I whimpered at the deep ache.

"You're in pain." Sark dropped his eyes when I met them, and wiped at a blood spot on the couch without much concern. "I have...things, Arie. Medicine. Ice for your hands, if you want it. You don't have to endure it all."

I started shaking my head again. "No, it's fi—" Another stab of pain in my arm cut me off. I softly pressed my palm against the sore spot, but that only made my hand throb worse. With a sigh, I closed my eyes and gave up. "Yes. Please."

I heard him get up and walk away, and the empty space in the room seemed to grow wider and wider, a giant chasm that I nearly fell into. The couch started slithering underneath me. I squeaked a half shriek and snapped my eyes open. The couch was still leather. No snakes.

Gritting my teeth, I forced myself to take deep breaths.

It was just a dream. It wasn't real.

The dark played tricks on me, though, and I found myself bolting upright when I heard claws tapping against the hardwood floor. Jerking my head around, I searched for any threat, my throat closing up when I swore I saw a hulking shadow move toward me, and I caught myself wanting Sark to come back.

It's not real. You're freaking yourself out. Get a grip.

I finally resorted to curling up in a ball with my hands over my head, fingers in my ears, and eyes squeezed shut, forcing myself to breathe. If not for my unwillingness to leave the safety of the couch, I would've trailed after Sark just for the sake of not being alone.

Though I knew he was coming back, I still jumped when he gently touched my shoulder.

"It's just me."

Lifting my head up, I cracked my eyes open to see Sark kneeling on the ground in front of me, spreading his assortment of supplies on an empty corner of the coffee table. Methodically, he gave me three pills that I swallowed down with a swig of flat soda while he started unwrapping a roll of thick gauze.

The second the pills slid down my throat, I realized my grave mistake. My body froze over. It was too late, though. I'd already swallowed.

"They'll knock me out." I couldn't bring my croaking voice louder than a whisper, but Sark still stiffened, hesitating a moment before meeting my wide eyes.

His returning whisper was unyielding yet cautious. "You need sleep. Real sleep."

"No." I shook my head, my hands shaking with it. "No, I can't."

Desperate, I reached my fingers for my mouth, like I could somehow yank the pills out of me, but Sark grabbed my hands and pulled them away from my face.

"You shouldn't experience something like that twice in the same night. Your mind needs time to heal itself from something so vivid before it can produce it again."

I searched his eyes for a lie, but came up empty. "You promise?" It was a stupid question, considering everything about this absurd situation, but I still asked it.

Sark studied me a moment before nodding slowly. He waited, and when I didn't say anything else, he turned his attention to wrapping up my hands.

Not wanting my mind to wander, I focused on what Sark was doing instead. It went against the grain to let anyone—especially him—touch me without bailing or putting up a fight, so I concentrated on staying still. Sark also focused on his work, refusing to meet my eyes. His fingers were gentle and experienced as he softly pressed mini ice packs to my burned palms and wrapped gauze around them. I knew he must've had a lot of practice putting himself back together, given his job and history, but it still struck me as odd that someone I'd seen be so heartless could fall into a routine of taking care of someone else. His movements were skilled and familiar, but uneasy in a way. He probably felt some discomfort, like I did, but there was another layer to it, like he was trying to retrace steps of an old dance he used to know by heart.

He was halfway through with my first hand—already the ice had cooled some of the throbbing—when a sound tore through the kitchen behind me. I jumped three feet in the air and almost fell onto Sark. He swore under his breath before glancing pointedly at me, and I realized it wasn't another attack but the dishwasher automatically turning on after its set delay.

Biting down on my lip, I closed my eyes and breathed rapidly through my nose, trying to calm myself down but it wasn't working. Conscious or no, I felt like I could never escape the corpse on the floor or what was slithering inside of me.

Sark finished wrapping my first hand and started on the second. I was so focused on the suffocating darkness that it took me a moment to realize he'd spoken to me.

"What do you do when you're alone and this happens?"

I blinked in surprise, momentarily forgetting the nightmare. "Um...I don't know. It's scary. Sometimes it gets ugly, but...I have to pull myself out of it eventually."

Somebody has to.

He continued to work without meeting my eyes. "Do you...uh, do you want to tell me about it?"

My mouth fell open. For a second, words almost came spilling out of it, and I almost told him how my brother had died around this time a year ago and left me completely alone in facing the vile formula inside me and the monsters that wouldn't let me have a moment of peace. For a second, I thought I might cry at the thought of how much I ached for Kieran to come back.

Instead, I swallowed hard and shook my head. "No." I waited a few seconds before asking a question of my own. "Why are you out here?"

His eyes flicked to mine for a fraction of a second. "In Chicago?"

"No, out here. In the living room. It's, like, three in the morning." My eyebrows furrowed. "Do you *ever* sleep?"

The corner of his mouth pulled up ever so slightly. "Not as much as I probably should."

I watched him, and he felt my expecting gaze without meeting it. Finally, he sighed and answered my question.

"Nobody is coming here. I know that. But I didn't want to leave you two out here alone.

Just...just in case." He twisted the last strip of gauze around my palm. "I almost moved you to your bed once you were asleep, but I assumed Alaina wouldn't appreciate the same courtesy, and I wasn't about to let her burn my house down when she woke up and found you missing."

"Oh," was all I said.

Sark taped the gauze on my hand, then placed it carefully in my lap before looking up at me. "Is there anything else you need before…" He trailed off uncertainly. The reminder sent my calming heart into overdrive as I felt the medicine slowly leaking through me and spreading grogginess in its wake.

"Too dark?" Sark asked me.

"What?"

"Do you want me to turn the lights on?"

I was both mortified and relieved that he knew I saw monsters in the dark, but I shook my head. "No, it'll wake Alaina up. But will—" My mouth stayed open even though I stopped the words from coming out. What was I *doing*?

Sark raised an eyebrow at me in question. Maybe it was the soft light of the TV against his face or the memory of the gentle way he'd handled my situation, but something about the moment drew the desperate plea from my mouth.

"Will you stay with me?"

He blinked with surprise, but didn't give any other reaction. Taking a breath, he nodded, then started untangling the blanket from my limbs, careful not to actually touch me. I laid down and curled into a ball; Sark spread the blanket out over me before sliding a pillow under my head, then sitting next to it.

My eyelids grew heavier. Every time I closed them, though, I saw Kieran's half-eaten body. Tears stung my eyes again, and I carefully put my hand against my mouth to stifle a dry sob that shook me.

I don't want to do this anymore. Especially without you. I can't.

Suddenly, I felt Sark's hand on my head. When I didn't move away from it, he started to slowly stroke my hair. The movements were awkward and hesitant at first, but grew into a steady rhythm, and I found my muscles relaxing. When my eyes closed, I felt the motion in my hair, not the snakes in my veins.

How does he know how to do all of this?

I wanted to ask Sark about his mom. I wanted to ask if when she was going through cancer treatments or the incessant horrors of domestic abuse she ever woke up crying in the middle of the night. I wanted to ask if he ever had to get her medicine, or wrap her hands up, or convince her she was safe, or stroke her hair until she went back to sleep. Something about the systematic way he patched me up and the concrete yet calm set to his face and voice made me think he'd had a lot of practice in these kinds of situations.

Despite my curiosity, I asked about someone else instead. "Where's Erika?"

Sark's hand stalled and I felt him freeze. "She's, uh, she's asleep. If...if you don't want me here without her, though, I can go—"

"Oh, no...no, it's okay. I just...I just need something to talk about. A distraction."

A beat of silence. "All right." Thankfully, he kept stroking my hair. It was so simple yet it made me feel so safe, and I couldn't help but think it was something Kieran would've done too.

"You like her," I stated.

"Is that the end of a question?"

"No, I don't need to ask. I can tell." A smile formed on my lips as my words slurred, and felt myself beginning to drift off. "Have you kissed her yet?"

I heard a smile in his voice too. "You really want these kinds of details?"

"Well, I'm curious. I love her too, in my own weird way."

"It's all a bit weird, isn't it?"

"Yeah, but not completely surprising. Erika's gorgeous."

"Yeah, I noticed," he said dryly.

The pain that had been vibrating through me was now the slightest feather in the back of my mind. My words came slower, my body heavier.

"Why aren't you all over each other then?" I asked, confused. The few young couples I'd had contact with had serious PDA issues.

Sark chuckled under his breath. "Common courtesy to you, though that can change if you don't have any objections."

I wrinkled my nose. "Ew. No thanks."

I thought I said something else, or maybe he said something else, but I didn't catch any of it before I slipped all the way under into peaceful sleep.

~~~

When my eyes flitted open the next morning, I found light streaming through the windows of the
~~~

living room—it was nearly afternoon. The place was clean now: no evidence of excessive food, medical supplies, or carnivorous dogs. My head held a wisp of grogginess leftover from the medication, and there was only a slight dull ache of pain in my shoulders, but otherwise I felt good and rested.

Bracing myself on my elbow, I half sat up, wincing when my neck popped. My eyes instantly searched for Alaina, but there wasn't a scrap of crimson anywhere.

"She's in the shower."

I jumped and turned to see Sark walking into the living room, buttoning the sleeve of his shirt. He was in fresh clothes, giving no indication he'd stayed up all night besides the laptop left on the chair he'd been sitting in.

"She asked me to tell you that," he continued as he scooped his laptop up without looking at me. "So you didn't panic when you finally woke up."

I tucked some loose hair behind my ear, noticing the gauze still wrapped around my hands. The ice had melted and the packs were sloshy with water now.

"Thank you," I told him, the words so genuine that Sark stopped and looked up. Then he cleared his throat and dropped his eyes.

"You're welcome."

He turned to go, but I pushed myself into a sitting position and spoke, my forehead creasing.

"Where are you going?"

Sark stopped again and glanced at me with a shrug, though it wasn't quite casual enough to be believable. "Nowhere."

I mulled that over, thinking of his behavior since the Lennon incident. It wasn't that Sark had avoided us, necessarily, but he'd stayed on the edges of everything, always watching but never really entering anything. He'd always been there, but not really *there*.

"You don't have to leave," I said, "just because I'm here. It's your house."

"It's not because of you."

I raised an eyebrow at him in a challenge. He pursed his lips before coming all the way into the room and sitting down in his chair, the movements a little too exaggerated, which made me roll my eyes.

"I'm infected, not contagious."

"I never said you were."

"You've been acting like it."

"It's on me, Arie," he said, opening his laptop back up and typing out his password. "Not you."

I cocked my head to the side, unable to let this one go. "Did I scare you?"

He laughed, a sound of surprise, but was still focused on his stupid computer. "What?"

"Did I scare you?" I repeated. "I wouldn't be that shocked, really. A lot of people get scared of me."

"Rest assured, I don't scare easily."

"Well a lot has happened."

"Perhaps, but they're not exactly things I haven't seen before."

My eyes narrowed. He wasn't giving me a straight answer. "If you're not avoiding me because you're scared of me, then why are you?"

He shot me an exasperated look. "I'm not avoiding you."

"Yes you are. Not *literally*, but kind of."

"That doesn't make much sense."

"Then why do I get the feeling you know exactly what I'm talking about?"

Finally, Sark broke his firm concentration to his laptop and met my gaze. "You're annoyingly perceptive."

I shrugged. "Everyone needs a hobby." My fingers grazed the edges of the gauze on my hand, and I felt myself shrink a little bit. "I just...I just want to know what I did wrong."

"What you did *wrong*?"

The icy fury in his tone made me flinch back into the couch. My body froze over and I watched him with wide eyes, every nerve on edge, waiting for a real explosion.

It never came. Once Sark saw my expression, he went rigid too and let out a long breath, then the anger seemed to drain out of him. I relaxed slightly but not completely.

"A lot has happened," he agreed, his voice even now as he nodded. "I assumed with the nature of the incident with Lennon, both you and Alaina would be more comfortable if I kept my distance." His tone hardened. "And *none* of that is your fault."

I scoffed when I realized what he was getting at. "And that makes it yours?"

He opened his mouth to say something, then shook his head and gritted his teeth, typing on his laptop again but with too much force.

I couldn't believe it. "You saved us." When he started to object, I continued. "Lennon would've found us. You know that. He would've found us, and dragged us somewhere else, and maybe even killed us. We weren't in any shape to defend ourselves. And it would've..." I winced just at the thought. "It would've been bad. You know that as much as I do. Maybe even better than I do."

Sark's jaw was clamped tight, the muscles in his neck tense. He stared at his laptop, without doing anything, and I realized I didn't like him like this. Sark could be stiff and unapproachable, but now that I'd seen him relaxed and personable, I wanted to get him back.

Finally, he let out another breath through his teeth and went back to his computer. "We'll have to agree to disagree on that front."

I folded my arms across my chest, annoyed he wasn't understanding the magnitude of what he did for us, putting his own neck on the line too. "You know, those things sound ridiculous coming out of your mouth."

His shoulders lost some of their tension, and he didn't look up from his screen. "My accent is perfect. I've convinced many people for years."

I made a face at him he didn't see, which was unfortunate. Sometimes I just wanted to let some hot air out of his head. "Not that. You act way too old. It's weird."

"It's only weird because you know how old I am. Anyone else doesn't look twice and believes me."

He *was* good at it, admittedly, but I wasn't going to tell him that. "You're not that old."

"I'm still six years older than you."

"That's not that many, really. You talk like you're some eighty-year-old British mob boss."

Sark actually laughed at that, and I gave a small smile that my plan worked.

"Most of my co-workers have at least ten years on me," he said. "You saw the way Lennon talked to me. If I acted my age, I'd never survive."

I shrugged. "I guess."

He looked at me now, computer forgotten, and settled back into his chair. "Well you had to grow up quickly, didn't you? You don't act like an infuriating teenage brat."

I raised my eyebrows and grinned at the near compliment.

He rolled his eyes. "Most of the time, anyway," he amended.

Footsteps sounded in the kitchen, saving me from having to quickly think of an adequately snarky response.

"It's nice to see you, sleepy head," Erika called from the kitchen. "I was beginning to think you'd never wake up."

Glancing from Erika's perfectly curled hair to Sark's amused expression, I broke into a huge smile.

"What?" he asked, sensing my smile wasn't all innocent.

"Oh, nothing." I pretended to nonchalantly flatten the gauze on my palm. "I just wonder if she'd still like you if she knew your accent was fake."

The amusement fell from his face. He stared back at me, accepting the challenge without blinking.

I called his bluff. Half turning toward the kitchen, I raised my voice. "Hey, Erika, did you—"

My voice got cut off by a mound of fabric, and a pillow fell into my lap. He'd thrown a pillow at me.

Sark glared. "Don't you dare."

I burst into laughter just as Erika and Alaina came in.

"Did I what?" Erika asked, looking from me to Sark in confusion. Sark just shook his head, the tiniest of grins on his face that he was trying to fight, while Alaina just gawked at us, red hair still dripping from her shower.

Erika put a hand on her hip. "What?"

I just shook my head too and smirked at Sark. "Nothing."

"Good," Alaina said, recovering herself. She swung over the back of the couch and landed in a heap in her spot in the corner, watching Sark the entire time. When he didn't care, she looked to me. "Because we're going on an adventure today."

14

Alaina's 'adventure' was a test. Well, it was a real adventure for us, and it also dueled as a test for Sark and even Erika.

She wanted to take me to meet her brother.

The fact that she even mentioned her brother's existence in front of Sark gave me an idea of how she was gauging his intentions. She trusted him more than I thought, but she was also climbing out on a limb to see whether or not he'd let her fall.

To her credit, Erika held up better than I thought she would. When Alaina first asked me to go with her—purposefully asking loudly in front of Sark and Erika—Erika's eyebrows shot up. She pursed her lips as she glanced from me to Alaina and back again, as if battling with herself on whether to voice her opinion or wait for me to come to the same conclusion. She opted to stay silent. That plan blew up on her when I told Alaina I would go.

After I failed, Erika looked to Sark, who just shrugged. Erika let out a frustrated breath through her teeth before leaning against the couch to talk to us, but mostly me.

"Going anywhere is a bad idea," Erika started. "How many times do we have to prove that?"

Alaina settled back into the couch and propped her feet up, clearly comfortable with and welcoming the confrontation. "Sark's here. Lennon's gone. A day trip downtown won't kill anyone, right? It's not like we're prisoners, after all." Then she looked at me, voice a little too sweet to be believable. "I haven't seen him in *years*. It's amazing that I have a free moment in my terrible life to safely see him again—especially since I get to introduce him to my best friend." She sighed in contentment and rested her head back. "What a dream."

Erika gritted her teeth at that. Sark, oddly enough, was doing his best to suppress a smile. When she saw his amusement, she shot him a glare.

"You know as much as I do that this is a bad idea," she said, a steely edge to her tone.

Taking a deep breath, Sark put his laptop aside and leaned forward, resting his elbows on his knees. I straightened up at the thought he was going to take us seriously, and I suddenly realized how much his approval mattered to me. If Sark said it wasn't safe, then it really wasn't.

Sark seemed to be mulling things over in his head—ignoring Erika's frosty look—as he glanced between me and Alaina.

"How far is it?" he finally asked.

Alaina shrugged. "I don't know. Downtown."

"Chicago is a big place," Erika cut in.

"But you wouldn't be able to walk, would you?" he went on.

"Well…" Alaina glanced at me, and I realized underneath her apathetic bravado, she cared about what he said too. "We *could* walk, technically."

"But it's stupid," Erika said, leaning further over the edge of the couch. "It's stupid, it's dangerous, it's cold, and while you guys are a lot better, you still aren't healed enough to go walking around Chicago for hours on your own."

I nodded to myself. She had a point, as much as I was itching to refute it.

Alaina opened her mouth to argue, but Sark beat her to it. "So, you need a car then?"

"Yes." Alaina beamed, triumphant. "Then it would be no big deal."

"Do you drive as well as Arie does?"

I rolled my eyes at him while Alaina deflated and Erika nodded in approval. So much for that idea.

"Then I'll drive you."

All three of us—me, Erika, and Alaina—said, "What?" at the same time.

Sark sat back in his chair, appraising us. "I'll drive you both where you need to go. No need to walk or worry about potential hazards on the way."

Erika opened her mouth, then shut it. Alaina blinked in surprise, then looked at me.

I just stared at Sark. "Really?"

"Yeah." He rubbed his neck, as if to stretch it out. "I could use a trip out of the house anyway. Letters on the screen are starting to run together."

"Should you be driving then?"

He gave me a wry grin. "Well, it's better than having you drive, now isn't it?"

I scoffed. "You know, I keep waiting for you to finally let that one go."

"Don't hold your breath then." Sark closed his laptop and stood. "I assume you'd rather go sooner than later?"

Erika finally regained herself, not able to keep the annoyed betrayal off her face. "Well, I'm going if you are."

Sark just shrugged again. "Company would be nice."

My eyebrows furrowed, my brain struggling to realize that *Sark* just said that, and it was Alaina's timid, cautious voice that snapped me out of my own head.

"Why?"

Her tone caused everyone to turn and look at her. Alaina had been all attitude since she arrived, and hearing anything other than sassy, sarcastic veiled insults was weird—especially since she suddenly sounded so small and...scared.

Sark didn't bat an eye at the drastic change in her. "Why what?"

"Why are...how can..." Alaina studied him, trying to hide the desperate fear in her expression, but she just looked like she was shrinking into the couch. After an endless thirty seconds, she finally blurted, "Lennon doesn't know. I've spent years...convincing him I don't have a brother. He...he can't know."

There was a few moments of thick silence. In that time, Erika drew back into herself, annoyance forgotten, while Sark's face softened. I'd never thought I'd use the word 'compassion' to describe him, but there it was, brimming in his eyes. Suddenly, he was the Sark that had helped me sleep after my nightmare last night.

"I would never think of it," he told her, and even I was taken aback by his sincerity. "I swear, Lennon will never hear of your family from me."

Alaina took that in slowly, analyzing each syllable. "You mean that," she said in near wonder, a statement more than a question.

"I do."

She couldn't hide her bewilderment, and her charade slipped further: she smiled, a genuine smile of gratitude, which, from Alaina, was impossibly rare.

At that, Sark gave her a nod, before going with Erika to get ready to leave. Once they were out of earshot, Alaina leaned closer to me, lowering her voice.

"Okay," she said, watching them go, "I can see why he's growing on you."

I grinned. "Told you. It's too awkward to be anything but real."

She just laughed once in disbelief, then smacked my shoulder, regaining her excitement. "We're going to see my brother!" She paused for a second, sobering up. "Is it weird that I'm so freaking nervous?"

"No." I shook my head. "It's been a few years, hasn't it? Makes sense. Is he...like, does he know...or care...about...?" I didn't know how to nicely phrase my question, but I'd heard stories of infecteds thrown out of their houses and disowned by their families because of what they were.

"He knows what I am," Alaina answered thoughtfully. "He doesn't understand it all, but who does, really? And he knows I have to stay away but...he doesn't have many details on Lennon. He only knows bare minimum."

"Ah." I nodded.

"Yeah. It's been hard on him, since Mom died, then me having to take off...I don't want to add anything to that." She blew out a breath. "We aren't really like PB and jelly, if you know what I mean, so I'm nervous, but also it's been forever. It's weird that I actually miss him. A lot."

I gave a half smile, suddenly overwhelmed by how much I missed my brother. "Of course you do. I'm excited to meet him."

She beamed. "I'm excited too."

The excitement I felt battled with my nerves as we all pulled on shoes and got in one of Sark's cars. My stomach squelched and grumbled, trying to decide if my anxiety was outweighing my eagerness, and the chemical reaction of the two emotions just left me nauseated. I just focused on the road and Alaina's hand gripping mine. The car ride didn't help, as Alaina only had vague directions, and we had to drive around in circles for awhile before she claimed she'd found it. Sark finally found a parking spot on the curb a block down.

He turned off the engine, then glanced at Alaina in the rearview mirror. "You ready?"

She took a deep breath, finally releasing my hand, and blood started flowing back into it. "As I'll ever be."

Erika took off her seatbelt and turned to look at us. "I'm coming in with you."

I raised an eyebrow, my stomach twisting painfully at the thought of Erika meeting Alaina's brother and how I would keep all the millions of possible disasters from happening.

Sark shook his head and muttered something under his breath—something about giving us space—but Erika wasn't going to relent.

Surprisingly, Alaina didn't put up a fight. She must've been too nervous to care.

"Fine, just don't do anything embarrassing," she muttered to Erika. "I don't really want to be affiliated with you."

Erika just glared at her in the mirror. "Likewise."

"Okay, then," I said, opening up my door before things accelerated. "Let's go."

I stepped out of the car and let Alaina lead the way, Erika trailing behind us, while Sark opted to turn off the engine and hang out in the car. I couldn't help the slight acceleration of my heart as I followed Alaina through an alleyway between businesses and stopped at a back door. Erika muttered impatiently under her breath, rubbing her hands together against the cold, while Alaina hunted around the broken pavement. Finally, she came up with a spare key underneath a loose brick. She gave me a last glance;

I tried to look as supportive as possible. Then with a deep breath, she turned the key in the lock, pushed the door open, and headed inside.

The room was dark. We stumbled along, tripping over shadowy objects that sporadically littered the floor, using the light spilling from the doorway ahead to guide us. Alaina ducked through the doorway, me right after her, and I had to squint for a second before I adjusted to the amount of light in the vast room. My eyebrows furrowed when I realized I'd been here before.

"Wait a second…" I murmured to myself, noting how different the club looked during the day.

I crashed into Alaina, who had skidded to a sudden stop right in front of me. We both stumbled off balance, but Alaina couldn't care less. Her gaze was focused on the eighteen-year-old kid in front of us with shaggy dark hair and mahogany eyes—eyes I recognized. When he saw Alaina, he dropped the box of cords he was carrying.

"Hey," Alaina said, miserably failing at trying to be casually cool.

Astonished, he shook his head slowly, expression glazing over in shock like she was the only thing in the world. "You're here." Then he came to himself, dashed forward, and gave Alaina a huge hug that lifted her off her feet.

I, for one, could not believe what I was seeing, and if it weren't for Erika's tiny gasp of surprise, I would've thought I was crazy.

When he caught sight of me over Alaina's shoulder, recognition flickered in his eyes, and my mouth fell open in disbelief when he remembered my name. "Arie?"

"Liam?"

Alaina pushed herself out of Liam's hug and looked between the two of us. "You two *know* each other?"

Liam and I both opened our mouths, but responses were cut short by a slew of new shouts.

"Alaina?"

"Ohmygosh, it's Alaina!"

"It's really her!"

"Alaina!"

Four other teenagers raced into the room, pushing each other out of the way in an effort to get to the redhead first. A giant group hug ensued, and Alaina laughed from the center of the bodies.

"Hey, you guys, you're smashing me to death!" she complained, but her laughter overtook any annoyance she may have actually felt. "Lay off!"

She managed to push off one kid—Mark—who turned and caught sight of me. His expression lit up like a strand of Christmas lights. "Hey, look!" he crowed, pointing at me. "It's the mystery guitar chick."

At that, everyone let Alaina go to stare at me and Erika, questions shooting from every which way, catching all of us in a firefight.

"Who is she?"

"She knows Alaina?"

"Why is she here?"

"How did you get here, Alaina?"

"Did she bring you here?"

"What's going on?"

Another voice broke through the chaos, as Neil, the owner (if I remembered right) came in from the kitchen. "Hey, Erika, what are you doing here?"

Erika waved her hand. "Oh, I'm just—"

"Liam's sister is here!" Mark shouted in delight.

Neil's bushy eyebrows furrowed and he pointed to me. "Liam, this is your sister? Why didn't you tell me?"

I shook my head and took a step back. "No, I'm not—"

Alaina pushed through her siblings until she was in the middle of everything. "No, *I'm* his sister, and I have zero idea what's going on right now." Her eyes shifted to me. "You first. How do you know them?"

Liam arched an eyebrow. "Why didn't you say you knew Alaina?"

"I didn't know." Now that I finally got in a sentence, my voice felt way too loud to me, especially in the large space. "I met Alaina way before you. She just asked me to come with her today."

"Bummer," Mark chimed in. "We were hoping you'd just come back one day 'cause you missed our faces. Or Erika would bring you back, at the very least."

Alaina shook her head. "Derailing, Mark. What am I missing here?"

"Um, well…" I scuffed my heel against the floor. How much should I say? "Remember how I told you about when I called…*him* and I ended up going to a club to meet up with Erika…?" Erika stiffened at that, glancing sideways at me. I decided to ignore whatever questions she might have had about the disaster with Dalton.

"*This* is the club you were talking about?"

I nodded.

She threw her hands up in the air. "Well, hello? Why didn't you tell me?"

"Well it's not like I knew. It was a total coincidence."

One of the girls—Chelsie, maybe?—stepped forward, cocking her head and glancing between me and Alaina. "What happened to your faces? They're, like, weirdly scabbed or something."

Now it was my turn to tense up. I hadn't thought it was *that* noticeable, but I guess I'd been wrong. Alaina and I exchanged glances, clearly caught, but I wasn't sure what I was and wasn't allowed to say.

Turned out, I didn't really need to say anything. Liam went back and forth between the two of us, connecting dots, then sucked in a sharp breath and focused on me.

"You're like Alaina?"

I shrunk into myself, automatically swaying toward Erika. Not that it *really* mattered what this kid thought of me, but...I hated the reactions. The judgment. The way I was suddenly put into a box marked 'different' and could never climb back out no matter how average I looked.

There's a reason I'm the epitome of anti-social.

Instead of answering, I looked to Alaina. It was her brother, after all. Ultimately, it was her call on how much she wanted him to know, and I would abide by that.

She just shrugged and nodded at me. I sighed.

"Yes, I am," I responded, voice now too quiet to fill up the space.

"How many of you are there?" Chelsie asked, the same time Mara questioned, "How does that work?" while Mark exclaimed, "*Please* tell me you actually have superpowers because Alaina only knows how to mega-annoy people." The quiet boy (I couldn't remember his name) just shook his head at Mark while Liam inspected me with incredible scrutiny considering I was three feet away from him. Meanwhile, Neil stared at both me and Alaina like we were drug dealers, clearly not knowing what they all did.

If you only knew.

"This is crazy," Erika muttered under her breath in the commotion, and I had to agree.

My voice got caught in my throat, though, when suddenly Liam surged forward and grabbed my wrist. Instinct took over. I twisted my arm and yanked back, successfully jerking myself free, which wasn't that hard because he wasn't really restraining me. He was looking at my burnt hands. Then he narrowed his eyes, turning back to Alaina and surveying her like he could see the bandages under her clothes and the scrapes on her skin before they'd scabbed over.

His face drained of color and his hands clenched into fists, making everyone go quiet so his words rang out. "It was him again, wasn't it?" Alaina went pale, which only confirmed his theory. "What did he do?"

"Nothing," she said, too quickly to be believable. "Nothing, this was just an accident." She gave me a hard glare. "Right, Arie?"

"Yeah." I didn't know where she wanted to go with it, so I stayed vague. "Freak accident. My bad." Erika scoffed. Alaina glared at her too.

"Kitchen fire," Alaina added. "Gas stove and everything—hard to work with. Arie nearly took her hands off when the flame caught. Crazy stuff."

"Uh huh." Liam did not look convinced. "Your ability to lie to me hasn't gotten any better."

Mark plopped himself on a stool at the bar, giving a mischievous wink to Alaina while feigning an innocent tone. "Speaking of fire, did you guys hear about Bernard's orchard burning down? It was pretty bad: they suspect arson." He held his chin in his hand like he was thinking hard. "Now, I wonder who would have *anything* to do with that."

Alaina scowled and swore at him, making Neil and Erika bristle and Mara mumble, "Language," but Mark just grinned. Liam, on the other hand, exploded.

"You set an orchard on fire?" Even I froze at his anger, but the others seemed bored, like they were used to this kind of thing. "What were you—"

"I didn't!" Alaina bit back, flustered instead of defiant.

"Do you have any idea what—"

"I didn't do it!"

"But you—"

"Arie did."

At that, every eye shifted to me.

"Oh wow, thanks," I said sarcastically. "Nice save."

"Well you *did*, technically," Alaina muttered, eyeing Liam.

"You set Bernard's orchard on fire?" Neil thundered at me, so harshly that I flinched back.

My throat closed up and I suddenly felt sick to my stomach, not even trying to deny my actions.

"Do you realize the consequences?" he raged on. "Thousands of dollars in property damage, not to mention the sentimental value. You should at least turn yourself into the police." He went on and I felt the guilt rising in me like bile.

Erika took my wrist in her hand, as if reassuring me, and I actually calmed a degree. "It was an accident, Neil," she said, the slightest edge of warning in her tone, as if subtly challenging him to yell at me again. "It's all been worked out."

"Hmph." Neil relented, but gave me and Alaina a skeptical glance before walking back into the kitchen.

"You'll grow on him," Mark told us. Alaina swore at him again.

"Language," Mara murmured again, a soft reprimanding.

Liam just looked me up and down, as if seeing me for the first time, and I hated the glint of apprehension in his eyes. "It was really an accident?"

I decided then that I was going to walk out and never come back, since I'd just been branded the freaky arsonist weirdo, but Alaina cut in.

"No, it wasn't, Liam. She set it on fire to save my butt. If she hadn't, then…well..." She trailed off, losing steam and deflating when she realized the trap she set herself in.

Liam just whirled and turned on her. "Then, what, Alaina? What exactly would have happened?"

"Nothing, just—"

"What 'nothing' is bad enough to warrant arson and hands burnt to a crisp, huh?" He turned to me again. "Did you really save her or were you—"

"Liam, back off," Alaina barked. Mark gave a dramatic yawn and Chelsie rolled her eyes at him. "She's my best friend."

The retort was aimed at Alaina, but his gaze was still on me. "Yeah, well I wouldn't know that anymore, would I?"

"Would you *ever* know?" Chelsie muttered.

"Shut up, Chels."

"Yeah," Marked echoed. "Shut up, Chels."

Chelsie glare shot daggers at Mark. "You're such an idiot."

Liam ignored them, shaking his head. "I'm going to murder Lennon one day."

"Get in line," I muttered.

"Everyone just stop." Alaina raked her hands through her hair in a gesture of being overwhelmed and asking for a truce. Then she turned in a circle to give everyone a meaningful look before resting her eyes on Liam, the corner of her mouth pulling up like sharing an inside joke. "Okay, can we start over?"

The question brought a somber stillness over the group, which was a feat since I didn't think they knew how to be that quiet. I didn't know what it meant, but eventually Liam blew out a long breath and chuckled, relaxing, which made Alaina—and me—relax too. Alaina's mouth pulled into a real smile as Liam walked up to me.

"Hi," he said, holding out his hand to me. "I'm Liam."

I raised a wary eyebrow, but shook his hand, careful not to let my burnt palm touch his. "Arie."

"It's nice to meet you, Arie." The line was too heavily rehearsed, and Mark snickered at how ridiculous it all was. Then Liam looked at Erika. "Is this your sister or roommate or what?"

Erika managed to give him a gracious smile and shook his hand. "We've met plenty of times before, but now you can meet me as Arie's roommate. I'm Erika."

"Nice to meet you, Erika."

Mark slid up next to Liam, appearing out of nowhere, and started quizzing me. I tried to give answers as fast as he asked questions.

"Parents?"

"Ran away."

"From?"

"New York."

"Boyfriend?"

"Long time ago."

"Oooh, okay, so there *is* competition." He elbowed Liam. "Might want to make note of that."

I could've sworn Liam's ears turned a shade of pink, but Mark pressed on.

"How'd you meet the Crimson Curse over there?"

Alaina stuck her tongue out at him. I stifled a laugh. "Let's just say we ran into each other and realized we had a lot in common. We stuck."

"So why in Chicago now?"

"Just passing through." I tried to be more nonchalant about it then I actually was. Erika twitched, and I knew she'd bring that back up later.

"Passing through, huh?" He glanced at Erika. "Then why a roommate? Do you just have a house full of transient girls?"

"No. It's me and Erika and another, um, guy, I guess."

"A guy? Yours or hers?"

Now Erika smiled a real smile, genuine affection lighting up her face. "Mine."

Mark gawked at me. "You live with your friend and her boyfriend?" He wrinkled his nose at the prospect. "Now that's gotta be weird."

"You don't know the half of it," Alaina muttered.

Mark continued to drill me, asking things like who my favorite US soccer player was or if I considered black a color. The others used that time to drag out some couches from the back room and settle into themselves, so by the time Mark ran out of steam they were all sitting around like they were home. Of course, once Mark was free, he antagonized Chelsie, and they got into it. Alaina mouthed 'sorry' to me, but I didn't care. It was fun to watch a family interact with each other.

Alaina had told me about her family soon after we decided we were actually friends, not just mutual survivors. She'd grown up with Liam and their mom in Rhode Island, and their dad left when she was eight, which, Alaina had admitted, nobody ever really got over. Shortly after, Mark and Mara, siblings as well as Alaina's cousins, came to live with them after their own parents died. Andrew (I finally remembered his name) and Chelsie had come separately—runaways who happened to run into a mother desperately trying to fill her house with love again. She took them in and they all became a family.

Everything shattered when their mom died. Alaina had gotten in a fight in the schoolyard and landed in the hospital. Crazy enough, Lennon happened to be at that hospital with his first assigned infected. Somehow the formula got mixed up in Alaina's IV, and that set her body off unexplainably while she writhed in pain. The doctors kept her for a few days to try and figure out what the heck happened, but when she woke up fine one day they finally just sent her home, baffled. She and her mom were hit by a drunk driver on the way. Alaina survived, probably because of her newfound durability. Her mom didn't.

Lennon showed up a few days later. His other infected assignment had died, so Alexis had reassigned him to the newbie: Alaina. She had no choice but to run.

Knowing they would likely be separated, Liam took his adopted siblings and skipped town before social services caught up to them, going off to find his father. I was pretty sure Neil wasn't their dad, but I didn't dare ask how that had all gone down.

Erika and I hung out for a few minutes before a flash of blonde made me stiffen. The bratty girl I remembered from the night at the club—the one that had a distaste for me and took a liking to Sark— sauntered in from the front doors like a model down the runway.

I turned to Erika. "We should probably get going," I said, catching Alaina's eye. "Sark's probably freezing in the car."

Alaina must've caught the gist of what I told Erika, because she frowned and opened her mouth, but a sing-song voice cut her off.

"Liam!" Claire gushed with a wave of her hand.

Mark's shoulders slumped and he let out a dramatic groan, and Erika nodded at me. "I think you're right," she whispered back.

Claire had her arms around Liam, who was trying to shrug out of them, when she caught sight of me. Instantly, her eyes narrowed, and I could've sworn her tongue hissed like a viper. "What is that trash doing back here?"

That's my cue.

Ignoring Claire entirely, I waved at the group. "See you guys later."

Alaina traded between looking at me with longing and Claire's hands on Liam with territorial resolve. Finally, she nodded at me and mouthed, "Tomorrow." I nodded back, a promise. Erika and I turned and left through the back room again, but not before I caught Claire acidically saying she was Neil's niece that had been around here *forever*, and Alaina introducing herself as her worst nightmare.

That's a disaster waiting to happen.

"How'd it go?" Sark asked when we got back into the car.

"Good," I said, softly rubbing my cold hands together. "I think."

"They'll all have a lot to work through," Erika added. "It's probably a good thing she chose to stay there with them instead of come back with us."

Sark and I exchanged glances in the rearview mirror, both of us realizing her real meaning, and I had to look away before I laughed.

"Can we take a detour?" I asked once we were in the throes of traffic, ignoring the pit in my stomach. "I want to check on something."

Erika probed me with questioning eyes, but Sark didn't hesitate. "Sure."

I only had my hazy memory to work with, so it ended up being a much longer detour than I'd planned on, but eventually we found it. A somber silence hung over the car once they realized where we were, and it was quiet except for the blowing of the heater. The pit in my stomach filled with acid as I took in the orchard.

At least, what was *left* of it.

The snowy field was littered with charred stumped and blackened branches, a graveyard of the beautiful orchard it once was. It seemed there was a pocket of trees toward the back that might have escaped unscathed, but it was too far away for me to tell how much had survived. A group of workers were loading burnt branches into the back of big trucks while an older gentleman looked on. Even though I couldn't really see his face, I could sense his grief.

"Okay." My voice was rough with the acidic guilt that was crawling up my throat. I turned around to look out the other window, unable to watch the cleanup anymore. "That's all." Then we drove off without a word for the rest of the ride home.

15

The next morning, I got up and dressed, a slight skip in my step as I made my way to the kitchen. Predictably, I found Sark reading the newspaper while drinking coffee and Erika already working on breakfast.

"Someone's in a good mood," Erika commented when I walked in. "Finally find the right side of the bed?"

I rolled my eyes, but I couldn't bring myself to actually be annoyed. "I have plans today and none of them include blood, guts, or monster dogs. So, yes, I'm in a good mood." Sliding into the chair next to Sark, I pulled the comic section out of the newspaper. He swatted my hand away without looking up.

"Yeah, about that…" Erika started. Her tone made me pause before diving into the comic strips, and she waited until I met her gaze. "I don't know if that's a good idea."

Sark took a breath as if to prepare himself for something, still not breaking from the newspaper. Erika twirled the wooden spoon she was holding in her hand, trying to look nonchalant and authoritative at the same time, which only irritated me more.

Pick a side.

"Is it because you don't like them?" I demanded. "Because that's just dumb."

She pulled back like she was actually shocked. I was getting good at figuring out when she was faking it. "Why would I not like them?"

"Oh please, you didn't say a word last night except to Neil. If your mouth isn't going a thousand miles a minute then something is wrong."

"First of all, rude." The wooden spoon made another arc. "Second of all, I don't like the idea of you leaving—for *any* reason with *any*one. Bad things just always happen, and I don't think any of us want to do it all again."

That stung a little, for reasons I couldn't explain. I tried to bury the feeling. "I know, but I'll just be with Alaina and—"

Erika's eyes flashed with disdain at Alaina's name. "Yeah and look what happened last time."

My eyes narrowed. That wasn't fair, and she knew it. "It wasn't her fault."

"I didn't say it was. I'm just saying it's a bad idea and I want you to stay here."

I was shaking my head before she was finished. This sounded way too familiar. Suddenly I felt like I was in my kitchen at my house, arguing with my mom over her disapproval regarding my choice in boyfriend. Except this was *so* different.

"No offense," I said with a tone that totally meant offense, "but you aren't my mom. You can't boss me around one second and then want to be my best friend like we're roommates or something. If I want to go, then—"

"I know you *want* to go, but—"

"I don't have a problem with it," Sark piped up while still reading.

Both of us turned to stare at him. He finished reading his paragraph, the silence forcing us to realize how stupid our arguments were.

"What?" Erika finally demanded, as if challenging him to repeat himself.

Calmly—a little *too* calmly, actually. He knew what he was doing—Sark folded up the newspaper and gave us his attention. "I don't have a problem with Arie going out today. I think it's a good idea for her to spend time with Alaina and her family."

I grinned triumphantly. Erika's mouth fell open in raging disbelief.

"She has no way to get there," she argued.

"I'll drive her." Sark went on before she could, standing up to rinse out his coffee mug. "It might be nice to have Arie out of the house anyway."

I swelled with victory, then my forehead creased and I realized I must've heard him wrong. Sark reached the sink just as I put it together and he smirked at me. Erika rolled her eyes, still mad, but a smile was unwillingly growing on her face.

"Ew." I shook my head, ridding my mind of what they'd be up to when I left. Suddenly I felt like skipping breakfast. "I did not need to know that."

Sark deposited his mug in the sink, then reached out and snaked his arms around Erika, pulling her toward him.

I made a gagging expression and stood up. "I'm driving myself. See ya."

"You wish," Sark called back, holding up the keys in his hand like he somehow knew it would all pan out this way. With a glare, I beelined it to the garage, snatching my shoes and coat on the way, just as he planted his mouth on Erika's.

Arrogant, disgusting know-it-all.

Once in the garage, I gave a dramatic sigh at nobody and got in the passenger side of Sark's car. Sliding on my coat, I put my shoes on and sat back in the seat. It was freezing out here. Each breath fogged up the windshield, and I tapped my fingers impatiently against the middle console.

Finally, Sark came out, eyes bright and cheeks colored. It was an effort to not throw up.

"You're welcome," he said as he slid into the car and turned it on.

I rolled my eyes. "Yeah, it looked like it was real tough for you."

He shot me a smirk as he turned his head to back out. "Someone has to make the sacrifices."

"I feel like I'm living with two majorly overprotective parents."

"Yes, well I feel like I unwittingly adopted a seventeen-year-old pain in the neck."

Folding my arms across my chest, I rolled my eyes again. "I don't think I'm meant to be parented."

Runaway infecteds aren't really prime children material.

Sark just shrugged. "I don't think I'm meant to be a parent period, but here we are."

I snorted. "What's my curfew?"

The corners of Sark's mouth pulled up. "As long as you don't come home bloody or with some riffraff, I don't really care."

"Riffraff?" I raised an eyebrow. "No hooking up for me, then, huh?"

"A good parent would say no, wouldn't they?"

"I'll have to resort to drugs for my high."

"I can run a blood test."

"Underage drinking?"

Sark shot me another smirk. "Would it be hypocritical or parental wisdom for me to say no?"

"Wow," I said, words laced with sarcasm. "I can't have any fun, now can I?"

Now he rolled his eyes. "Yes, because we all know your reputation as a partier, and this will really put you out."

I turned my head to look out the window so he wouldn't see me smile.

When Sark pulled up to the club, he gave me a slip of paper. I glanced down to see a phone number was written on it.

"If anyone offers you drugs," he told me, a half joking grin still on his face, "then call me. I don't care how long you stay, but know Erika will come break down the door at some point. I'll hold her off as long as I can."

I stuffed the paper in my pocket. "Again, I really don't need that imagery."

His expression didn't change, but something shifted in his eyes, and now they were too serious for his faint, teasing smile. "If you get tired of trying to make new friends, you can call me too. I'll come if you need anything." The tone of his voice dropped just a little, placing the slightest emphasis on the last word. I knew he meant it.

I gave him a real, grateful smile. "Thanks for the ride."

"You're welcome."

Unsure what to do, I ended up just going through the club's front doors, ignoring the sense of déjà vu I felt. Everything had turned on its head since the last time I'd opened these doors. I didn't have time to dwell on that prickly thought before someone shouted my name and a ball of crimson flung itself at me.

"You came!" Alaina squealed like a little girl, squishing me in a hug.

"Of course I did!" Then I lowered my voice. "How's it going?"

"It's…" She stepped away from me, thoughtful. "It's okay. It's going to be a long road. But we're back on the road."

I smiled at her. "Good."

Obviously, I'd come to visit Alaina, and my gut knotted when I thought about seeing anyone else. Of course, they *lived* there, so it was only a matter of fifteen seconds before I ran into her pack of siblings. I braced myself for the onslaught, for the initiation, for the territorial fights over whether I was allowed to be their sister's best friend.

"Hey, Arie," Chelsie called as she and Mara bounced up to me, her dark skin color a deep contrast from Mara's. They each held up two paint samples. "Which one?"

I picked a color. And just like that, they welcomed me in like I'd belonged there my whole life. Neil was still skeptical and didn't say much to me, but everyone else acted like I was just one of the crew. I could hardly believe it.

I spent every day that whole week at the club, going over after breakfast and leaving just before they opened for the evening. We just hung out, doing nothing but everything at the same time, and I was barraged with questions—usually from Mark—and I dodged them as best as I could with my own about them. Over the week, I learned more about Alaina's family.

Liam came to Chicago to try and find his dad, the only hope of survival they had after their mom died. They found him, but it wasn't the movie moment Liam had always hoped for. Their dad was nice, interested to see them, and saddened by the news of his ex-wife's passing, but wasn't eager to play dad again—that was part of the reason he'd left in the first place. Instead, he put them in the care of his good friend Neil, who needed cheap labor to keep his club afloat, with enough money to support them for years. It killed Liam to see his dad go again, and Mara told Alaina he hadn't been himself since.

Mark and Mara were actually twins: Mark was born seven minutes earlier, a fact that he never let her forget. They both had the same jet-black hair, but Mark's carefree mess didn't match the tight bun on the top of Mara's head. Mark was into sports, mostly soccer, and had the tan to prove it; but Mara was pasty white, a great contrast from her dark hair, and would rather sit inside. They were the only ones in the group who were actually related to Alaina (their moms had been sisters) and they moved in with them right before Alaina's dad left.

Chelsie was a runaway from New Hampshire and was completely devoted to her art. Her clothes were stained with splotches of paint and chalk as she was constantly working on a new project, using the medium to speak her mind. At first I thought she wasn't going to talk but I was soon proven wrong. She had the biggest mouth of all of them, jabbering to anyone who would listen and anyone who wouldn't. Mark informed me that everyone ignores her anyway so she wouldn't feel bad if I did too. Chelsie responded by throwing an empty can of paint at him.

Andrew always had his headphones on. Whether they were over his ears or around his neck, some sort of sound was always following him. He definitely talked the least out of all of them, but he wasn't quiet either. When he wasn't busy trying to write a new melody then he was kicking a ball around with Mark or cleaning the instruments with Liam. Music was his life and he didn't talk about much else, so of course it was just a matter of time before my first visit to the club was brought up.

Alaina and I were playing cards on the couch. Chelsie was touching up the paint on the stage, talking Andrew's ear off as he sat next to her, strumming a guitar. Liam was going through a bunch of equipment and instruments scattered around the space, bugging Mark to help him, while Mara kneaded bread dough. Mark wandered around, bored but not wanting to work. After an hour of annoying Mara, he made his way over to me and Alaina.

"So," Mark began, plopping next to me on the couch, "I recall you saying something about playing a guitar the first night we met you. True or false?"

I started to shake my head, but Alaina cut me off. "She's amazing."

"What?" Liam asked from his seat on a box speaker, a wounded expression on his face. "You told me you *used* to play."

Alaina smirked at me. "Liar."

"I'm not—" I started.

"We don't lie about music, Arie," Mark told me.

"Yeah," Chelsie called from the stage. "If you play at all then you have to play with us."

Mara perked up. "We should do a show with Arie and Alaina this weekend."

"Everyone's sick of Claire anyway," Mark added.

"Whoa, slow down." I leaned forward in my seat on the maroon couch. "No shows for me."

"Oh, come on." Mark batted his eyelashes at me in an overly creepy way. "Pretty please?"

I flicked a card in his face. "Nope. I don't do crowds."

"You can't intimidate talent," Chelsie scoffed, waving a paintbrush in the air.

Alaina put her stack of cards down on the table. "We haven't sung together in forever."

"I know," Liam and I said at the same time, then glanced at each other before looking away. Neither of us wanted to ask who Alaina had actually been talking to, and she didn't offer the information up.

Mark tipped his head back, trying to balance the card on his nose. "I say we book her anyway. See if the Crimson Curse can still spot talent."

I opened my mouth to protest, but was saved by Neil of all people. He came through the front doors with a covered catering tray. "Look who brought us lunch." I barely managed to contain my surprise when Erika waltzed in the door carrying a bag, and Sark entered behind her with two more catering trays.

Erika beamed at the group, apparently taking on the role of favorite mom now. "I hope you all like pasta." I raised an eyebrow, but Sark just shrugged at me, and Alaina gave Erika a thumbs up—something positive for once. Erika smiled back and she, Sark, and Neil started setting up the food on the bar while Mara thanked them.

Mark glanced from the food to me. "I'll play you for lunch."

At first I thought he meant a card game, but then I realized he was looking at two of the guitars set up by Liam. My hesitation lulled in the air, nerves making my fingers tingle at even the thought of touching a guitar again period, let alone in front of all these people.

"Oh, I get it. Can't keep up." Mark puffed his chest out in bravado. "I realize it's intimidating, being in the same room as me. The prospect of *playing* is probably too much to bear."

I rolled my eyes. He was baiting me, I knew that, but man I wanted to wipe that smirk off his face.

Alaina was not amused either. "Put him in his place, Arie, or I will."

Mark picked up a guitar and ducked his head underneath the strap, then brushed the strings fondly. "Yeah, well, I guess we all know girls can't play guitar anyway, so never mind."

My eyebrows shot up. Alaina and Chelsie both barked a curse at him—the same word at the same time, which was kind of impressive—and Mara rolled her eyes.

"Fine." I picked up a guitar and secured the strap on my shoulder, then jerked my chin out at him. "Let's test that theory."

They all went 'oooooh' at the same time, which made Alaina cackle and sprawl back on the couch. "I've missed you dorks."

"Okay, then," Mark said, standing toe to toe with me. "See if you can keep up."

"I'll do my best," I retorted.

"I'll go easy on you."

"Please don't."

He started with a basic chord. I scoffed and played it back. He went with a simple combination. I copied it. He sent a harder one at me. I pretended to yawn and duplicated it with ease, ignoring the slight sting of my healing hands.

Andrew whistled and Chelsie aimed a devious grin at Mark. "Now this just got interesting."

We went back and forth for several minutes. Eventually Mark's face twisted with concentration, but I made sure mine remained passive, like nothing he sent my way even fazed me. After I perfectly copied a complicated riff, everyone cheered for me, and Mark gritted his teeth.

"Okay, hot shot," he said, adjusting a string on his guitar before leaning down to grab a pick off the speaker. "Let's see how you handle this." Then he launched into a song, fingers flying through the complex chords to keep up with the quick tempo. He sang along with it too, his voice lower than I expected, and I was surprised to find he wasn't bad.

The best, though, was the surprise on *his* face when he finished the first verse and I picked up the second with ease, singing the words I'd learned in high school. He hadn't expected me to know it, and I smirked at his disbelief as my fingers flew just as his did.

Chelsie and Alaina whooped while Mara clapped her hands in excitement. Faces alight with animation, Andrew slid behind his drums and picked up the beat, while Liam plucked on his guitar and the girls followed with percussion. By the time I hit the chorus, the song was fully alive, and Mark and I sang the words as if aiming them at each other.

Caught up in the exhilaration of the music, I didn't really realize what I was doing until we hit the bridge. I got embarrassed and my voice went quiet. I managed to keep playing, though, and Chelsie took the harmonies for me. The song built and built, the melody thrumming through my veins and pulsing in my heart, and when we hit the last run of the chorus, everyone belted out the lyrics together.

It was *amazing*.

I couldn't remember the last time I felt so relaxed, so lost in the comfort and music, and so myself, especially in front of people I'd just met but somehow called my friends.

The song ended, Mark and I both breathing heavily. His siblings all laughed and slapped each other on the back, while Erika burst into rounds of cheers and applause, and Neil gave me a new look of half skepticism, half appreciation. I was still an arsonist, but at least I could sing.

Mark took the loss with grace. "You're all right, Arie." He did some hybrid clap-handshake thing with my hand and grinned at me. "Welcome to the club."

16

I thought Erika had reached a limit on what she could possibly surprise me with, but I found I was wrong. She did it again.

She apologized.

"I'm sorry," she said as she stood before me in the kitchen, wringing her hands while her eyes jumped all over. The words made me go rigid, but her nervous nature sent my insides buzzing.

"For wha—" I started, but she jumped right in and cut me off.

"I'm sorry I was so overprotective and tried to keep you from going to Alaina's. That was wrong and I shouldn't have been such a pain."

I blinked. "Oh."

"I just...care, I guess. A lot. More than I thought I ever would. After seeing you go through so much...I panic at the thought of anything else." She gave me a sheepish grin. "And I thought maybe...I don't know, maybe Alaina would convince you to run away. And that would...I would just be devastated. I would miss you so much. And I'd be sick at the thought of you alone and cold and hungry—not to mention what could happen if Lennon or somebody like that found you."

I tried to keep my face passive, hoping she wouldn't realize exactly how many times I'd wondered about taking off from the club.

Erika smoothed out her shirt. "Like you said, I'm not your mom and I swear I'm not trying to be. You deserve a life and freedom, and I shouldn't keep you from that. I'm really sorry. I'll try to tone it down, okay? Are you, um, are you going over there today?"

"No," I answered. "Liam is taking her on a walk around the city. They invited me but I think they need some time to themselves."

"Oh okay." She wrung her hands again. "Do you...are we okay?"

I couldn't help the half smile that stretched across my face. It was oddly cute to watch her be so nervous and flustered over my feelings. "We're okay."

She beamed. "Oh good." Then she surprised me by giving me a hasty but sincere hug, pulling away before I could really react. "I just love you."

I blinked in surprise again, but she mentioned something about washing her favorite shirt and vanished into the hallway before I could ask her my real questions—beginning with why we were both here in the first place.

Shaking my head at the encounter, I wandered into the living room where Sark was sitting in his chair on his laptop, per usual lately, hoping he'd break for a second so I could talk to him. I had been nervous when he and Erika had shown up with lunch at the club yesterday, knowing it was Erika's plan and unsure how Sark would handle such a normal situation. But he'd done great. He was still quiet, but he wasn't mean or scary, and even talked to the boys about cars.

He was good at faking normal, which made sense considering the last years of his life depended on him fitting in with those around him. But I wasn't looking for him so we could discuss social chameleon skills—I wanted to ask him about something I'd overheard Neil say in passing the day before.

Engrossed in his computer, he didn't acknowledge me when I climbed over the back of the couch and sat down. After a few minutes passed I considered throwing a pillow at him just to see if he would react, but he spoke when I reached for the closest one to me.

"No plans for the day, then?"

I sat back against the couch, abandoning my pillow plan. "No, but I'm kind of glad. It's nice to stay here for a day."

"Hm." The noncommittal sound let me know how little he was paying attention. Maybe I'd be able to catch him off guard.

Feigning nonchalance, I stretched my legs out on the coffee table. "Yesterday was fun."

He didn't even look up. "Mhm."

"Neil was kind of talking to us." He still didn't like me much, but he was trying to force himself to tolerate Alaina, since she was Liam's sister.

"Has he shaken off any of his pious distaste for you yet?"

I shrugged. "I don't know. Maybe a little. He brought up Bernard's orchard again yesterday."

Sark's eyes still hadn't moved from the screen. I hadn't even seen him blink. "Hm."

"Yeah, but he was happier than usual. He said someone gave Bernard a ton of money for rebuilding the orchard. Anonymous donation."

I waited for him to be surprised that I figured it out or take credit or give me a sly smirk. Nothing. I could've sworn his shoulders went kind of rigid but I could've been making it up.

Sark gave nothing away. He just typed something and said, "Lucky for him."

"It was you," I blurted. "I know it was."

He laughed once, and it was powerful enough that I doubted my conviction. "Really? And why would you say that?"

"Just..." I felt unbearably stupid now. "Just a feeling."

"It's too bad I'm not as noble as your intuition would suggest."

Narrowing my eyes, I stared at him, as though if I looked hard enough I would find evidence I was right. Why had I been so certain?

Sark must've felt my stare because he finally glanced up from his computer to look at me. I wasn't sure how he read my expression, but it wasn't right because he frowned and drew back slightly, like I'd tried to slap him.

I should've said something nice and reassuring, but instead I asked, "Why did you do it?"

He watched me for a moment longer than normal in conversation, and I noticed the slightest shift in his eyes—I was getting better at reading new Sark's emotions, especially considering it used to just be anger, hatred, or arrogant indifference.

His tone stayed light, as if discussing the weather, but I could sense the deeper meaning. "I'm never going to pretend I can make up for what has happened, Arie, and I'm never going to ask your forgiveness. You will never owe me anything, no matter what charitable causes might be taken up in your name."

It took me a few seconds to recover from such a packed statement delivered so casually. I brushed my hair behind my ear, twirling the end of it around my finger. "Erika...she said she was afraid I'd use going to the club to run. You let me go anyway. Why?" My stomach knotted at the thought that he'd somehow known I'd come back.

Sark leaned back in his chair, computer now forgotten and all attention on me. "I wouldn't blame you if you don't feel safe here anymore—if you ever did at all. With Felix and Lennon...I've always known it was a possibility. When you don't feel safe, you run. It's very understandable."

"Then why keep me here?"

"Have you checked the doors lately?"

I blinked. It never occurred to me to check. I just assumed they were all still locked.

I'm not a prisoner anymore? I took a shaky breath. *I'm not a prisoner anymore.*

A million thoughts spun in my head, and for a second I thought I'd get too dizzy and collapse before I remembered I was already sitting down. I was sitting down, here, on Sark's couch, and I should not have been.

I should be gone. I hated the true meaning behind that conviction, the glaring insecurity that I shouldn't have this, that I didn't deserve it, that I should do everyone a favor by leaving.

Now Sark's eyes narrowed as though he could hear my thoughts and was glaring them down. "You'll always have a place here if you want it, for however long you need. Don't worry about that. Ever."

"I'm a lot to deal with." I thought of what had happened to me just since I'd been here. How many tears had Erika shed over me? How much of his medical supply stash did Sark have to use on my injuries? How long would it be before what I was grew bigger than what I could contain and hurt them?

He shrugged. "Maybe. But I don't have much else to do, now do I?"

This conversation and all its implications—like the fact I was more scared of leaving this house than staying, or that I didn't know what would happen if

Alexis called on Sark, or that I was afraid that all my secrets would somehow end up hurting these people who'd locked me up in the first place—it was all freaking me out. So I changed the subject.

"Seems like you do." I nodded at his computer. "You're on that thing all the time now. I didn't realize you were such a computer game junkie."

My attempt at smoothing things over wasn't very successful, but Sark went with it anyway, probably wanting all the serious stuff gone too. He gave a small smile and relaxed slightly. "My work is much more than a computer game, thank you."

Instantly my blood went cold and the air was sharper, thicker, and harder to breathe. I could hear the silence between us like static, shocking us both.

Sark quickly tried to backpedal, but it was too late. "It's not what you're thinking. It's...other work."

I raised an eyebrow. "Other work? What, you're a skin care product salesman on the side?"

"No, I'm…" He sighed and ran a hand through his hair, deflating. "It's too much to hope I can talk my way out of this, isn't it?"

The revelation shouldn't have stung so much, and I hated myself for being shocked and hurt. Balling my fists to keep my hands from shaking, I shifted in my seat, prepared to jump over the couch and get out of here before Sark got any more 'work' done.

"Arie." Sark's expression was torn between indifference and desperation, as if he couldn't decide if letting me go was easier than trying to win me back. "I swear, it's not what it seems. You don't—"

"Then prove it." I hated that my voice was small and trembling. Gritting my teeth, I jerked my chin at his computer. "Show me."

Sark just pursed his lips. To my horror, my breath caught and I suddenly felt like I was going to cry.

You're an idiot, Arie Nolan. Seriously, what had I expected? *You're stupid and you're leaving now.*

I brought my legs up, ready to go, when Sark sighed and rested his forehead in his hand. He looked tired.

"Philo Castor designed the formula hundreds of years ago in an attempt to create the perfect human." The words were slow and heavy, as if they were a weight for him to carry now rather than his life work. "The average human doesn't use their potential ability. The formula was created to change that. Many people view Castor as some kind of religious prophet or leader of the supernatural, but anyone with sense can see it's purely science."

Then Sark paused and looked up at me, as if seeking permission to go on. I remained perched on the couch, knees to my chest, ready to bolt any second. Cautiously, I tipped my head.

"I've always hated biology," I muttered, nearly accusing.

Movements dense, Sark closed his laptop and placed it on the coffee table before easing back. "Think of it like a switch. Imagine every human has three switches. The general population has one switch flipped on, with typical mental and physical capabilities. As an infected, you have two switches on. In Castor's vision, everyone had all three. As you are aware, the formula is incomplete, which is why you are stuck in between average and supposed perfection."

In another world I would've shot off some sarcastic line in response, but paranoia was still pulsing in my blood. I just stared at him until he ran his fingers through his hair and kept going.

"Of course, we aren't entirely sure what that perfection entails. Physical and mental capabilities would be markedly superior, but it wouldn't equate to what some people consider superhuman or a paranormal. There are also notes regarding a severe reduction in emotional aptitude, meaning they'd be unable to feel or experience emotions any longer. Castor believed emotions help ruin humanity and stand as our greatest flaw."

"That's ridiculous," I said just because I needed something to say. "Emotions make us human."

He cocked his head to the side, appraising me. "Yet often your fear and panic are the things that ruin your ability to escape, right? Just like your emotional attachment to Alaina caused you to put yourself in harm's way in order to save her."

I didn't have a response for that, so I just shrugged.

"Granted, giving up your emotional palette can be a high price to pay for strength, but Lennon and I always wondered if there some way to control it: if you could go back and forth between yourself and a stronger, unemotional, formula-influenced self." One side of his mouth pulled up. "Of course, we never pursued it for fear you would figure out how to use it to your advantage. We weren't about to help you."

Despite the situation I actually laughed once. "*You* were afraid of *us*?"

His grin grew slightly, like I was missing a punch line to a joke. "Alexis has most of the infected world in the palm of his hand. Many infecteds are caught once by him and remain enslaved until they die. They just give up.

"And then there are the ones that became very good at fighting back, like you and Alaina. You may find it hard to believe, but that influence has spread. Lennon and I have been afraid for a long time that you would all band together and figure out how to use the formula in a way to completely beat us."

I imagined going up against Felix being an all-powerful infected ninja. I couldn't say I wouldn't enjoy it.

Sark sighed again, tipping his head back against the chair and looking at the ceiling now. "You know the formula is broken. It always has been. Supposedly a key exists somewhere—a key to fixing the formula. Finding that key is the essential objective of Alexis' organization."

Any wonder or satisfaction I'd found quickly evaporated into frigid panic. Having the sensitive subject out in the open made me feel like there was a knife in my ribs. I took a painful breath, hoping Sark took the anxiety in my expression as apprehension for this conversation in general.

"I've never understood why Alexis thinks the key is a person," I lied, like it was that easy to just throw everyone off track.

"Castor said it was," Sark responded. "A type of biological code. Apparently something in that code would give the key to fixing the formula." He shrugged. "Alexis likes to pretend he's got a firm agenda, but he truly wouldn't know what to do with the key if he found it."

I internally flinched at the word 'it' but kept it up. "So it's safe."

"Not necessarily. He'll find it. After that, there are many possibilities. Alexis likes the idea of an army. I've heard of others that want to infect everyone, since a minimal amount of people actually survive the infection process in the first place, as a type of evolutionist vision. Some just want it for themselves."

My bones felt like lead, my muscles glass, as bile rose in my throat. "Oh."

Sark closed his eyes and rubbed his forehead. "Regardless of motive, that power shouldn't be given to anyone, least of all someone as ruthless as Alexis."

I couldn't help it. I forced most (but unfortunately not all) desperation from my voice. "Is he close to finding the key?"

"It's difficult to say."

"How would he know who the key is?"

"I'd imagine the key would be no noticeably different than you and me, though Castor did say they'd be marked somehow. That's why Alexis believes the key needs to be infected in order to be found."

My throat closed up, and I was too afraid that if this conversation kept up I'd slip and he'd find me out. I did my best to sound annoyed. "Okay so what do switches have to do with what you're doing?"

Sark sighed again, lifting his head and opening his eyes. "With the biomechanics of it all, and—"

"English, Sark."

"I want to know if it truly is a switch." Conflict struck his features, and suddenly he tripped over his words, fidgeting with what I thought was nerves. "If...if we were able to switch it on through the formula...there could—there *might*—possibly...be a way to...to switch it...off."

I curled inward like I'd been punched in the gut, the blow of the revelation leaving me breathless. "You...you mean…"

Sark winced, as if the blow had left me a bloody mess and it was difficult for him to look at. "Reversing the formula."

"That's possible?" My mouth dropped open and closed again. I'd never even considered that, didn't know it was an option. It was too good to be true. "How?"

"I don't know. I really don't." His tone was mournful but careful, and he held up his hands in an apologetic gesture. "Arie, please don't look at me like that. I don't know. I didn't want to tell you until I was certain."

Suddenly the air was too warm and the leather couch was too hard, and I steadied my hands underneath me because it felt like the world was going to turn on its side. "Why?"

"Because," he answered, his face clouding over, "false hope is such a cruel way to kill a person."

"But I'm…" My heart started hammering in my chest, my mind filling with ideas and answers and so many questions. I leaned forward so far I nearly fell off the couch. "I need to know. I need to find it."

"I don't know if it exists."

I barely heard him. My mind was racing faster than I could keep up, trying to understand all the implications of this idea. Reversal. If we found reversal we could reverse everyone, free infecteds everywhere. I could be reversed. I could escape the key, escape the future that I'd be the one to help Alexis take the world for himself.

I wouldn't be the key anymore. Even the thought caused joyful tears to sting my eyes.

Would it work on me though? If I was the key, was there something inherent in me that would keep me from being reversed? I sucked in a sharp breath. It seemed overly optimistic to think there could really be a way to reverse me—the one thing that could make the formula permanent and whole.

It had to work. I would *make* it work.

I can be free.

I snapped back to reality like the crack of a rubber band, suddenly back on the couch in the living room, with Sark's anxious eyes on me. He was leaning forward with one arm half outstretched, as if he thought he might need to catch me.

Then another blow struck me across the face: Sark was researching reversal.

Sark.

Sark.

Embarrassed I'd made such a scene about everything, I rubbed the back of my neck and stammered, "Can...I can help. I don't...I mean I don't know very much, but..." I took a shuddering breath. "Please."

Sark pursed his lips and watched me, and I could see the debate playing out as he worked his jaw. I opened my mouth, then shut it, wondering if I should plead my case or not. I could do research on my own, but I wouldn't get nearly as far without his help.

He exhaled and nodded. "Start downstairs in the office. Once you get through that, we can go from there."

I crumpled with relief. "Thank you." Scrambling to my feet, I was over the couch and at the basement stairs before his voice stopped me.

"Arie."

I peeked back around the corner to see Sark rubbing his forehead again, then his piercing blue eyes met mine.

"Please be careful," he said. "All this...it's a rabbit hole. People get lost and they don't come back out, as you saw with your father. Please, just...be careful."

I nodded. "I will."

He watched me a second longer before waving his hand in dismissal, and I disappeared down into the basement.

17

Sark's office was a cavity of information overload. While meticulously organized to the point I was almost afraid to breathe on anything, the files were dense and difficult for me to understand. Trying to wrap my head around even the simple concepts gave me a headache. The hours went by quickly, and I got increasingly frustrated at my inability to just catch on. How was Sark able to keep up?

I made a pile of things to ask Sark about later, since I didn't want to keep going up and down the stairs, and I thought staying in the office without distractions would increase my productivity. Eventually, the 'questions' pile turned into two piles, and the cushy chair got old. I switched to sprawling out on the floor on my stomach, my eyeballs roaming over intricate diagrams and big words, trying to absorb any bit of information possible.

Suddenly, a door slammed, making me jump. I glanced up to see Erika stumbling through the library, and she stopped in the office doorway, her face stricken with fear.

"Erika?" I asked, lurching to my feet. "What's wrong?"

She flinched at my voice, and when she saw me her eyes widened in terror. My gut tightened at her expression—what was happening?

Her mouth opened, but no sound came out, and she stumbled backward, tripping over her own feet. I darted forward and caught her by her arm before she fell. The contact scalded my hand. I yelped and jerked away; Erika screamed and collapsed to the ground.

I looked at my palm, expecting to find the scabs from my burns back, and my own scream sounded when I saw it was blue. The color shot up my arm, painting the same pattern that enveloped me when my dad first injected the formula in me—the pattern that marked me as the key.

"Erika!" I cried, wanting to help her but unsure how. I fell to my knees next to her, and my heart leapt in my throat. She was convulsing, the blue vines taking ahold of her too. "Erika? Erika!"

I leaned away from her, holding my hand to my chest as my eyes filled with tears.

What have I done?

Then all at once she stopped moving. An eerie silence slammed in my ears, a harsh contrast from her agonized shrieks.

"Erika?" I whispered hesitantly. "Erika, please wake up."

I breathed a sigh of relief when she stirred. Slowly, she started pushing herself up on her elbows, and I tried to support her with my eyes, afraid of touching her again. Then she lifted her head, black curls framing her cheeks, and a choking sound ripped its way up my throat as I jerked away from her.

Her face was gone.

Her body, clothes, hair were all the same, but her eyes, nose, and mouth were gone. Just a blank slate of skin.

I scrambled back, colliding with another body. The second I touched them, they collapsed to the ground and screamed, just as Erika had. Suddenly a crowd of strangers engulfed me, each of them running from the new things I created. I kept getting shoved around, and every time I touched someone they turned into a faceless zombie bent on tearing me to shreds.

Horrified, I clawed at my hands and arms, desperately trying to tear the blue from my skin to keep it from spreading. The bodies kept building and building until I was pinned down in darkness, using the last of my air to scream.

My eyes snapped open. I was back in the office, a mess of papers and file folders around me, and I couldn't move. The zombies were gone, and Erika was kneeling on the ground in front of me—not blue and with a face, which was streaked with tears.

"I'm sorry!" I blurted, a sob bursting from my chest. "I'm sorry, I'm sorry, I didn't mean to! It's my fault! I didn't...I swear, I..." I broke off into sobs, trying to wrench myself away, which was when I realized Sark was behind me, pinning me against him. One hand was at my neck, holding my head against his shoulder, while his other arm was wrapped around my waist and securing my left wrist. My right arm had a bloody scratch that stretched from my elbow to my palm, and I had a pair of scissors clutched in my left fist.

"Drop them," Sark said, a quiet yet strained order in my ear. "Drop them right now."

Hysteria bubbled on my lips as I squirmed. "No! I have to get it off! I have to—it's my fault! I didn't mean to! I never wanted to!" When I couldn't worm myself free, panic seized my chest, and my sobs broke off into wheezes. My head got dizzy and my palms were slick with sweat. Hands trembling, I dropped the scissors, and Sark let go of my head. My shoulders slumped forward, shuddering with my airless gasps.

"Breathe, Arie." Sark's voice was still soft, but the urgency was gone. He kept a hold on my injured wrist, but put his other hand on my shoulder, trying to steady me. "It's okay. Breathe. You're awake now. Deep breaths."

I got enough air in me to cry again. The tears started streaming down my cheeks as violent sobs tore at my throat, and Sark wrapped his arm around me. I collapsed back into his chest, burying my face in his shirt as I bawled.

"You're okay." He stroked my hair softly, which calmed me a degree. "You're okay."

The steadiness of Sark against my shaking body helped ground me, and I felt secure enough to start working through what had happened: a dream. A terrible, cruel dream.

It wasn't real. It wasn't real. It wasn't real.

It wasn't real, the scared little girl inside me cried. *But it could be.*

When my sobs had tapered off to heavy gasping, Sark stretched out my arm to look at it, and I peeked out from hiding in his shoulder. Blood had mixed with tears and smeared all over my skin, so it was difficult to tell how big the injury actually was. I couldn't see Sark's face, but Erika was withdrawn in silent horror, bug eyes going from my arm and the stained scissors on the carpet. Sark gently probed the spot by my elbow; he made a small sound of disapproval when more blood oozed.

They were worried about me. They were worried about me when they should've been afraid of me. I was the problem, the monster, not a point of their concern.

I need to get away from them.

The realization sobered me right up. This was *the* secret, and here I was, parading it around with a bunch of tears and snot for all the world to see.

With a shuddering breath, I pushed myself to my feet, hating how alone and fragile I felt without Sark's arm around me. The files I'd been looking at were strewn out everywhere—so much for keeping his organizational system—but I managed to lean down and pick out the one I'd been most interested in before I slipped into insanity. I remained standing when I handed it to Sark, who was still on the floor, because it gave me the illusion of control.

"Who is he?" I asked, wiping rogue tears off my face.

Sark looked at me for a few seconds, the concern draining out of his expression and something harsh and dense slowly taking its place. After a moment, he took the file from me. My teeth snapped together when he just set it back on the floor.

I voiced the question again, biting like an animal. "Who is he?"

Sark closed his eyes and shook his head slowly, weary lines hollowing his face as he let out a long breath. "I don't think this is a good idea anymore."

My hands balled into fists. "Just tell me."

"Arie—"

"Now."

There were several beats of silence, and I nearly pulled my own hair out. Erika gave me a soft warning glance, but I ignored it, glaring at Sark like my eyes could draw the information out of him.

"It's Stephen White," Sark finally answered. He sounded exhausted. "He was the leading research specialist for Alexis."

"Was?"

"White is dead."

"Alexis killed him?"

"Yes."

"Why?"

"Because...because White was...conducting reversal experiments."

"Did they ever work?"

"Arie." Sark flinched, like saying my name actually hurt him. When he opened his eyes and looked back up at me, they were empty and cold, but not hateful—more haunted. "This is wrong."

"Well of course it's *wrong*," I snapped. "This whole thing is majorly messed up."

He ignored me. "This is too much. You need to separate yourself from the situation until you can—"

I pulled on the ends of my hair in frustration. "That's what I'm trying to do! This situation is my *life* and I can't just leave it alone no matter 'how much' it is. I'm sticking with this until I find answers."

Sark just looked me up and down, as if seeing me for the first time, before stopping to rest on my eyes. "No."

"No?" My eyebrows shot up. "What is your problem?"

Now Sark got to his feet, and though I came past his shoulder, I felt smaller at the sudden anger chipping the creases on his face. "My *problem* is that you've been down here for the better part of one day—one day—and I find you screaming and bleeding."

"That's not—"

"My *problem*, Arie," he went on, gaining steam, "is that you obviously can't handle this, and I'm not going to let you push yourself past the limit."

"You don't get to make that decision for me!" I shouted at him. "Nobody does!"

His eyes flashed and he squared his jaw, shutting me down. "I just did." Then he glanced around the room, his lip curling like he was suddenly disgusted with the place, and ran a hand through his hair. "Be gone by the time I get back."

My mouth hung open as he turned and nearly stomped up the stairs. I heard the garage door slam shut, and I winced. How had things derailed so fast?

In a daze, I opened a desk drawer and pulled out a roll of gauze, haphazardly wrapping it over my arm so I didn't get blood anywhere else.

What a disaster.

Slipping the gauze back in the drawer, I jumped when Erika spoke, having momentarily forgotten she was there.

"He'll come around," she said softly. "Just give it time."

I sighed and plopped down on the floor next to her. "I don't know. It's been a long time since he's been so…"

"Angry?"

"At me," I added quietly. I didn't get why I cared so much, but I did.

Erika nodded, leaning back against the chair behind her. "He's been telling me about it, all the reversal stuff. It sounds…intense." She gave me a sympathetic smile. "He didn't want to tell you until he had something more concrete, in case you freaked out."

I looked at the ground, avoiding her eyes and the red stained bandage on my arm that pretty much had 'freaking out' written all over it.

"I didn't *mean* to," I mumbled.

"I know. He does too." She paused for a moment. "It's amazing, you know, that he would look into this—derailing what he's worked on for so many years. He cares about you."

I flinched, remembering his words and scathing stare: *be gone by the time I get back.*

"Really?" I glanced up at Erika. "Because I can't...I mean, I don't know. He's done so much for me, but I..."

Erika nodded. "Of course he does. I never thought he'd care about you period, let alone care so much about you."

I caught the false note in her voice. "And you're bothered by that?"

"No, I think it's great. I never..." She smiled. "I never thought we could all get along like this, you know? It's such a huge relief. But sometimes, I wonder...I know he owes you your life, but sometimes it worries me what lengths he might go to...what he might do to try and save you. Or what he thinks is saving you, anyway."

"Really?"

She rolled her eyes. "He bought you a grand piano worth several thousand dollars in a drunken guilty stupor. And that was when I was still trying to get him to tolerate you."

"Oh."

"He's not only risking his job by helping you, but his life too. It's strange because he's so self-preserving, except when it comes to you he throws all that out the window." She looked at me. "I see you do it too, in your own way. Like you're trying to compensate for your existence or something. It's weird."

I quickly wiped the surprise off my face, hoping she didn't catch my likely guilty reaction. How did a girl like her pick up on something like that?

"Erika? Why are you here?"

She blinked, feigning misunderstanding. "Well you were screaming down here, so…"

"No, I mean why are you *here*. In this house with us. I've never understood…" *Why you started out crazy and now are kind of normal*, I wanted to say but settled with, "that."

"Oh." Erika nodded once, twice, then three times. "That."

"Yeah, that. Will you tell me?"

"Um, I…" She brushed a piece of hair behind her ear and glanced through the office door toward the stairs. "I…are you hungry?"

"Nope." Not to be deterred by her methods, I sat back against the desk, making a show out of settling in the mess of papers around me. "I've got nothing else to do."

"Right. Um, okay. Okay, I guess."

I couldn't help a laugh at her discomfort. "What? Is it really that bad?"

She laughed too, a nervous sound, still not meeting my eyes. "No, it's just…you're going to think I'm so pathetic."

"No I won't."

Erika bit her lip and thought for a moment, like she was trying to count something out in her head. Then she took a deep breath. "Okay fine. Yes."

"Well go on," I said when she didn't.

"Right." Finally, she looked at me. "I met you in the cab and didn't have a second thought about you, other than I was really annoyed you were trying to steal my ride. When I saw you at Sark's house…I don't know what I thought, I was so scared, but then you…you went into the box. For me. A stranger who'd spent our time together yelling at you from the back of a cab. I realized…I thought Sark was some kind of gang leader or something, and you'd gotten mixed up in it somehow. So I decided…I decided I wanted to save you."

I raised an eyebrow. She waved a hand at me and laughed.

"I know it sounds ridiculous. I don't know why…I don't know how I thought I could do it. But I was just so convinced I had to do it. Like I owed it to you somehow."

"So," I said, trying not to sound too skeptical, "your grand plan to save me was to steal my bracelet and then try to date my captor?"

Erika laughed again, but it was too high pitched. She was still nervous. "I know, I know. But I knew you probably weren't going to trust me, and I got the impression apprehending Sark wouldn't be a simple 911 call. So I made my own crazy plan. I was able to stop him that first night, and I thought I could do it again. I thought if I could somehow keep an eye on both of you, then we could…" She shook her head. "I don't know what I thought. I just believed it would work."

"That's crazy," I muttered in spite of myself.

"It was. But then…" Her cheeks turned faintly pink. "I spent some time with Sark and realized…there was more to that story. Desperation was probably key in my infatuation, but it was there. And then at the club, you called the authorities." She shot a halfhearted glare at me. "And I *freaked out*. I thought Sark would assume I'd set the trap for him, and he'd kill me."

"But he didn't." I still couldn't quite believe that.

"Nope." She grinned triumphantly. "We both survived."

"So then you decided to stay in his house?" I asked. "Because that doesn't make any sense whatsoever."

Erika rolled her eyes. "He wasn't going to let you leave. No way. So I improvised. I said I'd help him keep you here so long as he followed my rules. I thought…honestly I thought he was going to kill me then, but he didn't." She grinned again, the faint pink color coming back. "Now I know the feelings were mutual. He couldn't understand it, but he listened to me. And…" She shrugged. "The rest is history."

I bent my knees and leaned forward. "Let me get this straight: you really had some kind of romantic feelings for Sark *before* his whole one-eighty switch on us?"

The color in her cheeks deepened and she watched the ground. "Well…it's not really that simple."

That's insane.

Then Erika looked up abruptly, her eyes boring into mine with depth I'd never seen in her before. "Arie, do you believe in second chances?"

I blinked. A tangle of conflicted answers got caught in my throat, so I settled with a shrug.

"I used to be…" Erika smiled. "I don't want to say 'different' but something like that. More shallow. My attention span was, like, five seconds, and my main goal was to have fun. Be wild, be crazy, push the limits. I was *such* a drama queen."

"No," I gasped, pretending to be shocked. "*You?*"

She just laughed, holding her hands up. "I know, I know. Hard to believe, right? I wasn't nearly as mature as you are. My poor parents...I always wanted what I didn't have. We lived in the suburbs; I wanted the big city. I had to go to school and sit still and listen; I wanted to be traveling, working, bossing other people around. My mom stayed at home; I wanted my own career, my own company, even. It got to the point where I couldn't remember if I actually wanted something or if I just said I did to spite everyone.

"I graduated high school early. All my siblings are older, and I was the only one at home. I wanted out so badly. And I...well, my uncle had some contacts...so he got me an internship. I was ecstatic. I got to move out, I got to wear fancy clothes to my fancy job every day, and I dated the hottest guy there."

Then Erika slowed down, the bright glaze that had taken over her features as she described the past suddenly fading away. "I'll save you the sob story. We were together for a few years before I found out he was doing major illegal work within the company. He took off, pinning it all on his pathetically naive young girlfriend."

I gasped, for real this time. "What?"

She nodded, a new sharpness to her features. "Yeah, it was pretty bad. Thankfully I managed to bail myself out of trouble and stay with the company. I got demoted, of course, and never quite worked up from that. But they gave me a second chance. And I...I owe them for that."

She sounded more harsh than grateful, but I didn't press the point. "Meeting Sark...it was total infatuation at first, and I know that. Just wishful thinking of a girl who wanted attention again. But eventually I started to wonder. My dad is a developer, and he'd always say people are like buildings: they get built up and torn down. Sometimes a pretty tower has a rotting infrastructure. Sometimes a shack falls apart because it wasn't given the right blocks to build a solid foundation." She shrugged. "You just never know. After a few days with Sark, I started to wonder how he'd been built, and it turns out not very well. It's a miracle he's still standing at all."

I nodded. That was true.

"So my new philosophy," Erika finished, finding her real voice again, "is that everyone deserves a second chance." Then she rubbed her hands together and leaned forward, regaining her usual enthusiasm. "Okay, your turn."

"My turn for what?"

"Terrible boyfriend story. I hear you have one for the ages."

"Oh really," I muttered. "And where did you hear that?"

She scoffed. "Sark can be *way* too noble. I haven't managed to teach him the art of gossiping yet."

I rubbed my arms and looked around, suddenly very interested in the office around me. "You know, we should probably clean this mess up before—"

"Oh please, Arie, you can't get rid of me that easily. Besides, I told you mine."

I shrugged, choosing to look at the blank TV on the wall instead of her. "There's not much to it. Connor was my boyfriend. He was assigned by

Alexis to keep an eye on me because of my dad's involvement with the formula. After I was infected, he strategically distanced me from all my friends so that by the time Alexis came for me, I was all alone. That's basically it."

Erika took a few seconds longer than normal to respond. "Wow. Okay. Define 'strategically distanced.'"

I wrapped my arms around my legs and rested my chin on my knees. "It means Charlie was my best friend. Even after infection, he knew and he stuck with me. But then Connor noticed Charlie was acting strange. Connor thought Charlie was working against me, that he planned on turning me into the government or something as a freaky experiment. I didn't believe him at first but…Connor was very persuasive. Eventually I confronted Charlie about it. He was livid, of course, and denied everything, claiming it was all Connor, which it was. But I didn't believe him. We didn't…" My throat got tight. "We didn't talk again, for months, and then I had to run."

I sighed in frustration, raking my hands through my hair. "Everyone hated Connor. Well, no, everyone *loved* Connor, at first. Charlie never really got along with him, but tried for me, and I got used to his muttered comments. My mom was the first to say something to me, months after we'd been dating—that Connor was…wrong for me. Then Kieran got on that bandwagon. It used to be the only thing we'd ever fight about." I winced, remembering the needless arguing, me stubbornly adamant I was right when something in my gut knew I was wrong. "I just can't believe I didn't see it."

"It always makes sense in hindsight," Erika added, a faint trace of her earlier harshness coming back. "You can rarely see it in the moment."

"I didn't. Kieran used to tell me Connor was manipulating me, that he was borderline abusive. I'd defend Connor every time, even if I didn't know why. Deep down...I was scared of him, I think. Or at least intimidated, by his looks and charm and popularity. It didn't make sense that someone like him would even notice someone like me." I'd never said those words out loud, but there they were. "It wasn't that he ever threatened me, exactly, or hurt me, but...I was always confused, and he was always putting me down, and I'd just blindly follow him, even if somehow I knew it was wrong. Even when I caught him with all these other girls, and he would scoff and say I knew I wasn't enough for him, so why was I surprised? And I wasn't, really. I would just let him do anything, say anything, walk all over me. If anyone said anything about him, I'd defend him to my death. I just..."

I scoffed, shaking my head and letting harsh bitterness fill me up instead of the raw heartbreak. "Not my finest hour." Now that I was safely out of the story, I met Erika's gaze. "So, I can't say I necessarily agree with you, on the whole second chances thing. It's not so cut and dry."

She gave me a soft, sad smile. "Some things are just out of our hands."

"Yeah, I guess."

We fell into silence, each of us soaking up what we'd learned about each other in the last hour. Some kind of understanding passed through us, a current of what was unsaid, the implied heartache, connecting us together. Though we'd never understand each other's lives, she had an idea of what Connor had done to me, and that made me feel a little less insane.

"Erika?" I asked after a few minutes, watching my finger trace along the carpet. "What about…what do you think about my dad?"

Her tone was colored with surprise, but she did her best to drown it out. "What about your dad?"

"He, um…" My voice got progressively quieter as I shrunk in on myself. "I don't know…if he's…maybe…second chance material. You know?"

"Oh."

I glanced up to gauge her reaction. She pursed her lips thoughtfully, and her forehead creased with sympathy.

"Well," she finally answered, "I've never met him. What do you think?"

"That's the thing…he used to be a good guy. Annoying and difficult sometimes, but…he was good. He was a dad. I mean, he wasn't really the loving type, but we always figured he loved us, in his own way. At least…"

At least, I thought *he did.* Weren't your parents supposed to love you? What did it say about me if my own dad didn't care enough about me?

Erika leaned forward to put her hand on mine. "Your dad made a mistake, Aric. The mistake cost you a lot. But it's *his* mistake—not yours. I don't think it means he doesn't love you anymore; I think it means he got lost, and maybe his love for you did too. I think he got buried in his obsession. There's a chance he'll make his way out of it someday. I don't think that means you should go running back and trying to make something work, but I wouldn't give up just yet."

Of course I couldn't go running back to him. Not unless I wanted my nightmare to come true.

After that, I started cleaning up the office. Erika was nice enough to help, and we worked in silence, trying to put things back the way they had been before I'd screwed it all up. It took some time to find cleaner to get my blood spots out of the carpet, but I didn't mind the work. I needed it; I focused everything on it. My brain and body felt tired and empty by the time we finished.

Dragging myself upstairs, I tried to appease Erika by eating dinner, but I mostly just pushed my food around my plate. I was about to give up when the garage went up.

My heart nearly jumped out of my chest and my muscles all went stiff. Even Erika's eyes widened, but she quickly recovered and gave me an encouraging smile, which is when I realized she truly didn't know what was up with him either.

We waited in anticipation before Sark came through the garage door. I turned just as he walked in, and tried to curb my reaction. He looked like he'd aged years in the hours since I'd seen him last. His eyes found me first, and his voice matched their harsh emptiness.

"Go to your room. Now."

I didn't even blink. I stood and walked as fast as I dared down the hallway, making sure to shut my door behind me. His eyes were burned in my mind, his fuming voice on repeat.

Be gone by the time I get back.

Reaching underneath my bed, I yanked out a duffle bag I'd found in the basement weeks ago and stowed under there, just in case. My bones seemed to shake inside me as I started pulling clothes out of my closet and stuffing them in the bag.

I'd been here too long. I was leaving.

I threw the clothes inside with too much force, gritting my teeth against the raging emotions swirling around in my heart. My transient lifestyle was to keep myself safe—safe from Sark and others—but on some level I knew it was also to keep others safe from *me*. There was a reason I didn't stick with Alaina when we first met, even though she was hurt by it and refused to talk about it even now. There was a reason I never worked with her to meet other infecteds or try to make a temporary home. Deep down, I knew my future was insecure at best, and I could not stand the thought of making new friends only to hurt them down the road, whether they were the collateral damage of the hunt for me or I was the one that pulled the trigger.

Tears blurred my vision once the bag was halfway full. Where was I going to go? I'd been spoiled with a bed, food, and comfort for a month— with people to talk to that knew what I was and still talked to me anyway.

What am I going to do?

Images from my nightmare swam in my watery eyes. I sucked in a sharp breath and sat down on the bed, suddenly longing for Erika's company again. It still shocked and weirdly touched me that she did so much for me, even though I wasn't sure she'd given me the whole story. But in the last weeks she'd watched out for me, taken care of me, and become the first friend I'd had in so long.

How can I just leave her? But if I stay, what if I hurt her? I wouldn't be able to live with that.

And Sark...I couldn't even broach the thought. It was too confusing. I couldn't stop thinking about waking up in the office, and having him there, protecting me, hugging me. Out of everything, that's what stuck out to me the most, the ghost of the contact still on my skin. My gut ached for that sensation again, the feeling that I could crumble for a moment, and someone would take the burden off my shoulders and just let me cry.

I tried to remember the last time I'd had a hug from anyone other than Alaina, besides the awkward, quick one from Erika earlier today. This had felt different though, somehow: meaningful and understanding and fiercely protective.

It had felt like Kieran.

The wave of grief crashed into me so hard, I curled into a ball and moaned at the pain in my chest. It was too much. How many times had my body been picked apart and put back together again—and yet I was sure that this anguish in my soul would be the thing that killed me. Sure, bones broke and muscles tore and a person survived, but how could a human go on when their very heart and soul were cracked beyond repair?

I can't do this anymore.

A knock sounded on my door, short and soft. Peeking my head up, I looked at the door a moment before saying hoarsely, "Come in." I thought my voice might have been too quiet, but the knob turned anyway.

Sark entered, steps heavy against the hardwood floor. He looked exhausted: deep lines etched his face and he sagged like the core of the earth was trying to swallow him. Stepping inside, he softly shut the door behind him, and my packed bag was the first thing he saw. He stared at it for a moment, clearly reading my intentions, then looked up at me. I could see the echo of his own words in his eyes.

Be gone by the time I get back.

"I meant be out of the office." Even his voice was tired, and he barely managed to maintain it above a whisper.

I swallowed, willing my words not to tremble. "I know."

We stared at each other, both wary, as if expecting the other to bite. After a few seconds, he gestured to the bed. I scooted back a little, and he sat down next to me. We both stared at the floor.

"Your arm?" he asked.

"It's okay," I murmured. My forehead creased as I thought of him trying to make me drop the scissors I'd reached for in unconsciousness. "I'm sorry."

"Don't—" He shook his head and took a breath. "Don't say that."

Cringing, I bit my lip, almost wishing he would yell at me again. This heavy defeat was too much for me to carry.

Another few seconds of silence passed before he exhaled and spoke, still not looking up from the floor.

"You can ask me anything," he told me quietly. "We can talk about anything, and I'll tell you anything you want to know. But the things downstairs are off limits. You can still read the books, of course, but the documents in the office...you can ask me anything about them, I just don't want you near them, okay? This is your life, I realize, and you do have a right to know—I'll help with that as best I can, I will, but I..."

Sark trailed off and finally looked at me. I counted to three before I worked up the courage to turn my head and look at him, but even then I couldn't make my voice work. I didn't think I'd be able to promise him that—to me, a promise was binding—but it wouldn't matter anyway if I'd be gone tomorrow.

The train of thought seemed to be written on my face, because Sark glanced at my half-filled bag again and sighed, somehow deflating even more.

"I meant what I said: you'll always have a place here, should you need or want it. But if you decide you need to leave, I won't stop you and I won't follow." He reached into his pocket and rifled through his wallet, and my eyebrows shot up when he handed me a wad of at least five one hundred dollar bills. When I didn't immediately take it, he pressed it into my palm, his eyes deep enough to drown me. "Please take care of yourself."

I stared at the money, trying to think about the last time I'd seen that much at one time, let alone *held* it. "I think I should go," I said, even though the words were shaky and broken and scalded my mouth. "I think...I've been here too long." I had to swallow, swallow it all down, deep, but everything was too big and it got stuck.

But I don't want to go.

"Arie, I'm invested in your future." Sark flinched, then scoffed, closing his eyes and rubbing his forehead with his hand. "That sounds so...that's not what I mean. I..." He sighed. "My...my mom was good at this. Saying...expressing the right thing. I...I am not."

"It's okay," I told him, a small smile breaking through my tears. "You don't have to be good at it." Then I waited, watching him patiently as he struggled to find the words he was looking for.

"I...I understand why you..." He cleared his throat and started over, still holding his head. "My...Bryce was always telling me how...much I didn't matter, how I would never amount to anything...or be worth the space I took up. It made...it made me feel small and...undeserving. At first I excelled out of spite, just to prove I could be something, have more than he ever imagined."

He looked up and gestured to the house. "Now I have everything and more money than I know what to do with—ten times what he had—and most of the time I feel like I shouldn't have it." He shook his head and squared his jaw, a brief spark of anger lighting up his dismal features. "I hated that. I pushed myself harder, pushed *you* harder, trying to be the best and prove him wrong somehow, but all the success couldn't erase the feeling I didn't deserve to even be alive."

I clenched my teeth so hard my jaw hurt, and I couldn't tell what stung more: that a monster like Bryce existed or that Sark was somehow picking up on emotions I'd barely even admitted to myself.

He stumbled on. "You are...you are more than this. You deserve to feel safe and happy and...like a person. You deserve a bed to sleep in, and dinner every night, and friends to spend time with. And I...I care about what happens to you. I care that you...that you get what you deserve, even if you don't think you do."

My mouth was hanging open, my eyes burning with the tears I was fighting to keep inside. I snapped my jaw shut and shook my head, voice low and rough. "Don't look at me like that. I'm not...I'm not *that*." I closed my eyes so I didn't have to see his face anymore, how sincere he was, how he thought I was so much more than the reality.

"You don't deserve what's happened to you, Arie."

At that, my composure further slipped away from me, and a single line of tears fell down my cheek. "You don't know that." I took a shaky breath and scrunched myself smaller, wrapping my arms around my leg, raking my fingers through the ends of my hair, and rubbing the back of my neck. I hated feeling so exposed and vulnerable.

Out of the corner of my eye, I saw Sark open his mouth, then close it.

"Thank you," I told the comforter because I couldn't bring myself to look at him. "For caring." Then, without reasoning through my crushing loneliness, I leaned over and hugged Sark's arm.

He stiffened, surprised, and I jerked away, mortified. Before I could get up and run right then, he put his arm around me and gave me a hesitant, gentle hug. The gesture crumbled what resistance I had left. Throwing my arms around him, I buried my face in his shoulder and cried. Cried for everything. For everyone. I cried enough to fill oceans, and Sark didn't try to stop me. My sobs were ugly as I soaked his shirt, my empty insides pulsing with a kind of despair I couldn't put into words, a despair that had overtaken me many nights. It's different to cry alone than to cry with someone, though. They catch your tears, somehow validating your pain, for better or worse. Sark didn't use my tears against me, and something inside me knew he never would.

"I don't know what to do," I cried. Then I curled myself smaller and he held me tighter, and for the first time in what seemed like forever, despite everything, I felt safe.

18

Something collided with me, jarring me out of the darkness. I struggled to open my eyes, but they were heavy and crusted shut, grogginess making everything harder than it should've been.

"Arie!" Erika shouted so loud in my ear that I flinched further into my pillow. "Arie, get up now!"

Sensing her urgency, I pushed myself up on my elbows, feeling something crunch in my fist. My eyes broke through their crusted filth, my voice slurred. "What's wrong? Where…"

Where am I?

I managed to focus my blurry vision on Erika, who was already dressed for the day and bouncing on her knees next to me. What was going on?

Erika rolled her eyes. "Nothing's wrong."

Sighing, I shot her a mix of a groan and a hiss, and collapsed back onto the pillow. I was in my bed, I realized. Still in my clothes from yesterday too. My head felt lethargic, my eyes swollen, and throat scratchy. The blankets had been pulled up to nearly my chin; I opened my fist and peeked through my eyelashes to see the crumpled wad of cash Sark had given me last night. I didn't remember him leaving, so I must've cried myself to sleep. Awesome.

"Did you hear me?" Erika was talking with way too much animation for this early in the morning with my headache. "Get up."

I just buried my head further into the pillow, willing reality to melt away for a few more hours. But then the blankets disappeared and Erika was yanking me up by my arm.

"Come *on*, Arie! You're killing this!"

"Killing what?" I nearly snarled back, stumbling to my feet.

Erika just gave me a smug smile and grabbed my hand, pulling me along with her. I turned back in time to throw the chunk of cash on my bed before she dragged me into the hallway.

"What's going on?" Patting down the animal that was my hair, I tried to rub the sleep out of my eyes. "Erika—"

I skidded to a stop when I saw the living room. My head thudded harder and I sucked in a sharp breath, blinking, trying to understand what was in front of me.

"What the heck is this?" I finally asked.

Sark gave me a small smirk from where he was leaning up against the wall by the couch, the immense weight of last night gone from his eyes. Erika jumped in front of me and spread her arms like she was on a stage. "It's Christmas!"

My mouth fell open. I tried to count the days in my head. Then I closed my mouth.

Christmas?

"This is…" I gestured my hand to the mountain of gifts that took up nearly the entire living room. "Christmas?"

Some of Erika's bright enthusiasm faded, and she dropped her arms. "Yeah. You know, the twenty-fifth of December?"

I just stared at the heap of red and gold wrapping, mesmerized and shocked and a little nervous, like I was staring at an ocean of presents that could be fun to swim in, but also could bury me in its powerful waves.

Am I dreaming again?

When I didn't move, Erika took my hand and pulled me forward again. "Christmas is going to be *over* at this rate if you don't get going."

I still couldn't understand that word. It seemed a foreign concept from a different life—certainly not something that fit into my current existence. Christmas was for...normal kids with normal lives.

Once I got closer, I realized there were more presents than I originally thought. The bottom of the Christmas tree was stuffed, and from there it just spread out, creating a mountain range that took up half the couch as well.

Foreign land for sure.

My wide eyes looked to Sark, as if he could somehow explain this madness.

His amused grin just grew slightly. "I might've gotten a little carried away—"

"A little?" I asked. "Are you kidding me?"

He shrugged. "You spent last Christmas running from me. I had to do two years in one, and this is what we came up with."

My eyebrows shot up so fast I thought my forehead would split open. "They're *all* for me?"

"If Erika couldn't decide then we bought both."

Erika beamed at me. I just couldn't wrap my head around the idea of so much money, so much stuff, for me.

"When?" I asked, eyeing the ocean again.

"Well we haven't just been sitting at home while you're off with Alaina. These things take time." Sark straightened up and gestured toward the living room. "Now are you going to completely kill the mood or play along for us?"

I shook my head. "This isn't real." For a moment, I felt it so strongly in my gut that I felt sick. "I'm not awake, am I?" I took a shaky step back, wondering where I really was—maybe I actually had left Sark's house, and I'd wake up cold and alone in a ditch, dreaming with longing for a place that wasn't really mine to call home.

Deep lines creased Sark's face again, all amusement gone, and he looked like a ghost of last night. Erika didn't miss a beat, though.

"You're not asleep, Arie," she said, softer than normal but still with a smile. "You're not dreaming, you're here with us, and we're about to have the greatest Christmas ever. Okay?" Then her patient smile faded. "Did we do something wrong?"

"No." I took a breath, willing myself to get a grip so I didn't slaughter this amazing gesture. "No, you didn't. I guess…" I managed a small grin. "I guess I'm used to the Christmas where you get a couple gifts with a few socks and call it good. This is like...this is like the giant Christmas in the crystal mansion for the orphan Annie."

Erika's eyes sparkled and she laughed. "We can even break into musical numbers if you want."

I smirked. "Sure, and Sark can be the rich guy and shave his head."

Sark gave me a halfhearted glare, the brief moment of despair fading from his face. "Not a chance."

At Erika's insistence, I sat on the couch. She sat next to me, and Sark—after moving a few wrapped boxes—sat in his chair, handing one of those boxes to me.

And we had Christmas.

It took me a few presents to get into it, mostly because I couldn't shake the shock-slash-immense-guilt feeling I couldn't really place or understand. But Erika was so excited, and it was so cute, so I tried to just adjust.

Of course, *adjusting* was easier said than done when I was unwrapping absurdly expensive things, like a new laptop, tablet, TV, speaker, headphones, and two kinds of guitars, not to mention the DVD player and video game console—both of which came with at least a dozen movies and games each. My favorite, though, was the iPod. Back home, my iPod had been my life.

Erika clapped her hands in excitement when I opened the billions of packages containing clothes, shoes, and jewelry, some of which I could tell she picked out especially for me, and others I suspected she got so she could 'borrow' them.

It was insane.

An actual squeal escaped me when I opened up the giant box that had been pushed up against the mirror wall: a bookshelf. A big, black, beautiful bookshelf.

Eyes wide, I glanced between Erika and Sark, suddenly understanding why there were so many boxes she'd been unable to move because of their weight. "Does that mean…?"

Erika was radiating so much happiness, she could've been a star in the sky. "Keep going!"

I was right: the heavy boxes were all filled with brand new books. I abandoned all discomfort then, swooning, gaping, and laughing in disbelieving delight as I flipped through pages, breathing in their smell.

By this point, Sark was reclined back in his chair playing around on my tablet, making sure to look up every couple minutes so Erika knew he was still paying half attention. She showed no sign of slowing down, though.

"The rest is for your room," she told me, gesturing to the haphazard boxes left on the edges of the room, having been pushed farther and farther out by all my new stuff. I didn't know what she meant, but soon understood: there were mirrors, picture frames, paintings, paper lanterns, and little trinkets for decoration like mini glass animals and fake flowers. Already my mind raced with possibilities of where I could put everything.

Stranded on a tiny island of available floor space amid my sea of new belongings, Erika reached over the piles to hand me a small box I missed.

"More?" I asked, incredulous. "What else on this planet is left?"

Erika still smiled, but there was a more serious note to her expression. "It's more for us than you. Try to be open minded about using it."

Curious and slightly nervous, I ripped apart the wrapping to find a small cell phone. Nothing grand or (hopefully) expensive, just enough for the basics. It had already been set up and two contacts were saved: Erika and Sark. Since I'd left home, I'd never really liked the idea of having a cell phone. First, I didn't have a way to pay for it; second, I didn't have anyone to call; and third, it was so easy to be tracked by.

Erika cocked her head at my skeptical expression. "Just consider it, okay? If you're ever in trouble, or need anything, or…" She shrugged, not wanting to spoil the atmosphere by naming terrifying possible situations.

A noncommittal nod from me was enough to appease her for now, and she climbed over my presents to get to the kitchen in the name of finding breakfast.

"Heads up."

I glanced up just in time to catch a little square box Sark tossed at me, hearing a jingling sound inside. Lifting off the lid, I scoffed and rolled my eyes when I saw the joke.

"Very funny," I muttered dryly as I flung the car keys back at him.

Sark gave an amused grin, managing to catch the keys while still playing on the tablet. Then he just threw them right back. "Not a joke."

I blinked. "You're giving me a *car*?"

"Were the keys too subtle for you? I couldn't quite fit it in here."

"But…" I shook my head. "Why?"

He just shrugged, like he'd given me a half empty pack of gum he'd found on the street. "I don't really need four. Besides, you might learn how to actually drive one day."

It took me a few moments to soak that in, ignoring his teasing. Then I finally just laughed once and shook my head. "I didn't even get you guys anything." Heck, I'd forgotten about the whole holiday in general.

Sark chuckled under his breath. "We didn't expect you to, neither do we need anything. It was enjoyable enough just watching you open them."

"You're just saying that to make me feel better. That's like word for word from the handbook."

"What handbook?"

"The 'This Is What You Say To Make People Feel Better' handbook. It's a staple."

Sark just raised his eyebrows at whatever game he was playing. "Well I've never read it."

"It's probably in the giant pile of books you bought me. You can look if you want." Standing up, I extracted myself out of the field of gifts and stepped carefully around things until I made it to the couch. "Can I watch what you're doing?"

Concentration still focused on the screen, Sark stood and pivoted, somehow managing to avoid kicking my new guitar over, and plopped down on the couch next to me. I loved when he sat like that: sprawled and unkempt, feet hanging over the arm. It felt more like Aiden, rather than the practiced and poised professionalism of 'Mr. Sark', and I loved the thought he found moments he was comfortable enough that his real self shone through.

I watched over his shoulder as he played some retro space game where he had to blow up the enemy ships without getting hit himself. After a moment, I noticed something sticking out of Sark's pant pocket that looked suspiciously like another present.

"Holding out on us?" I asked, nodding toward the tiny package.

Sark stuffed it back in his pocket with a smile, lowering his voice so there was no chance we'd be overheard by Erika,`. "She's not expecting anything."

I couldn't help my own smile. "Is it a diamond?"

"A huge one. On a bracelet."

Sark grunted when his ship blew up, bringing him down to the last in his arsenal, and I snickered. He managed to flick me before returning to his game.

After pancakes provided by Erika, they helped me move everything into my room. With the TV mounted, the bookshelf up, the clothes in my closet, and the decorations placed, I realized they'd given me something else without having to wrap it up: a home.

The thought made me swell with some hybrid of gratitude and nausea. In the excitement, the bag I'd started packing the night before had been kicked under the bed. When Sark and Erika had momentarily left the room—Sark to find a different screwdriver and Erika to check on the cake she'd put in the oven—I dragged the bag back out. I'd been so certain, so terrified, so desperate last night. Glancing around, a familiar pit formed in my stomach at all the stuff that turned this room from an empty guest prison suite to a teenage girl's place of refuge.

Someone cleared their throat, making me jump. I turned to see Sark in the doorway, screwdriver in his hand but forgotten somehow, and whispers of the same ghosts he had in his eyes last night.

I dropped my gaze. I couldn't meet those eyes, full of so much. Not with everything I was considering—and not with all the secrets I kept locked up tight.

Sark cleared his throat again; he was buying himself time. "I realize all this, it's...poor timing, I guess, with what you...may have been considering last night. I swear I didn't intend it that way, nor is all this a bribe or meant to guilt you. Just...a better offer than we could give previously. But if you decide not to take it, there won't be any hard feelings."

Biting my lip nearly hard enough to bleed, I just nodded, still staring at the floor. I didn't know what else to do or say.

"Hey, Sark?" Erika called from down the hallway. "Can you come help me pull this out?"

"Yeah," he told her. I waited until he left before I moved or really breathed.

With a sigh, I collapsed back against my bed—*the* bed. It wasn't mine. None of this was, really. This room, this house, was the closest thing to a home I'd had in so long, and now that it was here, reaching for me, asking me to take it...why was I hesitating? Why couldn't I just accept the good fortune and be grateful for however long I had it?

Because you don't deserve it, a mean little voice inside me whispered. *You know you don't, and if they knew everything, they wouldn't offer.*

Before I'd ran away, a thought like that would always have been followed by Kieran's voice in my head, telling me I was worth so much more than all this. That voice had quickly been snuffed out after he'd left—after I realized he truly didn't believe that either. Now, for the first time in months, I heard another voice. Sark's.

You don't deserve what's happened to you, Arie.

Tears sprung in my eyes, and I forced them to stay inside. Kieran had been my best friend forever, my real brother, the person that promised to fight for me until the end. How could I believe Sark and Erika would do the same if it really came down to it?

If they knew. The question was, should I leave and avoid that eventual pain, or stay while I could?

"Okay, Arie," Erika said, waltzing into my room with Sark behind her. "What's next?"

What's next, Arie?

Her voice snapped me out of my momentary pity party. I needed to get a grip. This was pathetic.

"What's next, Arie?" Erika asked again. Sark watched me, expressionless, but Erika thankfully didn't catch on to my funk. "I've got to let that cake cool before frosting. What do you want to do?"

What's next, Arie? Make your choice.

"Um, well…" My voice was soft and raspy, so I cleared my throat, clearing my tears and indecisiveness as well. "I kind of wanted to play a video game."

"Yeah?" Erika wandered over to the stack of games on my dresser. "Which one?"

"The racing one. Sark thinks because he used to beat the kid down the street ten years ago that he can beat me." The corners of my mouth pulled up. "I've got a point to prove."

Sark just shot me a challenging smile. "Ten bucks says you lose."

"Do you have ten bucks left to bet?"

"Doesn't matter; I'll win anyway."

"I don't know," Erika said. "She's got a chance."

Sark didn't take to that well, so we immediately set up the game to settle the score. We sat on my bed until after the first round: Erika moved for safety precautions. Turned out, Sark was just as competitive as I was, and it took about four seconds for the bet to go to trash talk, to insults, then to sabotage. Pillows were thrown in between shouting. Erika joined my cause, and after attacking him from behind, we ended up shoving Sark onto the floor. Just as I was about to cross the finish line, Erika shrieked a warning to me in between her laughter; Sark snatched my ankle and yanked me off the bed too, allowing him to sail past me and win.

Laughing so hard my stomach hurt, I noticed my half packed bag still on the floor and kicked it under the bed. I was already home.

19

Despite the drastic changes that had come into my life—namely having Erika become one of my best friends, Sark giving up his sadistic habits, and me finally finding stability—there was still a part of me that was always coiled with anxiety. Even though I had shelter and food, felt safe and loved, and divided my time between Sark's house and Neil's club...there was a sense of fear I just couldn't shake.

Today I felt it more than usual, and that set me on edge. I'd barely managed to make it through the grocery store trip I'd made for Erika. Andrew's birthday was coming up, and I wanted to get him these vintage records I'd found in an old music store. When Erika had said she'd needed more flour and vanilla, I'd volunteered to grab them for her while I was out.

My driving skills had drastically improved, but I still clenched the steering wheel too tight as I pulled into the parking lot across from the small music store. Turning off the car, I counted to four in my head and took deep breaths before stepping outside.

The February afternoon was grey and cold, the overcast sky showing signs that snow would be coming tonight. Zipping my coat up, I stuffed my hands in my pockets and ducked into the store. Cheap coffee and old paper tainted the air as I went straight to a record display and scanned the place. There weren't very many people inside: a couple teenagers, a guy in a suit, and the cashier.

I found what I was looking for and made my way up to the counter. The cashier was friendly, thankfully ringing me up fast. I wanted to act natural, but I found myself tapping my foot against the ground and glancing around at the strangers. Hastily handing over cash, I grabbed my bag full of purchases and threw a hopefully nice smile at the cashier before heading back to the car.

The second my foot hit asphalt, an uncomfortable sensation washed over me. A familiar one.

Someone was watching me.

I glanced over my shoulder as I walked, looking for someone that stuck out. Besides a couple ducking inside the bar next to the music store, there wasn't anyone else. It didn't feel right.

Chill Arie. Things had been going good lately. I didn't need a streak of paranoia to screw that up. I'd get in the car, go home, and I'd be fine. If I really needed to, I'd go over to the club to hang out with Alaina, or find Sark. Just sitting next to him for awhile helped me to relax a little.

Turning forward again, I noticed a man standing casually next to his car about two rows ahead of me, talking on a cell phone. I might not have cared about that, if he hadn't been parked next to my car.

Automatically, I turned right and headed for the sidewalk rather than my car. Just in case. Out of the corner of my eye, I saw a man from the record store had been walking behind me, but he stopped when I changed directions. Like the man by my car, he was muttering into a cell phone and wearing a suit.

Familiarity struck, more than just spending ten minutes in a store with him. I'd seen both of them before. But where?

I turned onto the sidewalk and started walking down the block, trying to think. I could picture their faces in my head; I tried to mentally zoom out from the image, to remember where we'd been. It was at night. I knew that. The memory was me looking down on them, so I must've been watching them from a rooftop or something. Watching and waiting...for what? For them to find me? No, I hadn't been hiding from them. I'd likely been hiding from Sark.

Sark. That was it. They were there for Sark. It was his hideout in Philadelphia, and I was waiting for those men to catch Sark after I'd called them. They were Dalton's men—specialized government investigation agents.

Relief came as I remembered, but then it slammed to a halt.

Why would Dalton's men be following me?

It couldn't be for Sark. As far as Dalton knew, I was still running from Sark. And if they did somehow know where Sark was, they wouldn't follow me—Dalton always made it clear he didn't value me above the gum stuck to his shoe.

Cutting behind the music store, I circled back into the parking lot. Both men were gone.

It took everything I had not to break into a run. I walked as fast as I could without drawing attention to myself, just wanting to get in the car and get out of here.

I was three stalls away when they reappeared, each closing in on either side of me, and they'd intercept me before I reached the vehicle. Prepared to just ask what the heck Dalton had them doing, I looked up at the one on my right and froze at the harsh glint in his eyes. I knew that glint so well.

They weren't here to follow. They were here to hunt.

My breath hitched, getting stuck in my throat. The man's eyes just narrowed at my response, like my reaction had confirmed something to him, and I felt like my bones would shatter inside me.

They know.

They weren't here for their criminal mastermind that always evaded them, or the useless infected that would calmly talk to them if they just asked. No, they were here for something much more valuable than that.

They were here for me.

They know.

Dropping everything I was holding into the snow, I whipped around and sprinted in the opposite direction. The men shouted behind me—one of them shouted my name—and I nearly combusted right there at the bark to his tone. He wasn't here to reason or gather information. He was here to stalk and capture.

They know.

My feet struck the cement over and over, and I thought a giant fissure would open in the earth and swallow me down. Dalton knew I was the key. How could this happen? I'd been so careful. I'd tried so hard to avoid his probing questions, to evade his curiosity, to keep my damning truth far away from his greedy and exploitive hands.

I ran flat out for years, not caring about the people who had to jump out of my way or how they'd remember a girl racing down the streets of Chicago with utter terror in her eyes. I ran until my legs hurt and lungs ached, and, by then, the men weren't chasing me anymore. I'd lost them. For now.

Ducking in an alley, I collapsed to my knees behind a dumpster. My throat felt like it was being compressed, my chest smashed, bits of me splintering everywhere. I couldn't get enough air, and I wheezed against a brick wall, my body shuddering.

What do I do?

Leaning over, I dry heaved until I fell into a coughing fit. Tremors shook me and I had to bite down to keep from screaming.

What do I do?
What do I do?
I'm alone.
They know.
WHAT DO I DO?

Slumping against the wall, I felt something shift in my pant pocket: my cell phone.

Indecision struck me for a second, and I went still as a statue. I wasn't alone. Not completely. Not anymore.

What do I do?

I thought of the men chasing me, men that would likely watch my car and be scouring the streets for me. Men that were hunting me.

Men that *knew*.

Panic surged through me again, taking control of everything, and I yanked the phone out. My vision was blurry—it was then I realized I was sobbing—so my trembling fingers pressed random buttons until a call screen came up. The ringing sounded in my ear.

What do I do?

Erika answered. Her voice was airy and distant, on speakerphone, and she nearly shouted over the sound of running water and clanking dishes. "Hey, Arie," she called. "Are you okay?"

"Erika!" I sobbed, verging on hysteria despite the fraction of relief that came at the sound of her voice. "Erika!"

All pleasantries evaporated from her tone and the sound of the running water disappeared. "Arie, what's wrong? Are you hurt?"

I couldn't get enough air, couldn't find the words to explain. "No, no, they...I...the car...it's…" My breathing caught again and I squeezed my arms tighter around myself.

How could this happen?

Erika's voice went up an octave with panic. "Arie? Arie, what's wrong? Please tell me. Are you hurt? Are you okay? What's happening?"

I gulped in air, and vomited words in between sobs. "I was in the car and then the store and back and they were there and then chasing me and I know them and it's Dalton and he's here and—"

Something crashed on the other end of the phone like she'd dropped something. Now her voice was raspy with fear. "Dalton? Richard Dalton? That government guy?"

"Yes." I nodded rapidly, so fast it made me dizzy. "Yes, him."

"But..." Erika's breaths came in quick gasps. "But why is he following *you*?"

I opened my mouth, then snapped it shut. I'd never told anyone. Never in my life had I even said the words out loud. Even the thought of the admission made me choke.

How could this happen?

"Arie?" Erika was crying now too. "Arie, why is Dalton there? Has he talked to you? Has he hurt you? Please, Arie, you have to tell me *now*."

"They know." The confession silenced me, halting my breaths and stilling my heart.

"They know? Know what? That we're with Sark?"

"They know?" My voice broke and I started crying again. "They know."

How could this happen?

"Arie, they know what? I don't underst—"

"It's me!" I nearly screamed into the phone. "It's me. It's my...body, biology, something, it has codes for the key, and I...it's me. It's me." Sobs overtook me again, and I folded myself as small as I could get. Erika replied, but I wasn't listening anymore, unable to hear over the roaring panic in my ears.

"Arie!"

I lifted up my head, hoping Sark's voice was real and he was here with me, before realizing he was on the phone now.

"Arie!" he yelled again, and I shrunk away from the harsh fear that frayed his voice, breaking his accent into pieces. "Arie, pull yourself together and answer me now!"

"They know," I whispered.

"Are you sure?"

I nodded, then realized he couldn't see me.

"Arie, are you sure?"

"Yes." My voice shook so hard it was a miracle he could understand me. "They were following me. They know what I am and I'm hiding and don't know where they are and I...I'm so scared. I'm so scared."

That softened him up. The harsh bleakness to his tone melted into a warm kind of calm that could only come during a complete eruption. "I know you are. I need you to listen to me very carefully, okay?"

"I can't...I can't get caught. I can't breathe, I can't...I don't..."

"Arie, take deep breaths and listen to me. Now."

I nodded rapidly, taking his advice. I pretended he was here with me, holding me and stroking my hair and telling me to breathe.

Sark waited for a few moments until I got myself in control, then started railing off an address for a parking garage and instructions. "Don't go back to the car. Stay near thick traffic and use unpredictable patterns—just like you usually do. Erika and I will meet you there, okay? We'll get you somewhere safe. You'll be okay."

I sucked in another deep breath, my senses sharpening, as I slowly found myself again. "Okay."

"Arie?"

"Yes?"

Sark's tone hardened again, every word emphasized and sharp enough to cut through steel. "Do. Not. Get. Caught. Do you understand?"

I bit my lip. "Yes." I understood perfectly.

"You'll be okay." It sounded like he was telling himself more than me. "You'll be safe."

"Okay."

"Start moving."

"Okay."

"Be safe." Then there was a clicking sound and the line went dead.

I stared at the crumbling brick wall for a moment, everything slowly coming back to me: the chill to the air, the uneven cement underneath me, the taste of salt in my mouth, the bustling of traffic just a few blocks away. I only allowed a second to wallow in my stupidity—these last months I'd been careless and lazy, and now everything was falling apart, culminating in the day I'd had nightmares about for nearly two years.

The cell phone was a heavy weight in my hand: a reminder. I wasn't completely alone in this. Not anymore.

Rising to my feet, I wiped my eyes and pulled my hood over my head, then stepped out onto the

street. My hands shook in my pockets as I raced for
the parking garage.

He's here.

He knows.

Be safe.

~~~

It seemed the parking garage was halfway
across the planet. No matter how far it seemed,
though, I didn't allow myself to panic. I squashed
my panic into a little ball in the bottom of my
stomach and forced it to sit there. I was in survivor
mode now, and I was going to get out of this. I
didn't have a choice.

I will not get caught.

Rounding the last corner, I finally saw the
parking garage Sark had been talking about. Several
cars were coming in and out, so I went around until
I found the door, then took the stairs two at a time
to the near empty bottom level. Heart pounding in
my chest, I headed straight for the back corner.

A ghost of a sob caught in my throat when I saw
them. Sark was shoving boxes from his backseat
into the trunk while Erika paced next to him,
wringing her hands. I ran to her and threw my arms
around her. She yelped in surprise, then squeezed
me back, holding me like she'd never let me go
again.

"You're going to be okay," she whispered in my
ear as I breathed in the familiar scent of her jasmine
perfume. "We're going to be fine." And for that split
second, I let myself be comforted, and I believed her.

We'll be okay.
~~~

Suddenly, tires skidded as a big silver van screeched next to us. Erika and I jumped out of the way just in time, nearly tripping over each other, then a hulking man snuck up from behind. I didn't have time to sound a warning before he had his arms around Erika, and she screamed before he slapped his hand over her mouth.

I went to shoot forward and punch him off her when a crushing blow to my head knocked me to my knees. My vision went blurry as I struggled to get to my feet. Another blow, and I collapsed. My limbs felt like noodles as someone bound my hands behind me and hauled me to my feet.

They're here.

Clenching my teeth, I scanned the space, searching for Dalton. He was an idiot. I could talk him out of this, at least to let Erika go. Sark would be a much tougher sell. And me…

Nausea bubbled in my stomach and my palms went slick with sweat.

I can't get caught, I can't get caught, I can't get caught.

I saw a man dragging Erika into the van as she gave muffled screams and thrashed violently. Following her lead, I kicked my legs and squirmed, looking for Sark. Had they already apprehended him? Taken him into custody? A pit formed in my stomach. Dalton wouldn't have the authority to shoot on sight, would he?

Flailing harder, I craned my head in a desperate attempt to locate Sark. He could beat Dalton—he always had before.

"Well, it's about time."

The voice froze me over. All sounds echoing in the garage went silent in my ears, my heart stopping. The man handling me jerked me back around to face forward. To see him.

Jefferson.

He sneered at me, his round face contorted with a hatred that didn't quite match the maniacal animated glint to his eyes. I stood taller than him; the guard forced me to my knees. I was too paralyzed with terror to put up any kind of resistance.

Jefferson took my chin in his warm, fleshy hand, squeezing it too tight. My mouth went dry. I could see him planning in his head, imagining all the things he wanted to do to me, how he ached to snap me in half in retribution for what I did to his leg. Instead, he raked his eyes over me before slapping me hard across the face.

"Get her in the van," he ordered, the same insane glint in his shrill voice.

Cheek stinging, I didn't thrash when the man started hauling me toward the van again. Jefferson was *here*. Now. With me, with Erika, with…

Horror shot through me, freezing the blood in my veins. Sark. Where was he?

An airless scream escaped me, and I was fighting again, straining to turn and find some sign that he'd escaped. That Jefferson hadn't already ordered he be ripped to shreds for his betrayal. For helping me.

Don't be dead don't be dead don't be dead.

When I nearly managed to slide out of the man's grip, he hit me and barked an order, and another man came to help. Between the two of them they were able to force me into the van. I collapsed on the floor next to Erika. The van door slammed shut.

I bolted upright, desperation strangling me. "Erika," I whispered harshly, glancing wildly out the windows, looking for him. "Erika, where's Sa—"

My searching screeched to a stop. I choked on air. My mouth stayed open, but my voice stopped working, unable to find words for the horrifying scene in front of me. Each cell inside me buzzed and trembled, threatening to implode.

"What?" Erika demanded, leaning forward. "What's wrong? Is he…?" When I couldn't answer, she finally tracked my gaze, following it out the back window. She went rigid. Still as ice, as glass, a sculpture of a kind of pain beyond description, poised to shatter.

"No," she murmured. "No."

Neither of us could tear our eyes away from Sark's face, twisted beyond recognition. His face was sharp and indifferent, eyes cold and hateful, shoulders poised and straight with arrogance. My Sark was gone. The Sark from my nightmares, from the past, stood there, shaking hands with Jefferson, who was beaming from ear to ear with too straight teeth. Then Jefferson swept his hands around to the other guards and started applauding Sark, shouting 'amazing work' and 'this is how it's done' and how their boss Alexis will be so thrilled.

Erika was so still, her body stiff despite the deep sobs that were building in her chest. She just stared and shook her head and cried. "No, no, no, no, no, no." When Sark nodded back at Jefferson in some kind of thank you, his aura oozing with pride, Erika crumpled, her head smacking against the van floor as she drowned in her tears.

"No, Sark," she whispered, a mix between a moan and a cry. "No, Sark, no."

I still couldn't get my limbs to move. I still couldn't breathe, couldn't open up my airway because I couldn't swallow the fact that Sark had just left us and we were on our own.

Though he hadn't really left us, because he was never really ours. It wasn't a betrayal as much as it was a huge oversight. The scalding of his sellout battled with the cold numb in my heart that wasn't even surprised. And in that moment, I hated myself nearly as much as I hated him.

Because I knew exactly how it had happened. I knew exactly how he had bided his time, played each part, said all the right things to gain millimeters of trust with every astonishing performance. I knew exactly how he waited until I was most vulnerable to sell me the toughest lies, how he had squeezed those details about Kieran from me just to turn around and attack me with them. How he'd been exactly the person I needed most, how he'd perfectly filled the void that made me feel like a black hole. How he'd wrapped me around his finger, pulling me around like a puppet until he got what he wanted.

What he wanted.

What he wanted.

My gasp hitched in my throat, the sound of me screaming in the alley roaring in my ears, the only time I'd ever voiced the truth I'd dedicated my life to hiding.

It's me! It's my...body, biology, something, it has codes for the key, and I...it's me.

It's me.

It's me.

It's me.

Sark knew. Sark knew my secret, and now he was gift wrapping me for Alexis, handing over the key to get what they both always wanted.

I crumbled. The waves of agony gave one last heave and swelled over my head, suffocating me, dragging me down to the deepest pit of misery and blackness it could find.

20

September 24th

Dear Diary

Today was just your average Friday. Nothing to report, really. Life can be so boring and repetitive—sometimes I wonder why I even keep a journal at all. Mr. Barton droned on forever about expanding an equation, and I swear he messed with the clock because there's no way that was just one period. I finally gave up and put my earbud in and doodled in my notebook to keep myself awake. The only good thing was he was so focused on his lecture that he didn't have time to assign homework before the bell rang and everyone ran out. Midterms are coming up and I'm practically drowning in papers and projects, so no extra math homework was a plus.

In English, everyone conveniently forgot to do the reading, so I spent the whole time listening to Mrs. Bower review the chapters I read last night. WASTE OF TIME. Seriously, does nobody care about their education? I get some people don't care as much as I do, but come on. It's annoying when their apathy slows me down, especially since I've started looking at college applications. Kieran says it's early for me, but I don't care. I'm getting out of here and getting my degree, and if that means planning ahead a little, then I'll do it.

Oh, I guess there is one new semi-interesting thing that happened today: we got a new kid. In between throwing grapes at Charlie all through lunch, Erin told me about him. I guess his name is Connor and he's in her physics class, and then he happened to be in our social sciences class the next period. He reminds me so much of Kieran: spiky blond hair, bright blue eyes, muscles built for football, etc. Anyways, Erin kept trying to get me to ask him out, but I just laughed. I'd never find the guts to even speak to him, and since he's a shoo-in for the football team, Mandy will be all over him. Yuck. Stupid high school social class system.

Oh well. We can't have everything, I guess.

Yeah, so that's it. Dad was still holed up in his office when I got home—no surprise there. I don't think he's even moved since yesterday. Usually he'd already be off on something else right now, but he's keeping to himself, which is really strange. The other day he was stomping around and muttering to himself and refusing to look anyone in the eye. I don't know. I tried asking Mom about it, ~~but that was about as helpful as asking a styrofoam box for help.~~

Sorry, I shouldn't have written that. I miss Grandpa too. So much it hurts.

We're doing the best we can. Hopefully Dad will snap out of whatever funk he's in for five seconds to comfort his grieving wife.

~~~

They brought us to a warehouse. It was dark by the time we got there, so I couldn't get a good idea of where we were even if I tried. Knowing my history of attempted—and successful—escapes, Jefferson ordered I be shot up with some kind of drug that made me lose all use of my legs. They were just numb and tingly, like they were asleep, and if I tried to put any pressure on them I'd collapse. No walking for me. I couldn't bring myself to care.

After that, they dumped Erika and me in the basement, shutting us up in adjacent cells where time stopped and started and never ended. It was damp and dark, with no windows to keep track of the passing days. Any kind of time was marked by the single tray of stale food that was brought for us to share—I think they hoped we'd fight over it, but Erika had to beg and force me to even take a bite— and the guard that would come for us.

They never took us at the same time, so we never had to witness what they did to the other. Just the aftermath. It started with interrogation. They dragged me upstairs and tied me to a chair and put
~~~

a bright spotlight on me. Jefferson asked me questions. I let his words slide in one ear and go out the other, not even bothering to concentrate hard enough to attribute meaning to his syllables. He hit me when I didn't answer, and when my silence stretched out for decades, he brought out knives and let the aggressive guards have a go at me.

I didn't care what they did to me. I didn't care that while I knew I was the key, I didn't know how to use the key, which was probably what they were asking. I just made sure my eyes stayed glued to the ground, putting all my effort into ignoring the penetrating gaze from the monster that always stood in the shadows, watching everything. I would not give him the satisfaction of even acknowledging his existence.

Several days passed—which I only knew because the people around me had changed clothes—before they finally gave up on getting answers from me. Shaky, bloody, and aching, they dumped me back in my cell.

I'd gotten used to pain. I'd gotten used to seeing my body bruised and my skin streaked red. But nothing could have prepared me for seeing Erika, her beautiful pale skin swollen, purple, and crimson. The man dragged her back into her cell, and I started crying after one look at her.

"Arie," she rasped through her own tears. They'd even broken her beautiful voice; she must've screamed so much. "Arie."

Despite my own pain, I dragged myself to her, and she did the same. We reached through the bars and clasped hands tightly, then leaned up against the bars like we were snuggling together on the couch.

Except we weren't on the couch. We were in a cell after being tortured for information we didn't have.

"Arie," Erika whimpered again and again, like the chant hurt her but kept her alive. "Arie. Arie."

"I'm here," I croaked back, the first words I'd said in days. As softly as I could, I brushed my blistered fingertips over the back of her hand again and again, in an attempt to comfort. Truthfully, I hadn't known if she'd come back at all. Jefferson usually didn't care about bystanders—he would've shot Erika within five minutes of not providing anything useful. "I'm here."

Her words shuddered with her body as she huddled closer to me, soaking my shoulder with tears and blood. "I don't know anything, I don't...I don't know anything. I'm not important enough. I don't know. I don't *know*."

I cried harder into her hair. The smell of jasmine was gone now. She just smelled like blood and waste. "I'm sorry. You shouldn't...you shouldn't even be here. I'm sorry."

"He was there. He watched. He just..." Her voice splintered further, sobs nearing hysteria. "He would barely look at me. Didn't even...didn't talk to me. They asked him about me, once. He said...he said I was easy. He kept me for you. Like a pet. He said...he said he kept me to help gain your trust and for...for his own pleasure." She shuddered in revulsion now, like he was acid and she needed to wash off every touch and kiss he'd left on her skin.

I clenched my free fist so hard that my palms bubbled with blood. "I'm sorry," I said because I didn't know what else to say. "I'm so sorry."

Erika just buried her face in my shoulder and sobbed harder.

~~~

<div align="right"><em>September 30th</em></div>

Dear Diary,

You'll never ever ever ever guess what happened today. Like, ever. If Erin hadn't talked about it nonstop all day, I totally would've thought I made it up daydreaming during Algebra.

Get this: that new kid, Connor, talked to me. To <u>me</u>! And not just a polite hello in the hallway either. We had an actual conversation.

The scene opens at lunch. I'm quizzing Charlie on the periodic table for his test while Erin is popping Pringles like pills. Then Connor just sits next to me out of nowhere, looking right at me. Me. He glanced at Erin, who choked on her chips, and didn't acknowledge Charlie. It was just me.

Me.

Okay, imagine a hot football player saying this with a charming voice:

"You're Arie, right?"

Cue me nearly fainting.

(Thankfully, I did not actually faint. Unfortunately, I was suffering from shock, and therefore could only nod).

After my pathetic nod, he said, "Hey, I'm Connor" (like I didn't know that!) "and I think you're in my math class. Period three, right?"

Instantly, I was crushed. He was a hot football player asking the nerd for math answers. This
~~~

wasn't a daydream love story—it was a stupid rom com. But I still said yes and then he said "cool."

Cool??? What does that even mean?? Math isn't cool!

When I didn't answer, he said, "Okay, this is embarrassing, being the new kid and all, but I was hoping you'd be able to explain synthetic division to me. I felt like Barton was speaking Arabic during the last lesson and I really can't bomb the first test."

At this point, I was flattered he picked me, but still disappointed, which was utterly stupid. What had I really expected? So I agreed to help him out during lunch tomorrow.

Then, the miracle: instead of just ditching and pretending like he didn't know me, he stuck around for the rest of lunch. Erin recovered and talked with him too, but Charlie claimed he had to study and didn't offer much to the conversation. But there was conversation!!

After lunch he walked me to class, then we bumped into each other after school and he walked me to Kieran's car too. When I told him I'd see him at lunch tomorrow, he winked at me (WINKED!!!) and said, and I quote, "It's a date."

It's. A. Date.

!!!

Look, I know it's waaaaaaay too soon to say, but I think this maybe could possibly be the start of something.

~~~

After interrogation failed to get anything out of me, Jefferson vetoed those pleasantries and moved
~~~

on to testing. If I wasn't going to tell them how to access the key power to fix the formula, then apparently they were going to dissect me into pieces to figure it out themselves.

They took so much blood that I passed out. They took samples of everything to test: skin, muscle, tissue, bone, spinal fluid...everything. Every day someone dragged me out of my cell for something horrible, every day I stayed silent except for screams of pain, and every day I went back with my body shaking and voice gone. I'd press myself against the freezing cement floor and hold Erika's hand. I still didn't know how she was alive. They'd stopped interrogating her regularly, but I still held my breath every time I heard the latch down the hallway open, knowing I'd give anything to take her place but also knowing every time I did they were one step closer to solving the mystery that could end everything.

Today, the guard that came to get me was grouchy and impatient. He tried to stand me up and make me walk, but I just collapsed to the ground, my chin bouncing painfully against the pavement.

"She can't," Erika snapped at him, quiet but still sharp as steel.

He gave her a glare that screamed murder and snapped back, "Shut up, or I'll make you."

Erika stayed silent, but didn't drop her stare. He called her a nasty word before grabbing me by my arm and dragging me down the corridor.

This time we didn't go upstairs. Instead he brought me to an empty loading area on the other side of the bottom level. A massive garage door stood across from us, presumably leading outside, and there was a mini stairwell that led to a regular door. I didn't know what was on the other side—if there was an arsenal of guards and guns just outside—but I made note of it in my head.

A large glass box stood in the center of the space, and several wires and pipes were attached to it. There was a computer screen and a keyboard, as well as a few tables, one of which was covered in medical supplies that made me shiver. Jefferson was there; I sensed a few others but didn't allow my eyes to focus on any of them. I returned my stare to the ground.

The guard pulled me to my knees, forcing my head up by my hair. I didn't look at Jefferson when he pressed something against my neck. I didn't respond when he spat some insult at me. I didn't flinch when he slapped me again.

Nothing matters anymore.

Jefferson gave an order, and the guard picked me up and threw me into the box. I thudded hard on the ground, and was suddenly hit with such a strong sense of dread that I almost threw up the stale bread Erika had forced me to eat half of this morning.

For once, I sharpened my hearing and forced myself to listen to what they were saying. The glass on the box was thick, distorting some voices, but I managed to catch Jefferson at the computer saying something like 'this better provide us with some kind of useful data.'

Data? He made it sound like they didn't have any, like they hadn't been extracting body parts from me for the last week. Hadn't they been able to tell I was different by this point? Not that I was itching to end the world, but even I had to admit this was taking a long time. *What are they doing with it all?*

Jefferson gave the order to start. My heart stopped, then started pounding when I heard a rushing sound. Then water started pooling underneath me.

The dread in my stomach exploded into terror, and I gave a scraping scream, snatching everyone's attention since it was my first and only scream that hadn't come directly from pain—my first real response to anything.

Water rose higher and higher, freezing my bones instantly, but this time I couldn't stand. I shrieked and pounded my fists on the glass, then shrieked louder when I hurt my hand.

I couldn't do this. They could beat me, starve me, freeze me, break me apart piece by piece, but I could not do this again.

I can't I can't I can't I can't I can't I can't.

Searching wildly for an escape, I screamed again when the water hit my shoulders, splashing it around with all my thrashing. My skull hit the back of the box hard, making me dizzy and stop for a second. In that moment, my eyes landed right on his.

His gaze paralyzed me. I'd tried for weeks to bleach the memory of it out of my brain, but there it was, deep and blue and piercing me to my core. I stared at him, unmoving, as the water rose over my head.

Something snapped in me. After days of excruciating pain and numbing despair, the rage felt white hot and scalding in my veins, warming me despite the freezing water. I was so angry that I was here, trapped in another box of water, and none of it mattered. I was so angry that I'd somehow trusted a demon, that Erika would likely die in this prison, and that we'd never see the light of day again. I was so angry that my brother was dead and my life had been ruined and there were so many awful monsters in this world that pretended to be humans.

I was so angry in that moment, and I knew they were measuring how long I could go without oxygen, so I held his stare with the most defiant glare I could muster and opened my mouth.

I was so angry, that I didn't care that the water rushed into my lungs, and I didn't care if they couldn't save me in time, only hoping that I'd screwed up all their twisted data.

I was so angry, that when they freed me from the box and got me conscious again, I swatted and kicked and made the biggest scene in the whole world, knocking all the medical supplies to the ground.

I was so angry, that I managed to swipe a small scalpel that fell and hide it in my sleeve, and they were so shocked and mad at my reaction, that Jefferson hit me a few times before ordering I be taken back to my cell without food for three days.

I was so angry, that when the guard dropped me in my cell, slammed my door and sauntered away, muttering to himself about getting a drink, I stuck the scalpel out so the door clanked against it, but didn't shut all the way.

And the guard was still so annoyed he had to be the one to deal with me, he didn't even notice the different sound and kept walking.

21

April 22nd
Day 14

Today was a joke.

In PE we had to run the mile, which is a form of hell itself. I came so close to ditching, especially since I never ditch class, but Erin convinced me to go. She's ditched too many times and couldn't miss for her grade, and since she's moving away next week she wanted to maximize our time together. So I agreed. I went to class, changed behind a shower curtain since everyone still stares at me (and I have nightmares about that blue thing on my skin coming back and I don't know and start stripping and boom: someone calls the CIA) and we went to class. Coach read off our previous mile times for 'motivation to reach a PR.' How twisted is that? Really, it's just public shaming at its finest. The education system is so messed up.

Anyways, I've always been able to hold a nine minute mile, which means I usually finish about third to last since the whole track team basically is in my class. So, prepared to take another loss, I lined up at the start and Coach shouted go. And I started running.

I beat everyone.

Coach asked me if I'd somehow cheated, but we both know I didn't. Nobody would come within five feet of me. People whispered just loud enough for me to hear, theories ranging from drugs to witchcraft. Even Erin was unusually quiet, and by the time we got to lunch nearly everyone had heard about it. Charlie tried to make a weak joke out of it, but Connor shut him down and took my hand instead, saying this was bigger than a joke. When the miserable day finally ended, I met up with Kieran at his car. I didn't even have to say anything since he already knew. He gave me the longest hug and we went home without talking. I didn't know what to say. I don't know what to say to anyone.

It's been two weeks since 'infection' (I hate that word) and already things have spiraled faster than I thought they would. If it weren't for college and Erin, I probably would give up on school.

Okay, that's an exaggeration. I still want college, even if there's no way any university would accept a science experiment.

And Erin. She leaves on the twenty-eighth and I have no idea what I'll do without her. But her dad got transferred to West Virginia, so she has to go. It's kind of a joke that nobody actually knows what he does—every time he starts explaining it, I end up more confused than when he started—and that makes Erin mad. She feels like there isn't a real reason for them to go. And I wish with everything I have that she could stay.

In other terrible news on the Arie Nolan Show, Kieran went through more of Dad's stuff while he was gone today. This cult he's involved in sounds crazy dangerous (and crazy in general) and Kieran worries what he dragged me into. I mean, there are scary people who hunt infecteds. According to what Kieran found, it sounds like Dad thinks I'm hidden enough that nobody will find me, and nobody will ever know I'm their precious key. But what if someone found out? What if those scary people started looking for me? Or what if he decides to do something with me? What would I do then?

I told Kieran we should call the police, but he thinks this goes deeper than that. Plus, we don't have any actual evidence besides the notes of an unstable father, and we have no way to know how they'd react to what I am. Anyone could easily turn against me.

And I don't <u>want</u> to hurt people. I don't. I don't want to help anyone hurt anyone, I don't want to be infected, and I don't want any of it. But good intentions don't matter. I've seen the TV shows. If more people start to suspect something is really wrong with me, they'll lock me up for experiments and stuff.

I don't know what to do.
I'm so scared.

<div align="center">~~~</div>

Despite the rage burning in my veins, I forced myself to wait. We had one opportunity—one precious chance—and I would not let myself waste it.

Erika and I waited for what we guessed was a few hours. Once we hadn't heard an echo of human life for a considerable period of time, we decided (hopefully) that night had fallen, and it was time to make our move.

I whipped my cell door open as fast as I could to keep it from creaking. Then I waited. Nothing happened.

Gritting my teeth, I started dragging myself across the ground. It took everything in me, and I struggled not to scream at the pain that shot through my body as I strained what muscles I had left. Erika started to say something—to object, probably—but stopped herself and let me keep going. It wasn't like we had another choice.

I managed to drag myself out of my cell and over to Erika's door. Using my stolen scalpel, I reached up and tried to pick the lock, but I couldn't kneel for more than a few seconds and wasn't able to get the right leverage. After a few tries, Erika took the weapon from me and started working on it herself.

Sweat beaded on my neck and trickled down my back as I glanced toward the empty hallway.

Please stay empty.

After what seemed like years, Erika finally got the door open. Both of us cringed at the faint squeak the hinge gave; both of us snapped our heads toward the hallway.

Silence.

Using the bars, Erika pulled herself up, wincing as her bruised and skeletal body tried to work, then walked out and glanced at me. The returning look I gave was grim, but full of resolve. We were getting out of here.

Of course, that would be a lot easier if I could *walk*.

Erika reached down and tried to pull me up, but I was too heavy and she was too weak. Raising the scalpel like a sword, she walked down the dark hallway until I couldn't see her anymore, scouting the area. My hands balled into fists, my heart pounding, as I strained my ears for any sign she'd come across someone. A few minutes passed, and she came back signaling the coast was clear.

I took a breath. This had to work.

Erika leaned down and put one arm around me, holding me halfway up. She gripped the scalpel in her other hand; I used my other hand to haul myself across the floor. My muscles strained with effort, my very bones shrieking in protest, but I locked my cries behind my clenched teeth and kept going.

We made it through the hallway—arguably the easiest part. Now we had to make it through the hangar with the hope they'd given up on the water tank and the place was empty. Then out the door I'd seen with the hope it would go outside. Then a way to get out of this place with the hope nobody would catch us.

The plan had too much hope involved, and I hated it for that.

Softly, Erika lowered me to the floor, then took a breath and inched the metal door open, peering through the crack.

"It's empty," she whispered to me. "It really must be night." She opened the door all the way, propped it open with her foot, then reached for me again.

I pulled myself through to see she was right: the loading area was empty of people. The computer screen was still there, now dark, as was the glass box. Even in the shadows, I saw Erika go paler than she already was. Her fist tightened around the scalpel, and she scowled.

"I hate him," she breathed, so quietly I wondered if I made it up. "I *hate* him."

Getting across the vast space took considerably longer. With each thudding heartbeat, each tug on my muscles, fear pounded inside me. The scuffling of my body against the cement was deafening in my ears; I was sure someone would hear it.

Once we got about three quarters of the way across, Erika scampered ahead, checking around the corners with scalpel raised. I kept going during her investigating, my arms threatening to give out, and we met up at the base of the stairs that led to the door. Hopefully the door to our freedom.

I began the agonizing climb up the stairs with Erika half dragging me by my arm. There were only three stairs, then a small landing followed by another three stairs, but it felt like they went on for eternities, and I realized Hell was probably just a never ending staircase. Once I reached the second to last stair, Erika surged forward and cracked the thick door open.

My heart leapt at the brief gust of fresh air that hit my face. We were so close.

We're getting out of here.

Movements stiff, Erika opened the door enough to slip half her body through, keeping watch while extending her arm toward me. I reached for her hand to help pull me up the last stair, when I heard her gasp. I looked up just in time to see her disappear through the crack, and the door slammed shut, the sound reverberating through the warehouse.

Choking back a scream for her, I hauled myself up the last stair and reached for the door handle. At first, I could barely get the door to budge—it was so freaking *heavy*—but the desperation at who had Erika gave me strength from somewhere. Groaning through my teeth, I managed to crack the door enough to wedge half of me through. The door slammed painfully into my ribs, and I bit back a cry of pain. That cry got swallowed up when I took in the scene outside.

It was raining. The ground was a mess of dense mud, creating a dirty sea that stretched to the companion warehouse that stood several hundred yards away. Erika was pinned up against the wall just a few feet from me; the silver scalpel glinted in the mud at her feet. And keeping her there, hands clamped tight on her frail shoulders, was *him*.

They were both mostly dry, thanks to the small lip of roof over our heads, but Erika was deathly white and shaking as if she'd been left out in the storm all night. Motionless, her eyes were trained on the monster in front of her, her mouth open without sound. I couldn't tell over the rain, but I thought he was saying something to her.

Outrage roared in my ears—how *dare* he touch her. Growling, I crawled the rest of the way through the door, snatched up the scalpel, and went to stab his leg with it. My hand slipped in the mud, so it slashed across his shin. He shouted in pain and jumped back; I used the momentum to shove his legs, sending him to the ground. Erika fell—I hadn't realized he had been holding her up—and gave a muffled cry when she crumpled into the reddening mud.

The shout had drawn attention, and I caught a glimpse of several guards coming around from the other side of the second warehouse. I gave Erika a glance, telling her to run. She just stared at the blood flowing with the rain, in a daze.

She wasn't leaving me. Our escape failed.

Furious, I took the scalpel and climbed on top of him before he could get up, pressing the weapon to his throat. He went still, his face expressionless. Somehow, though, I found myself wondering if he'd stop me if I decided to shove the blade through his neck.

He's trying to use you again. Don't buy into it.

Knowing we had seconds at best, I forced the cracked words out of my mouth as water soaked every inch of me.

"Was she real?" The guards were coming now, and my stomach twisted at their shouts. But I had to know. I pushed the blade harder against his throat. "Was Kristen a lie too?"

Even buried in his vacant face, I saw it—I'd gotten too good at reading him. The slightest flicker in his eyes that told me enough.

Rage scalded my blood as the rain splattered and chilled my skin. "You don't deserve her," I spat with all the hate coursing through me. "After everything she did, every abominable thing she went through, she'd be horrified to know her son turned out just like the scum that murdered her." The flicker in his eyes cracked, and for a second I actually felt guilty I'd hit that nerve. Livid I still felt guilt for him, I snapped my teeth together. "You're exactly the monster your father was, and that will *never* change."

The second the words were out of my mouth, someone behind me grabbed a fistful of my hair and yanked me away. I lashed out with the scalpel, slashing one guy's arm, but someone else twisted my wrist and smashed it against the wall until I dropped the weapon. Another guard grabbed Erika and forced her deeper into the ground. I thrashed and she screamed and *he* shouted, and I was prepared to die right there in the rain rather than go back inside the hellish warehouse.

"Enough!"

Instantly, the scene froze. Everyone stopped. Even the rain seemed to stop, as if Mother Nature herself wouldn't dare cross the man standing in the doorway.

Alexis.

His wavy dark hair framed his square face as he glared at each of us, exuding a kind of power that rendered even *him* speechless.

None of us moved. None of us spoke. We all just stopped and stared, paralyzed. Alexis surveyed each of us with endless black eyes that could suck the life out of the entire planet if left unchecked.

Those eyes rested on me. My mouth went dry. My insides squelched and melted, I nearly threw up my guts right there.

"Bring it inside," Alexis ordered, his voice somehow soft and sharp at the same time, like the low growl of a hunting lion. I flinched. He just jerked his chin at Erika. "Her too." Then, as quickly as he appeared, he was gone, the door slamming shut in his wake.

Instantly, the tension lifted and we all found our range of motion again. The guards grabbed me by the arms, prepared to haul me inside for who knew what else.

But Alexis was *here*. And if he was here, it had to be for something important. Something worth his precious time.

I froze, realization smacking me in the face, and I felt *him* look at me in the same instant. I didn't care. I didn't care because I knew exactly what was so important for Alexis to be a part of.

They figured out how to use me.

An earth-shattering scream tore through my throat. I flailed and jerked and twisted, desperately trying to escape, and sobs wracked my chest when I realized there would be no escape. This was my fate, the fate I'd been running from for nearly two years, and it had finally caught up to me.

How many people would suffer because of this failure? How many people's lives would be ruined because I couldn't keep my secret safe? Another useless shriek left my mouth as three guards hauled me through the door, and I went limp. I'd never been qualified to do this, to protect something so important. I wasn't a survivor; I was a walking disaster. For this catastrophe, I deserved to be locked up, tortured, and killed.

I tried! I wanted to scream up at the sky. *I tried so hard, I tried with everything I had.*

But trying didn't matter. Sometimes you could kill yourself trying, and the universe just scoffed at the pathetic offering and didn't care one bit.

It's all over.

22

December 19th
Day 255

Kieran is still dead.
He left me, and now he's dead.
It's been three days since I read the letter. I haven't slept much, but every time I finally fall asleep, I wake up thinking it hasn't happened. Somehow, my brain tricks itself into thinking he's still here. I put the bracelet back on, which may have been a mistake, because feeling it against my wrist again makes me think this nightmare never

happened, and he never even left me in the first place.

Then seconds pass, and it hits me all over again, like there's a real dagger in my heart, twisting with every pointless breath.

What's the point of anything? What's the point of building a happy life you're proud of with people you love if it's all just going to get taken away?

I feel so alone. I don't talk to my parents. Erin's long gone, and she doesn't email back as often as she promised. I haven't spoken to Charlie for months, ever since I accused him of trying to turn me in as a mutant science freak. And Kieran's not just gone, but dead. Dead. I haven't even told anyone. And Connor...

I went to his party tonight. I don't know why. It's not like my brother just died and I'm wallowing in a kind of grief I can't even describe. But Connor really wanted me to go, and it was the first real interest he's shown in me in a long time, and I guess I just wanted to make him happy. So I went. And he didn't even show up. Pretty much the entire student body was there, but no Connor. I left after a half hour, and now I'm sprawled out on my bed in the pretty blue dress I rented to go in. He texted me with some excuse about work and told me he'd come over later to 'make it up to me' but I told him not to. It's not that I don't want him to, I just feel like being alone.

I don't know. I feel like something's wrong. I keep thinking about one of the last things Kieran said to me, and it was about Connor. He insisted again that Connor isn't good for me, and our 'relationship' isn't right. And now...I don't know, sometimes I start to wonder if Kieran's right. ~~I mean, there's a good chance Connor lied about work and really had his tongue down Mandy's throat. Wouldn't be the first time.~~

But he's all I have left. If Kieran really wanted me to stay away from him, then he shouldn't have left me with no other option. I should be grateful Connor will stand by me at all, even if it's not in exactly the way it used to be. And I shouldn't rail on him for wanting someone else, even if I don't like it when he's with other girls and my 'boyfriend' at the same time—it's not like an experiment is at the top of anyone's prospect list.

Maybe it's just the grief messing with my head, but I feel like something is really wron—

The doorbell rang. I ignored it despite the fact it was after midnight: Dad was always up, and usually Mom was too. One of them would get it. Probably prankster teenagers or something.

It rang again, pealing long and loud, as if someone were holding down on the button. When it rang for the third time, I sighed in exasperation and slammed my journal shut before pushing myself up off the bed. My dress swished around my ankles as I unlocked my bedroom door and crept down the hallway. The house was eerily silent, but I was used to that, especially since Kieran left and Dad spent most of his time in the office.

The floor creaked underneath me as I padded down the hallway. I was surprised to see the office door slightly ajar—usually it was shut tight whether he was in there or not. Stopping, I held my breath and counted to three before timidly poking my head around the corner.

I sucked in a sharp breath. The place was a disaster. Sure, the office wasn't very big or organized to begin with, but all the drawers in the filing cabinet had been pulled out, and most of the desk contents had been dumped on the floor.

The doorbell rang again. A pit formed in my stomach as I continued down the hallway, stopping again at the door to what had become just my mom's room. It was shut. Turning the knob as softly as I could, I inched the door open and peeked inside. Mom and Dad were sleeping soundly in the bed.

The pit in my stomach turned to acid. They hadn't slept in the same bed for months, and neither of them were ever asleep before one in the morning these days.

Something isn't right.

The doorbell rang three more times, impatient shrieks that didn't even rustle my parents. Dad was a light sleeper—one sneeze from Mom and he was jerking awake.

My hands shook softly as I closed their door and stepped out into the living room. I peeked through the hole in the front door, then deflated with a sigh at the familiar flash of blond. Steeling myself, I opened the door to see Connor.

"There you are," he said, unable to brush all annoyance out of his tone that I'd made him wait. "Took you long enough to answer."

I started to tell him to go home, that I was tired, but he ignored me and pushed his way inside. Automatically, I stepped back and let him in despite the lead weight inside me, making sure to stay arm's length away. I tried to think back to when I'd started dreading the idea of him kissing me, or even touching me.

Again, Kieran's voice sounded painfully in my head: *he's not good for you, Arie. It's not right.*

Thankfully, Connor seemed to have different things on his mind, for once. He reached for my hand; I hated myself for letting him take it.

"I've found someone," he said quietly, eyes shifting all over my shabby living room. "Someone that can help you."

My blood went cold. While Connor knew I'd been infected, Kieran had made me promise I wouldn't tell him my secret, and now I nearly collapsed in gratitude I'd listened to my older brother.

"What?" I stammered, trying to sneakily pull my hand out of his. "What do you mean?"

Rather than answering, he went to the front door and opened it. Momentarily confused, my jaw dropped when I saw two strangers standing on the porch. One younger but taller, one older but shorter; one with pristine hair and a nice jawline, one with a crooked smile and odd glint to his green eyes. One watching me with a fathomless expression, the other with a broad grin. I didn't know the younger one, but I recognized the other from rifling through Dad's documents. He was one of them—one of them that looked for people like me.

Connor had brought them here.

Now.

The frigid outside air prickled at my face, but I just stared, unable to really breathe. When I didn't do anything, the shorter one gestured toward me.

"Hello, there," he said, his voice higher than I expected. "My name is Jefferson, and this is my associate Mr. Sark. We don't mean to intrude, but I believe our services might be of use to you."

My brain froze. It wouldn't work. Something inside me wanted to scream, but somehow I knew that wouldn't help—someone had made sure my parents wouldn't hear.

When I continued to just stare, paralyzed with terror, Connor cleared his throat loudly as a signal for me to get my act together. I was embarrassing him. The ridiculous idea helped me to see reason, to focus.

"Arie Nolan, isn't it?" Jefferson offered.

Numbly, I nodded and swallowed hard. "Sorry, I wasn't...expecting...um, come in." I gestured to our pathetic living room and battered couches.

Despite the laughable offering, Jefferson's eyes brightened, like I'd pleasantly surprised him. "Why, thank you." His associate, Mr. Sark, looked less than impressed, but it was hard to tell—it was like he wore a cool, expressionless mask.

As the three of them sat on our fraying couch, I stayed standing and focused on breathing, in and out, in and out. My lungs wouldn't work on their own. I felt like I'd pass out.

"Tell me, Arie," Jefferson started, perched on the very edge of his seat. "Have your parents spoken to you about our organization? What we can do for you?"

I know that you're all here to dissect me like a frog.

I swallowed hard, willing my tone not to tremble too much. "We, um, we don't talk a lot."

"Ah, I see." He cocked his head, his tone turning sympathetic. "It's difficult for common people to understand your situation. Infection is rather exceptional; most don't know how to handle it. We can help with that, Arie. We represent a man named Donovan Alexis. I don't know what you may have heard about his organization, but your father is doing you no favors by keeping you locked up here for whatever purposes he has in mind. There are more people like you, and we can help you like we've helped them. You may not have a place in society, but you will with us."

My eyes widened, and I found myself perking up without my own permission. What if Dad had been lying to me? What if these people could actually help me, and he wanted to make sure I never found them?

I need help.

Connor was staring at the floor. Mr. Sark was studying me. Jefferson smiled at the flame of interest catching in my expression.

"We can help you, Arie," he said again. "Come with us."

Wringing my hands, I stared at a spot on the stained coffee table, still barely able to talk above a whisper. "Um, can I...can I get you water? I want to...I want to hear. What you have to say."

Jefferson nodded in encouragement. "Water would be great, thank you."

I hid my shaking hands in my skirt as I stumbled into the kitchen, ignoring the odor rising from the stack of dirty dishes that hadn't been touched in a week. Taking a breath, I flipped the sink on and watched the water run, counting in my head. When

I hit four, I tiptoed across the tile floor, opened the back door, and took off.

The streetlights were dim, but I knew these sidewalks well enough to navigate in the dark. Wintry air bit at me through my thin dress, and I whimpered at the gravel that dug into my bare feet.

My mind went on autopilot, taking me to the one place I had left to ask for help. Scampering through the snow on the lawn, I scrambled up the stairs of a red brick house and pounded on the door, just realizing the impossibly late hour.

Please be awake, please be awake, please be awake.

When Charlie answered, I let out a sigh of relief that sounded more like a dry sob. He was in a wrinkled t-shirt and boxer shorts, dark hair sticking up everywhere, and eyes bloodshot. They widened when he saw me, freezing to death in a dress without shoes, terror written all over my face.

"Arie?" he asked. Despite the situation, part of me relaxed at the sound of his voice. We hadn't talked in so long, and now I knew that had all been a mistake. "What's going on?"

"It's Connor," I let out in a rush. "He—"

"Did he hurt you?" Charlie had never been a fighter, but his hands clenched into fists as he looked over me again, the ends of my blue dress soaked and ruined.

I glanced behind my shoulder. The street was still deserted. "No, he just came over and—"

"Look, Arie." I turned back to see his expression darken with his tone, hardening his face in a way that was totally uncharacteristic. "I don't know why you haven't picked up on this by now, but I don't care about your boyfriend. And I don't want to hear about all his drama, okay? Just leave. Deal with it yourself."

He started to shut the door, but I stuck my hand out to keep it open. My heart cracked when he took a step back as I took one forward.

"Charlie, please." I checked behind my shoulder again. Empty. "He talked to these people, and I...I think they want to hurt me. I don't know what to do, and I—"

"Like you thought I was doing?" Charlie's indigo eyes flashed. "Really, Arie, I'm starting to think this 'condition' of yours is actually paranoid schizophrenia. How many more people are there left for you to accuse of turning you in?"

There's no one left. Everyone is gone.

"No, Charlie, this is different, I swear. Please just—"

Charlie leaned forward, striking with his words. "It's different because he's your scumbag boyfriend you chose over everyone despite the fact you knew him for two seconds and he treats you like crap. It's different because I was your *best friend*."

"Charlie." I choked, my eyes filling with tears. "I'm sorry, I was wrong and—"

"It's too late for all that." He sighed, some of the anger draining out of his system. Unforgiving sadness took its place. "Now get out. Go deal with your drama yourself. I'm over it." Then he slammed the door.

A sob caught in my throat, but I didn't get the chance to break down. Distant headlights illuminated the quiet street, getting closer each second. Shivering, I scurried off of Charlie's porch and across the street, stowing myself in the Maeve's giant bushes in their front yard. It was hard to make anything out in the shadows, but before the car passed I caught sight of a flash of blond. Connor knocked on Charlie's door, and in that moment I hated him for knowing me so well.

I can't talk to Charlie. I can't get anyone involved. The thought hit me like a semi-truck. If those men really wanted me, they'd probably use any means—or any person—necessary. And if they really knew what I was…

Bile rose in my throat. I watched long enough to see Charlie's mom answer the door this time, but I couldn't wait.

My bones seemed to rattle inside me as I extracted myself from the bushes, my mind buzzing with panic. Where would I go? What would I do?

Finally freeing myself, I turned to run in any direction away from Connor, but skidded to a stop. The guy from earlier, Mr. Sark, was standing a few feet away, blocking my path. Though he'd been impassive in my house, he seemed to have shifted slightly, and suddenly I couldn't even meet his hateful eyes. Just his presence made me shrink in on myself, my shoulders hunching with the weight of his calculating stare that was colder than the snow freezing my toes.

He didn't say anything. He just watched me, and my skin prickled despite the modesty of my dress. I felt like I was turned inside out, my whole being visible to his scrutiny.

Swallowing hard, I whipped around, only to find Jefferson on the other side. He held his hands up in surrender—a shocking contrast from Mr. Sark's blatant distaste for me already.

"There's no need to run," Jefferson told me. "We didn't mean to scare you. Though, your speed is rather impressive, despite no training, as Connor tells me. You must be pretty special if you can run faster than him without really trying, don't you think?"

I clenched my numb hands into fists, cursing the fact I'd just proved a point. If there had been any doubt that I was different, it was gone now.

Jefferson took a step toward me. I matched with one back, very aware of Mr. Sark much too close to me now, then awkwardly sidestepped so I wasn't sandwiched between them anymore.

"You're special, Arie," Jefferson continued. "Nobody here understands that. We can help you—"

"Help me?" My voice was too high and cracked with panic and cold. "If you wanted to help me, then why send Connor?"

"To watch your father, of course. We wanted to make sure he didn't do anything with the formula that he'd regret. Unfortunately, we missed it, but that doesn't mean things are over for you. We can help. We sent you a friend, didn't we?"

I narrowed my eyes, a buried truth bursting out of my mouth, scalding and soothing as it came. "Connor has been awful to me."

For once, Jefferson lost a degree of pleasantry and his jaw set with irritation. "Yes, well teenage boys tend to get distracted, now don't they?"

No. I'd given Connor plenty of pathetic excuses. I wasn't going to let this Jefferson guy give them too. Jerking my chin out, I took another meandering step away from the men, keeping a mental tab on Connor still at the front porch. He hadn't noticed us yet.

My resolve must've shown on my face, because Jefferson's mouth pressed into a hard line. All the friendliness evaporated from his expression, and a deranged kind of hostility brutalized his features.

"Arie Nolan," he sneered, "ask yourself what you have left to fight for. You friends are gone. You're a ghost in your own house, and your parents obviously don't care about you if they did this to you. You are alone." He took a step toward me, and with shaking hands I held my ground, which made him scowl at me. "We can either be your only ally or your worst enemy. The choice is yours."

I never had a choice.

Gritting my teeth, I cocked my head to the side, toward Connor, who had just wrapped up his conversation with Charlie's mom and was making his way over to us. Slumping my shoulders, I took a couple slow steps toward him, lacing my countenance with submissive acceptance. Like the obedient, pathetic puppy he'd trained me to be.

I counted down in my head.

Three.

Two.

One.

I whipped around and kicked with my frozen foot. Snow sprayed into the air, and I used the fleeting distraction to make a break through the Maeve's yard and jump their fence, landing in a sprint that sent me worlds away.

I ran, not recognizing the true danger of the monsters behind, how they'd stalk my every step and haunt every nightmare.

I ran, not realizing that was the last time I'd see my house, my parents, Charlie, or any shred of the life I had.

I ran, not knowing that I'd never stop.

23

The guards dropped me on the floor, purposefully letting my body slam against the solid concrete. My eyes went blurry for a second as I took in the unfamiliar room: it was narrow and dim, with several cracked mirrors lining one wall. They dropped Erika next to me. She dissolved into a defeated heap, her feeble body shaking. Then the guards left. I refused to lift my head up, knowing I'd find three devils standing in front of me, and I dreaded their judgement. My wet body felt so heavy, I thought I'd sink into the concrete and never be able to climb out.

It's over. It's all over.

The taste of mud clung to my mouth as a hand gripped my chin and forced my head up. Jefferson.

"Despite the *considerable* amount of time and resources we've spent on you, results remain largely inconclusive." The bite in Jefferson's voice was vicious, but I had the impression it wasn't for me. "So I'm only going to try this once."

Jefferson released my chin. I slumped, refusing to look at Alexis or the sopping wet monster next to him as I tried to figure out what Jefferson meant.

"You know what we want," Jefferson went on, straightening up and wincing slightly, then stretching out his injured leg. "We will find the key eventually, one way or another. Tell us the truth, and this will be over."

Even in my numb desolation, confusion bubbled. Tell the truth? I'd already slipped up. I'd told the traitor exactly what he wanted to know, and that information was why I was here in the first place. Why would they go to this trouble if they already knew?

"Arie," Jefferson added in caution. "Your clock is ticking."

Suddenly, my sluggish mind was racing. Was it really possible that they didn't know?

Huffing through his teeth, Alexis surged forward and produced a gun from his expensive jacket. He stalked right up to Erika, grabbed a fistful of her hair, and pressed the weapon to her temple. She gritted her teeth to trap a whimper, locking her eyes on mine.

It's okay, she seemed to tell me. *Do what you have to.*

So I did.

Hesitantly, I forced myself to meet Alexis' soulless black eyes. "Please," I rasped, my voice long since spent. "I don't know. I don't know what a key is, or what that means." Tears started flowing down my face, the panic and desolation in my tone real. "All I know is my dad shot me up with something and now I'm different and you won't leave me alone. I don't know. I don't know the point. I'm just like every other infected I've met, I...I don't know. Please don't hurt her. I don't know."

Alexis narrowed his eyes, weighing my answer. Then he pulled the trigger.

I gasped; Erika flinched. Even *he* stumbled forward a step in what must've been surprise.

Instead of a bullet, though, there was an airless click.

Empty.

A test.

Tossing the useless gun, Alexis released Erika and stalked toward the door. "Kill them and move on," he ordered over his shoulder. "We're done here."

It worked. My limbs went numb with euphoria, taking all pain away. I didn't understand, couldn't comprehend what just happened...but it worked.

Relief struck me, suffocated me, and it was so thick that I instantly succumbed to it, falling into a peaceful pit of darkness that only death could bring.

24

Eons passed before the darkness ebbed, pain pouring in and filling all the cracks in my soul. That wasn't right. I was dead: everything should've stopped hurting.

Slowly coming to myself, I tried to make sense of what had happened before I admitted to consciousness. I was stretched out on something long and soft, but stiffer than a bed. There wasn't a sound besides a steady beeping of some machine in time to my heartbeat. I barely turned my right wrist and felt a slight tug: an IV.

I'm in a hospital. Maybe Jefferson had thought he'd killed me, but underestimated my talent for durability. Maybe they thought they had done me in and didn't dispose of my body well enough, and now I was a Jane Doe under the care of some doctor.

Where is Erika? I couldn't even broach the thought. *One thing at a time.*

Despite the pit in my stomach, I forced my breaths to stay even, my heartbeat smooth. If I spent too much time in a hospital, someone would eventually figure out I was infected—not what I wanted. I had to get out of here before someone caught on.

I counted to fifty-five, and when I hadn't heard or sensed anything or anyone, I cracked my eyes open.

Then I blinked.

Blinked again.

Nothing changed.

A scream got caught in my throat and the machine started beeping erratically. Bolting upright, I ripped the IV from my arm and lurched off the couch, as if the leather cushions burned me.

How was I back *here*? How could I be in this despicable house *again*?

Lurching to my feet, I staggered two wobbly steps before crumpling to the ground, the effects of Jefferson's crippling drug still lingering. I hit the floor hard, and suddenly footsteps thumped behind me.

"No!" My voice was dead and scratchy, barely audible. Even without looking, I could sense it was him, and I dug my fingernails into the hardwood floor to drag myself away.

"Arie."

I flinched, hating the sound of my name is his mouth, hating that he sounded like mine when I knew he wasn't.

"Arie, please. You're going to hurt yourself."

Clenching my teeth, I closed my eyes and slammed my fist against the mirror wall, feeling the hopelessness crash into me. "Don't! Just kill me! Just *let me die*!" Falling into cries, I curled against the mirror and covered my head with my arms. "Please just let me die. I can't...I can't do anymore. Please."

"I'm not going to kill you." The words were softer and shakier than I expected from him. I hated them. "I won't hurt—"

A mix of a sob and a growl went through my teeth. I lifted up my head and glared, my tears blurring the sight of him kneeling in front of me. Such strong revulsion shot through me, I nearly threw up right there. "I won't be your key pet," I snapped in a blubber. "I won't. Just kill me and be done. Kill me like you killed Erika."

In my blurry vision, I saw him shake his head. "Arie, she's okay. She's alive."

It was a carefully crafted lie, and I wanted it to be real so badly that I paused—I paused just enough for the water in my eyes to drain so that I could really see him.

He sat on the ground in front of me with his arms wrapped around his legs. The position looked strange on him, the boyish stance not matching his nice clothes or tough shoulders. His piercing blue eyes bore into mine. They paralyzed me, shocked me to the core, because they were a raging storm, wet with moisture he was fighting hard to keep inside.

One thought echoed in my head: the Sark I was scared of could never look like that.

Sark watched me for a moment, so hesitant and so careful and so *scared*, in a way I'd never seen before.

"It's okay," he finally whispered, wincing against his own cracked voice like he couldn't tolerate the sound. "I swear, I won't hurt you. I won't touch you. I'll stay away from you." I took a shuddering breath and he nodded. "I won't hurt you. I promise."

Shaking with shallow gasps, I looked him over once, twice, huddling closer to myself, farther from him. I swallowed hard, but my voice was still coarse. "Where's Erika?"

He deflated slightly, as if in relief. "She's asleep now. She needed..." He clenched his teeth and ducked his head. "A lot."

I remembered the bruises on her face, the blood on her skin, the shadows in her eyes. The memory sent my body aching, though it was much fainter than it should've been. "What did you give me?"

"Morphine." He glanced up in apology. "I know, I shouldn't...I should've asked your permission. But you...you were..."

I swallowed again. I knew exactly the bad shape I was in. I knew exactly how vulnerable I was right now, and I knew exactly how great of an actor Sark could be.

But his eyes. Those stupid eyes of his made it so hard for me to turn away, to believe the agony in them was fabricated.

"Get away from me," I whispered, my own eyes watering in response to his. "Get away now."

He clenched his jaw and nodded, barely keeping himself stitched together. "Okay." Slowly, he got to his feet, half raising his hands and taking deliberate steps backward.

I worked to keep my glare up, to keep myself from hysterics for just a little longer. "Where's Erika? What did you do to her?"

"Nothing. She's asleep." He glanced up at the ceiling. "She, um, wanted to be outside, so she's up—"

Suddenly, a crashing sound echoed down the hallway, coming from the foyer. I jumped at the sound and whimpered. Sark's eyes widened, his lips pursed, and he froze for a half a second before springing into action.

I'd never seen him move so fast. He jerked the mirror door open and picked me up, slapping a hand over my mouth to silence my built up scream, then practically threw me inside. Before I could scramble out, he grabbed the IV supplies and machinery while tapping on his phone. Chucking all of it in with me, he shut the door. I yelped when he broke the knob off from the outside and slid it in his pocket.

Trapped. I was trapped in here.

Prepared to beat the door down with whatever strength I could find, I paused when I saw his phone on the floor next to the piano. Sliding over, I picked it up to find the screen was flashing with emergency. It was synced to the house—he'd just enacted extra security measures, locking all the doors and stopping the elevators. A small box was in the bottom corner of the screen, playing some kind of feed. I tapped it. The screen enlarged and I recognized the roof. And curled up on the couch, breathing peacefully, was Erika. The sight of her alive sent an aching relief washing through me.

He wasn't lying.

The next moment, another crashing sounded. I glanced up to see Sark facing the hallway expectantly, all emotion gone from his face. A robot compared to the fragmenting young man that had been in front of me moments ago.

"I don't believe it."

I squeaked in horror when Felix and Vega appeared from the hallway, their eyes narrowed and bodies tense. For a harrowing second I felt hideously exposed, before I remembered that I was safe behind the mirror wall—they couldn't see or hear me.

They stopped halfway into the living room. Felix shook his head at Sark. "I really don't believe it. I knew something was up, but this? Unbelievable." He held up a black box with a speaker—some kind of recording device—and I heard Sark curse under his breath as he clenched his hands into fists.

Felix pressed a button on the device. My stomach dropped when my own voice erupted the tense air.

"They know."

"They know? Know what? That we're with Sark?"

"They know?" My voice broke and I started crying. *"They know."*

"Arie, they know what? I don't underst—"

"It's me! It's me. It's my...body, biology, something, it has codes for the key, and I...it's me. It's me.

The conversation continued, ending with Sark's instructions to go to the parking garage. A clicking sounded; Felix threw the device on the floor, and it landed at Sark's feet.

"Clever," Felix continued, "using her like that. So clever that nobody bothered to wonder why you hadn't called Jefferson. You weren't planning on meeting him there at all, right? *He* found *her*, and followed her to you. And you just went along with it, and nobody questioned daddy's favorite boy."

Sark's jaw twitched at that, but he just stared at them, motionless, a statue of calm expectation.

Felix scoffed in disgust. "Even if it makes sense now, I still don't believe it. You were really going to help her get out, even after you knew what she is. After everything you've worked for, everything you built, you were just going to let her walk away."

Finally, Sark spoke, steady and cool. "You missed her. She's not here."

"Figured." Felix and Vega started walking forward, calculating each step. "Alexis has already started the hunt for her. He has a far reach—you know that. He'll find her in no time. Too bad you won't be around to see it." They stopped a few feet in front of Sark, in front of me, so close I could see Felix's crooked nose as he gave a cruel grin. "I'll enjoy this."

I sat there frozen, watching as Felix rolled his neck and Vega clenched his fists and Sark's shoulder went tense. They had a brief standoff, the atmosphere taut with hatred and anticipation, then

Felix took the first swing and something clicked into place in my brain.

Sark was sacrificing himself for me.

Paralyzed by the opposing emotions raging inside me, I watched in a kind of incredulous horror as they fought. Sark held his own against Felix and only suffered a couple blows when Vega joined the fight, clearly used to unfair brawls. My limbs were rigid and motionless as I watched the sick show, unsure what to hope for, flinching every time Felix or Vega landed a hit.

In one second, though, the tide shifted. In one second, Vega managed to punch Sark hard in the ribs once, twice, three times. Sark went down and Felix grabbed him from behind. I gasped at the glint in his eyes as he snatched Sark's arm and jerked it backwards. The breaking sound was sickening. Sark's roar of agony was worse.

The scream snapped something inside me. Suddenly, all my movement came back to me in a rush and I pushed myself up on my weak legs, beating myself against the door as they beat up on him. The door didn't budge; my knees gave out.

I caught a glimpse of something metal.

Felix had a gun.

Desperation burst through me, giving me a rush of energy. Not knowing what else to do, I grabbed the piano bench and slammed it against the door, crying out at the strain on my body. But I slammed once, twice, five times. On the sixth, a hinge came loose. On the eighth, another hinge cracked.

By the tenth it was open.

I used what strength I had left to chuck the piano bench at Felix. He looked up when the door broke, and the bench hit him right in the face. He lost his grip on the gun and toppled over, crashing into Vega, and the three men gaped at my form crumpled up on the floor. I saw stars for a second, swallowing down bile. Sark's eyes widened with horror.

Felix just grinned, rubbing his jaw and starting toward me. "Now this is just too perfect."

"Don't touch her," Sark snarled. He tackled Felix to the ground. Vega glared at me, then both of us glanced at the gun on the floor in between us. We both lunged.

He got there first, but I was prepared for that. I drove my foot into his stomach and punched him in the face. He squeezed the trigger, blindly letting off a shot, and I heard glass shatter behind me. Then I twisted the gun from his grip and shot him in the shoulder. He howled and clutched the wound.

I turned to Sark only to have Felix slam into me. The gun slid from my grasp, and when I reached for it Felix plowed my head into the floor. I blacked out momentarily. I came to just in time to see Vega standing over me, blood rushing from his shoulder, and Sark rolling around with Felix. Felix gained the advantage and pummeled Sark's face. One punch. Two. On the third, Sark went limp, his eyes rolling up in his head.

I let out a broken scream. Jerking myself around, I threw my elbow into Vega's kneecap, then drove my knee into his groin when he buckled. The gun clattered to the floor. Felix and I dove for it; this time I won. My hand closed around the weapon and I bashed it as hard as I could into Felix's head. He crumpled, disoriented. I hit him again and he went out, then I turned and smashed the gun into Vega's unsuspecting skull. He sagged, unconscious. Tossing the gun, I dragged myself over to Sark.

Don't be dead don't be dead don't be dead don't be dead.

I winced in spite of myself when I saw his face up close: it was bruised and bloody, one side of his jaw swollen and one eye purple. I couldn't look at the odd angle of his arm.

Softly, I tapped his uninjured shoulder. No response. Harder. Nothing. I shook him as hard as I could. He didn't budge.

"Sark?" My voice was scratchy, my shoulders heaving with near hyperventilation. "Sark, please wake up. Please. I'm sorry." The word caught in my throat and my eyes watered. "I'm sorry. Please get up. Get up. *Get up!*"

I shoved his shoulder again, then drew back when he groaned. His fingers twitched, his forehead creasing, and his eyelids fluttered open.

"Arie?"

I dropped my head onto his chest and burst into tears.

"Arie, what…" His voice was low and hoarse as he panted in pain. I felt him shift slightly, probably taking in the scene, and he groaned again. "Arie, what were you *thinking*?"

I just shook my head, my skin scraping against the buttons of his shirt, and cried harder.

He wrapped his good arm around me. "It's okay. You're okay. I'm—" The words caught on a gasp of pain he forced through his teeth. "I'm so sorry. I should've known they might find out. I didn't think to check her phone. We should've left already. I'm sorry. For all of it."

"How?" I sobbed because I didn't understand how I could want to kill and hug someone at the same time.

"I didn't set you up, I swear. They surprised me. I had to go along with it to stay alive, or they...they would've..." He sighed, a deep aching sound that seemed to come from the very core of him. "They were going to give her to the guards. Erika. After her interrogation, they were going to let them kill her, however they wanted. I had to...I had to claim some disgusting possession over her, so they wouldn't..." He shuddered, and his voice broke. "Her face, when I said that..."

"They kept her alive for you?" He must've made a persuasive case for them to keep a useless civilian.

"Yes." He sounded miserable. "After Alexis left, I said I wanted to be the one to kill you both. They all...it took convincing, but Erika played it perfectly, and I managed to bring you both back here. That was stupid. We should've left."

"And Erika...she..." My tears lulled as the truth hit me. "She knew?"

"I told her. While you were trying to escape. I gave her keys to a truck, but the guards noticed before you could get out. I swear, Arie, I didn't mean for any of it to happen." Another tremor went through him. "I didn't. I'm so sorry I let them do so much to you, but it was already so suspicious, and I didn't dare do more than ruin the data, but I still can't..."

He kept talking, but I didn't hear. I froze. My bones turned to lead, my heart stalling, as the forgotten reality crashed its way back into me.

Sark knew.

Sark *knew*.

Slowly, I held my arms to my chest and sat up, leaning away until I wasn't touching him anymore. Our eyes locked. His were laced with confusion and sorrow, then widened with understanding. My breath caught and I dropped my gaze, hunching my shoulders against the crushing shame I felt.

"I'm sorry," I choked out, because I felt the world deserved an apology for having to house me. "I'm sorry."

Sark reached his hand toward me. "No, Arie—"

"No." I jerked back, wrapping my arms around myself. "You should stay away from me. Now that...now that they know, they'll come for me. I can't hide forever." Tears started streaming down my face. "They'll find me. I know they will. They'll find me and I'll be the monster and you'll all hate me. It was my responsibility and I—" A deep sob choked me off and I cried into my hands.

I failed.

Sark shifted next to me, and I heard him curse under his breath. Peeking through my hands, I found him sitting up, cradling his hurt arm. Then he looked at me, staring right down into my soul.

"I've seen monsters." His eyes were haunted but genuine. "You aren't one."

I shook my head. "You don't know that."

"I do. Arie, in all the time I've known you—in some of the worst times of your life, no less—you have never once shown the capability of being a monster, even set against the backdrop of being the key, and that won't change. You are the most human person I've ever met."

New tears were forming at his blind faith in me, but I sucked in a sharp breath when I realized what he'd said. My mouth snapped shut and I drew back. "You knew."

Sark shut down. All human emotion left his eyes, replaced with careful calculation, as he realized his mistake. He watched me a moment before saying, "I guessed."

I curled inward, the blow leaving me breathless. I'd tried *so hard* to keep my secret a freaking secret, and really I was just deluding myself. "How? How did you know?"

Sark sighed and rubbed his forehead. "From day one, I...I wanted it to be you. I wanted to be the one to find the key so badly, that I convinced myself it had to be my infected. Of course, nobody believed me. Jefferson thought I was too eager to solve it, that I needed to give it time so I didn't make a fool of myself. So I watched you closely for any kind of evidence."

"And you found it." My lip curled with revulsion for myself.

"Not necessarily. You were just...different. Different than any of the others. The other infecteds seemed to operate on the fear of pain, while your concerns were more internal. You had different priorities. It was subtle, but it was there, and I was sure it meant something. Again, Jefferson, and later Lennon, thought I was just making things up, and I hated you for keeping it all from me. I thought eventually you'd break and just admit it to me. That's why Jefferson came to the parking garage that day—after months of me badgering him about you, he finally decided to give me a chance, and he caught sight of you going inside the parking garage on his way into the city. He was irritated, to say the least, when I denied everything, claiming that I'd been wrong. It took weeks of keeping up the charade and faking the data before they started to believe me, but by then..." He trailed off and shivered.

I shook my head. "And when I was here, just living in your house?"

Sark adjusted his arm and winced. "After our...truce, I guess, I put it all on hold. Eventually, I realized I didn't *want* it to be you anymore, and the likelihood that you were actually the key seemed so small. The idea left my mind. And then..."

"And then?"

He sighed. "And then I found you in my office, surrounded by reversal files, bloody and screaming everything was your fault. That's when I knew."

I blinked in shock, my mouth falling open. "But that was *months* ago."

"And?" His eyebrows furrowed.

"And you let me stay?" I couldn't understand that. I was the key—nobody in their right mind would dare take that on. My mom hadn't. Kieran hadn't. I'd just accepted the idea that if anyone found out what I was, it was over. They'd hate me.

I'm a monster.

Sark just stared at me, mouth open in an airless gasp as if I'd dug a blade in his side. Then he took a deep breath through his teeth and adjusted his arm. "I'm taking Erika and we're leaving. I have a place we can stay for awhile, one Alexis doesn't know about. And you..."

I dropped my eyes, forcing back a sob.

Sark placed a finger under my chin, so lightly I hardly felt the touch, and lifted my head to meet his gaze. "I don't care what you are, Arie. I don't. I just care that you're safe, and that's the whole truth. Of course, the choice is always yours and I'll never force your hand, but…"

But they'd come after me. Now that he had a name and face to target, Alexis would pour every resource at his disposal to tracking me down. How long could I hope to last on my own? But how could I force all that danger on the two people I cared most about?

"I can save you," he said, the rawness to his eyes holding me captive. "I can. If you'll let me."

I watched him with rogue tears rolling down my cheeks, measuring the words. My last test for him.

"Saving me won't bring her back."

Sark flinched. I didn't have to say her name, and somehow I was grateful for that: Kristen's name seemed too reverent for this scene.

His voice was rougher, his head bowed slightly. "I know. It's not about that anymore." Gingerly, he took my hand and squeezed it. "You saved me—not just today. Let me save *you*."

I closed my eyes, my forehead creasing with the weight of everything I was carrying. It was all so heavy; I thought I'd get crushed underneath it. But right as the blackness threatened to swallow me up, there was one thing tethering me in place: Sark's hand in mine.

Numbly, I nodded. "Okay."

Sark squeezed my hand again before letting go. "I'm going to get Erika. You have three minutes to change your clothes and pack a bag. We have to get out of here."

I cried again when I saw Erika. She held me tight against her gaunt body, dampening my greasy hair with her own tears. It was only when Sark came up from the basement with three bags on one arm and the other in a sling that she let me go. They loaded up a car while I leaned up against the wall, supporting myself as I limped down the hallway and left the disaster zone behind.

I cried yet again when we drove away. Wrapped up in a fresh hoodie that smelled like soft laundry detergent, I huddled in a ball on the seat and cried as quietly as I could, breathing in the fresh scent of the fabric and trying to stay somewhat calm. The morphine was wearing off, and my body was paying the price.

Sark spoke on the phone as he sped down the street, driving despite Erika's mild protests. The guy had been nearly beaten to death twenty minutes ago, and yet he was still breaking traffic laws left and right to get us where we needed to go. Erika held up his phone to his ear so he could arrange the money and resources he'd kept hidden from Alexis all these years. He'd been saving it for a rainy day, and today was a hurricane.

Watching the city blur by, I wondered how long it would take for anyone to realize Felix and Vega never came back. In just a few hours, Alexis' men would be crawling all over Chicago, searching for us.

The realization hit me so hard, the wind got knocked out of me. Sark finished up his last call and I leaned as far forward as my seatbelt would let me.

"What's wrong?" Sark asked, noting my expression in the rearview mirror before I even said anything. Erika took my hand in hers.

"What about Alaina?" I rasped. "We can't just leave her here."

Sark shook his head halfway through me talking. "She won't come with us."

"But still, we have to warn her. Lennon will know you lied and he'll come looking for her."

"You can call her."

"Anyone can track the club's landline—it's too easy. We have to stop there. I have to talk to her before we go."

"No."

I opened my mouth to protest, and Erika squeezed my hand. "But—"

"I have to get you out of here," Sark snapped, decision clearly made. "I've kept you too long as it is, and the risk is too high." His tone softened slightly. "I'm sorry, but no. They'll be fine."

I clenched my jaw so tight it hurt, torn between being grateful for all he'd already given me and demanding he do what I say. "You don't believe that."

Sark started to argue, but Erika put her hand on his arm. "Sark," she murmured, her low voice still cracked beyond repair.

We came to a stoplight. Sark and Erika locked eyes for a few moments before he let out a long breath and rubbed his forehead. "Arie," he groaned through his teeth. Then he looked at me in the mirror. "Fine. Three minutes. No more."

I sagged in relief. "Thank you." Pulling back, I curled on the seat again, desperately trying to keep my body together, hoping I could hold out until we got to wherever we were going.

The light turned green. A few beats of silence passed before Sark glanced in the rearview mirror again and asked, "What are you going to tell her?"

I knew what he was really asking, but I didn't have an answer for that yet. Closing my eyes, I rested my throbbing head against the window. "I don't know."

We had to backtrack to get to the club. My empty stomach had worked itself into a frenzied knot, and I nearly threw up with the car stopped in the back alley.

What am I going to tell her?

"Three minutes," Sark told me, parking the car and leaning back in his seat.

Steeling myself, I took off my seatbelt and stepped out of the car. The afternoon sun was bright overhead; I squinted and ducked my head, using the car, then the wall, for support as I shuffled to the door that had been dubbed mine months ago.

The lights were on in the back room. Chelsie and Mara were painting the walls, and they both screamed when they saw me.

"Arie?" Chelsie gasped as Mara trembled. Then she shouted, "Arie!"

The shout was like a beacon. Mark burst into the room with searching eyes, a flash of red behind him, and Liam and Andrew skidded in from the stage area. They all gaped and gasped until Alaina shoved them out of the way.

A mangled cry escaped her lips when she saw me, her black eyes huge. Then she lurched forward and hugged me. The sensation felt safe and painful at the same time.

"I'm sorry," I whispered. "I'm so sorry."

"What happened?" she demanded. "It's been *weeks* since I saw you, and you disappeared off the face of the earth." She leaned back, glancing over me again, and a single tear fell down her face. "What happened?"

I held back my own tears. "Alexis. He found out about Sark. We were able to escape but they're after us now, and we have to go. We're leaving now."

Alaina pursed her lips, giving me her answer without me even voicing the question, but I'd already known that would be the case: she would never leave her family, and her family would never leave Chicago.

I nodded. I understood. "I just wanted to warn you. Lennon will know Sark lied about you. He'll come looking for you too. They'll all be here. Just...please be so careful."

Alaina raised an eyebrow. "They'll *all* be here? Why?"

"Arie."

I turned to see Sark in the doorway, expression mournful but resolute. My time was up.

Alaina went pale at the sight of Sark, and I heard the others gasp. It hurt my heart to leave them, to know I had friends here, and I had to abandon them in such danger.

I swallowed hard and looked back at Alaina. "Just be careful, okay?"

"No." She tightened her grip on me, searching my face. "Something else happened. What's really going on?"

She's my best friend. I could tell her now. The secret was out anyway—if Lennon found her, he'd make sure she knew what I was. *You know you can trust her.*

But I met her gaze and froze, unable to force the words out of my mouth, to face her reaction. "I...I..." My tears spilled over and I shook my head. "I'm sorry. I'm just so sorry." Taking a shuddering breath, I stepped away from her, out of her grasp. "Be careful. Be so careful. I'm sorry."

I'm sorry I can't be the friend you deserve.

Alaina protested, demanding to know what really happened and reaching for me again. I stepped away, heading for the door, but Mark bombarded me in a giant bear hug, holding me tight. I hugged him back and cried into his shoulder.

"It's not goodbye forever," he promised in my ear, voice thick. "Just for now."

I nodded. *It's not forever.*

"Thank you," I whispered back. There was no way, no time, no words to adequately express what I felt for all of them, how grateful I was that they had accepted me into their lives.

"Make sure Sark takes care of you, okay? We'll be back jamming together in no time."

I cracked a small smile. "Okay."

With my arms still around his neck, Mark carried me to the car so I didn't have to walk. I waved to Mara, Chelsie, and Andrew over his shoulder; Chelsie's mouth just hung open, Mara burst into sobs, and Andrew returned my wave. Now in a mess of tears, Alaina started for me, but Liam held her back. Our eyes met. He nodded at me. I nodded back.

Take care of her.

Mark slid me into the backseat of the car, forcing a grin and making some quip about wearing my seatbelt. Then he shut my door and waved until we turned the corner, watching as we disappeared.

Three Months Later

The cool water washed over my feet in small waves as I buried my toes in the sand. It was a beautiful day, a staple for this place: the sun shone in a clear sky, the blue ocean sparkling and stretching on forever. If I looked at it long enough, I could almost convince myself that I was the only person in the whole world. Funny, how I always daydreamed of a secluded beach, and now here I was.

I didn't know where exactly in Florida we were. I didn't really care. The house here was less than half the size of the one in Chicago, but it was homey and easier to manage. It stood on a deserted area of the beach, miles away from the nearest town and just a minute walk from the coast. The empty stretch of sand was a perfect place for me on days like today.

The gorgeous weather did little to shake off the nightmare that had been plastered to my eyelids since I woke up. The dreams had been coming more often and with more cruelty than ever before. They all started different but ended the same: with Alexis showing up and murdering Sark and Erika before taking me. Every single time. Then Sark would wake me up and calm me down, waiting minutes or hours with me until I fell back asleep. Every single time.

This morning, though, I couldn't fall back asleep, even though it wasn't even four yet. I told Sark he could go back to bed, but he stayed with me, and we ended up on the floor in the kitchen—Sark with a cup of coffee, and me with a carton of ice cream. It was easier for both of us to talk in the dark, and even though it was terrible and he had to be at least as exhausted as I was, we had some of our best conversations during those early hours. Sometimes it was about the formula. Sometimes our childhoods. Most of the time it was about things like whether we believed in God or what kind of cereal was the best without milk.

Once the sun came up, though, the spell broke. I helped Erika with breakfast that I didn't really eat, then wandered out to the beach to watch the ocean. Sometimes I thought if I stared at the horizon enough, I'd see an attack coming from miles away.

I stayed outside until the sun had crested and began its slow descent. It was a Monday, which meant Erika was cleaning the house, Sark was hiding in his office, and I had chores to do. He'd been hiding out down there a lot more recently. Sometimes I caught myself daydreaming that he cracked reversal and I got to have a normal life again.

Stop. Going down that road was never good. Instead, I wiped the sand off my feet on the doormat and went inside to start sweeping.

The kitchen was empty. I went for the pantry and rifled through it, searching for the broom and dustpan. I found the silver dustpan on top of a pile of papers tucked into the bottom shelf, and a brief smile crossed my face when I saw one of the pages on top was a marriage certificate, complete with Sark and Erika's sloppy signatures.

What a night that was.

They had been drunk—the first and only time I'd ever seen Erika drunk—and had started by daring each other to do ridiculous things, culminating in a marriage ceremony. I was the officiator, butchering my lines as we laughed through the whole thing, and we downloaded a certificate off the internet. It had been a weird night, but it was one of the only real good, stress-free times we'd had since coming to Florida. And it must've been binding in *some* way, even if unofficially, because they both had worn rings ever since.

Something clattered behind me. I extracted myself from the pantry, expecting Erika to be there. I was alone. Confused, I dropped the dustpan and peeked around the corner into the living room. Also empty. The mirror door to my new piano room was shut, so Erika likely wasn't cleaning in there, especially since she usually saved that for the end of her routine so we could do it together.

I bent down to retrieve my dustpan when I noticed the dishes from breakfast piled in the sink. That wasn't right. Erika would've done those hours ago.

Skin prickling, I flipped on the kitchen sink to the coldest setting and splashed my face, then dried myself off and stared out the window above the sink.

You are so paranoid, I told myself. My suspicion about everything increased every day, so I knew I just needed to chill. *Erika's probably downstairs trying to convince Sark to come help. It's fine.*

Taking a breath, I picked up the broom and started sweeping the floor. The bristles scraping against the tile was the only sound besides the distant waves crashing on the shore.

It's too quiet. Not that the three of us were ever loud, but this silence was too much. I managed to sweep for another thirty seconds before my hands were shaking too hard.

This is ridiculous, I told myself, leaning the broom up against the counter. *Look, I'll prove it to you.*

I walked through the kitchen, stopping at the top of the stairs. "Erika?" I called.

I waited. No response.

"Erika? Sark?"

There was nothing but the waves.

"Okay, guys, you're really starting to freak me out." Hesitantly, I started down, taking a step at a time. "Sark? Where are you?"

I hit the third step when someone pushed me from behind. A yelp of surprise escaped me as I tumbled down the stairs, hitting my head against the wall on the way. I landed in a heap at the bottom, only to find a man in a suit waiting there for me, and I kicked him down before he could grab me. Turning, I prepared to bolt back up the stairs, but another man was there, stopping me in my tracks. And he had a gun.

My throat closed up. He jerked his chin out at me, and I held up my shaky hands. Following his gestured command, I walked slowly up the stairs, aware of him and his weapon right behind me, as I tried to place where I'd seen him before. Both men carried themselves differently, somehow, than Alexis' cronies did, and were dressed too nice.

Who are you?

He marched me straight through the kitchen. I froze over when I saw the living room.

It was no longer empty.

The mirror door was ajar, and it seemed men in suits had spilled out of it, filling up the space. Erika sat at their feet with a strip of duct tape over her mouth, wrists bound and eyes wide. Sark was on his knees next to her, handcuffed. The man behind him had a gun pressed to the back of his head.

I sucked in a sharp breath. Where was Alexis? Jefferson? Even Lennon?

"Interesting."

My blood went cold. I turned to see an older man enter from the hallway, sunlight bouncing off his round, bald head, and shoulders straight with superiority.

Richard Dalton.

"I have to say, Arie, I'm a little surprised to find you here," he said, his lips pulling into a smirk, which looked odd on top of his tiny chin. "Since when do you affiliate yourself with these kind of traitors?"

My mouth went dry. He stepped fully into the living room and I stumbled back, gauging his every breath.

When did I become so scared of him?

My eyes did another sweep of the room, and the memory came back to me: I recognized two of his men from the day in Chicago when they'd been tailing me. When I'd spilled everything because I thought they knew my secret.

Finally, words trembling, I asked, "What do you want?"

"What do I want?" His eyebrows pulled down and his expression darkened. "How about the truth. Let's start with that."

"The truth?" I felt sick. "What...what do you want to know?"

"You're not the innocent little girl you claimed to be. I see that now. You're hiding something— something big, I'd wager. You wouldn't be out here in the middle of nowhere if you weren't trying to protect yourself."

I felt a molecule of relief I'd been wrong. *He doesn't know.*

"I don't know what—"

"Stop lying to me!" Dalton exploded, making me flinch back. "You've been lying to me for months now, I know it, and it stops now. You hear me?"

I held up my hands, very aware of the gun at Sark's head and Dalton's history of a temper. "Okay, okay. Is this about Sark? I can explain that." Really,

I didn't know how I'd explain, but I'd have to come up with something.

Dalton scowled at me. "It's about everything, Arie! It's about the fact that Sark, one of the best in his disgusting field, is obsessed with you, more than just a worthless infected. It's about someone as inferior as you managing to convince a notorious criminal and one of my own to turn traitor and disregard everything for *you*. Unless you're actually a captive here, in which case, you're well provided for—and still worth something."

I shook my head, my shoulders slumping slightly. "I'm not worth anything."

"Liar!" His face turned a shade of red, and I stumbled back when he surged forward. "Sark wouldn't give his life up for nothing, and Erika wouldn't turn on me after everything I've done for her."

Drawing back, my eyebrows furrowed, sure I'd heard him wrong. I glanced at Erika, startled by the pleading tears in her eyes.

Dalton watched our brief exchange with a raised eyebrow, his face lightening up a degree. "You didn't know?" He actually laughed, and a couple of his men snickered when I just stared, dumbfounded. "She really didn't tell you? Well, now, Arie, maybe you aren't as smart as I thought."

My heart thumped painfully in my throat, prepared to crack. "What are you talking about?"

Dalton grinned, puffing up his chest with arrogance that he could talk down to me. "Erika has been my assistant for years now. The night you commandeered her cab, she recognized Sark and called me once she got out. I made her go back to keep tabs on both of you. When she stopped calling, I assumed she lost you and didn't want to admit it to me." His amusement faded, and he squared his jaw. "I didn't guess you and Sark had managed to turn her."

I took a shaky breath, the chunk of information cutting up my throat as I tried to swallow it. I searched for reasons to deny it; my body felt heavier as more things started to make sense. Erika's behavior, her knowledge, her fear...or why Jefferson had taken so long interrogating her.

Dalton's assistant.

Every inch of my body stinging, I forced myself to look at Erika. She was crying now, muffled whimpers coming from her mouth as she leaned forward, begging for forgiveness. For a chance to explain. I glanced at Sark for signs he felt betrayed too. His eyes were closed and he was breathing intently, as if trying to convince himself this wasn't actually happening. He must've felt me looking at him because he opened his eyes, and I found them holding the same expression, pleading for trust.

He knew. They both knew and they didn't tell me.

Dalton cleared his throat, snatching back my frayed attention. I stiffened when he pulled out a gun from his waistband. "Now, Arie, I believe it's your turn to talk."

Mind reeling, I couldn't remember how to use my voice. I couldn't think a coherent thought without the revelation pounding that everything I knew about Erika made sense and was a lie at the same time.

A shot rang out, jarring me out of my daze. The bullet burrowed into the flooring next to Erika's leg; she, Sark, and I flinched.

"Don't be difficult," Dalton told me. He fired another shot that narrowly missed Sark's shoulder. "When you're difficult, things get ugly." He stalked up to me and I scrambled away, until he'd backed me up against the far wall.

"I don't know what you want." My voice wavered, and I left the next part unsaid, for fear of further angering him.

And I don't think you know what you want either. Dalton had always been a short fuse, but this kind of erratic behavior was extreme for even him. *What happened to you, Dalton?*

"I want you to tell me what I need to hear."

I raised an eyebrow at that, in spite of myself. Noticing his mistake, Dalton growled through his teeth and brought his gun up, aiming at me. I squeezed my eyes shut as the cool metal barrel pressed against my forehead, pinning me against the wall.

"Dalton," I breathed, my voice shaking with my hands. "Dalton, think. Be rational. I don't know...I don't know what you mean."

There was no rationality in his tone, no pause for reason. "Something tells me you know exactly what I mean."

Clenching my jaw, I counted to ten, grounding myself, reminding myself of the pact I'd made ages ago.

Don't give him anything. You can't tell him anything.

Resolve set, I opened my eyes. He glared at me, willing me to say whatever magic words he was looking for. I jerked out my chin and stared back.

Fury exploded across his face. He slammed the gun against the side of my head, hard enough to knock me to the floor. I felt blood trickle down my temple as the room spun. Hands seized me by my arms, and someone shouted. I recognized the sound.

Sark.

He was handcuffed with a gun to his head, but his eyes were on me. Shoving his shoulder back into the guy behind him, he jumped to his feet and smacked another guy in the face with his restrained hands as Erika used her legs to trip him. Suits surrounded Sark just as the men holding me threw me into the mirror room. The door slammed behind me.

Disoriented, I bolted upright only to have more hands on me, restraining me, tying me up and gagging me. I thrashed and fought until they pricked me with something. My body lost the ability to move for under ten seconds, but it was long enough for them to secure me. My attention tore in half between the three men in a piano room I no longer recognized, now overrun with two tables and medical machinery, and the scene outside.

They'd gotten Sark back on his knees. Blood ran from his nose and a wound over his eye, but he looked as defiant as ever—even with three guns on him now and one on Erika. Dalton stood over him, and I could practically see his head inflating by the second.

"You're after me," Sark told him, his tone assertive and complacent at the same time. "You have been for years now. Don't drag her into this just for your personal vendetta."

"Honestly, Mr. Sark," Dalton responded as he inspected his gun, "I gave up on you a long time ago. If the agency still wants you—and I'm sure they will—they can have you. My priority is the little freak."

As if in response to the word, one of the men came at me with a needle. I shrieked and jerked, but I'd been tied down too tight, and could only watch in horror as the man took my blood. My eyes traced the red liquid through the clear tube, but instead of being collected in some kind of container, the tube connected to a lump that took up most of the long table. A black tarp had been thrown over it, but even still my nose wrinkled at the stench emanating.

I just fought harder against my restraints, the cords rubbing the skin of my wrists away.

We have to get out of here.

Sark's voice stole my attention again, claiming the spotlight in the room while Erika discreetly tried to peel the duct tape off her face with her bound hands.

"I know you, Dalton," Sark said, meeting his eyes evenly. "I know your kind. It kills you to have lost so many times. To come so close to catching me—the one job they gave you to do—only to fall short. To be the joke of the office, and have nobody take you seriously."

Dalton snapped his jaw shut so hard that even I heard it. His fist clenched the gun, and Erika shot Sark a warning glance, but Sark went on like they were just talking.

"She'll only make that worse. I don't know what you think she is, but she can't help you. Not with what you're looking for. You bring her in as your solution, and you'll just be branded more absurd than you already are." He was so calm, so logical, except for the stolen glances at the mirror. "Take me in. That should be enough."

"Really? Then you wouldn't mind telling me what you're doing out here, would you? Why did you care so much about her in the first place?"

Sark just glared back, the muscles in his neck taut. "My job. You know that. Nothing more."

The man finished taking my blood. I glared at him as he removed the needle from my arm, and he met his cohorts at the table. One of them pulled the black cover off. The stench hit me like a hammer, making my eyes water, and I gave a muffled gasp when I saw the thing underneath it, the thing holding my blood.

It was a lump. A burned, blackened lump. My eyes worked with the shape, noting the four limbs, the ten fingers, the two eye sockets. It was a person, or it used to be. A girl, I thought, based on the outline of the figure. She didn't flinch or move or even breathe.

She was dead.

My stomach dropped, bile rising in my throat. I shrieked through the gag and jerked myself around, rattling the chair against the floor.

Oblivious to my panic on the other side of the wall, Dalton shook his head at Sark, as though correcting a pupil. "Contrary to popular belief, Mr. Sark, I'm not an idiot. I know something else is going on here. My men are testing her as we speak—I'll know soon enough if she's worth my time."

Sark flinched at the word 'testing' and I screamed for him to help me. As if hearing my cry, Erika managed to rip off enough of the duct tape to talk.

"You're wrong, Dalton." The words trembled, but she held them strong, lifting her head with confidence I knew was fake. "You know you're wrong. Just go home."

"I'm *wrong*?" Dalton's face went pink, then red, then hovered dangerously on purple as he waved his gun around. Even some of his men were watching the weapon with unease. "Tell me, Erika, was I *wrong* to rescue you from federal prison? Was I *wrong* to assume you'd be a half decent assistant rather that a traitorous tramp that shifts allegiances with the wind?"

Erika cringed at the unchecked rage in his voice, but it didn't stop her. "This has always been about us. From day one, it's been about us catching him." She tipped her head at Sark. "Not Arie. It never has been. Don't make this into something it's not. She's just a kid."

"As are you, Erika. But you seem to forget that, don't you?"

"Right now, Dalton, I'm your voice of reason." Her forehead creased, imploring. "Please listen to it. You aren't yourself."

The man that had taken my blood knocked on the mirror door, freezing Dalton's anger in place. His face stayed a shade of red, but he smoothed out his expression, then nodded toward the mirror.

"Voice of reason, you say?" he asked.

I watched as two men lifted the burned girl into their arms. The third man opened the door enough for them to get through, but not enough to reveal me, and closed it up again. Once in the living room, the men dropped the body on the floor. It gave a loud thud, then brittle silence filled the air.

Erika opened her mouth as if to scream, but nothing came out. A choking sound escaped Sark despite his blank face, and he blinked once, then twice, three times, as if he couldn't comprehend what was in front of him. Their reaction solved the puzzle.

They think that's me.

I screamed and kicked twisted, desperately trying to escape, to be heard, to tell them I was okay.

Sark clamped his jaw and clenched his fists, slowly tearing his gaze from the body to glower at Dalton.

Dalton just smirked and tapped the girl's head with his foot. "I guess you were right: she isn't the answer to my problem."

Sark growled, a guttural, animalistic sound, and jumped to his feet. The guards let off warning shots, which was their mistake: Sark took three of them out in one swing, despite still being handcuffed, his murderous eyes on Dalton.

Erika's voice cut through Sark's commotion. "What did you *do*?" she gasped in horror, tears streaming. "*What did you do?*"

Dalton shrugged, attempting to appear calm through Sark's violent efforts to get through the line of guards and squeeze the life out of him. "She was infected trash. Expendable."

Erika's eyes flashed and she lurched to her feet, striking Dalton across the face with her bound hands.

His head turned deep purple, his eyes nearly bugging out of their sockets. "Why you little—"

"You never deserved that badge." Erika glared him down evenly, despite being a head shorter than him. "You never did, and you never will."

The next moment happened in slow motion. A guard hit Sark on the back of the head with a gun. Sark crumpled to his knees, glancing back up just in time to see the frenzied violence light up Dalton's expression as he raised his gun. Just as I saw.

I screamed.

Dalton fired.

Sark shouted.

Erika fell.

Her body landed hard next to the burned body, red pooling underneath her. Limp. Motionless.

Dead.

Time stopped around me. I saw things, people, but they were distant. Murky. Like I was underwater, trapped in a nightmare world. Through the mirror wall, Sark caught one look of Erika and lost what little he had left. He erupted in a hurricane of violence, savagely taking down any body within reach. Some guards stared at Erika or Dalton with anxiety, exchanging glances. Until Sark managed to get hold of a gun—then the moment of incredulity passed, and they were fighting for their lives as their comrades were mowed down.

Then Dalton was there, in front of me. He looked back at Sark with alarm, then barked orders at his remaining people. I heard sounds. I couldn't make them into words. I just stared at Erika.

Erika.

Gone.

Two remaining guards picked me up. I tried to move, but my brain wouldn't give the command, too swallowed up in shocked grief to do anything else. I watched Erika until they'd dragged me away, not realizing I was crying until the fresh air kissed my face, as if paying its respects for my loss.

The men shoved me into the back of a car. Dalton slid into the passenger seat, hastily telling his driver to step on it.

Erika's dead, I finally managed to think.

Even from inside the car speeding away I could hear the gunshots still ringing, could still hear Sark fighting for everything he'd just lost.

Erika's dead and I am too.

I am alone.

ACKNOWLEDGEMENTS

This book has come a long way in the years I've been working on it, and I owe so much of that to a lot of incredible people I'm extremely blessed to know:

FAB FIVE: To my parents, for loving me unconditionally and raising me to love others the same way. To Nan, for getting me through it all—emotional breakdowns and writer's block included. To Court, for always reminding me to keep myself young as I continue to grow old. To Odie and JJ, for snugging me even when I'm a brat and giving kisses that heal so many wounded souls.

To #303, for worming your way through my walls and somehow liking the person you found hiding behind them. I can't describe to you what you all mean to me.

To Robbin, Kesley, my excellent teachers, and everyone that has helped me bring my stories to life and become the writer I am.

To NaNoWriMo, for saving my life through stories. I wouldn't be here, writing this book without that incredible program #storiesmatter

To my family, friends, and fans that have been with me from the start or helped push my wagon along the way. YOU ARE ALL AMAZING. Thank you so much for your support.

To past 2012 me, thank you for being brave enough to choose to write instead of give up. You'll never know how you changed the course of our lives.

And last (but not least) to you, the reader, for picking up my book. These stories are my life, and sharing my words with you is what makes writing truly rewarding.

Turn the page for

SURVIVING ON A WHISPER

bonus materials

"Arie"
by Kesley Moore

"Lennon's Dogs"
by Kesley Moore

"Nightmare"
by Kesley Moore

Questions for the author: Emilee King in conversation with popular blogger (and sister! Lucky me!) Savannah King, who writes for 'In the Mind of a Nan' (which you should definitely check out).

Q: So some may already know, but if not, this anniversary edition isn't special just because of the bonus content inside. This girl actually rewrote her entire first novel and republished it! We are talking updated manuscript, cover, synopsis—plus extra bonus content that wasn't in the previous edition. How did you come to the decision that you wanted to redo *Surviving on a Whisper?*

A: When I wrote the first draft of *Surviving on a Whisper*, I was a junior in high school, and while I had been an avid reader my entire life, there was a lot I still had to learn. I reworked the draft a few times before self-publishing it about five years ago. Since then I've grown immensely as a writer and learned so much. I loved the first book for what it was, but I struggled with it, knowing it wasn't even close to my best work—and I wanted people's first impression of my writing to be my best, not my worst. When I had some time, I went back to look at some of the criticism I'd received from readers, and then I checked on what they were saying...and they were so right! It was incredibly hard to swallow, but once I accepted the fact that I needed to shape it up, it was super fun! I hadn't realized how embarrassed I was of the draft...kind of like reading an old journal...except the whole world has access to it. So, yeah, once I had the idea 'well I could rewrite it' then it just took off from there. I'll always have a place in my heart for that (awful!) first draft, but I'm really happy with how it's all turned out. It just needed some extra love.

Q: Okay so obviously the rewrite is different than the first version, but how much of the plot and character development changed along with that? Was it difficult to stay true to the original story?

A: Yes and no. The story will always be what it is—and Arie will be the heart of that—and that would be something difficult to change unless I completely went off the path I'd set for myself. The basic plot is the same, but some scenes were cut and other areas revamped so it made more sense in the storyline and added the depth that was missing. Especially after finishing the last book, I realized how much character development was missing in the first book—things I'd thought I'd explained well, but later realized it hadn't come across like I'd hoped. For the rewrite, I focused a lot on character work, especially with Erika, and Sark to a degree. I also wanted to explore Arie's relationships a little better, specifically with Kieran, Connor, and Alaina, just to give readers a better look into the characters they already knew. And I underestimated how much I would love going back and fixing little things (and big things) that had bothered me for years. While the rewrite is definitely different in ways, I think it's an even better representation of Arie's story, which was my main priority.

Q: When you first starting writing *Surviving on a Whisper*, did you know that five years later you would have published four books in the series?

A: Not at all! The idea that I could write a book at all was rather insane—at first my goal was to just write one and go from there. I distinctly remember the day I was writing out an outline and put the note 'maybe save this plotline for book 2?' and then I laughed at myself because I thought it was crazy. But I'd say about halfway through writing the first book, I realized I had enough for a sequel, maybe even a trilogy. But, yeah, if you would've told me it was going to be four books, I would've either laughed or did a ridiculously embarrassing happy dance.

Q: Let's talk about the setting—Arie could be anywhere. Why Chicago? What importance does setting play in this story?

A: I've never actually been to Chicago (though I hope to fix that someday) and the decision was actually pretty last minute in my planning process. I knew I wanted a big city, but that was the extent of it. Chicago ended up being my choice because of you: you're *obsessed* with Chicago, and it's your lifelong dream to go there. So, I picked it for you. In a lot of stories, the setting plays a major role in forming everything, but I tried to do the opposite in these books. The foundation of the book, and Arie's character, is that she's lost. She's alone. She doesn't have a home. The world feels big and foreign and unsafe. I wanted to use the setting to heighten that. I didn't get very specific most of the time because I wanted the reader to feel that unsettlement too—the feeling that it doesn't matter if you're in Chicago or Salt Lake or San Francisco, you're still lost, you're still hunted, and you still don't have a place. I think those themes are a prevalent part of the foundation of the story, and I used the setting to reflect that.

Q: I'm sure there was a lot of fun scenes to write—there were a lot of fun ones to read!—but what was your most favorite? What about the most difficult?

A: That's such a hard question. I really really really love to write Arie and Sark together. I don't even care what they're doing, as long as they're in the same room—especially after things get weird and uncertain between them. I. Love. It. They combine two of my passions: deep sibling connections and love/hate relationships. A specific scene that sticks out to me is when she has a nightmare after the movie night, and Sark coaches her through it. I'm just a sucker for those two. As far as difficult, I'm not sure. There were pacing issues to work out, but I can't think of a specific part that bothered me to actually write.

Q: I saw little bits of myself in many characters (I'd like to comment that the characters you created are so real and easy to connect with), so what character, or characters, do you identify with most?

A: Aw thanks pal. Obviously, Arie. While she stands on her own, she's also like an extension of my being. But that's an easy answer. I like to think I can find bits of myself in every character, but, yeah, Arie is my homegirl.

Q: This book left us with quite the cliffhanger (and lots of tears). What can we expect in the next book?

A: That ending! I know, I know, I get a ton of grief over it. The second book picks up about eight months later, and so many pivotal things have taken place that change the game a little bit. It's a really dark time for a lot of the characters (it's called *Surviving through the Night*, after all) so there's a lot for them to work through. There are also some new people that I'm very excited for you to meet, and plenty of emotionally-charged Arie and Sark moments, because that's basically what I live for these days.

Q: Now that Arie's Story is finished, what are your plans for writing in the future? Any other projects you have in mind?

A: I have so many possible projects that sometimes I get overwhelmed by it all, but writing has become such an integral part of my life—so of course there will be more. Closing this series was extremely emotional for me, so I'm going to take a break for a bit and try my hand at some new things. I just finished writing a Cinderella murder mystery (which was SO fun), and there are plenty more fairytale-inspired ideas floating around in my head, as well as a couple other stories I can chase. I do plan on coming back to Arie in the future though. This world has such a hold on me, and there are so many stories that haven't been told yet—yay for spinoffs!

Q: What advice would you give any futures writers out there?

A: Don't stop. Ever. A lot of writing is trial and error, so don't stop practicing and stretching yourself. Even when I'm not actively writing, I'm still thinking about stories or characters or possible plotlines. And if you aren't writing your own stories at the moment, then you should be delving into others', whether in books or movies or TV—whatever. The basis of writing is stories, so if you surround yourself with them, things will rub off a little eventually. Also, I think it's super important to learn how to take criticism and grow from it. I struggled with that for a long time, and my writing really suffered a ton because of it. Of course, it still stings to take sometimes, but I'm so much better because of it. And, lastly, make sure you write for you.

ALL SURVIVAL COMES AT A COST

**The second installment of Arie's Story is available now!
Turn the page for a sneak peek.**

I'm alive.

I silently crept down the winding road, acutely aware of my shoes pressing against the asphalt. The street was deserted; I was the only one in sight. I kept reminding myself that I was alone and concealed. In the night, the inky black sky created almost total darkness, which I knew kept me perfectly hidden in the shadows, but I did not feel hidden. I felt hideously exposed, naked, and unprotected. The starless sky seemed to be reaching down, mouth agape as if to swallow me whole. There was too much space to move in, too much air to breathe, too many sounds to hear.

I can't handle this. I hadn't been outside since May. Since Florida. It was January now. After eight months of dark walls in square rooms, the world felt disgustingly huge and foreign, making my compulsion to curl up in a ball and close my eyes almost impossible to fight.

Of course, that wasn't really an option at the moment. For all I knew, Dalton was following me right now. It had been a few days since I'd escaped and he probably had guessed where I would go first. I knew it was stupid to be this predictable—especially since I wasn't sure this would work or end well—but I didn't know what else to do. This was what I would've done eight months ago and that old judgment was the only thing I had to go on. I was just going to have to trust myself.

Or trust who I used to be, I guess.

Finally, my destination came into view. The one-story building looked vacant and forgotten, hallways spreading out from the main entrance like lifeless fingers. I stopped at the set of concrete stairs that led to a glass door secured with metal bars.

Office of Cultist Intelligence—Colorado Division, the sign read. The capital 'O' had fallen off and Colorado had only half of its 'C'.

This is it.

I pulled out two narrow plastic pieces from my hoodie pocket and tiptoed up the stairs. My fingers fumbled as I began to work on the lock. For a second I wondered if I would be unable to get the door open—it had never taken me this long before—but I finally heard a click. Both relief and disappointment hit because I almost wanted the excuse of not being able to get in. Brushing the thought aside, I pulled the heavy door open. It gave a piercing creak and the sudden intrusion of sound made me jump. I lost my grip on the door and it slammed shut. Automatically, I froze and glanced around, sure that I had just compromised everything, but I was still alone.

Calm down, I told myself, *before you ruin your only chance.*

Taking a deep breath, I opened the door again and slipped inside. The reception area smelled musty and stale, the walls painted in ugly shades of green. All lights were off except one in a long hallway, so I clenched my fists and went in that direction.

I passed by all of the closed doors and kept moving until I heard the buzz of voices. An urgency exploded inside me, overtaking all fear. I needed this *now,* despite any consequences.

I didn't stop as I turned a corner and walked straight into a conference room. At a lengthy table, two men—an early thirties guy and an older fifties one—were sitting across from each other, bouncing a small red ball back and forth as they argued. A younger woman sat at the head, drumming her fingers against the table in frustration, her shoulder length brown hair swept to the side and her chin in her hands. All three of them gaped at me when I appeared in the doorway.

"Who are you?" the finger drummer asked as she stood up from her chair. Her voice had more power and authority to it than her appearance suggested. "How did you get in here?" The two men gave me questioning stares, the silver-haired one dropping the red ball. It bounced three times on the floor before rolling out of sight.

The woman started toward me, and my instant reaction was to retreat. As she came closer I automatically started to walk backwards. She stopped when she saw my sudden fear, folding her arms across her chest, studying me. Her face softened slightly.

"How did you get in here?" she asked again, less harshly.

You're going to have to answer, I tried to tell myself. *You're going to have to talk to her. You can't blow this.*

The anticipation of wanting to and not wanting to was eating me away, making me dizzy but resolute: this was my only chance. I hadn't risked everything to find this place just so I could screw it all up.

"Are you Lindsey Carter?" I blurted, my voice hoarse.

She nodded once, a fleck of surprise in her eyes.

I cleared my throat and it sounded like a dying engine. "So you're in charge of this place, right?"

She sighed. "Unfortunately, yes."

"You have a prisoner here, right? That's why you're here in the middle of the night."

A faint gasp went through her teeth as the two men stood up from their chairs—apparently they'd been expecting something else from me. Instantly, any molecule of friendliness that might've existed toward me was replaced with suspicion.

"How do you know that?" Lindsey asked, taking a step forward. I stepped backward again, wrapping my arms around myself, trying to stay calm.

Keep it together. You can't blow this.

"Look, uh, Lindsey, or, um, Ms. Carter…" How was I supposed to explain this? "I know that you don't know me, but…I, uh, need you to do me a favor."

"A favor?" She narrowed her eyes. "How about you do *me* a favor and tell me who sent you here?"

"Sent me? No, nobody…" I shook my head. "I mean, I'm here by myself. I'm on my own and I need your help. Please."

Her body relaxed slightly, but the two men weren't convinced, leaning forward slightly as if at the ready to neutralize me at any moment.

Just pretend they aren't there. They aren't. It's just you and this nice Lindsey lady.

"And how can I help you?" she asked, her tone a bit more resigned.

"I need to see him." The words came out faster than I meant to.

She raised an eyebrow. "You want to see Sark?"

My heart ached at the name, both in longing and anxiety.

"Yes. I need to see Sark right now."

About the Author

Emilee King is the author of the Arie's Story survival series and the Elarian Chronicles. She loves fairy tales, superheroes, fantasy, and murder mysteries, and is constantly on the hunt for good stories. When she's not writing, you can find her reorganizing her bookshelves, eating pasta, beating the high score on Galaga, or spending time with her family. Visit her website at emileeking.com